I0613319

Train to Laramie

Andrew Roth

PUBLISHING THE POSITIVE

ELK LAKE PUBLISHING INC
Plymouth, Massachusetts

Copyright Notice

Train to Laramie

First edition. Copyright © 2020 by Andrew Roth. The information contained in this book is the intellectual property of Andrew Roth and is governed by United States and International copyright laws. All rights reserved. No part of this publication, either text or image, may be used for any purpose other than personal use. Therefore, reproduction, modification, storage in a retrieval system, or retransmission, in any form or by any means, electronic, mechanical, or otherwise, for reasons other than personal use, except for brief quotations for reviews or articles and promotions, is strictly prohibited without prior written permission by the publisher.

This is a work of fiction. Names, characters, businesses, places, events, locales, and incidents are either the products of the author's imagination or used in a fictitious manner. Any resemblance to actual persons, living or dead, or actual events is purely coincidental.

Cover and Interior Design: Derinda Babcock

Editor(s): Cristel Phelps, Deb Haggerty

Author Represented By: Hartline Literary Agency

PUBLISHED BY: Elk Lake Publishing, Inc., 35 Dogwood Drive, Plymouth, MA 02360, 2020

Library Cataloging Data

Names: Roth, Andrew (Andrew Roth)

Train to Laramie / Andrew Roth

344p. 23cm × 15cm (9in × 6 in.)

Identifiers: ISBN-13: 978-1-64949-065-0 (paperback) | 978-1-64949-066-7 (trade paperback) | 978-1-64949-067-4 (e-book)

Key Words: Western, abuse, transcontinental railroad, 1860s, romance, coming of age, values and virtues.

LCCN: 2020944475 Fiction

DEDICATION

To God, our Creator, able to transform lives and redirect paths. Thank you, Savior.

"… And I will build you up again and you will be rebuilt."—Jeremiah 31:4

CHAPTER ONE

Tess lifted a hand and shielded her eyes, studying the mass of black clouds forming across the open prairie. A peal of distant thunder rumbled in anger. She dropped her hand and turned away, hurrying toward the well in the center of town. Mama would need this bucket of water for her special birthday dinner.

A sudden gust snapped Tess's loose-fitting dress snug around her slim form. She almost stumbled as her dark hair whipped across her eyes, momentarily blinding her, but the growing storm couldn't dissuade her from her errand. She stepped expertly left and right, dodging the heavy freight wagons rolling through the dusty streets, loaded with various metal parts for the railroad. The shouts of men and ring of steel on steel came to her from the distant train yard down by the station, but she ignored these familiar noises.

Finally, she reached the wooden platform that covered the deep hole and set the bucket below the spigot. The pump creaked as she moved the rusty iron handle up and down, drawing the water from the depths of the town well. A smile tugged at the corner of her lips as she worked. Despite her slight frame, she thrilled in the exertion and enjoyed the test of strength the pump demanded. Soon the bucket brimmed.

Grasping the rope handle, Tess cast another glance at the swelling bank of gloomy clouds. She hoped she would make the short trip back to the cabin before the rains came.

The gale increased, pushing Tess through the narrow gaps between the haphazard shanties and shacks of Omaha, toward the small shack she shared with Mama and Frank Mercer.

Tess grimaced at the thought of her stepfather. If she were lucky, the foul man wouldn't make an appearance at her celebration this evening.

The heavy bucket swayed, and Tess leaned with its weight. She slowed to prevent spills.

A frown settled on her face when she sighted Mrs. Burlington waving from her door as Tess passed the plump woman's small shack. Tess wondered what tidbit of information she would share today?

"Oh, Tess," Mrs. Burlington called, protecting her own stiff, silver hair from the wind with one hand while her other grasped her billowing apron.

Tess lowered the wooden bucket. She had no interest in gossip and didn't require a break from the cumbersome load, but she would be polite and allow the elderly neighbor a few moments of her time. Mama would expect her to act accordingly.

"Good evening, Mrs. Burlington."

"Your mother told me this was a special day for you, lass. Seventeen and a grown woman you are now." The nosy neighbor's remark seemed nonchalant, her voice raised above the wind, but Tess noticed the purposeful gleam in the old woman's eye.

Tess had known Mrs. Burlington long enough to recognize her methods. Although the old woman had befriended her and Mama when they'd arrived in town, it became evident the town gossip only sought new listeners. And new speculations. Tess was wise to the old woman's seemingly innocent tactics now.

Again she threw a worried glance at the approaching

storm. Would the rain hold off while Mrs. Burlington went through her ritual of commenting on random issues, preparing for the true purpose of the conversation?

Tess flexed her fingers and waited for the morsel of chinwag. She leaned closer to the old woman as the wind snatched at Mrs. Burlington's words.

"Of course, the Indians are always a concern as the line moves west," Mrs. Burlington continued. Tess realized she'd missed the initial remarks. Oh, well, they were probably insignificant to the true purpose of this delay. Tess nodded and pretended to listen.

"Surely looks like we are in for a humdinger of a storm," the old gossip prattled on. "Those clouds ain't black for nothing." Another rumble of thunder seemed to validate her observation.

Tess nodded again, waiting.

Mrs. Burlington took a step forward, drawing closer to Tess. Her dark eyes suddenly widened and flashed as she looked furtively over her shoulder before she went on.

"There's talk among the men that Frank Mercer has an unnatural eye on you, lass. Not as a stepfather should, mind you, if you catch my meaning. And he gets angry if any man talks of you." Mrs. Burlington straightened, her juicy tidbit shared.

Tess pursed her lips as she reached for the rope handle. "Thank you, Mrs. Burlington. I'm sure I'd better be getting this water to Mama," she called over her shoulder as she swiftly moved away.

Rounding a corner of another shack, Tess allowed her rapid gait to slow. So, the cat was out of the bag. It seemed even the neighbors knew how Frank Mercer looked at her. Her brow furrowed and she chewed the inside of her cheek as the strong wind pushed her homeward.

She drew a deep breath. Frank wouldn't change, so

she would have to leave. She'd thought about this for a long time, but now the desire boiled like a tea kettle in her stomach, preparing her for … for what?

Tess frowned and squinted once more toward the coming storm, wondering what God had in store for her life. She leaned against the back wall of a shack, the heavy bucket swinging, and looked down at herself. She hoped her baggy dress hid her blossoming figure from Frank's piercing stare. She cringed.

What would happen to her if Frank persisted? Tess could feel something building inside her, pushing her toward something, but what? Her frown deepened as she shook her head. The Almighty was almighty quiet, she thought, her annoyance growing with her sense of anxiety.

A hard drop of rain struck her cheek, and Tess pushed from the wall of rough-cut planks. She needed to hurry. She could think of these disturbing thoughts another time. Today was her birthday, and she wanted to enjoy it.

Besides, she had already some plans in place. The hidden bundle of belongings gave her some comfort. And surely God would aid her in this endeavor to flee. Hadn't the Lord protected her thus far from Frank's clutches?

She turned another corner and sighted her shack down the lane before her. She stopped abruptly in the narrow path between the railroad workers' small houses, a bit of water sloshed from her pail. She lowered the heavy bucket for an instant, feeling again the push of the increasing wind at her back. Turning, she looked westward. The darkening clouds were now a huge wall moving toward her. Distant lightning streaks stabbed from the black mass to the plains below. Thunder rumbled louder as the storm neared Omaha.

The black cloud reminded her of a train, she decided. Then again, everyone compared everything in this railroad hub to trains. Trains came and went daily. She and Mama were here because of trains. Frank had dragged them here because of his job in the train yards, the blacksmith forges and fabrication shops ringing the station.

Tess turned her gaze from the coming tempest to the weathered shack at the end of the lane. Her chest tightened as she stared at the drab shanty. Usually, she would remain outdoors as long as she could, helping her neighbors with their chores or simply walking the open prairie west of town. She always felt reluctant to return home where Frank might pester her and cause her to fear, though he rarely came home early anymore. The demands of the Union Pacific as the rails pushed west kept him busy. His responsibilities in the machine shop at the Omaha train yard were expanding and often he was away from the little shack he shared with Tess and her mother for days at a time.

He wouldn't be here now, she reminded herself. He would still be at the train yard. Thank God, she breathed as she bent to retrieve the bucket once more.

Her steps quickened, aided by the blustering gale behind her and the excitement of her birthday. No doubt, Mama had prepared something special for her this day, her seventeenth birthday.

Her anticipation faded as she approached the dingy shack. Tess thought back on the increasing references Frank had made about her becoming a woman as this day grew closer. He seemed to be counting down the days to this significant date.

Another loud clap of thunder caused Tess to jump and lent motivation to her hesitant steps as she neared her shack. Another thick raindrop struck her. Soon the rain would be upon her if she didn't hurry inside.

The door latch lifted easily under her hand and she

stepped into the dimly lit room. A single lantern sat upon the table, burning low. Her heart sank as she counted three bowls on the small table. Apparently, Frank was expected to join them for supper.

"What took you so long, Tess?" The accusing, irritated ring in her mother's voice could not be missed. "You know how Frank hates to be kept waiting for his coffee." Her mother glowered as she snatched the water bucket from Tess.

Tess didn't reply but frowned as her hands sought her tangled hair. She didn't want Frank to see her with her hair down. She deftly divided the long tresses into three strands and began braiding. She tossed the single braid over her shoulder and glanced again at the three bowls. "Is Frank really going to be at my birthday dinner?"

Her mother shot Tess a warning glance. "Frank Mercer is my husband and your father." She poured water into the coffeepot then handed the bucket back to Tess before moving the black enameled container to the small pot-bellied stove. She stirred the soup and continued. "And he provides for us. He takes care of us."

"He is not my father." Tess poured water from the bucket as her chin lifted. She eyed the tin cups she filled. "And we could take care of ourselves. Don't we make a good income from the laundry we take in? I could make more if he didn't keep the change I earn from haircuts." She glanced up at her mother, her eyes narrowing. "I still don't understand why you ever married the man."

Her mother turned on her, anger flashing in her tired eyes. "I did the only thing I could do after Papa died. Lots of men didn't return home after the war, and I figured Frank was our only chance of being taken care of. Don't hold it against me, Tess, that he's not your true daddy."

Mama seemed drawn to men that didn't respect her.

Tess scowled as her mother turned again to the little stove. Then the tight squeeze on Tess's chest loosened as she watched her mother work. Cathy Mercer was one of those types who would always need someone to protect her, someone to take care of her. She was not strong like Tess. She was weak and often afraid, but still Tess loved her dearly.

The mention of Tess's father had recalled visions of drunken violence. He'd never been foul or inappropriate toward Tess, but she still had felt happy when he'd left for the war. Papa could be tolerated unless he'd been drinking, but Frank Mercer was ten times worse even when he was sober, which was rare enough. Tess lowered her gaze and arranged utensils on the table. Not long ago, Tess had been very much like her mother, afraid and uncertain. Now her strength came from God, not from within herself. If only her mother would lean on the Lord, Tess thought, and not on Frank Mercer's tentative protection and provision. Silently, she shot a prayer for Mama skyward.

She finished placing the spoons and knives on the table and sighed. Too late now. Mama was married to Frank and that was all there was to it.

The door burst open and a strong gust of wind rushed inside with Frank. The big man shoved the door closed against the squall. His ruddy face alerted Tess and she inhaled deeply, catching the strong odor of liquor. His watery blue eyes leered openly at her, ogling her from head to toe.

With a casual flip of his bowler derby, the big man tossed his hat toward the hook on the wall. He missed the intended target, and the brown hat fell to the dirt floor. Cathy scurried to retrieve it, dusting the brim before placing the hat carefully on its hook.

Without a word of greeting, Frank lurched toward the

table. He pulled out a chair and dropped into it. "It's going to be quite a storm tonight," the big man remarked to no one in particular, his slurred speech revealing his swollen tongue.

Tess watched as he reached for the tin cup of water, his shoulders bulging under the filthy shirt.

"Will the storm slow down work for you, Frank?" Her mother's gaze darted from her husband to Tess and back to the soup on the stove.

The dirty man didn't bother to look at his wife. "Nothing slows down the Union Pacific, not even mountains or Indians. Talk around the shops is that they've already reached into the Medicine Bow Range. Crow Creek has been a base camp for months now, but they've completed the Dale Creek bridge and have pushed on to Laramie. Soon, they'll be over the divide and into Utah," the drunken man boasted.

"Do they have enough workers now?" his wife continued. Tess could tell her mother attempted to keep him focused.

Tess scowled. Her mother was wise, although her wisdom was born of fear. If she continued to press, he'd become agitated and Tess had hoped they could avoid one of their heated arguments on her special day.

"The Irish have proven to be good workers," Frank said as Cathy moved to spoon soup into his waiting bowl. "With the immigrants and the blacks and even some Johnny Rebs, the line is pushing on."

"That's good to hear, Frank," Cathy murmured. She turned to Tess and indicated one of the empty chairs. "Sit, Tess, and we'll enjoy one of your favorite dishes. Potato soup. Then, I have something special for after supper. Fresh bread and honey."

"Where's my coffee?" Frank growled. Dishes rattled as he pounded a huge fist on the rickety table.

Tess wanted to say something, to interfere and protect her mother, but she knew it would only make him angrier. She bit her tongue.

Cathy wheeled and hurried for the steaming pot.

"Right here, Frank. I wanted to make you a fresh pot for the evening," she explained as she poured the liquid into a new cup she placed on the table.

The big blacksmith reached for the coffee and sipped. He sputtered and slammed the cup down, spilling its contents. "This is cold!"

Cathy wiped the mess with her apron as she shot an accusing glance at Tess. "I'm sorry, Frank. It won't take but a minute to make it hot. Please give me a little time."

"You've had all day to prepare a simple meal, woman. Are you stupid?" he thundered, his eyes bulging, his thick words rolling from his wide mouth.

Tess dug her nails into her palm and willed herself to stay quiet. If she said anything, the brute might take it out on her mother.

"I'm sorry, Frank," Cathy whimpered as she rushed to clean the spilled coffee and fuss around Frank like a darting hummingbird.

"*I'm sorry, Frank,*" he mimicked. "That's all I ever hear about your constant shortcomings. I'm sorry. I'm sorry. I'm sick of it!"

With a sudden lunge, the big blacksmith leaped to his feet, upsetting the entire table. Soup bowls and cups of water flew in every direction as the turned table crashed on its side. The lantern sputtered out before shattering on the floor, spewing oil. The room was thrown into near darkness, lit only by the red glow from the small stove in the corner.

Tess had also jumped to her feet. Now she took a step toward Frank, unable to remain silent. "You're a rude little man, Frank Mercer," she flung at the towering hulk "Screaming at a woman makes you feel so mighty, doesn't it?" Her anger and annoyance at this crude man had finally burst its bounds. The way he treated her mother infuriated her, but her mother's weak demeanor and excuses for him angered her too.

"Tess, don't," her mother warned, her voice pleading.

Tess knew her arguments with Frank only made things worse, but she couldn't control herself.

"Don't stick up for her," Frank turned on Cathy. "She's a woman now, able to say what she wants from that pretty mouth of hers, ain't you, Tess?"

Tess could feel her anger grow along with the familiar fire in her stomach. "You're drunk," she replied, attempting to calm herself.

"Right you are, Tess girl. Drunk enough to have my way with a pretty thing in my own house." His small eyes glittered with that odd gleam Tess had observed in them before when she'd caught him staring at her.

"Frank, that's my daughter you're talking about," Cathy said as she faced her drunken husband.

"She's no kin of mine," he snapped and waved a dismissive hand. "Besides, she's living under my roof. I'll do what I please in my own home." As if to prove his authority, he raised a hand to slap Cathy.

Quick as a cat, Tess pushed Frank backward with a tremendous shove. The unsteady man staggered. Arms thrashing wildly, he tripped over a chair and toppled with a crash, lying still in the darkness.

Silence filled the small shack. Tess could hear the faint crackling of the wood within the little stove. The clapboard shack shuddered under the force of another powerful gust of wind. The full force of the storm had broken over Omaha.

A low groan came from Frank. Cathy stared at her husband sprawled on the cluttered dirt floor of the small shack. Her eyes widened as she turned her gaze and stared at her daughter.

Tess trembled and clenched her fists. Exhilaration swept through her.

Cathy leaped to the sideboard, wrapped a loaf of bread in a towel, and thrust the bundle into Tess's arms.

"Go, Tess, before he gets up. Write to me when you can."

Tess took the outstretched loaf and glanced at the prone figure on the floor. Frank Mercer would kill her for this.

She gritted her teeth and turned back to her mother.

"Come with me, Mama," she pleaded. "Leave this man and come with me to Chicago. We have friends there in the old neighborhood."

Cathy crossed her arms over her chest and shook her head, her eyes shining in the semi darkness. "No, daughter. I can't go. But you can. Go. I love you." Her mother shoved at her arm, encouraging her toward the door.

A louder groan came from Frank. Tess glanced at him and then back at her mother.

Something flashed in her mind and she knew the time had come. As if released from iron shackles, she flew behind her curtain. Despite the complete blackness behind her concealing cloth wall, Tess knew exactly where her packet of things lay hidden. She grabbed her few belongings and reached for a blanket before turning to run toward the door.

Frank struggled to his feet, grabbing the chair he'd tumbled over for support. Tess saw his bleary eyes widen as she raced for the door and he suddenly threw himself forward, snatching at her trailing blanket. His big hands held the quilt firmly and he halted, holding the blanket and grinning victoriously at Tess.

"You can't get away from me that easy, Tess girl. You're a minor, and I'm your legal guardian."

His words struck her like a fist, and her blood chilled in her veins. He was right. She had no way of stopping him.

An evil smile spread across his flushed face and Tess let go of the quilt. Frank fell backward, unable to keep his balance on the furniture strewn floor. He bellowed as he crashed once more to the floor.

Tess turned and stumbled out the door.

Wind whipped at her face, and the rain pelted her with cruel force. She leaned into the gale, forcing her legs to run as fast as she could. Behind her, Frank's mad roar mingled with Cathy's scream. Tess hesitated, wondering where to turn. Should she help her mother? Frank could be vicious when either angry or drunk.

He was both tonight, but Tess lowered her head against the gale and plowed on. She could do nothing for her mother now. Mama was probably doing all she could to prevent Frank's pursuit and aid Tess's escape.

Within a minute, the driving rain soaked her dress. A large tumbleweed loomed and tripped her. Tess staggered and dropped her belongings, the towel-wrapped loaf skittering across the mud. A howl of frustration behind her made Tess scramble to her feet, quickly scooping her scattered things into her arms.

Despite the darkness all around, Tess kept her bearings. The sound of Frank's bellows lent wings to her feet as she maneuvered among the familiar shacks and down muddy paths.

The train station. She must get to the machine shops that bordered the train station.

The east bound train would not be here for hours, she well knew, but to get near the railroad would be her best means of escape. There were friends and kind neighbors back in Chicago. They would take her in, Tess was certain.

A jagged fork of lightning illuminated her path, allowing Tess to see everything clearly for a split second, then the light was gone. A shadow moved and a man towered before her, snake-like arms reaching for her. A scream gurgled in her throat, masked by an ear-splitting crack of thunder as Tess recognized the bloated, bearded face of Frank Mercer.

Tess twisted away and dodged into a narrow chute between two shacks, her shoulders rubbing roughly against both walls. The big man bawled his frustration and relief swept over Tess in a wave as she realized he couldn't follow her through the narrow gap. She sidled on, fear driving her to Herculean efforts.

Her elbows scraped the coarse clapboard walls, but she ignored the pain and pushed herself through the small opening at the other end.

A large shadow rushed toward her, and Tess flung herself forward, her legs pounding the muddy ground as Frank slipped, his grasping arm going wide.

She must get to the train yard where the numerous shops huddled around the station. Surely she would find a hiding place among the forges and worker's shops.

Water splashed as Frank's boots kicked puddles, the drunken blacksmith only a few yards behind Tess.

Her long braid lay heavy across her back now, soaked with the powerful rain. Her dress and shoes were as soaked as if she'd swam in the well. The driving wind pushed hard at her, but she forced her way onward, committed to reaching the protection of the train station.

Another tumbleweed reared ahead of Tess, driven by the relentless wind, but she evaded its entanglements. As if a gift from above, the large plant rolled behind her and

Frank snarled as he collided with the obstacle. He called her name again, barely audible above the howl of the wind. Tess turned a corner and sprinted as another lightning strike revealed the beckoning train yard, dark sheds in a row beside the station.

The big yard seemed deserted as Tess rounded the corner of the first machine shop and ran beside the glistening tracks. Her heart pounded as she searched for a hiding place, anywhere she could lay low until the east bound train arrived.

Her eyes narrowed when she sighted the large engine, smokestack bellowing. Steam hissed at her feet as she ran past the big locomotive.

Something nagged at her mind, some detail she couldn't place. The train wasn't due for hours. Yet, it whistled shrilly at that very moment and again steam shot out from under the engine.

Darting between two cars, Tess scrambled under the connection and raced along the opposite side of the flatbed cars, looking for a ladder or an open boxcar. Gone now was her plan to hide and wait for the morning train to carry her to Chicago and to safety. The train had apparently arrived early and was attempting to leave Omaha before the storm grew worse.

Another shrill whistle split the night and a brilliant shaft of lightning lit the empty yard around her. Tess caught sight of a ladder to a flatcar piled high with building supplies.

She glanced over her shoulder before she scrambled up the wet ladder, her feet slipping once on a wet metal rung. The bundle of bread and clothes under her arm shifted, but she managed to maintain her hold.

Finally, she gained the platform of the car just as the train lurched below her. Tess staggered and dropped to her knees.

Keeping low, she crept among the wooden crates. Tess could hear Frank calling and running beside the train, still searching for her. If he found her, she would suffer his anger and frustration. She had before.

She must hide.

Dull light glistened on a wet tarpaulin. Cautiously, she lifted the heavy edge of the thick canvas and slipped under to lean against the rough wooden crate there. She pulled the protective tarp back into place and sat in total darkness, glad to be out of the rain and wind.

Frank's voice drew near, and Tess held her ragged breath. Her heart pounded and then rose in her throat as he approached. If he found her now, …

The train jolted again beneath her as the locomotive picked up speed. The slow *chug, chug, chug* of the powerful steam pushing the heavy wheels made Tess thrill with hope. As every second passed, her hope grew.

Frank Mercer would very soon be out of her life forever.

She huddled closer to the dry crate and shivered as Frank's voice faded into the night. The train gained speed and her breathing slowed. She drew a deep breath.

"Thank you, Lord," Tess whispered into the gloom.

Again, she felt something amiss, a foreboding she couldn't name. But the train clattered along the tracks, and Frank had been left behind at the Omaha train station. What could be wrong?

Tess grinned into the darkness and exhaled deeply. Excitement filled her, sending tingles down her arms. She had broken her chains and fled. She was now free to choose her own path and follow her dreams.

She reached for the edge of the tarp. Slowly, she lifted the canvas and peered out.

The rapidly retreating border of Omaha showed dimly in the distance, yellow lantern light streamed from shacks on the west end of town. But wait … The vast train yards lined both sides of the tracks along the *east* end of town. She gasped as a sickening shudder ran through her. She was headed in the wrong direction.

CHAPTER TWO

Tess had heard the men around the train yards speak of the Rocky Mountains far to the west. But how far? Where was the end of the tracks? She knew Frank had mentioned how far the twin rails stretched at her disastrous birthday dinner, but she couldn't remember his words.

Was it too late to jump off the train? She nibbled her lip and watched the darkened plains roll by. If she didn't kill herself leaping from the speeding train, Frank would certainly find her as she awaited the proper eastbound train.

The rhythmic, metallic clack-clack of the heavy flanged wheels sounded in Tess's ears as she lowered the sodden tarp over her. She leaned against the hard crate and forced herself to think.

Despite the strong winds and rain, the train rolled on at an even speed, unaware of the storm or the stowaway that rode the last flatcar.

Tess scowled into the darkness as she tried desperately to recall any pertinent information about the building of the tracks to the west. She reprimanded herself now for not paying better attention. She'd concentrated on points east, not the tracks stretching toward the Rockies. Oh, she had been so foolish not to learn more.

Pushing the wet tarp away from her face, she held it above her head as protection from the torrent above and breathed deeply of the cool air. She saw nothing beyond the edge of the flatcar. The lights of Omaha had faded.

Not even stars showed through the fierce storm that raged all around her and in her head.

Tess shivered in her wet dress. The canvas tarp had soaked through, leaving her little protection or warmth. She dragged a nearby box into position to allow the tarp to settle back down and yet still provide ventilation. The small box felt extremely heavy. No doubt filled with steel spikes for holding the iron rails in place. If there was anything Tess did know about, it was the details of the machine shop where Frank Mercer worked, providing the metal parts for the railroad construction. Boxes of these steel spikes were produced daily and shipped west for the workers to secure the heavy rails to wooden cross ties.

Thunder clapped overhead and she jumped.

Tess cocked her head, realizing that despite her unknown situation, she was finally free of Frank Mercer. A thrill of exhilaration raced through her, and she marveled at her unexpected predicament.

The overwhelming sense of freedom dominated her spirit, mingled with the chronic fear that plagued her and her mother. It had been so ingrained in her. Only keeping her eyes fixed on Jesus and the courage that came from above could she ever have attempted such a liberation.

Although almost summer, her wet dress felt heavy and chilled her completely. She felt warmer if she moved the box of spikes aside and lowered the tarp, but then struggled to breathe the stifling, stale air trapped under the damp canvas covering.

Tess hugged herself tightly, pressing her arms against her chest as she leaned her head against the hard crate at her back. She could see nothing through the thick canvas, but her mind raced.

What would she do? Her mistake nagged at her continuously. All her well-made plans of returning to

Chicago were suddenly worthless. Not only did she not know her destination, she would also know no one to help.

Over the past two years, as Frank Mercer's furtive glances become more brazen, Tess had constructed an escape strategy, which included the train taking her east to familiar friends and surroundings. Now, Tess rode the rails west toward lands and towns she had only heard about from locals as they discussed the growth of the Transcontinental Railroad.

The crews that laid the rails atop the fresh gravel beds lived in tent cities. These temporary villages only lasted a few months, depending on the ease of the geography, the abundance of water, and how quickly the rails were laid. Besides sleeping quarters for the numerous workers needed to build the railroad, the wild towns included dining tents, saloons, and gaming halls. Aptly called Hell on Wheels, these hastily constructed camps of canvas and lumber boasted little law and order. Peace was tentatively maintained using guns and fists. A man could do anything that he could back with strength and ability.

Tess knew that robberies and killings were a matter of course in these camps. As long as the rails continued across the open prairies, little could be done to impede these lawless men and events. They were simply a necessary byproduct of progress.

It was accepted that the hard work of these men demanded they have some way to let off steam—a chance to relax and have a little fun before they had to rise the next day and do it all over again.

Freezing cold winters and blistering hot summers, raiding Indians, stampeding buffalo herds, deep ravines and rivers, tall mountains, all proved obstacles of formidable measure for these mighty railroad workmen. Yet the tracks went on.

Tess recalled Crow Creek was a Hell on Wheels camp that had endured the longest. Had Frank mentioned if the workmen were finally finished with the Dale Creek bridge? Tess scratched her ear. Yes, he must have said something about the lengthy bridge, because she remembered the tracks had stretched farther west.

She tilted her head. That's right. The tracks were creeping slowly up the grade toward the Continental Divide. Frank said the managers were driving the men to Herculean demands, racing for Utah.

Tess frowned in the gloom, trying to recall more facts Frank and others might have revealed about the lands ahead, feeling angry with herself now that she hadn't listened more attentively when folks shared information about things going on in the west. Tess regretted thinking solely about the rails east of Omaha, where they crossed the Missouri River, the plains of Iowa, and on to Chicago.

Then it came to her, and she remembered the unique name Frank had mentioned at dinner. Laramie.

Sighing, she pushed her leg against the edge of the canvas covering and lifted the wet cloth. Fresh air rushed into her cramped position. The chill invaded, also, and she quickly lowered her leg as a shiver shot through her.

It still rained, although the wind had subsided. The gentle swaying of the car kept her aware of her surroundings and her stomach tightened. This was no dream, no illusion of something unreal. Tess would never forget the fateful night of her seventeenth birthday.

For the thousandth time, Tess wondered at the Lord's will for her life. She'd believed her plans for Chicago had been from him, but, in an instant, her plans were tossed aside for a completely new set of circumstances.

Tess thought back to something Mrs. Sellers, her schoolteacher, had shared with her. Tess had told the interested teacher about Frank Mercer and his sudden and violent drunken tirades. Not only did she not want him in her home, the hard man made no effort to be kind to his new stepdaughter.

"He doesn't love me," Tess had confided to her teacher.

Then Mrs. Sellers had spoken of Christ's love and his sacrifice for all people. "Jesus loves you, Tess. For all times, he will love you, no matter what you do. But he hopes you will choose to follow him." She had showed Tess a Bible, allowing her to turn the thin, onion skin pages and ask questions.

Tess had heard about Noah's ark and the baby Jesus born in a manger. But how did these old stories fit into the message of Holy Scripture?

For frequent lunch breaks after that, Mrs. Sellers had spent time with Tess and explained Bible stories. Not only with Tess, though. Many other students were led to the Lord by this faithful servant of God.

Tess's stomach growled, demanding attention. It had been hours since she'd last eaten, not even enjoying a bite at her birthday celebration. Frank had ruined her special night. Not that it was the first time he'd done that, Tess mused, recalling other events that had ended in calamity because of the drunken blacksmith.

Her stomach growled impatiently, disturbing her reverie. She searched the space around her until her fingers touched the sodden towel her mother had given her.

Tess peeled back the edges of the towel. The loaf had been pressed flat by the rain and her frantic escape. She tore off a chunk and shoved the piece into her mouth. She grimaced at the taste of the soggy bread, but it helped satisfy her craving. She ate half of the wet loaf, chewing slowly as the railroad car rocked. Where would she get more food?

Again, she considered the Lord. She'd hoped to return to Chicago and be among friends who would look after her. Now, she was going in the opposite direction, out into the open prairie of the Great Plains. But Tess knew God was everywhere. He would certainly be with her now. He would even be at the construction camp at the end of the tracks. She must steel herself for what lie ahead. God would not be surprised about her predicament. The Lord knew everything, right?

Taking a deep breath, Tess calmed herself with a few favorite Scripture verses that encouraged her. Be strong and courageous. Do not fear or be dismayed. God knows the plans he has for me. He will never leave me or forsake me. He will be with me to the ends of the earth.

Even when Joseph had been thrown into a pit and his brothers sold him into slavery, God used that horrible event for his glory and provision for Jacob's sons during the famine.

The promises of God always comforted Tess when she was in dire straits, either from Frank's merciless pestering or from her own doubts and concerns about her future. She could feel herself relax as she turned her troubles over to the Lord. He would be with her, wherever she went. God had a plan, and she would see it through with faith and courage.

She yawned. Despite the intense chill, the roar of the continuous rain, and the swaying railroad and bumpy car, she felt lulled to sleep by her encouraging thoughts.

⁂

The slowing of the train awakened Tess. The stiffness in her limbs told her that hours had passed. She pushed the thick canvas aside and peered cautiously into the dim gray light. The rain had stopped. Were they at Laramie?

Tess scanned the land she could see between the piles of supplies. She scowled when she saw nothing. Not even a tree.

Slowly, she lifted her head and studied her surroundings further. She could hear the gentle huff of the resting engine at the head of the train. Through the semi darkness of early dawn, Tess could make out piles of rubble and tumbled down shacks littering the ground beside the tracks. It seemed to be the abandoned site of an earlier end-of-tracks town. Now, only a water tank and a single solid building marked the isolated town.

Her scowl deepened when she saw the high water tank and the rope dangling from the spout. This would likely be the only jerkwater stop on the railroad. The fireman would pull on the rope and lower the spout to refill the huge boiler on the engine.

Voices sounded ahead, and Tess scurried back under her tarp. Probably the brakeman or the engineer checking the cars. She heard the men call for additional wood or coal to be loaded into the fuel car behind the powerful locomotive.

Tess considered leaping off the flatcar into the darkness beyond the train but feared she might be left in a worse predicament. Perhaps it would be better to wait and jump from the train in a metropolis where she could expect some aid.

The taste of blood as she bit her lip startled her. Metropolis? There would be no urban center out here.

She waited nervously as the fuel car was loaded, the sounds of cursing and laughing men coming to her on the breeze.

The train lurched again and continued, the huge beast gaining speed slowly as it pulled from the water tank. She wondered how much further they had to go and if they were near the new town Frank had mentioned last evening at supper, the end of tracks with the odd name. What had he called it? Laramie, that was it, she reminded herself.

Her teeth chattered. Her wet hair hung limp. Again, she wrapped her arms around herself and regretfully recalled the blanket she'd lost to Frank. If only he hadn't grabbed the quilt. Still, that blanket had allowed her to get away from the shack. If Frank hadn't fallen, he surely would have caught her.

Still shivering, Tess dozed to the continuous clack-clack of the wheels and the rhythmic swaying of the flatcar.

Again, the slowing of the train stirred Tess, and she jerked wide awake at the shrill scream of the engine's piercing whistle. She shoved the wet canvas away from her and peered around. Dull gray light penetrated lowering clouds. But still, nothing but vast, empty prairie and a bare, high slope to the north greeted her vision. She turned and looked south. Dark, shaggy beasts grazed, their huge heads bent to the new grass of spring.

She scrambled to her knees and craned her neck, peering farther forward along the supply cars and past the smoking engine. The buffalo spread far in advance of the train, covering the twin rails of the tracks. In the overcast light of day, Tess watched as the herd of giants ignored the whistling locomotive and quietly grazed, blocking the train's progress.

Her eyes widened. This was her chance. She'd needed to use the outhouse for hours and her back ached painfully.

Black and dark gray clouds hung low, hiding any sign of the sun. The lull in the storm appeared only temporary.

Another whistle blast sounded, and the engine crept forward a few paces. A pair of buffalo lumbered off the tracks, but the herd remained, resistant to the threatening locomotive.

Her discomfort increased and Tess's brow furrowed. She desperately needed to relieve herself, only there was no outhouse. She bit her lip. Perhaps she could climb down from the flatcar and go behind the train where the engineer couldn't see her.

Her stiff legs protested as she stood and moved toward the metal ladder rungs. Silver fish danced before her eyes, and she felt lightheaded, but she grasped the first rung and slipped over the edge of the car.

Tess lowered herself on shaky limbs to the ground, her toes searching for the gravel bed before releasing the final rung.

She glanced anxiously over her shoulder as she moved to the rear of the train, her shoes crunching noisily on the loose gravel.

Tess stumbled behind the cars and looked east toward Omaha. The twin rails merged and disappeared in the distance. The vastness of the empty plains overwhelmed her, and she shivered. She clenched her teeth and lifted her dress as she squatted on the tracks.

An unexpected whistle blast made her jump. The train gave a sudden lurch and moved forward again, then stopped. Would the train leave her?

Fear filled her and Tess finished quickly before hurrying back to the ladder, her legs struggling to obey her commands. The train shifted again, and Tess had to run to keep her grip on the bottom rung. Another longer, shrill whistle sounded, and the train moved faster yet.

Buffalo streamed away from the tracks now and Tess knew the herd was on the move. The large, shaggy beasts ran, their massive, dark heads hanging low, their hooves pounding the prairie.

The train gathered speed. Tess thought of being left out

here alone with these frightening animals and she lunged, kicking off the ground and grabbing a higher rung. Her feet dangled as she pulled herself up, sweat pouring from her as she found a foothold and clambered up.

Tess collapsed on the wooden floor of the flatbed car, panting heavily and leaning on her hands, watching the plains fly by.

What if she hadn't climbed aboard again? Was there any water out here? It could be days before another train passed this way. She would starve to death or be trampled by buffalo. How could that be God's plan for her after escaping from Frank?

She narrowed her eyes and studied the threatening clouds. "Well, it didn't happen. I made the train." She stretched out, the cool wind whipping around her. She stared up. "Thank you, Jesus," she whispered.

A single drop fell on her face, warning her of more rain. Slowly, Tess rolled over and crawled to the protection of the wet canvas tarp just as the rains fell with increasing force. She pulled herself into her sitting position with her back against the hard crate, trying to stem the shivering that rocked her. She felt like she would be sick, her stomach rolled with the swaying train. Her cheeks felt heated.

Tess pulled her knees to her chest and hugged them, her teeth chattering uncontrollably. Was it a fever? Could the dampness and chill have caused her to get sick so quickly? She wasn't sure, but she certainly felt awful.

Perhaps the bread would give her strength. The half-eaten loaf wouldn't last much longer, anyway. She tried to eat a few bites, but her stomach heaved at the smell of the wet bread. She almost tossed the remainder of the loaf away, but then reconsidered and wrapped the offending soggy mess again in the towel. It might be all she'd have for a while.

Now, the bumpy train ride irritated her and increased her ill feeling. Thirst choked her. The rain continued and Tess dozed fitfully all day.

Dim shadows stretched long the next time Tess awakened. She guessed it was evening now as the train pulled from a little tent town. Probably Crow Creek. She'd hoped to disembark here and find shelter or employment or even a ride to Chicago. But the train was already leaving the village when Tess peeked from under the tarp and saw the last of the town disappearing. She felt too weak to jump from the moving train.

Tess wrapped the damp tarp around her, letting the cool rain fall on her burning forehead.

They passed another smaller camp in the night. This time, the train barely slowed, allowing Tess only the briefest glimpse of the small village. Large stacks of railroad ties lay along the rails, ready for loading. It was the last she saw before passing out.

The sudden whistle blast didn't make her jump this time. Tess felt too out of her head, lethargic and feverish. The train slowed. Could they need to stop for fuel and water again so soon after Crow Creek? Tess could not be sure she thought clearly anymore.

She looked around, surprised to find she no longer lie beneath the tarp. The dark night had hidden her from prying eyes, but not the rain. Every item she wore had been soaked through.

A large town loomed ahead, lantern lights glimmering from dark buildings. Tess pushed herself up and brushed her wet hair aside, peering over the crates around her. Rows and rows of dirty canvas tents and shacks lined both sides of the tracks, giving way to wooden loading docks as the train neared the brightest part of town.

The locomotive puffed and slowed even more and

finally crept alongside a long loading platform. A wide street led from the train yard, music and shouts drifting to Tess's ears as she crawled to the edge of the flatcar. Yellow lantern lights glowed along the long, main street of the mobile city.

Laramie.

A steady drizzle pelted Tess as she stumbled and almost fell down the ladder, her hands slipping on the wet rungs. The train whistled once more and released a head of steam. From main street, a gunshot rang out, then another.

Tess pressed her bundle of spare dresses, her Bible, and the little chunk of soggy bread to her chest and leaned against the rail car. She swayed and fell to her knees, her belongings spilling to the muddy ground. Sharp rocks cut into her legs, but she couldn't move, her arms trembling as she heaved bile from her empty stomach.

She stayed there a long moment, trying to gather her strength and stand. She could hear men talking and she feared being discovered. Rain fell into her eyes as she looked up at the murky sky. Not even a single star peeked through the dark canopy overhead. Somewhere down the main street, she thought she heard a banjo.

Her anxiety grew as she heard steps approaching. Ignoring her nausea and her injured knees, she forced herself to roll over and crawl into the brush alongside the tracks. She lay there, panting, her eyes searching for the men. They were a little distance away, a lantern swinging as they strode. Then she remembered her things.

Tess scrambled from her hiding place and grabbed her dresses and Bible. She backed into the brush once more as the circle of lantern light neared. She held her breath.

"I heard it was Big Steve again." The first man spit loudly.

The second man snorted. "Well, he can shoot whoever

he wants, him being marshal and all."

The first man chuckled as they moved past Tess and out of earshot.

Through the drizzle, Tess saw the dull yellow lights of the main street beyond the train tracks. Numerous canvas and wooden buildings lined the wide street. Tess listened a moment longer, the banjo music sounding out of place in this muddy, wet night.

The gurgle of running water sounded above the din of the downtown, and Tess detected a nearby river, although she couldn't pinpoint its exact location.

As if she were a moth drawn to a flame, Tess started walking toward the lighted saloons. Help lay in that direction. She no longer felt hunger pains, but her thirst drove her. She must drink.

Smeared mud covered her baggy dress. What would Mama say about her rough appearance? Tess didn't care. She had to have water.

A shiver passed through her as she reached the first building.

She lifted a hand to her cheek, the heat radiating from her face like a furnace. The shivering wouldn't stop. Her fingers felt numb as she mindlessly smoothed her filthy dress.

Swaying, she walked down the lighted main street of the noisy town.

CHAPTER THREE

Despite the late hour, men crowded the muddy street of the tent town. Tess vaguely noticed them, garbed in rough workmen's clothes. Many were bearded, all were booted. Many of them stared at her as she passed, but she walked on, intent on finding water.

Fear mingled with the intense thirst that pushed her on. Was she safe? Nothing seemed to matter as much as getting something to drink. Not even prayer or favorite Scripture verses came to her clouded mind.

Again, the dull roar of swiftly racing waters reminded Tess of a nearby river. It seemed too far away, though. She needed a drink—now.

Men streamed in and out of a large building on her right. Music floated from the wide doorway, along with the tinkle of glass and the clamor of crowds. The memory of the saloons of Omaha came to her and she thought of Frank Mercer. Tess walked on.

A burly man in a red flannel shirt halted and peered at her. "Are you all right, miss? You don't look well."

Tess desperately wanted to ask for help, to seek some place safe where she could simply lie down in a dry place and sleep for hours. She looked cautiously at the railroad worker, unsure if she should or could speak to him.

Then she saw a horse trough in front of the saloon. She staggered to it, catching the rim of the rough planks to hold herself steady. Her few belongings tumbled to the ground as she dropped to her knees and plunged her free hand into the dirty water.

Gulps of the cool water dribbled down her parched throat as Tess lifted handful after handful to her mouth.

Tess sagged in the mud, unable to venture further. Her weak arms held her above the edge of the trough. Then she drank again.

A drunken man and his friend pointed at Tess sitting in the puddles and the rain. They laughed and slapped one another on the shoulder as the pair continued down the street to the next saloon.

Tess narrowed her eyes. She knew the ways of intoxicated men enough to know things would get worse for her as the night wore on.

Grasping the splintering edge of the trough with her left hand, Tess forced herself to her feet. She was still shaky, but the water had revived her. Slowly, she surveyed her surroundings.

Throngs of men sloshed through the rain and puddles, moving from one saloon to another. Yellow light glowed from every window and door. The roar of hundreds of voices came from each building. Laramie was in full swing, despite the rainstorm.

Tess glanced down, past her filthy dress to the bundle of goods at her feet. Slowly, she lowered herself and retrieved her belongings. As she stood, a man laughed.

"Look what the cat dragged in, Steve."

Tess clasped her things to her chest. She trembled and her head felt like a log afire.

A group of men stood before her, watching her intently from the boardwalk. A tall, wide-shouldered man stood in the center, a metal star pinned to his vest.

The men chuckled again, and Tess realized what she must look like. A young, slender girl of seventeen in a filthy dress too big for her, soaked to the bone. Her long, dark brown hair lay plastered to her head. Her slouched shoulders making her appear even smaller. She straightened a little.

"Why, the girl looks like a drowned rat." A short, thin man in a derby hat pointed at Tess.

"Don't be so rude to the little lady, Ace." A man in white shirtsleeves and black vest spit into the street and then replaced a cigar between his teeth. "Perhaps she's looking for a job in the cribs."

More laughter.

Tess shrank as the group of men fanned out on the boardwalk above her, facing her expectantly, wanting to see the show as the men made crude remarks.

"She's too skinny to work at the Bucket of Blood." Ace snorted with disgust.

At the mention of a job, Tess perked up, but then thought better of it. These men frightened her.

"Don't be too sure," the tall man with the star spoke up. His gray handlebar moustache drooped. "Some of the boys ain't too particular when it comes to the girls in the cribs."

The thin man in the derby frowned. "That's true, Steve. I saw the Chinaman has taken in a colored gal."

"Well, Ace, you know the Chinaman has no standards. He'll sell whiskey to anyone," the man in the white shirtsleeves said around his cigar, a note of contempt in his tone.

"Now, Con, don't be so rough on our little yellow competitor," Steve said as he turned to his friends. Tess saw light from the window glint on his star. He narrowed his eyes and leaned toward her. "Are you looking for work, girl, or are you a runaway? I'm the marshal here in Laramie and if you're a runaway, I'll have to arrest you."

The small group of men chortled and slapped each

other on the back.

A wagon rumbled behind Tess, and she glanced over her shoulder. Two powerful mules halted as the reins were pulled, and Tess shielded her eyes from the rain to look up at the driver.

A chiseled face, high cheek bones above dark stubble, gleamed with rainwater in the dull light of the saloon lamps. His hat was pushed back, revealing piercing eyes that bore into the small group of men on the boardwalk. A thrill raced through her.

Boots shuffled as the group spread out even more. Tess back stepped into the shadows, her presence forgotten. She moved between two buildings and watched the newcomer as he glared down at the marshal and his companions. Her scrutiny shifted to the crowd on the boardwalk. They stood beneath a roughly painted sign that read Bucket of Blood. Their humorous manner had vanished.

"Long, I heard you killed Cranston tonight," the man in the wagon accused.

Tess's gaze swung back to him. His hands held the reins idly, as if ready to grab a weapon quickly, but Tess saw no gun.

Steve Long stepped forward. His short, gray hair was slick from the tapering drizzle. He leered openly at the young man on the wagon. "Yeah, Calloway, I shot Cranston. He called me a liar and went for his gun. What concern is it of yours?"

"Everyone knows you and your brothers were after his land," Calloway continued. "It sounds like it was another convenient shooting in your own saloon, if you ask me."

"Well, no one asked you, Calloway." The man called Con spoke quietly from beside Steve Long. He leaned forward and spit into the street. "Besides, it's no secret I've made a fair offer to Cranston for his land, same as I've made you and your partner. It's no crime to buy land," Con added, a hard grin creasing his hard face.

Tess watched from the deep darkness of the narrow alley. The rain had stopped, but her shivering hadn't. Exhaustion filled her, making it a struggle to stand. She wondered if she had the influenza. God knew she'd seen it often enough back in Chicago as the deadly disease swept through the tenement housing. She needed to get somewhere dry and rest.

"It's not a crime to buy land," Calloway agreed. "Only when the owner doesn't want to sell, it is, Con Moyer. I know Cranston turned down your offer. He wouldn't sell his land willingly."

"Well, there you're wrong, Calloway." Long spread his left hand toward the man beside him. "He sold his land tonight to Con here, proprietor of the Bucket of Blood. There were plenty of witnesses present to that little event and the fair shooting that followed."

Calloway shook his head. "I know all about your witnesses, Long. I'm sure your friends will swear that Cranston went for a gun and forced you to draw. Let's see if an investigation from the sheriff will find such witnesses reliable." Calloway slapped the reins and the wagon lurched forward.

"Sheriff Boswell has no jurisdiction in Laramie, Calloway. You know that," Long called after the departing wagon.

The knot of men grumbled and shuffled into the saloon. Only the marshal remained in place, watching the wagon roll farther down the street. Finally, he, too, turned to follow his cohorts into the noisy saloon.

Tess turned and watched the wagon disappear into the gloom. She bit her lip and hugged her wet belongings tighter. Calloway seemed young, not much older than herself, and she thought his face appeared honest.

His coat had stretched over powerful shoulders, and his piercing eyes blazed as he spoke. She'd noticed his short-cropped beard in the dim lighting. But something about him struck her on a deeper level, and she trusted the sensation.

What made her consider him? Why should she care about these men and their issues? She was a stranger here and certainly had no loyalty to any faction or person. Yet something had made her warm to the fight in Calloway's voice.

Tess looked down the street. Lamplight from the various businesses revealed the again-halted wagon. A loud shout and breaking glass in the saloon next to Tess helped her make up her mind.

With a furtive glance toward the door of the Bucket of Blood, Tess stole from the shadows of her hiding place and hurried down the street. Additional shouts and cursing lent wings to her stumbling feet as she moved through puddles and mud toward the wagon.

Tess heard voices as she neared. Calloway spoke to someone in a shack at the edge of town. "Long is running unchecked in Laramie."

Tess slowed, moving cautiously through the shadows. Calloway continued, "He does what he wishes. Even Mayor Brown resigned last week when he realized he had no real power. Big Steve Long is the power here."

"Now, Brett," a calmer voice cautioned from the small shack beside the road. "It's no concern of yours. Stay out of it. You have a job to do. Stay focused on your dream, lad, and don't forget to remember your mother waiting on you back home. Don't let outside forces sway your resolve."

Tess moved through the muddy street, listening closely to the conversation, gliding unseen. Dull light shimmered on a puddle and she skirted the small pond. She crept to the tailgate of the tall wagon and slowly hoisted herself over the board and into the bed, high wooden sides hiding Tess from any chance observers. She rolled into a tight ball, clutching her bundle to her chest. The floor of the wagon was wet and smelled of grain sacks and sawdust.

Tess worried that Calloway might hear the chattering of her teeth. The sound seemed loud in her ears.

"Goodnight now, Brett. I'll talk of these things to you again soon. God bless." The man in the shack closed his door.

"Goodnight, Mr. Warren." Brett Calloway slapped the reins and the wagon moved.

Tess gritted her teeth and tried to ignore the bumpy ride as her woozy insides jostled. Despite the turbulence, she felt grateful to lie down.

The hollow sound of hooves on wood told her they crossed a bridge and Tess wondered if it was the river she'd heard earlier. She peered up at the darkness overhead. Only one star shone between ominous storm clouds. Tess fixed her eyes on this lone star and prayed.

"Heavenly Father …"

She yawned and her eyes fluttered. She laid her weary head on her arm and went to sleep.

CHAPTER FOUR

Frank Mercer chased her. A giant, his grotesque form dark and menacing in the fog. Tess screamed, but no words came out. She ran in the haze, darting one way and then another, never able to elude her pursuer.

Then a young man in a brown coat stepped beside her, took her hand, and led her through the murkiness. His strong hand gripped hers, reassuring her. She slowed and felt secure, safe, although she didn't know the stranger. Yet he was not a stranger. Somehow, she knew him, and trusted him.

He lifted her from the wagon, and she wondered if she might find a man like this one day, a man to trust and to love. She snuggled against his chest as he carried her away.

Strangely, the dream state of unclear events and hazy faces with beards continued for Tess. But now, there were two such men with hair on their tanned faces.

They took turns spooning soup into her and holding her head so she could drink. The dreams continued and Tess grew weary of remembering Frank Mercer, thinking of him chasing her through the Omaha train yard. Memories of her mother, and occasionally thoughts of her home in Chicago so long ago, flitted in and out of her head.

Once, Tess recalled her father. She didn't remember him well. She had only been nine years old when she last saw him. However, the memory remained of his rough and abrupt nature. She didn't remember missing him when he'd gone off to war.

Sunlight awakened her as bright rays streamed through a clear glass window across from her bed. Only, it wasn't Tess's bed at all. The thick woolen blanket felt unfamiliar. Slowly, she caressed the rough blanket and allowed her gaze to travel around the room. Long, yellow timbers, peeled pine logs, stacked artfully up each wall. The cabin smelled fresh, as if newly constructed. A large fireplace of native granite stones lay at one end of the cabin. Red embers glowed on the hearth, and a tiny tendril of smoke drifted lazily up the chimney.

Her eyes wandered to the opposite wall. A door of fitted planks, the latch string out, the bar leaning in the corner. The window had been cleverly crafted into the wall next to the door. Tess knew only wealthy folks could afford glass, especially a piece of this size. Bright light streamed through the tall window, at least two logs high, and splashed across the gray flagstone floor and across the bed.

Three planks had been nailed across a similar opening in the south wall. A glass window was intended here one day too.

A long table stood in the center of the room with benches on either side. A single chair rested by the fireplace. Both an elk hide and an antelope pelt covered wall space above Tess's head. A large deerskin lay in front of the open fireplace. Plank shelves lined the walls near the fireplace, stacked with various cooking utensils, plates, and cups. Although many of the items in the cabin appeared handcrafted, the quality was obvious. Whoever built this cabin and the furnishings knew how to work with wood.

Her own dismal shack in Omaha couldn't compare with this lovely cabin. Oh, how her mother would be jealous to see this room, Tess mused.

Something nagged at her, and she realized she was still in bed with the sun shining through the window. When had she ever been in bed this late? Tess eyed a wooden bucket on the nearby table. It was evident she'd been sick. Weakness and thirst lingered.

Moving tentatively, Tess tossed back the thick blankets and slowly swung her feet to the cold stone floor. Her head swam and she leaned against the bed post, still surveying the spacious room.

Another quiet minute passed, and she attempted to stand. Her legs wobbled, but she steadied herself and carefully made her way to the table.

She dropped onto one of the long benches and dipped an empty cup into the water bucket. Her hands shook as she held the tin cup to her lips. She drank deeply, the cool water sliding down her parched throat. The water refreshed her, and she quickly filled the cup again.

She leaned her forearms on the table and rested, her gaze traveling out the front window. A bare yard lay just outside the cabin door to a foliage-choked stream. Beyond, a thick forest, green and lush. How had she come to the woods?

Her scan continued and she took in the walls, stone floor, and the bare timbers once more. Although she didn't recognize her surroundings, she didn't feel frightened. The cozy, warm cabin comforted her.

Tess bobbed her head and peered out the window again. This time she looked across the stream and noticed a cabin nestled in the forest there.

Two cabins? Was she in a town then?

She pursed her lips and tried to think. Tess remembered the train ride from Omaha to Laramie, the men at the Bucket of Blood.

Her eyes widened as more details flooded over her. The Bucket of Blood? The saloon. The group of rough men. Steve Long. Con Moyer. Calloway. Memories swept over her as her stomach tightened. She had escaped Frank Mercer to end up in Laramie, the frontier town at the end of the railroad construction.

Her gaze roamed around the cabin once more, and her shoulders relaxed. Still, she felt safe here.

Dark green branches swayed gracefully as Tess watched the forest beyond the stream. The tall pines blocked much of the sunlight, but still some filtered into the open east window.

The forest was new to her—she'd only known the open plains around Omaha and the crowded city life of Chicago before that. This new experience thrilled her. The freshness of the clean cabin and the deep forest around her made her feel she had indeed left her old life behind. Perhaps she would find work here in this place and not return quickly to Chicago like she planned.

Wasn't it the Lord who had orchestrated the wrong train to bring her west?

Tess bit her lip and frowned. She was afraid to travel back through Omaha. Frank was there and the train would have to stop for refueling and water. Frank would never know she was on the train passing through Omaha, but what if he were to see her somehow?

A shiver ran down her back. No. Chicago could wait.

Her gaze fell to the smooth, gray flagstones at her feet. The large stones felt cold on her toes and fitted together so intricately. She thought again about the clever man who must have built this cabin.

Her gaze traveled from the floor and up her bare leg. Suddenly, her eyes widened in shock and a heated blush rose to her cheeks. She wore only her underclothes. Even her stockings had been removed.

Who had taken her dress off? She frantically searched the cabin for a clue. A workman's coat dangled from a peg in the wall and a rifle stretched over the door, mounted on a rack of elk horns. A spare shirt and a pair of breeches hung on more pegs driven into the crease between logs. Obviously, a man lived in this cabin, probably Brett Calloway.

Then she spotted her dress. The big coat almost concealed the garment completely.

Tess stood again, this time less dizzy, and made her way across the smooth stones to the clothes on the wall. Brushing aside the coat, she held her dress and studied the clean fabric.

Tess remembered now how filthy the garment had been the night she arrived in Laramie. Her other dresses hung on the same hook.

She tilted her head and released the dress. Her hand lifted and she touched her hair, marveling at the soft feel. Her hair, too, had been cleaned and brushed. How? Who had done this? Her nose wrinkled as she remembered the tangled and wet mane from that same terrible night.

She dropped her hand and walked slowly toward the fireplace. A pot simmered on the back of the glowing embers. Someone had left soup for her. Brett Calloway or someone else?

It took only a moment to scoop stew into a bowl. The smell made her mouth water. She thought over the confusing situation while she ate.

Mama would be worried about her, but there was nothing Tess could do about that now. In time, she would figure out a way to get word to her mother.

She recalled her fervent prayers the day on the train. Had God answered her plea for help? Was she now safe, or was she in worse danger than before? Certainly, the crowd of men outside the Bucket of Blood made her nervous and frightened. She hoped she was not at one of those men's cabins.

Tess peered again at the bright yellow logs and the big window. The cheery room convinced her that this cabin could not belong to any of them.

She glanced at the door and frowned again. It would not be fitting if someone entered now and found her in her underclothes. She wrapped a blanket around herself and sat in the chair beside the fireplace. The stew tasted delicious.

She tossed a stick on the embers and watched until it blazed, tiny flames licking the dry wood. Then, she added more sticks. She saw a half loaf of bread on the sideboard, but her stomach turned at sight of the small portion. It might be a while before she could eat bread again.

She narrowed her eyes and looked down. What if the man who lived here returned while she was parading herself half naked around his cabin? Mama would be horrified to have someone see her like this.

But hadn't someone already seen her this way? She blushed again, the crimson staining her pale cheeks. The thought made her angry. Who had the right to undress her?

Feeling satisfied from the warm soup, Tess felt drowsy. She still felt weak, although the food settled well in her stomach. A yawn escaped her, and she peered over her shoulder at the unmade bed.

Leaving her bowl near the fireplace, Tess moved toward the bed. She no longer felt dizzy but suddenly extremely tired. A little nap might do her well, Tess decided with another yawn as she stretched out and pulled the blankets over her.

The anger she'd felt at the man who'd taken her dress off slipped away as she snuggled deeper into the mattress. She would take care of that later. Right now, she needed to sleep.

Her final thoughts before she slipped back into sleep were of God. With closed eyes, Tess mumbled, "Thank you, Lord." She yawned again. "Thank you for bringing me here. I pray for your protection, and I hope you will use this experience for your glory. Let me serve you with my life. Give me faith to believe it was you who brought me here and that it was for a specific purpose. I love you, Father," she concluded.

Tess pulled the blankets higher. She felt so tired.

<hr>

The door opened with a creak, and she awakened. Shadows stretched under the trees beyond the window, and dim, drowsy light filled the quiet room. The sun had traveled far to the west.

She froze, excited and afraid, a thrill running through her. She would meet the man who lived here.

He stood in the doorway, a man of medium height, silhouetted by the fading light. She recognized his broad shoulders and short beard. He hesitated, peering through the gloom toward the bed. Tess didn't move, not sure what she should do. Should she speak? She held her breath.

The man moved on quiet feet to the fireplace and knelt. He poked at the ash, searching for glowing coals. She stared hard at his broad back. Tess couldn't be sure the man was Brett Calloway, although something made her wish it was the young man she'd seen in Laramie.

He reached for kindling, poking the fire with the small sticks and finally throwing them on the ashes. His hand lifted to the mantle for the matches.

A scratching sound and the stick flared. She saw his outlined face and recognized Brett Calloway. Tess thrilled anew at sight of the young bearded man, and she released her pent breath, relief coursing through her.

Tess rebuked herself for not banking a fire after lunch time. The few small pieces of wood she'd used had been quickly consumed and now the fire lay dead. She knew better than to allow a fire to die out completely. It was easier to keep a fire alive than to start one from kindling.

Brett fed the small blaze. He glanced over his shoulder, and Tess closed her eyes, pretending to be asleep.

She opened her eye a slit. Brett had returned to his task at the open fire, but then stood abruptly, startling Tess with his graceful movement. He took the bucket from the table and strode from the cabin, closing the door quietly behind him.

Tess was alone again, her thoughts in tumult. Why hadn't she spoken?

The door opened again, and Brett reappeared, the bucket swinging easily in one hand. Tess covertly watched him pour water into the coffeepot and place the blackened metal pitcher on the fire. He stood there a moment, staring into the flames. Then, throwing some more wood on the blaze, he turned to glance at Tess.

This time, she stared directly at him, challenging him, wanting answers. She gripped the woolen blanket and held the covers to her chin.

"Oh," he began, moving slowly toward her. "I see you've finally come out of it. You surely had us worried, miss."

He scooped the chair as he passed, bringing it with him. He settled the seat between the table and the bed, his eyes on her, his movements slow, as if he didn't wish to frighten her. He smiled and kindness shone in his eyes.

She liked his voice, Tess decided. His words rolled musically off his tongue and there seemed to be a note or lilt to it she didn't recognize. Irish? Norwegian? She couldn't be sure. Living in Chicago had allowed her to hear many foreign languages, but his seemed unrecognizable.

Tess stared into his clear, dark eyes. Brown? Perhaps hazel, she mused. His beard was scant, revealing his youth. Did the dark stubble conceal a firm jaw?

"Where am I?"

His grin widened. "Why, you're in my cabin."

"And who are you?" Tess persisted, even though she knew him.

"Brett Calloway. I found you in my wagon. We think you had the fever. You were much worse three days ago. But some rest and some food seems to have brought you through it."

"Who is 'we'?"

Brett nodded. "My partner, Sandy. He lives across the creek at his cabin. We're tie cutters for the Union Pacific. We've homesteaded joint parcels and hope to bring our families out here soon. Perhaps by winter, if all goes well." Brett arched an eyebrow and shrugged. "Well, I should say my family. Sandy doesn't have one yet, but someday."

Flames sizzled as the coffeepot boiled over. Tess watched as Brett hurried to the fire and lifted the pot from the flames. After adding the coffee, he sat the blackened pot on the coals.

He glanced over his shoulder. "Let me put dinner together, and then we can talk more. I'm hungry enough to eat a bear, and Sandy will be joining us soon. He's putting the mules in the barn."

Tess lay quiet, her mind whirling with questions for this stranger. Yet, somehow, she didn't feel he was truly a stranger. Not to her.

Brett moved about the cabin, lighting the candle for the center of the table and placing three plates around the scrubbed planks. He indicated the single candle. "I can't afford a lamp yet. All my money went into the glass window. I'm saving for the south window." He indicated the covered hole in the south wall. "Sandy says I'm a fool to buy glass before a lamp." He grinned, laughing at himself, and Tess couldn't help smiling.

It took only a few minutes to fry bacon in a skillet and add beans to the pan. Soon, the aroma of frying meat filled the room. Her stomach growled and she pressed a hand over her belly. Surprised, she realized she felt hungry again. The soup from lunch had only whetted her appetite.

The door opened, and a man entered. He halted when he saw Tess, his eyes boring into her over the bundle of wood he carried. He stood taller than Brett and looked older, judging by the lines on his face and his graying, sparse hair.

He smiled shyly, and Tess saw the relief in his eyes. He glanced at Brett. "So, the young waif has awakened."

Her brow furrowed. Tess didn't like being called a waif. It made her feel like she had no home or was somehow lost.

But then she pursed her lips. Well, wasn't she?

The image made her grimace. Perhaps Sandy's assessment was more correct than she cared to admit.

"Dinner's almost ready. Will you take the skillet while I carry the coffeepot?" Brett moved toward the table while Sandy dropped his load.

Quickly, they brought the food to the table. Benches scraped as the two men seated themselves. Brett glanced at her. "Will you join us, miss?"

Tess thought she noted a hint of impatience in his voice.

She lowered her eyes and felt the heat stealing up her neck. "I'm not decent," she mumbled, wanting to ask right then who had taken her dress from her.

They were silent a moment, so Tess looked up. The two men frowned at one another, and Brett shuffled his feet. Sandy coughed.

Finally, Brett nodded. Tess thought he looked uncomfortable. "I see. Perhaps we should step outside for a moment and allow you to dress."

His bench scraped loudly as he stood. Sandy didn't move, his eyes glued to the bacon in the skillet.

"Come on, Sandy," Brett called as he moved to the door.

Sandy scowled, which made the lines on his face crinkle even more. He glowered at Tess as he stood and followed his partner outside, slamming the door a little too loudly.

Tess waited a moment before tossing the covers back. She hurried to the window and glanced outside, careful not to show herself. The porch was empty.

She reached for the floppy dress on the hook and slipped into the clothing, her fingers racing through the long row of buttons. Her hand went to her hair. It didn't feel tangled, but she wanted to see it. Her gaze swept the room, searching for a mirror. None. She bit her lip. She would have to make do.

Where were her shoes? She found them, near the fireplace, along with her clean stockings. She picked them up and studied the gleaming leather surface. They certainly hadn't been clean the last time she saw them.

Again, she wondered who had cleaned them. Hastily, she sat on Brett's bench and tugged them on, then stepped to the door and lifted the latch.

"You can come in now." She waved to the two men, standing on a small bridge that spanned the stream.

Sandy took his seat at the table, but Brett hesitated at sight of Tess in the shapeless dress. She could feel his eyes on her as she turned the chair and sat down, her back rigid, waiting for him to take his seat. She kept her gaze averted as he lowered himself to the bench.

Brett cleared his throat. "Let's pray." He bowed his head.

Tess put her hands in her lap and closed her eyes. She trembled, feeling both nervous and excited. She'd escaped Frank, but what would happen now?

Brett cleared his throat again, and Tess opened one eye. His eyes were pressed closed tightly, his jaw set firmly. She peeked at Sandy.

Sandy scowled at her but said nothing as he folded his hands, elbows on the table.

"Lord, thank you that this young girl is all right. You surely answered our prayers. Thank you for this food and this good land. Amen."

Sandy reached for the skillet with one hand, his fork stabbing bacon with the other. Then he shoveled beans onto his plate and handed the skillet to Brett.

Tess watched as the two hungry men ate, absorbed in the meal. She had seen hungry men before. She stood and walked around Brett to the coffeepot. He narrowed his eyes at her, his mouth full as he chewed. She poured herself a cup of coffee and then filled each man's tin cup.

Brett swallowed. "I could've passed that to you."

Tess took her seat again and smiled. "You looked busy."

Brett handed the skillet to her, a guilty look in his eyes. Sandy said nothing.

"So, miss," Brett went on, forking more bacon into his mouth.

"Tess. My name is Tess."

She almost said her last name, but perhaps Frank had telegraphed information about her to Laramie. Were the authorities already searching for Tess Randle, runaway?

Brett nodded and glanced at Sandy. His partner nodded

in return, still chewing.

"I'm looking for work," Tess went on in a rush. Maybe these men knew of some place looking for new workers.

Brett and Sandy exchanged glances again across the table.

Sandy swallowed hard. "What type of work do you do?" He eyed Tess a moment and then dropped his gaze to his plate.

She scowled. What was that about?

"Oh, anything," Tess replied, oblivious of his meaning. "I'm a hard worker. I can do laundry or cleaning or cooking. Most anything that needs to be done, I guess."

"Oh," Sandy said in an exaggerated tone. "That's good."

Brett shot his partner a disgusted look that was not lost on Tess.

"What?" She bit her lip. Had she said something wrong?

Brett ignored her, his eyes on Sandy. "She's a bit young for that type of girl."

"You never know out here, especially a runaway," Sandy snapped.

Tess could feel the color drain from her face. So, they knew. She was a runaway, and they would turn her in.

Her stomach muscles tightened, and her hunger disappeared. Hadn't Frank told her he was her legal guardian since she was a minor? Tess also recalled Big Steve Long's remark about her being a runaway. Suddenly, Tess felt wary of this situation and these two men.

She determined to play it off and act innocent. "I'm not quite sure what you're talking about, but I'm a hard worker. No one would say different about me."

The two men fell silent and Tess grew increasingly anxious. Did they know? Could they have already heard about her? Was Frank even now on his way to claim her?

She sensed they thought she was only a little girl. Tess straightened in her chair and looked at Brett. "I'm seventeen."

Brett nodded, his eyes cold where they had been so kind before. "Really? I would've guessed younger," he mumbled under his breath. "That dress looks too big for you."

Tess dropped her gaze and pushed a piece of salt pork around her plate. The cabin grew eerily quiet.

She glanced up, studying the rafters. What was God doing? Hadn't he orchestrated her escape from her stepfather? She chewed the inside of her cheek. What could she do to convince these men she couldn't go back?

Tess jumped to her feet and started clearing the table. She moved quickly, not allowing them to stop her even if they tried.

Dizziness made her head swim and she dropped to the bench beside Brett. The weakness from the fever still hampered her abilities if not her desire.

Brett stood, concern clouding his face. He gripped her arm, steadying her. "We'll take care of clean up tonight." He took the plates from her limp hands. "You can help when you're feeling better."

He gathered the remaining dishes and started for the door. He paused and turned, his eyes softening as Tess stared after him. "That is, unless you're planning on leaving here soon," he added.

Tess blinked, unsure what to say. What were her plans? She had considered staying in Laramie at least for a while, until Frank quit searching for her and she felt it safe to go east. But what about right now? Where would she live?

She hesitated. "I have no real plans. I mean, I'm not sure where I'll live. I need to find work, of course, but I have nowhere to stay."

"You can stay here," Brett interrupted. "I mean, for a

little while, if you want."

Sandy growled. "Brett, think about what you're saying. Long is after us and we need to still cut ties if we intend on making the homesteads work." He glanced at Tess and scowled. "No offense, miss, but we're far too busy to play nurse maid anymore. I need Brett to give a hundred percent and stop fawning all over you."

Brett's eyes widened. "I'm not fawning over her, Sandy."

Sandy rose with a huff and snatched the dishes from Brett on his way outdoors. He thumped into the gathering gloom of twilight.

Now they were alone, and Tess lowered her eyes as Brett shifted nervously on his feet. She hated making Sandy angry, but she needed help. She tried to smile as she looked again at Brett. "Thank you," she whispered.

Brett nodded. He shot her a halfhearted grin and hooked a thumb out the door. "We just rinse our dishes in the stream. It's quicker than heating water."

Tess didn't reply. She wondered if Sandy would allow her to stay. Where would she go if he didn't?

Brett seemed to read her thoughts. He stepped toward the table and sat down, leaning across the smoothed planks. Their faces were only a foot apart. She could read the worry in his eyes. Worry for her or for himself?

"Look, Tess, we're between a rock and a hard place, but don't worry about Sandy. You can stay here awhile. I know Sandy and he's all bark. He's solid, though."

Tess merely nodded, not sure what to believe.

Sandy returned and stacked the dishes on the sideboard. He put the freshly filled coffeepot near the hearth and straightened, brushing his hands. His gaze shifted from Brett to Tess and back to Brett again.

"I'll be saying my goodnights." He stared intently at his partner. "Remember what I said, Brett."

Sandy left the room, the door closing softly behind him.

Firelight played on the walls, their shadows dancing gently amid the silence. Brett stood. "I'll sleep on the floor. You can have the bed." He pulled off his shirt and tossed it over the back of the chair.

His bare chest shone like chiseled marble in the dim light. Tess could feel her eyes widen, and she turned away in haste.

"What are you doing?"

Her words came out too quickly. She could hear the panic in her tone. Would Brett undress in front of her?

He hesitated and Tess looked at him, directing her gaze to his face, attempting to ignore his naked chest.

"I mean, I thought you would sleep in Sandy's cabin," she said, her voice lowering as she regained her composure.

Brett grinned. "I can't. The Homestead Act says you must live and build on your own land. Big Steve Long and his half-brothers, Con and Ace Moyer, are looking for any excuse to get my land. I have to sleep in here." He turned away and tugged off his belt. He glanced at Tess over his shoulder. "Besides, I slept in here the whole time you were with fever."

She frowned and turned away. "That was different. I didn't know you were here." She folded her hands in her lap and studied them. "It's not proper for me to sleep in a cabin with an unmarried man. What would people think?"

Brett chuckled and sat on the edge of a bench while he pulled off his boots. "We're on the frontier. No one cares what's proper out here."

"Well, I care." Her chin came up as heat rose to her cheeks.

Brett dropped a boot with a thump, and he sighed loudly. He looked at Tess, his eyes clouded. "Look, I said you can stay, but I have to get some sleep. You heard Sandy.

He's counting on me. So, what do you need me to do so we can both go to bed?"

She bit her lip. She needed a place to stay. She had nowhere else to go. Her gaze shifted to the bed in the corner farthest from the fireplace and she turned back to Brett.

"Where's the outhouse?"

"Any place north of the swimming hole."

Tess tilted her head. "What does that mean?"

"We don't want to muddy our drinking and bathing water. Use any tree on the far side of the swimming hole. It's just past the foot bridge."

"You mean you don't have a proper outhouse?"

Brett shrugged. "We haven't gotten to it yet. We've been busy."

Exasperated, Tess stomped to the door.

"Watch for bears," Brett added when her fingers touched the latch. She froze.

"Bears?"

"They run all over these mountains. Grizzlies too. I've heard it said they eat people."

Tess gulped and released the latch. She would wait until morning.

"Give me a few minutes to prepare." She nodded toward the bed and then pointed at the door. Brett arched an eyebrow, and, with a grunt, he rose and padded to the door, his bare feet making no sound on the flagstones. She could smell his musky scent as he passed, mingled with wood smoke. She closed the door behind him.

Tess waited a moment and then poured a cup of water and placed the mug near the bed. She glanced at the door again and pulled her dress over her head. Not until she was safely under the covers did she call to him.

Brett barred the door and threw a few logs on the fire.

He spread his blankets before the hearth, not looking at Tess as he worked. Then, he stretched out with a sigh, his hands laced behind his head as he stared at the ceiling.

Tess watched him from the bed, her hands gripping the blanket tightly. Only the sound of the fire crackling disturbed the silence.

"Goodnight, Brett," Tess called softly.

He didn't reply. For a moment, Tess considered repeating herself. Then, she thought better of it.

She stared at the rafters. Was Brett serious when he'd said they didn't wash their dishes? She shivered, thinking of that. Disgusting.

Then she relaxed and watched the swaying shadows play across the wall.

"God, help me," she whispered to the still night.

CHAPTER FIVE

Tess stood a moment, listening to the soft murmur of the stream at her feet. She couldn't see the cabin on the opposite side of the creek, but she knew the house was there, screened by the thick wall of foliage around the swimming hole.

This was the first time she'd been outside since … since when?

Tess tilted her head. She had no idea how long she'd been unconscious with fever. Probably only a few days. She would have to ask Brett about it this evening.

Sandy had awakened her earlier with his noisy search for food in the gloom of dawn. He had tossed items in a canvas sack, his dark form moving about the cabin. Tess had watched him with narrowed eyes, only the dim glow from the fireplace allowing Tess to see him. He glanced at Tess when his hand touched the latch.

She pretended to be asleep. Part of her wanted to ask him who had undressed her, then she remembered the way the older man had glared at her the evening before. The question could wait.

The lumberjack shut the door behind him, the latch falling into place. Tess listened as his heavy boots thudded across the porch and then died away in the silent morning. Not even a bird stirred this early. Brett must have slipped out beforehand without disturbing her.

She had lay alone in the darkness then. Panic threatened to envelope her, like a storm swirling about her. She gripped the blankets tighter.

What would she do now?

She forced herself to breathe and, slowly, she relaxed again, allowing the Lord's presence to fill her. For now, she would make herself busy. There were plenty of things she could do around the cabin before the men returned. She would show them how helpful she could be.

She wouldn't think about her future. Today, she would pray. Give the day to the Lord. Allow him to speak.

Hours later, she stood beside the swimming hole. It had been easy to find, the worn trail leading to the hidden pool. Piles of rocks hemmed the tranquil pool, signs that someone had cleared the area.

She stood there another moment, staring all around. The stream, the foot bridge, the dark forest ... all these things spoke to her of her new surroundings. She was far from home.

The encouraging words she'd remembered on the westbound train came to her now. "Be strong and courageous," she muttered, telling her timid heart to heed God's advice.

Joshua had spoken these words to the Israelites before they crossed the Jordan River and entered the Promised Land. Was she entering her own Promised Land? Had she escaped her own Egypt?

The angel Gabriel had said to Mary, "Do not be afraid." Even the shepherds outside of Bethlehem were told to fear not.

"So do not fear, for I am with you." Tess recalled this favorite Scripture verse from the Book of Isaiah. "Enough. God says not to be afraid, so stop being afraid," Tess chided herself. She held the armload of laundry to her nose and sniffed them once more. Her face wrinkled in disgust, and she dropped the pile at her feet.

Would Brett mind if she washed his clothes and the bedding? They obviously needed the attention. She wiped her hands on the front of her dress. With a final glance all around, she lifted her dress and tossed the garment on the grassy bank. She kicked off her shoes before stripping off her under clothes and, wading into the pool, waves splashing around her as she lowered herself into the clear water.

A gasp choked her, but the chilled water felt refreshing, and Tess swam across the shallow pool a few times before reaching for the dirty blankets.

Her teeth chattered as she worked. She washed the blankets and piled them on the rock ledge. As she hefted a faded work shirt, she noticed a tear in the shoulder and another in the elbow. She would mend the shirt if she could find a needle and thread.

Her thoughts strayed to Brett Calloway, imagining the way his broad shoulders would stretch the tattered shirt. His wagon in Laramie had allowed her escape. What would've become of her if he hadn't been there?

A shudder ran through her. Tess wasn't sure if the chill had come from the cool water or the anxiety of being left alone in Laramie.

She thought of Steve Long and his companions, and she shuddered again.

She continued to shiver as she hung the wet laundry from the rope line nailed to the corner of the cabin. The under garments and her floppy dress were hidden behind wet blankets, concealing them from anyone who might come to the cabin. Her wet hair hung loosely, soaking in the warming rays of the sun as sunbeams filtered through the tall pines around her.

Her gray dress fit her better. She glanced at her sleeves, noting the better condition of the material as Tess draped another sodden blanket over the line beside her worn dress and her white linens. She promised herself to remove the under things before the men returned. Also, she would take in the seams of the floppy dress that had concealed her figure. The ballooning garment was unnecessary now, what with Frank no longer around to pester her.

She stepped onto the porch and studied the inside of the spacious cabin through the open door, her hands on her hips. The space could use a good cleaning.

A broom leaned in a corner, wild oat stalks bound tightly with rawhide. At least someone thought of picking fresh oats recently, Tess mused as she started sweeping the flagstones.

The water bucket lay on the hearth and Tess wiped her brow with the back of her hand before hefting the rope handle. She would need to put water on to heat if she wanted to clean properly. She frowned at the memory of Sandy rinsing the dirty dishes in the stream. Bachelors lived like pigs.

She peered across the stream and studied Sandy's cabin. Only a small window had been cut into the logs, covered with greased butcher paper. He had no real porch, only a flat stone that served as a stoop.

Her eyes scanned Brett's cabin again. In contrast, his seemed so warm and inviting, the glass window letting sunlight dance across the gleaming flagstones. And the wide porch felt like an extension of the big room. She wondered if Sandy had a proper floor or if he simply had dirt.

A glance around the pine-scented cabin made her shake her head. Brett Calloway did not live like a pig. The lovely cabin wasn't as clean as she would have it, but the house wasn't filthy, either.

A path directly in front of the cabin led to the stream.

Tess watched a bee fly clumsily over a flower as she strode to the water's edge, the bucket swinging beside her. She smiled, pleased to see another sign that spring was truly upon the land. But it was early June now with summer just around the corner.

Water gurgled musically as Tess approached the creek. A narrow plank stretched from the bank to a flat stone midstream. A small waterfall shot over a rocky ledge and swirled around the stone island she stood upon. Undoubtedly, this must be where Sandy had rinsed the dishes. She smiled again as she lowered the bucket, filled it, and pulled the pail from the water.

A blue jay called to her, watching her from a nearby branch, and an irritated squirrel chattered noisily, telling her he didn't appreciate her presence. A gentle breeze whispered through the trees, and Tess breathed deep, letting the unfamiliar aroma of dry pine needles fill her lungs.

Sunlight glittered like diamonds on the droplets of water that spilled from the bucket. Tess wanted to sing as she turned, happy for the first time since she could remember. She was free of Frank Mercer and his disgusting stares.

She halted for a moment and caught her breath, studying the tall pines around her and the majestic peaks towering above. Her heart swelled. This was not the flatlands around Omaha. She stood among the mountains now. She drank in the clear air as her gaze traveled over the cabin. She noticed the cleverly fitted logs and the tall glass window. She knew Brett planned for a second window when he could afford one. She thought of the swimming pool where she had cleaned the laundry and the little path where fresh water could be drawn, right outside the front door—not like the long walk in Omaha to the town well.

Her critical eye measured the forest setting. She liked it

here and appreciated the location and the improvements Brett had already made to the land. What a perfect place for a homestead.

Tess tilted her head. Brett had mentioned his family hoped to come here soon. Had he built this cabin for a special someone?

A stab of irritation pierced her, and she pushed the sensation aside. That was none of her business. She needed to find work, but she also needed to show Brett her appreciation at letting her stay here. Nothing more. Soon, she hoped to return to Chicago where friends awaited.

Off in the distance, Tess heard a faint train whistle. She lifted a hand and shielded her eyes, looking through the trees toward the noise. Was Laramie that way?

The forest island she found herself in made her feel secure somehow, like she stood far away from anything that could harm her. But if Laramie was that close …

She pushed the threatening thought away and returned to the cabin.

The afternoon passed swiftly as she scrubbed the stone floor and washed all the simple homemade furniture, marveling at their shrewd construction.

Soon, though, fatigue caught up with her and Tess decided to rest for an hour. A nap would do her good. The fever had taken a lot out of her.

She gathered the damp blankets and moved them indoors. A glance at her dress and the linens revealed they could do with a little fresher air. She draped the blankets on additional rope lines within the room. Heat from the small fire would dry them thoroughly by nightfall, but they would smell of wood smoke. She didn't want the same for her personal clothes.

In the evening, she prepared a hearty meal, keeping the food warm until the men returned. She kept an anxious vigil, peering out the window every time she heard a sound.

Finally, she heard the wagon rumble into the clearing. Tess nudged the coffeepot deeper into the coals and hurried to the door. She stepped onto the porch and searched the surrounding forest until she sighted the two men leading the team of mules.

Sweat streaks carved little paths through the grime on their wearied faces.

They walked slowly into the clearing. "Whoa, Tip." Brett patted the big mule and smiled at Tess, his white teeth flashing in the fading light. "We've got one wagon load here and at least two more waiting in the woods. Tomorrow, Sandy will deliver to Tie Siding while I continue cutting." He patted the mule again. "Good job today, Tip. You too, Mike."

Sandy unhooked the team from the wagon, leaving the heavily loaded vehicle standing in the yard while he led the tired mules behind the cabin.

"Is that where the barn is?" Tess pointed after Sandy.

Brett chuckled and accepted the dipper of water she handed him. He gulped half and poured the rest over his head. "Well, it's not really a barn. More like a stable. We plan on building a proper barn someday."

She led the way into the cabin. Brett stopped when he noticed the clean cabin, his gaze roaming over the arranged table and the pots steaming on the hearth.

"You made dinner?"

Tess lifted her chin and smiled. The look on his face indicated his pleasure at the prepared meal. He would let her stay for sure now.

"Sit down," she commanded and hurried to the fireplace. She poured two steaming cups of coffee and handed one to Brett.

He stared at her, as if seeing her for the first time. His

eyes softened and he grinned. "You cleaned the cabin too. Thanks, Tess. A man could get used to this."

She looked at him, their gaze meeting and her glad heart leaped into her throat. What did he mean by that?

Sandy pounded his boots on the porch before entering. He halted when he saw the set table, a slow grin spreading across his weathered face. "Well, I'll be." He moved slowly to his bench. "I'll be," he repeated under his breath as Tess handed him the other cup of coffee.

They ate in silence. Hungry men, they were intent on completing the meal so they could move on to other tasks. The sun set over the western mountains, and the cabin grew even darker before Tess lit the short candle and placed the glowing stub in the center of the table.

"I will do the dishes tonight." As Tess cleared the table, she could feel Brett's gaze follow her.

"Don't forget to fill the coffeepot for the morning," Sandy ordered gruffly as he stood. "I'm beat. Brett, help me hitch the team first thing tomorrow and I'll deliver to Tie Siding. You go back to that notch and keep felling timber. I should meet you there by afternoon."

The tall man waved to Tess but said nothing more as he closed the door behind him.

The fire crackled as Tess continued gathering dirty pots and plates. She stole a glance at Brett as he sipped his third cup of coffee, his eyes darting to the fire. "Sandy doesn't speak much."

Brett nodded and drained the tin cup. "Let me help you, Tess." He leaped to his feet and took half her load.

Her breath caught as he stood so near. She could smell sweat and pine mingled with the fragrance of fresh cut lumber on him, a wild scent of the mountains and woodwork.

They left the cabin door open, dim light showing the

way as Brett followed her to the stream. They knelt side by side and rinsed the dishes, Tess making sure she washed them thoroughly. She dried the wet dishes and put them away while he retrieved the bucket of fresh water for morning coffee.

Tess pursed her lips, sure that she needed to know tonight. This would be a good time to ask.

Brett spread the clean blankets before the hearth and tossed a couple logs on the flames. He then stepped outside while she quickly undressed and jumped into bed. She leaned on one elbow while he finished stripping to the waist.

A contented sigh escaped Brett as he stretched out, his bare toes wiggling in the glow of the fireplace.

"Goodnight, Brett," she whispered.

"Goodnight, Tess." Firelight played over the stretched muscles of his powerful chest. Tess looked away.

She rolled onto her back and stared up into the rafters. "Brett, can I ask you something?"

He yawned. "Can it wait?"

She thought about it, her brow wrinkling. "No, not really."

He grunted, and Tess wondered if that meant he would listen. She bit her lip and considered remaining quiet. No, she had to know. "Who undressed me when I first came here?"

Silence filled the cabin, and Tess wondered if Brett had fallen asleep. Anger spiked, and she was about to call out to him when she heard his low chuckle. "That's what is all powerful important?"

Tess shrugged. "Of course. It's very important to me. Did you or Sandy take off my dress?"

"Which of us do you think it was?"

She narrowed her eyes, his teasing tone annoying her.

Was he playing games with her? Her anger flared. "It's not appropriate for you to see a lady in her underthings." She could feel the heat creep up her neck. How embarrassing. This man had seen her almost naked, certainly seen the shape of her.

Silence. Had he fallen asleep?

Now she was livid. Her stomach tightened with shame. He'd seen her, looked upon her, and didn't have the common decency to apologize?

She was about to give him a piece of her mind when he spoke. "Tess, neither of us undressed you. I carried you into the cabin and left you alone to prepare for bed. You undressed yourself and passed out in bed."

Relief swept over her like a tidal wave. Why hadn't he said that in the first place?

She listened and could hear nothing except the tiny rustling of the fire. Then, the distinct sound of even breathing came to her. Brett had fallen asleep.

She was going to call to him when she remembered how tired he looked when the men had returned home. They worked hard. He needed his sleep.

"Goodnight, Brett," she whispered and closed her eyes.

CHAPTER SIX

Tess pushed the coffeepot into the coals. She brushed a loose strand of hair from her face and yawned while she poked at the logs, coaxing flames and feeding the small blaze with sticks. Brett tugged on his boots, neither of them speaking in the morning gloom. He stomped his feet before removing the bar on the door and departing for the stable.

Tess hurriedly mixed dough and sliced bacon into the skillet. The men would need something to eat.

Tess watched from the porch, a blanket draped around her shoulders, as Sandy met Brett in the clearing and helped hitch the team. The forest lay quiet and dark. The chill of the mountain morning surprised her.

The men worked in silence, pushing the mules into position and harnessing them with deft fingers.

She poured coffee while they ate. She would eat later, after they had left for the day's work. They were in a hurry and spoke little, although Sandy did arch an eyebrow at her and nod when she asked if he wanted more coffee. Tess had been there long enough to tell he seemed pleased with her attentions.

Soon, they pushed back from the table, and Tess followed them out into the early gray of dawn. A dull light hovered in the east, and Tess could barely discern the shape of things. The bridge, Sandy's cabin across the stream, the tall mules hitched to the loaded wagon.

Sandy stepped onto the wheel and climbed to the seat.

He wrapped the long reins tightly around his gloved hands while Brett scratched the mules' noses and ears.

"Can I see the ties?" Tess stepped from the porch, not waiting for a response. She leaned over the wagon sides, peering at the stack of squared logs.

She knew various details about the railroad construction and had seen wooden cross ties before, but never freshly cut for delivery.

"It was Sandy's idea to go ahead of the railroad and homestead land that would become valuable and provide ties for construction." Brett left the mules and stepped beside her, his nearness disconcerting her somehow.

She nodded, not sure what to say, and backed toward the porch. "Have a good day. I'm going into town to look for work, but I should be home to get supper ready."

"Take this road until you come to the tracks, then go left. Laramie isn't far," Brett explained, gesturing toward the dark avenue through the woods.

Sandy lifted the reins. "Brett, I'll see you later."

The older man didn't say anything to Tess but eyed her for a moment. Tess wondered if the twitch on his lips indicated a grin. He slapped the reins and the wagon lurched, the team turning into the rough road through the woods.

The clatter of the wagon drifted away, the sound muffled by the thick mat of pine needles scattered over the ground.

Brett glanced at Tess and then reached for his axe, the long saw, and his canvas bag of tools at his feet. Metal files and heavy wedges clinked inside, but Brett swung the bag easily to his shoulder.

Tess shifted, surprised at her nervousness. She certainly hadn't felt any of this when Sandy departed.

Brett stared at her, and Tess thought he wanted to say

something. He shifted, too, and his gaze roamed past her to the woods beside the cabin. Suddenly, he squinted and tilted his head, peering at something behind her.

"Tess, are those your underwear on the clothesline?"

Her heart stopped beating and a chill swept through her. Her underwear?

Realization flooded over her and her hands flew to her mouth, her eyes widening in horror. Brett had seen her linens on the clothesline. She had forgotten to bring them in.

Heat stole up her neck and she felt her face burn crimson with the embarrassment of the moment. With a lunge, she raced to the line, snatching the under garments, and concealing them under the blanket around her shoulders.

"Tess, I have a younger sister." Brett's words did nothing to slow her pounding heart.

As she stumbled onto the porch, her only thought was to get inside the cabin, to escape his piercing scrutiny. She could hear him laughing. She slammed the door firmly behind her, leaning against the heavy planks and staring heavenward.

First, she had been worried that Brett had undressed her when she came to his cabin. Shame had tormented her. Then she found out he was innocent, only to have him see her private clothes anyway.

Her hand went to her heated cheeks. They still burned.

She leaned into the door, listening for any sound from Brett. Silence. Perhaps he'd gone to work.

Tess threw another log on the fire. She would eat something before launching off for town. After a bath, she told herself, recalling the hard work of yesterday when she'd cleaned the cabin. She must look her best.

Tentatively, she opened the door and scanned the clearing. No sign of Brett.

The bath felt wonderful, and again she thought of the improvements to the homestead that anyone would appreciate. A wash pool with clean water was a luxury.

Tess studied the stone dam of the wash pool, so cleverly fitted together, retaining the water for washing or swimming. These two men had built a true homestead in the woods, one where someone intended to stay permanently. Which of the men intended to stay here? The railroad was being built at an alarming rate, nearly a mile a day. Soon, the need for people in this region would pass.

Or would it? Tess had seen with her own eyes how men had begun to farm the open prairies around Omaha. Perhaps there were jobs men could do out here on the edge of the mountains. Maybe Brett had a plan.

Tess knew the former days of the fur trappers had passed. Long ago, men had ventured into these wild, rugged mountains to take the fur of the beaver and other animals. Now, that time was gone.

Even the era of the Indian who roamed and dominated the vast plains was passing. Certainly, Tess had heard all about this while she lived in Omaha. How the military, released from fighting the Civil War, had turned their attentions on the hapless Indians of the Great Plains. Bows and arrows could not compete with the guns and cannons of the cavalry.

Regardless how history would play out, white men were on the prairies now. They would build and settle, all in the name of progress and ownership.

Tess recalled how Frank had ridiculed such settlers, men who moved west to build their own farms. He had called them suckers and fools.

"Who would wish to live in such a hard land where money will be scarce? Better to take advantage of the time that is here. Work for the railroad and get out when they're finished. It's all about money and who gets the most. Doesn't Doctor Durant say the same thing and he runs the Union Pacific."

Frank had laughed while he spoke, full of his own wisdom.

Yes, Tess remembered the mean and ignorant things Frank had said. But Tess also remembered the proud and resolute look upon those pioneers who'd struck out for the open prairies. They were creating something that would last. They had come west to build and to stay.

Were Brett and Sandy like those pioneers? Would they settle here or only work for the railroad and leave when the tracks were completed?

By the quality of the construction, Tess believed at least one of them intended to remain behind after the building of the iron rails were finished.

Tess pulled herself from the pool and slipped into a clean dress, her yellow cotton one. She hadn't washed her hair today, so she draped the brown locks over one shoulder, allowing the dark tresses to hang while she sat on the porch and stroked through her hair with the comb she found on a shelf near the fireplace.

Sunlight fell around her, sprinkling the dirt yard with dancing shadows as the branches overhead swayed in the breeze. Her hands moved easily through the long hair, relaxing her as she worked. This was a beautiful place, this cabin among the big pines, and she wondered if she might one day find a place to call home as Brett Calloway had.

The desire to walk to town and look for work dissipated as she studied the dwindling wood pile. Only a few logs remained. She put her hands on her hips and chewed the inside of her cheek. She needed to cut wood for the men. They would come home expecting a hot meal. Perhaps she could also prepare something special.

She would walk to town tomorrow. It could wait another day.

Hours passed as she cut wood, occasionally checking on the simmering ham and potato soup. Another afternoon rest perked her up for the evening. Tess was surprised how the unfamiliar fatigue of the fever persisted.

Long shadows lay across the clearing when Tess heard the returning team. The meeting she had dreaded all day was at hand. Brett had seen her underwear and her embarrassment threatened to overwhelm her. But she needed to show them she intended to help them, serving them for the opportunity to stay at the homestead. She couldn't fail now.

She stepped onto the porch, careful not to meet Brett's gaze. "Supper's on," she called with false cheerfulness. She retreated into the cabin before they could reply.

Tess paced the room, checking and rechecking the coffeepot and the stew. Cornbread would have to do again. She'd found no yeast for bread.

Tess averted her eyes as she served the two hungry men. She could feel Brett's eyes on her as she poured his coffee and felt irritated when she noticed her hand shook. What must he think of her?

They spoke little. Tess did manage to ask Sandy about dropping the load of ties at Tie Siding. He replied with a noncommittal grunt.

"Where is that, Tie Siding?"

Brett lifted his head quickly. "It's a small supply depot a few miles east of Laramie. There was talk of abandoning it and using the docks at Laramie, but the railroad is reluctant to take the time and build something they already have. I'll bet Tie Siding will last, at least until the construction camp leaves the region."

The trio lapsed into silence again as Tess cleared the

dishes and poured more coffee.

Finally, Sandy broke the quiet. "This is the best food we've eaten in months. Sure beats the slop Brett throws together."

Tess stared, surprised by the lumberjack's lengthy speech. Sandy usually seemed somber and quiet.

He nodded at her and stood. "Early day tomorrow, Brett. I want to get another load to the rails." Sandy stretched and held his empty cup out to Tess. "One for the road. This is the best coffee too."

Tess filled his cup, too stunned to respond.

He closed the door behind him, the latch falling into place with a sharp knock.

Brett chuckled, his hands gripping his tin cup as he rested his elbows on the table. "You really impressed Sandy, Tess. I've never heard him say nice things to anyone, not even me."

She said nothing, aware again they were alone.

"I'm on dish duty tonight." Brett pushed back from the table.

"Oh, no," Tess said, reaching for the remaining dirty dishes. "I want to earn my keep. Dishes are my job."

Brett lowered himself to the bench with a grateful sigh.

Tess hurried outside, relieved to get away from her silent observer. Shame drove Tess, convinced Brett had stared at her throughout the meal, heat rising to her cheeks as she recalled his earlier words. She frowned, disturbed he had seen her private linens.

She only needed a few minutes to rinse the dishes. As she stacked the clean dishes beside her on the little plank, she caught a glimmer of light over her shoulder. She glanced across the stream.

A dull glow came from the greased butcher paper in Sandy's tiny window. There was no sign of smoke from his chimney, and Tess wondered if he'd retired to bed without taking the trouble of starting a fire.

As she watched, the light went out. Sandy had a candle like Brett, neither man willing to pay the high price for an oil lantern.

Only a dim light remained in the western sky. A few stars already appeared, reminding Tess she must hurry and allow Brett to go to bed.

Reluctantly, she gathered the dishes. Her legs felt heavy as she made her way back to the cabin.

Brett had tossed a blanket atop the deerskin hide before the fireplace. He looked at Tess as she entered, but she turned away, stacking the dishes on their proper shelves.

"I'll fetch water while you get into bed." He lifted the bucket and the coffeepot, closing the door softly behind him.

He returned to find Tess in bed, the blanket pulled tightly beneath her chin. He placed the coffeepot beside the fireplace and stretched on his blankets.

The fire burned low, casting a deep glow on the yellow logs beside her. Tess nibbled her lip, wondering, hoping he didn't think poorly of her. Her stomach clenched.

Finally, Tess broke the uncomfortable quiet. "Brett." She could barely make out his dark form on the other side of the table. "Are you still awake?"

He shifted his position on the floor. "Yes." His voice held a note of curiosity, an eagerness she had not noticed before.

"Thank you for not laughing or saying anything to Sandy about earlier." She tensed, worried he might tease her.

There was a long pause. "That's all right, Tess. I told you the truth when I said I had younger sisters. It's nothing I haven't seen before."

She scowled into the gloom. His casual response irritated her. "Well, you haven't seen mine before," she snapped.

He said nothing at first and then laughed. "Well, I've seen them now."

A pitch knot popped in the fire and Tess fought back the embarrassment. She breathed out, forcing herself to relax. Brett was only teasing her. She stared at the rafters overhead. "Is that how you knew to brush my hair when I was sick?"

Again, a long pause. "My pa died when I was young. I had to help Ma with my sisters. I've gotten real good at braiding hair and cleaning dresses."

"Where are your sisters now?"

Brett rolled over and leaned on one elbow, peering into the darkness toward Tess. "My youngest sister died of the pox when I was fourteen. Ma took it real hard, her already having lost Pa. Me and Ma and Becky were all that was left. That's why Ma was mad when I joined the war. I stayed home until I was seventeen and couldn't stay out of it any longer. Folks were questioning my honor."

Tess sat up, watching him. "Where are they now?"

"They live with friends in Minneapolis. I finished up with the war and took a job with the Union Pacific laying rails. But its wood cutting I really enjoy. I worked with Sandy, and he convinced me to come ahead west and cut ties. We knew the railroad would get here eventually, so we just cut and stacked ties all winter. Now, the railroad is at Laramie, and our ties are fetching a premium."

Brett lay back, his hands folded beneath his head. "I homesteaded this tract from the creek to the west. One hundred and sixty acres and it's all mine. Sandy did the same from the creek going east. We had it specially added to our deed that if anything happens to the other, he would get first chance at buying the property before it goes to open land again. I plan on moving Ma and Becky out here by the end of summer, if all goes well. Sandy is hoping to find a wife when he goes back east this fall. If he does, he'll return here to work with me. If he doesn't find a woman, he might decide to stay back east. He isn't sure what he'll do yet."

Tess lay back down, her gaze searching the dark rafters once more, allowing the information to sink in. Where would she and her mother wish to live if they could? Would they go back to dirty, overcrowded Chicago if Frank were not in the picture?

A scowl furrowed her brow and she let her gaze wander around the spacious, clean cabin. Brett had built well. His mother and sister would be proud of what he'd created for them.

"I'm getting my strength back," Tess said suddenly. "I'll clean and cook for you for a while longer, if you don't mind, until I can get a job and make some money." She chewed the inside of her cheek. He wouldn't kick her out before she was ready, would he?

The fire crackled and Tess felt the anxiety grow. Was he thinking of asking her to leave? Where would she go?

Finally, he spoke. "I saw how you hung the laundry on the line and cleaned the cabin, Tess. Dinner was delicious. It was real nice eating something other than what I had to cook."

He paused and Tess thrilled at his compliment.

"You stay as long as you need," he added softly.

Tess blinked. Brett's gentle words touched her deeply. He'd noticed her efforts. She was unaccustomed to such kindness.

"Thanks, Brett," she whispered into the darkness. A tear slid down her cheek as Tess smiled.

CHAPTER SEVEN

"Brett," Tess lifted the bubbling coffeepot from the coals and turned to face him. Sandy was at the stable while Brett packed food for lunch. He stood near her, shoving cornbread and ham into a canvas sack. Not even a dim gray showed through the window to the east. "I know you intend to bring your mother and sister here, but what then? Will you stay in Dakota Territory?"

He held out an empty mug. "It's called Wyoming Territory now." He smiled at her before blowing on the steaming cup. "I'll stay. I hope to build a sawmill eventually. There's lots of good timber, and lumber will be needed. Not only for towns around here, but I heard talk of a new railroad branch to Denver one day. I can ship lumber wherever the rails go."

Tess nodded, but something bothered her. She pursed her lips and tilted her head. Brett had plans. What about her? Was she simply going to find work to save enough money to go to Chicago? What then? What goal did she have for her life?

"Brett," she continued. "I heard a train whistle yesterday. Are we close then?"

"Very close. We cut a lane through the woods to the main road that follows the rails. A left will take you to Laramie, a right to Tie Siding where we leave our ties."

Tess forked ham slices onto a plate. "How far is it to Laramie?"

He reached for the meat and then stopped, his fork held

in midair. He glanced up at her and arched an eyebrow. "Tess, I don't know if you should go into Laramie alone."

The worry she saw in his eyes pleased her for reasons she couldn't explain. She appreciated his concern, but it nettled her somehow too. She wasn't a child that needed looking after.

Tess narrowed her eyes. "I'll be all right. I can't just do your laundry and cook your meals and clean the cabin. I need a job if I'm going to make money so I can move on. You have plans for your future, and I need to be thinking of doing something myself."

Brett frowned. "All right," he said, taking another sip from his cup as he peered at her over the rim. "I guess I can't stop you. I have no hold on you. But be careful," he warned.

His condescending manner irritated her, and she bristled.

"I'm not your little sister, Brett Calloway." She turned away suddenly, her loose hair twirling as she moved to the fireplace. She whirled again to face him. "I don't need your protection or permission to go to town. I'm seventeen. My mother was having children by this age. I can look after myself."

As the heat rose within her, Tess leaned forward, her eyes flashing. Brett stared at her, eyes wide. Tess relaxed, aware she held a ladle like a sword, ready to battle. She took a step backward.

Sandy's boots sounded on the porch and then the door opened.

Tess moved to serve Sandy. The room quieted and Sandy kept his eyes down, intent on eating. Tess glowered silently across the table at Brett.

Finally, the men stood, benches scraping as they stepped to the door. A dim gray appeared through the window, dawn's early light.

Brett shot Sandy a worried glance and then leaned close to Tess. "I never said you were one of my sisters, Tess. You do what you want, but Laramie is a rough town." He walked into the gloom and joined Sandy.

Tess rested her hands on her hips and watched them disappear into the forest before she turned and entered the cabin. She leaned against the plank door and sighed, her gaze traveling to the rafters.

Why had she attacked him that way? Why did she allow him to get under her skin?

"I'm sorry, Lord. I should be grateful. Thank you for bringing me here."

She tidied the cabin and took an extra minute to put on her best dress and brush her long brown hair. She pulled the locks behind her and expertly worked the mass into a single braid.

The sun was just topping the trees when she started out on the road to Laramie. Tess almost skipped with the excitement of this adventure. She'd been regaining her strength these past few days, and now she believed she was ready to strike out for town and see what she could find in way of employment.

Only the blue jays watched her walk from the glade. They squawked loudly at the intruder in their forest home, but she only smiled at them, enjoying their company.

She passed the foot bridge that crossed the creek and strode past the wash hole. The narrow lane through the woods led downhill and toward the railroad tracks at the bottom of the mountain. She could hear the small stream in the thickets to her right as the creek wound around boulders and deadfalls on its way down the mountain.

The cool air felt pleasant, but Tess knew it would warm by afternoon. June in the Rocky Mountains was still not too hot, unlike Omaha.

A flash of white tails alerted her to a pair of retreating deer. Tess watched their graceful leaps as they disappeared into the deeper forest beyond the road. She knew Brett or Sandy would have shot these deer if they could. The tie cutters sold meat to the café in Laramie when possible. They were always looking for ways to make extra income.

Tess studied the woods as she walked, enjoying the coolness and the dark shadows of the trees. Her steps made no sound on the thick carpet of pine needles under her shoes. Her thoughts turned to Brett Calloway, and she remembered now what he'd told her. Sandy hoped to return east in the fall and find a wife. She thought of the wonderful cabin, admiring Brett's work on his homestead. His dream of moving his family out here and one day opening a sawmill drove him to build for the future.

She felt her anger stir as she recalled Brett telling her she shouldn't go to Laramie. Then she grinned when she remembered her fiery retort. She'd given him a piece of her mind.

Soon, she felt her anger subside as she recalled his tender touch when he'd nursed her back to health. He'd been kind. His thoughtfulness at the way he had brushed and cleaned her hair while she was unconscious touched her. Also, he had washed her dirty dress. That was something, right? Perhaps she did need a little help, she surmised with some reluctance.

The sight of the tracks startled her. They truly were close to Brett's homestead. The wide, well-trodden road extended both to the right and left. The iron rails glistened on their four-foot high gravel bed, safe from floods.

Tess had learned a lot about the train in the years she lived in Omaha. Probably more than she wished to know. The railroad men she knew, and the friends Frank occasionally had over to the shack, always talked of the Union Pacific and the great work they were achieving. Their goal was connecting both distant shores of the continent, and they were confident they would succeed. A deep sense of pride and belonging to something grand permeated the air of Omaha.

Tess halted when she came to the crossroad. A glance over her shoulder told her the forest concealed all that Sandy and Brett had built on their homesteads. Only the dim trail of a road gave any indication that man had penetrated this section of the woods.

A bleached tree stood sentinel beside the road, and Tess studied the dead monarch closely. This would signal the turnoff to the homesteads.

The stream that wound and raced down the mountain was nowhere in sight now. Tess wondered if it connected with the larger Laramie River that flowed through town.

She raised a hand, shielding her eyes as she squinted, studying the tracks to the east. No sign of Tie Siding, either.

Tess dropped her hand and faced west, squared her shoulders, and started walking. This was the way to Laramie.

CHAPTER EIGHT

The forest banked steeply on her left as Tess walked toward town. Sometimes, the deep woods melted into the edge of the trail she followed, and Tess could peer into the eerie thickness of the dark forest.

The thick woods appeared almost impenetrable, the rugged land folded with rocky ravines and dense undergrowth. Her respect for Brett and Sandy grew as she realized the difficulty of carving a road through this rough terrain.

The pine trees stood tall and straight, perfect for lumber. Perhaps Brett's idea of a sawmill here was wise.

Brett worked to bring his family west. Tess wondered what it would be like to have a sister, to share clothes and secrets with. It had always been just her and Mama, she felt, especially after Papa went off to the war. Tess had only been nine then. She wondered how old Brett's sister, Becky, was.

Then, after the war, there had been Frank.

Tess shivered and glanced at the twin rails beside her. They gleamed brightly as she walked, their brilliance keeping pace with her. The rising sun warmed her back, and Tess hurried on, her curiosity growing with every step.

She had only been in Laramie the night she arrived. She didn't remember much, only the wide, muddy street and the row of saloons and businesses.

Tess walked on, letting her thoughts wander. Usually, she was too busy to indulge in idle dreams and memories.

Train to Laramie

Once, when Tess delivered lunch to Frank down at the train yard, he had grudgingly allowed her to explore a passenger car. Tess had studied the brass lanterns adorning each wall and had caressed the red velvet seats and cushions. Surely, famous people or the president himself rode in cars like this one.

She remembered how Frank had not really wanted her to look into that plush, elegant passenger car but had eventually given in. He didn't like Tess to see or know about nice things. Perhaps he was ashamed of their dingy, shabby shack.

Tess clenched her fists, and she could feel the short hair prickle at the back of her neck. No, that wasn't it. Frank never really cared about her or her mother. He only wanted to keep them near, not letting them see nice things that might tempt them to leave him. He knew Mama was timid and had only to fill her already frightened mind with scary thoughts of the outside world to keep Cathy Mercer around.

Tess pitied her mother. Too bad Mama couldn't push her timid nature aside and risk a little, take a chance for a better life.

Tess knew this and the words she read in the Bible confirmed that God never wanted her to be timid or afraid. God said continuously to not be afraid, to be courageous. St. Paul even refers to Christians as God's soldiers. Brave and resilient, Paul commands Christians to stand firm in their faith, fight the good fight, to train hard through discipline and practice. A spirit of timidity was not allowed for God's children.

She smiled with a hint of sadness as she reminded herself of the ride on the flatcar in the rain. Tess felt brave for leaving Omaha and she lifted her chin. She was a soldier for Christ.

Yet, the feelings of fear and dread continued to plague her, despite these battling resolutions to be strong, to be a warrior for Jesus. Tess wondered if she would ever achieve the confidence and strength she longed for in the Lord.

She hesitated when she stepped onto the wooden bridge spanning the Laramie River. The raucous town lay sprawled before her, busy and loud.

She peered down at the rushing, clear water, turbulent and wild. Later, it turned to the east and joined the Platte River, eventually joining the Missouri River at Omaha.

Laramie served an important purpose in the building of the railroad. Perhaps this was the ideal place to discover her purpose. Maybe it was here that God would reveal what he wanted for her life.

Her heart swelled at the thought of an adventure, her adventure.

Tess glanced again at the racing water below. Funny that this very water would soon be flowing through Omaha where she used to live.

A shrill blast of a train whistle disturbed her reverie. Tess turned and looked toward town. Fear threatened again, but she pushed the worry back down. She would trust God. He had brought her here as part of his plan.

Smoke bellowed from the stack of a black engine, steam hissing as it spewed from under the train's belly, the big wheels starting to move. The locomotive was departing town, probably on its way to Omaha for more supplies. The rails would continue west, progress marched on. And so would she.

A wagon rumbled over the bridge, forcing Tess to step to the edge of the narrow wooden crossing. The driver peered curiously at her from his high perch atop the tall wagon, but he said nothing to her.

"Well, Lord, here we go," she whispered to the cool

morning air as she faced town. "I know you're with me. Please lead me."

Tess had been lost in her own thoughts. Now, she stood in Laramie and the noise of a small but bustling city surrounded her. A chorus of hammers on anvils came to her ears. The familiar sound comforted her, and she knew blacksmiths were busy at their forges, making and shaping necessary brackets and tools.

Men in rough trousers and boots moved from shops to wagons which carried the finished items to the end of tracks, barely forty miles from town. Tess knew no expense was spared to keep the tracks moving west.

Tess stepped from the bridge and walked ahead slowly, surveying the busy activity around her. Few men looked at her, Tess realized with relief. She hoped to remain unnoticed by these railroad workers. Memories of Omaha and the rough men of the train yards reminded her she needed to be careful. These men were, for the most part, uneducated and hard-working, but the railroad turned a blind eye to lawless behavior. There were no laws west of Omaha, Tess had been informed. Only those enforced with fists or guns. Out here, might made right.

Tess passed the spot where she'd hidden in the brush, remembering her sickness. She thought of Brett again, grateful for his kindness. The big livery loomed on her left and she only glanced at the barn, her attention riveted on the long row of saloons farther down the street. Sight of the water trough where she'd taken a drink sickened her. Flies hovered over the horse droppings scattered in the mud around the trough.

She hesitated before the Bucket of Blood, her teeth clenching. Loud laughter and the clinking of glass filtered through the canvas walls of the saloon. She studied the boardwalk, remembering Steve Long and the Moyers. A shiver ran down her arms, and she looked away, her gaze moving down the street.

Tess glanced at a gaudy structure further along. Yellow and red swirls covered the canvas walls and two brightly painted posts stood on either side of the wide doors. She chewed the inside of her cheek and studied the colorful building. The Chinaman's saloon?

An intricately drawn likeness of a dragon hovered above the double doors just below the sign that announced The Palace.

Past this saloon, Tess noted the stage station across the street—The Overland Stage. The squat log cabin doubled as the land office for the area. This is where Brett had probably registered his claim on his homestead.

She squinted farther along, dimly recognizing where Brett had halted his wagon the night she'd arrived in town. He had spoken to someone in that shack, which stood next to the café.

Without a job, Tess would never raise the money she needed to return east. She wondered what employment opportunities abounded in this end-of-tracks town.

A scowl crossed her face as her gaze drifted again to the saloons. No, not in there. She turned toward the café and continued on.

If not the café, she could always take in laundry. She could sew and mend clothing. Workmen always needed repairs to trousers and shirts. But pay would be slow coming in. The café promised the fastest income.

Tess left the red and yellow building behind her. She'd heard of girls working in the saloons. People whispered about them and Mama always made Tess hurry when they passed the painted girls on the streets of Omaha. She wouldn't look for work in the saloons, even though Laramie boasted more of these than any other business along the main street.

A fast-moving freight wagon rumbled beside her, dangerously close to running her down. A hand gripped her shoulder and pulled her from its path. Tess stumbled backward, but the stranger's hold kept her upright. She peered into his weathered face, gray whiskers concealing all but his startling bright eyes.

"Watch out, miss. You have to keep a sharp eye around here." He released her and turned to watch the heavy wagon disappear down the street.

Tess nodded, liking the familiar old man immediately. He smiled at her, like a grandfather might, and Tess warmed to him.

"I'm Ivan Belmont," he said as he turned back to Tess. "I own the livery." He gestured to the large barn and then lowered his voice. "Even though I'm forced to pay lease to the Moyers."

Although she didn't understand the sharp bitterness in his words, she stuck out a hand. "I'm Tess Randle. I'm looking for work."

Could she work in a livery? Tess glanced again at the big barn. She was strong. Perhaps she could muck out stalls.

"In Laramie?" Ivan's bushy brows arched, and his bright eyes widened. "Not much work available here for a nice girl, if you catch my meaning." He limped to a nearby bench and sat stiffly, favoring his left foot.

Tess followed. He sighed as he leaned back, grinning as he pointed at his boot. "Lost my foot at Pittsburgh Landing."

Tess nodded. "Pa died at Pittsburgh Landing." She didn't bother to mention she didn't miss him.

Ivan peered at her closely but said nothing for a long moment. Then he rubbed his whiskers and narrowed his eyes as he glanced at the clouds. "Listen, Tess. Go ask at the café for a job. Tell them I sent you. Warren is a good man. If you can't find work, come back and see me. We'll figure something out."

Relief filled her and Tess lifted her head. "Thanks, Mr. Belmont."

She glanced over her shoulder at the café and again noticed the small shack beside the restaurant. Was Mr. Warren the man Brett had spoken to? A crowd milled outside the diner, encouraging Tess with its popularity. Surely a busy place like this would need help.

With a grin at the liveryman, she stepped into the street.

Tess dodged two wagons and moved carefully across the wide street, avoiding puddles and horse apples.

She wormed her way through the line of waiting men until she stood inside. Customers at long tables clamored for plates of food. A plump woman moved among the rows of people, serving as fast as she could.

Tess watched her a moment, noticing the wide apron stretched over her ample belly, one hand continuously pushing strands of loose hair from her red face. Tess pitied the large woman.

A square hole in the back wall of the big room drew Tess's attention. Steaming platters lined the shelf and the woman with the sweat-streaked face hurried to distribute them.

Tess waved at the big woman as she passed. "Ma'am, I would like a word."

The bustling woman ignored Tess completely, intent on retrieving fresh platters and delivering them to the boisterous and demanding crowd.

Tess scowled. She would have no opportunity to speak with the woman now. Perhaps it would be wise to return later and seek a chance to ask the woman about a job. Disappointment settled in her stomach like a cold ball of ice, and Tess bit her lip. She'd been so hopeful. She dropped her head and turned to leave.

"Miss?" A burly man nudged her elbow. "Hand that platter to this table. It's our turn." He pointed to the shelf behind Tess.

Her eyes widened and she looked from him to the frantic waitress then back at the workman. Tess rolled up her sleeves and grinned. "Yes, sir. I believe it is your turn." She grabbed a platter and placed it on the table.

It was only then she realized the platters were piled high with doughnuts. Her mouth watered.

Another man from a nearby table handed Tess some coins as he rose to leave. Immediately, other men filled his seat on the long bench.

Tess dropped the money into her pocket as another customer lifted an empty cup and called to Tess. "Coffee, miss," he yelled above the din of the crowded café.

Again, Tess glanced at the large woman, still racing wildly around the room. Then she rushed to the big, black coffeepot on a side stove. She moved among the crowd of workmen and filled empty cups.

A man in a dirty apron waved an empty pot in the air, glowering at Tess. "Girl, there's a pump out back. Fill the pots and put them on to boil."

Tess nodded and followed him into the kitchen. A black man stood over a wide stove, shoveling doughnuts onto platters. He shot Tess a grateful grin as she grabbed three empty pots and went through the back door. The pump handle creaked as she hastily filled the containers.

"Throw some wood in the fire and get back out there," the man in the dirty apron ordered after Tess had set the pot on the stove. She did as he said, filling orders from waiting customers and refilling empty coffee cups.

At one point, the big woman and Tess met at the

window. "What's your name, dear?" the sweaty woman asked as she brushed hair from her round face.

"Tess." She took the platter of pancakes and turned away.

"I'm Mrs. Warren," the big woman called after her.

Tess continued to work hard, taking orders and delivering food to the tables as men came and went. She collected so much money that her pockets sagged heavily. She emptied them repeatedly into a coffee can in the kitchen.

Finally, the crowd thinned in the early afternoon. Tess deposited another coin into her pocket and walked to where Mrs. Warren sat fanning herself, her face flushed.

"Henry, put another pot on to boil and then take a break. You deserve it." The man in the dirty apron spoke to the black cook and then removed the stained cloth and tossed it in a basket. He poured himself a cup of coffee and joined Mrs. Warren. "Well, Ma, I don't know if I could do that again." He sighed loudly and then blew lightly on the cup in his hand. "I never saw such a rush in all my life."

The big woman nodded, her heated cheeks shining like apples. "I know what you mean, Mr. Warren. Thank God you hired Tess."

Tess arched an eyebrow as Mr. Warren scowled. "Tess? Who's that?"

Mrs. Warren pointed at Tess.

She smiled weakly as the pair stared at her. "Well, I wasn't actually hired by either of you. I saw you needed help and I lent a hand."

Mr. Warren bristled. "And the payment for the food? I saw you taking money."

Tess hurried into the kitchen and retrieved the coffee can full of coins. She handed the heavy can to Mr. Warren. "It's all there, Mr. Warren. I had to keep emptying my pockets."

Mr. Warren looked into the can and held it out to his wife. They both turned and stared at Tess. "You're hired, dear," Mrs. Warren said. "I was just telling Mr. Warren this very morning how I needed someone to cover the café while I work around the house. I'm no spring chicken anymore. I can handle breakfast and dinner if you can commit to the midday meal."

Tess nodded eagerly, then silently thanked God for this opportunity. Soon, she would be on the train east.

Mr. Warren tilted his head and looked at his wife. "Are you sure, Ma? We don't even know this girl."

"Mr. Belmont said to give his name. He said to mention him," Tess interrupted. "And I saw you speaking with Brett Calloway last week. I think he might be a friend of yours. He is a friend of mine."

The scowl disappeared from Mr. Warren's lined face. "You know Ivan? Well, that changes things. And Brett is a good friend. All right, miss, you can work the midday meals. Say ten to two o'clock in the afternoon. I'll give you four bits a day and a meal. What do you say?"

Tess nodded again, smiling. "I say that sounds good, Mr. Warren." She grasped the café owner's hand and shook it firmly. "I'll be here every day, you can count on me."

Tess had not realized how hungry she was until she sat down to a meal with Mrs. Warren. The plump woman ate and talked at the same time and soon had Tess filled in with most of the town's scant gossip. She reminded Tess a little of Mrs. Burlington back in Omaha.

"Of course, most of the honest men don't like the marshal. Big Steve Long is not a good man, but he got himself elected marshal when the train hit town in early May, and there's little we can do about it now," Mrs. Warren explained around a mouthful of cornbread.

The big woman glanced over her shoulder, then leaned closer to Tess and lowered her voice. "They say he takes land from men who own homesteads he wants. They say he's growing his holdings and hopes to be a big landowner hereabouts. They say he even pushes men into fights and then shoots them for their land."

Mrs. Warren leaned back and reached for her mug. Tess wondered who "they" were.

After her meal, Tess left the café and wandered back up the dusty street. She needed to hurry home and prepare dinner for Sandy and Brett.

She frowned at her choice of words. Home? Why had she called Brett's cabin home?

Well, it was the only home she had now, she figured. The word sounded permanent and warm to her. After all, the bright yellow cabin with the glass window and the deerskin rug was cozy and would make someone a wonderful home one day.

Mrs. Calloway and Becky were supposed to arrive at the end of summer or even this fall, Tess knew. But what about a wife for Brett? Would he search for a wife like Sandy intended to do? There certainly weren't many choices around here, Tess thought as she glanced up and down the main street. Mrs. Warren was the only woman Tess had seen in Laramie so far.

She walked down the busy street, ignoring the open stares of rough men, unaware she passed the colorful saloon with the dragon over the door and the Bucket of Blood. Her thoughts turned again to Brett. His hazel eyes danced when he spoke about his homestead and his plans for the future. He was strong and had manners, unlike many of the workmen she had served in the café. He'd been a complete gentleman with Tess in his cabin.

"I saw you go into the café." Ivan sat on a different

bench than earlier, his clear eyes twinkling at her. "But I didn't see you come out until now. That must mean good news."

Tess looked up at the tall barn. She'd been so engrossed in her own thoughts that she hadn't realized she stood before the livery. She blushed, thankful Mr. Belmont could not read her thoughts. Tess dropped her gaze, hoping the older man didn't notice her sudden discomfort. She sat beside him.

"How did the Warrens treat you?"

"They gave me a job," she shared, excitement lacing her words, her thoughts shifting from Brett to her new opportunity. "They said I can work the noonday meal. Fifty cents a day. At that rate, I can make plans to head for Chicago."

"Is that where you're from?"

Tess hesitated. "Well, I used to live there," she said. "And I hope to live there again soon. We had friends there."

"We? Who else was with you then?"

Tess bit her lip. She knew Mr. Belmont was only being kind, but his persistence annoyed her. She glanced at him out of the corner of her eye. Could she trust him?

"My mother," she confided cautiously. "After Pa died, we moved to Omaha. I didn't like it there, and I want to return to Chicago."

Ivan pulled a stick and a knife from his pants. He began whittling, the wood curling as he removed narrow strips with the sharp blade. "What brings you to Laramie?"

Tess frowned, angry for allowing the old hostler to push her into conversation about herself. "Work," she said quickly, as if the answer were obvious.

"Well, Tess, I'm pleased you landed a job." He skinned another long curl from the stick, watching as the strip fell at his feet. "Where are you staying?"

Tess rose quickly. "Mr. Belmont, thank you for your help. I think Mr. Warren only gave me the job because of you. I'll see you tomorrow," she called over her shoulder as she threaded a path into the crowd.

Jostling workmen surrounded her as she made her way down Laramie's main street, intent on leaving town. Tess walked swiftly, her shoulders hunched against the nagging worry that plagued her. Was Mr. Belmont on to her? Did he guess she was a runaway?

She pursed her lips and hurried on, the westering sun warming her back. Why did he have to ask where she lived? She knew what men would think if they knew she was living with an unmarried man.

Brett was nice to her when she needed a friend. He had taken her in and allowed her to live in his cabin. There was nothing inappropriate in his behavior toward Tess, but others would assume the worst.

A scarlet wave of shame crept up her neck, blotting out her tan. The men in the road blurred in her sight as she felt the hot tears begin to slide down her cheeks. She hurried across the bridge, eager to leave Laramie behind.

Sure, she'd gotten a job at the café, but she felt afraid. Afraid of life, of starving, of being alone. Brett had welcomed her in, but she could not take advantage of his hospitality and kindness. Folks would talk, and although she was not worried about her reputation, Brett intended on living in Laramie and bringing his family west. It would not do for him to have his good name tarnished with stories of him living with a single woman.

The hubbub of the busy street fell behind her, and the crowd disappeared as Tess rushed past the last tents and shacks down the road toward the turn off to Brett's cabin. Tears of fear and frustration fell unheeded as she hurried through the afternoon, shadows from tall trees laying across the road now, shielding her from the hot rays of the sun. The calls of the watchful blue jays and the chirps of the squirrels went unchecked as she strode on, head bent to hide her tears from any who might see.

Anguish bubbled, a sense of panic swirled in her chest. Nothing around her seemed to register except her own lack of belonging. If only Frank had not been so wicked. None of this would be happening to her now if she were still safe with her mother. Only it was no longer safe with Mama. Frank had made that very clear at Tess's birthday dinner.

A large freight wagon lumbered past Tess, and she suddenly slowed. She watched the wagon wheels roll by before she lifted her eyes and halted, her gaze traveling to the clouds.

Think on what is pure, what is good, what is wholesome. The Scripture words came to her like a soothing salve on an open wound. Be strong and courageous, she reminded herself again. Remember how Joshua was about to cross the Jordan River and take the Promised Land. He had every right to be afraid, but his strong words floated to her heart. Be strong and courageous, he had told the Israelites. In the face of danger and possible death, be strong and courageous.

I will never leave you or forsake you. God's promise to Tess through his Holy Word came to her then, reminding her she had nothing to fear. If God was for her, whom could stand against her?

She drank deep breaths of calming air, her chest rising as she relaxed. Tess could feel the rapid beating of her heart begin to slow. She had become anxious without realizing it, and her chest heaved from the labored breathing. Slowly, she regained her composure.

The tall, stately pines stood all around her like sentinels.

Their dark green crowns barely moved in the slight breeze, yet the gentle sound of wind through their branches calmed her. The mountain spoke to her, a song of peace and strength. God was with her.

The distant melody of the rushing river came then to her eager ears, and Tess felt the musical sound penetrate her soul. God, the creator of nature, called out to her. *Be at peace, child*, the majestic voice of God whispered down to her from above. *Trust me*, he said with reassurance and power.

She looked around but saw nothing. Her ears had not actually heard any sound—as if the voice lay only in her head. Tess smiled as she remembered how Moses did not hear God's voice in the mighty storm but in the whisper of a gentle wind.

She peered all around again and saw she stood alone, yet she felt comforted and not alone. God was with her.

Tess tilted her head back and looked up at the tops of the pines and the wide blue sky above. Her smile widened, her tears forgotten, and she praised Jesus for his love and encouragement.

Strength welled within her and Tess closed her eyes, soaking in God's presence.

As she opened her eyes and looked along the road, the figure of a small man stepped from the brush, a derby hat cocked on his head. With a start, Tess recognized him.

CHAPTER NINE

Ace Moyer stepped into the road, his derby pushed jauntily on his narrow head.

Tess frowned, panic trying to well up within her as she fought valiantly to curb the fear. She clenched her fists, forcing calm. This would be an opportunity to show God how her faith grew. She would trust him. It was no accident this man stood here on the road from town. Tess would meet this situation with strength and faith, she resolved, setting her teeth firmly and turning to face the approaching little outlaw.

Hastily, she wiped the back of her hand across her eye. Again, Tess could feel the fear wanting to grow inside her, trying to swell like a storm cloud on the horizon. She pushed the terror back, leaning on God's strength. She would not fear. She would not succumb to panic. God would protect her.

She clenched her fists as she watched the man approach, remembering her first night in Laramie and how this man had frightened her. His group of friends had openly sneered at her. They had treated her with contempt, not caring what happened to her. She well remembered that night now. The complete despair she had felt. And now this man walked toward her.

Ace smiled as he drew near. She could see his small, weasel-like yellow teeth. "Well, Tess, I saw you in town today," he said easily, his beady eyes traveling over her slender form as he slipped his thumbs behind his belt.

Tess shivered from the disgusting scrutiny, so like Frank Mercer's back in Omaha. But this little man held no fear for Tess. She drew a deep breath, standing tall. God was with her.

"So?" she challenged quickly, lifting her chin. "I want nothing to do with you. And how do you know my name?"

This felt good, Tess thought. Not being afraid felt freeing. She could sense the strength in her body. Courage pulsed through her veins.

The insolent grin fell from Ace's thin face. He took a step closer to Tess. "I heard it in the café. And say, girl, I'm Ace Moyer. My brothers and me own the Bucket of Blood saloon. Big Steve is marshal of Laramie."

Tess rolled her eyes and turned away. "What do I care for you and your brothers?" She began walking again toward Brett's cabin. "I remember how rude you were to me when I first came to town."

Ace fell in step with Tess. "We run Laramie, in case you haven't noticed. Soon, we'll have all the good ranch land around here, then we'll go into ranching on a big scale. We'll be big men in the territory, wealthy men."

The thick smell of stale beer and sweat covered him, and Tess wrinkled her nose, leaning away from Ace. She glanced at him from the corner of her eye, noticing she stood as tall as the ruffian.

She laughed. "That's ridiculous." Tess stepped out a little faster. "Brett Calloway cuts ties for the railroad. That's the real power in this land. The Union Pacific runs this show."

Ace moved quickly ahead, spinning to halt her steps. Tess heard him snarl and his small eyes narrowed as he grasped her arm. Tess struggled, but to no avail.

The little man pulled her closer, pressing his face into hers. His dark eyes gleamed with malice. "We're the power here, girl. And Brett Calloway will get his soon enough, just you wait."

She stopped struggling and glowered at him, not saying anything. His scowl deepened, but finally, he let her go. Tess rubbed her arm and stared at him with narrowed eyes. He dropped his gaze and shifted his feet, looking away. Then, he turned back to her and tried once more to stare her down.

Tess merely looked at him and crossed her arms over her chest, surprised she didn't feel any fear of him. She knew she was in danger, but she felt protected.

She shrugged, indifferent. "I want only to be left alone. Go away."

Moyer's eyes blazed, and the shock he felt at her words was evident on his swarthy face.

Tess looked away and began walking again.

He grabbed her arm and spun her around to face him. Tess stumbled and was almost knocked off her feet by the sudden attack. Her eyes widened, and she tilted her head. "What are you going to do now, Ace Moyer? Slap me? You're so tough, aren't you, Ace? I know someone like you. You and your brothers are bullies. No one really respects you."

Her taunting speech seemed to infuriate him, and he raised his other hand, his open palm hovering for a long moment.

Tess wanted to shrink back, but a force greater than herself checked her movement and made her stand fast, looking Ace squarely in the eye.

The little man hesitated, his arm quivered, and Tess knew he would strike, reading the look in his eyes. A sudden yell halted the swinging of his arm. Both he and Tess turned as Sandy stepped from the forest. The lumberjack held the big Spencer rifle in his hands, and the gun was pointed at Ace.

"What's going on here?"

Ace released Tess and stepped back, the color draining from his face. Tess could tell he wondered if he could draw his own gun before Sandy shot him.

Sandy must have guessed the little man's intent. He stepped closer, disturbing Ace's plan.

"He grabbed me, Sandy. He said he would get Brett's land soon." Tess stepped away and rubbed her arm, her eyes never leaving Ace.

The tall woodcutter stared hard at the smaller man. "So, that's your game, huh, Moyer? You and your brothers have taken land from other homesteaders and now you have your greedy eyes on mine and Calloway's. Well, you can't have it."

Ace took a step backward and then another. "Well, we'll see, woodcutter."

He glanced at Tess, and she read the threat in his eyes. A shiver ran down her spine as she watched him hurry away. But as soon as he was far enough away, the little man turned and walked backwards, his hands thrust into his pockets. "I'll be watching you, girlie."

He spun and hurried on, casting only a single frightened look over his shoulder, quickly making his way toward town.

Tess watched him go, pleased somehow, and then looked at Sandy. "It's a good thing you came along when you did, Sandy."

The tall man still stared after the retreating outlaw. Then he glanced at Tess, and a hint of a smile creased his leathery face. "Brett and I needed to knock off early today. We can't keep up this pace for long. We've been working too hard. I told him I would go hunting for meat, and he's working around the place."

Tess suddenly remembered her good news. "I got a job at the café in Laramie. I work every day for the noon meal."

Sandy stroked his chin but said nothing.

"And I met Mr. Belmont at the livery barn. He seems very nice," she added quickly.

Sandy nodded. "Ivan is a good man. I don't know the Warrens too well, I never go to the café to eat, but Brett says they're good folks." He looked once more down the lane, but Ace had disappeared around a bend in the road. He turned to Tess. "You go on home now, Tess. Get something on for supper, and if you have a chance, I need some mending done, if you are willing."

Tess could feel her mouth drop open. Sandy's request signaled a shift in his thinking. He had finally accepted her. She straightened and smiled, then nodded, eager to comply.

"Of course, Sandy. What needs mending?"

He arched an eyebrow and a muscle twitched in his jaw. "Oh, you'll see my clothes hanging on pegs in my cabin." He waved a casual hand. "Look them over and see which ones need a stitch or two. I'll see you later."

Without another word, he glided noiselessly into the forest.

Tess watched him vanish, branches concealing him as he faded into the forest. She pursed her lips. If he hadn't come along when he did …

A little farther along, she located the bleached tree and turned off the road. Taking the dim trail, she followed the small stream up the mountain to the glade where the two cabins sat on either side of the swiftly flowing creek. Her eyes darted, searching for signs of the young homesteader as she approached the little bridge that spanned the stream. Her disappointment surprised her when she couldn't locate

Brett.

Not wishing to explore those feelings further, she hurried across the bridge, her shoes clattering on the rough boards. This was the first time she'd even crossed the stream.

Tess hesitated as she stepped from the bridge, her gaze studying the cabin before her. She glanced over her shoulder, across the stream to where Brett's cabin nestled among the trees of the clearing, comparing the two houses before facing Sandy's cabin again. The same peeled and squared logs, the same shake roof overhang stretched beyond the door. But Brett had built a plank floor on his porch, and he, of course, had the big window with the glass. The bare earth was tamped firm under Sandy's overhang. A single flat rock served as a step over his threshold.

The light must be very dim through the dark paper, Tess thought as she glanced at the greased butcher paper tacked over the small window cut into the log wall. She crossed the hard-packed dirt and stepped onto the flat stone. The latch lifted easily under her hand, and she swung the door wide, peering into the gloomy room.

A stub of a candle stood on the plank table, and Tess frowned at the ring of melted tallow around the base. Her frown deepened as she noticed the unmade bed. Brett always folded his blankets and stowed them properly.

No kitchen utensils hung beside the stone fireplace, no animal hides decorated the walls. The floor was dirt, old harness and broken tools piled in a corner. Where Brett's cabin seemed so light and open, Sandy's was dark and bare.

She surveyed the silent room. Not even a coffeepot was to be found. The two men had agreed to cook in Brett's cabin, a chore Tess had taken over since her arrival. She shrugged. Perhaps Sandy had no need of those items.

Tess grinned when she thought of the ongoing

argument between the two men over who was the worst cook. It sounded like it might've been Brett, if the reports of burned and tasteless meals were to be believed.

Tess felt pleased at Brett's compliments about her cooking. Even Sandy asked for seconds, although he rarely praised her openly. She wondered why Brett's approval warmed her.

She saw the few articles of clothing hanging on pegs just as Sandy mentioned. She crossed the unswept floor, wrinkling her nose as she rifled through the dirty garments, searching for rips and tears. Why hadn't Sandy asked her to wash them with Brett's clothes?

Tess decided to wash all the clothes, and while she scrubbed the garments, she would discover where mending was needed.

She gathered the bundle of spare clothes and marched back outside, closing the door behind her with her foot. She dropped the pile of dirty clothes near the path to the wash hole and hurried to Brett's cabin to fetch soap.

It took only a little time to wash Sandy's few articles of spare clothing. She did locate some minor tears, which she quickly repaired while the garment was still wet. Then, she threw them over the clothesline.

Tess decided soup and cornbread would be good for dinner. Her lunch at the café had showed her how routine and dull their dinners had become. Bacon and beans or venison and beans had begun to wear on her and most likely on Sandy and Brett too. Perhaps she could occasionally bring some variety of meals home from the café. She was sure the doughnuts and pies would be greatly appreciated by the lumbermen.

She stirred the simmering pot and added the few potatoes Mrs. Warren had given her. The yellow mixture for the cornbread she smoothed into a pan. She placed the pan on a stone beside the coals.

Glancing around the bright, clean cabin, Tess felt glad she lived here rather than with Sandy. The older bachelor cared little for cleanliness and light.

The door opened and Brett stood there, his wide shoulders filling the frame. He stopped when he saw her. "Tess, what're you doing here?"

She smiled at his foolish question. "I live here."

He strode forward, leaving the door open behind him. She tensed as he stood near her, the smell of pine and sawdust clinging to his clothes.

"Where else would I be, silly," she demanded playfully. He bent abruptly and sniffed her hair then moved to the fireplace, still sniffing.

Tess narrowed her eyes, her gaze following him. What was that about? Why had he smelled her hair?

For a long moment, he said nothing, appearing engrossed in the soup simmering on the fire. But Tess wondered if he thought of something else.

"It's done by now."

Brett glanced at her over his shoulder, his eyes questioning.

"The soup. It's done," she repeated, unable to take her gaze from him.

He took the wooden spoon and stirred, then tasted the broth. He smacked his lips appreciatively and used a faded rag to move the pot from the coals to the stone hearth.

He knelt beside her, slowly stirring the spoon in a circle, intent on the pot's contents. She looked away, pretending not to care, but watched him from the corner of her eye, her heart beating like a drum. His nearness unnerved her, made her feel uncomfortable somehow, as if she couldn't trust herself.

"I mean," he explained as he handed the spoon to Tess.

"I mean, Sandy and I returned home early today, and you weren't here. That's what I mean."

Tess nodded, but was unsure about his comment. She couldn't resist and looked deeply into his hazel eyes. Then she remembered and gulped, nodding again. "I was in Laramie. I told you I was going," she said. Why did she feel as if she needed to explain anything to this man? She wondered at her feelings as she turned to place plates on the table. She decided not to say anything about her encounter with Ace Moyer but was eager to share the update about her new job.

"I was hired at the café to work the noon meal. That way, I can still work around here, doing the laundry and cooking and cleaning. I really do appreciate you allowing me to stay here, Brett."

He peered at her and his head tilted. "The cabin wouldn't be the same without you," he said softly, a light in his eyes.

Tess turned away, feigning disinterest and continued fussing over dinner, her heart still pounding loudly.

"Come on, Tess," he called suddenly as he straightened, taking the spoon from her hand and leading her to the open door. "It's a glorious day, and I want to show you something."

He tossed the spoon, the utensil clattering on the table as Tess followed Brett. He held her hand tightly, and she tried to get free, but his grip only tightened, dragging her around the cabin to a well-worn path into the forest.

Finally, with an effort, she pulled her hand free. Brett glanced over his shoulder, chuckling as he plunged into the narrow trail. Tess frowned as she tagged behind, regretting her hasty decision to let go his hand.

"This is my special place." Brett spun in the trail and walked backward, beaming at her for a moment before turning around again. Together, they maneuvered around the rocks and brush that bordered the noisy creek. "I made it as soon as I settled the land."

Tess wanted to ask about this special place but was forced to watch her step as she leaped over fallen logs and trudged through small ravines. A startled deer raced through the woods, its white tail bobbing as it vanished into the dense forest.

"I'll clear the trail more when time allows," Brett went on, scrambling atop a large tree trunk that lay across their path. He peered down at her, a reckless grin creasing his bearded face as he held out a hand to Tess.

She hesitated only a moment before placing her small hand in his. He hoisted her up, pulling her to him as they balanced on the smooth trunk of the massive tree. A thrill raced through her at his touch, and Tess looked away, worried he might read the excitement in her eyes.

He still held her hand, but she reached for his shoulder with her free hand, balancing on the rounded surface. She peered at the ground, avoiding his gaze.

"I've wanted to show you this place since you arrived." His warm breath whispered into her hair as she steadied herself against him.

Tess said nothing, afraid to spoil the moment.

Brett released her hand and dropped to the other side of the big tree. Turning, he reached for her, his big hands encircling her slender waist. The unfamiliar touch made her tense, but then he lifted her easily to the ground.

What would Mama say about a stranger walking with her in the woods? What would her mother say about her sleeping alone in his cabin each night?

Tess bit her lip and followed Brett on the narrow path. She knew exactly what her mother would say, and she didn't care. It felt so good to have a friend again, someone to enjoy time with. Tess was sick of being lonely.

The trail ended at a large boulder, as an open glade spread before them. Tess stared, marveling at the small waterfall cascading into a pool. The stream narrowed here, its channel pouring through a gap between two rocks, spilling into a clear pool. Reflections of tall trees shimmered upon the ripples and Tess could only stare, amazed at the peace, the reverence the sylvan spot stirred within her.

Brett smiled at her and then led her to a stone bench, a natural shelf cut into a massive boulder that faced the quiet glade. They sat beside each other, and Tess gazed around the little park, drinking in its beauty. She gasped.

Across the stream, nestled in the green ferns and granite boulders, stood a tall cross.

"I come here when I need to pray or just be alone," Brett said softly.

Tess relaxed and leaned back, her gaze roaming the clearing, the waterfall, and the wooden cross.

"I discovered this place when I was exploring my land," Brett went on, his voice quiet. "There's no church in Laramie, so I made this place my church. I read my Bible here sometimes and spend time praying. At night, the stars are so brilliant. I truly feel the Lord's presence here."

Tess said nothing but let the peacefulness of the special retreat soak into her. The clearing felt like a natural cathedral among nature, adorned by the creator's artistry. Across the creek and at the edge of the space, the tall cross drew her gaze again and she could see Brett's touch in the carving—a wood lover's handiwork.

"I love this place," Tess breathed. "It's wonderful, Brett. I can feel God too."

Brett sat completely still, staring up at the tall cross. Tess studied him from the corner of her eye. His chiseled profile, the rugged beard along his firm jaw, the high cheek bones. Brett Calloway was handsome, she had to admit. But it was not a grudging confession. She felt pleased at his handsome qualities.

He turned and looked at her. "I need a haircut. Will you try your hand at it? We have no mirror, or I'd attempt it myself. And I won't let Sandy near me with a razor and scissors." He chuckled at his own comment.

Tess silently returned his look, imagining her hands rifling his dark hair. He wanted her to cut his hair? A nervous giggle escaped her.

He stood. "Come on, let's go back. I'm hungry and need a haircut."

Not waiting for Tess, he moved off down the trail, leading the way home.

CHAPTER TEN

Tess glanced back once as Brett climbed the big fallen tree. The afternoon was far advanced and dark shadows painted the little glade among the trees. The tall pines seemed to stand guard around the quiet dell, protecting the place like sentinels. Something warm and spiritual permeated the small clearing in the forest.

This time, Tess stood back from Brett as he pulled her onto the big tree. She shied away from him, suddenly shy and aloof to his closeness.

Brett must not have noticed, for he leaped down and turned to help Tess, lifting her again as before. When her feet touched the ground, however, Brett did not immediately release her, peering into her face with those piercing hazel eyes.

Her gaze dropped, and she moved hastily away, leaving Brett standing beside the fallen monarch. She led off now, needing to put distance between them. She could not allow her feelings to grow for the kind woodcutter. He was merely being nice, letting her stay temporarily at his cabin. Soon, she must leave for Chicago.

She weaved through the rocks and trees, breathing hard as she raced for the cabin.

Once, she heard Brett call her name, but she didn't slow until her shoes clattered on the porch.

Breathlessly, Tess rushed into the room, noticing immediately that the soup had boiled over and spilled into the dying fire. Brett was on her heels, and she turned on him. "Look what you've done." She pointed at the mess on the hearth. "The soup is ruined."

Brett skidded to a halt, looking from Tess to the soup pot and back to Tess. "Me? How is this my fault?"

Anger burned in her gut and Tess felt like she might cry. She narrowed her eyes and stared at him, wondering who she was truly mad at, him or … herself?

Her feelings confused her, and she didn't want Brett to see her this way. His presence, his strength, his kindness made her angrier still, and she turned and fled from the cabin.

The path to the foot bridge lay before her and she bolted for it without further thought. She thundered across the narrow bridge and ran around Sandy's cabin to fall in a heap among the ferns.

The tears came harder now, and Tess wiped them away with her sleeve, trying to understand her conflicting emotions. On one hand, she enjoyed being with Brett. He made her feel warm and safe. On the other hand, she felt wary of him, not trusting her feelings and not wishing to get too close to this fascinating new friend.

Tears ran down her cheeks, the salt stinging her eyes. Why should she cry over Brett Calloway? He was a stranger to her, nothing more. She wanted only to save money and return to Chicago. Those folks back there were her true friends, not this bearded woodcutter in the mountains.

Yet, something drew her to this peaceful, strong man. He was kind and looked at her in such a way that made her knees weak. What was happening to her?

The heavy weeping slowed, and Tess wiped her wet face, peering up at the fading light of evening through the dark trees. Was God trying to tell her something?

A sudden thought came to her. She would return to the little glade beside the large boulder and ask God what he wanted from her. The chapel in the woods seemed the perfect place to bring her questions and concerns. She would go tonight after Brett had gone to sleep.

Tess stood and smoothed her dress. Resolved, she marched back to the creek and bathed her face in the cold, clear water. Her eyes felt puffy and sore, but she determined not to allow Brett to ask her any questions.

The door creaked when she slipped into the cabin. Brett looked up quickly from his seat on the bench, his elbows on the table, a spoon in one hand. Two bowls lay on the table.

She dropped her gaze and walked slowly to the opposite bench. Without a word, she sat and began to eat.

At least he had the sense to hold his tongue, she thought as she ate without tasting the burned soup. A glance at the cornbread told her it had not fared as well as the soup. A blackened brick of coal filled the bread pan.

Tess avoided Brett's searching eyes. She could sense the concern there but ignored it. Her anger had passed. Now, she wondered what had gotten her so upset in the first place. It wasn't his fault he'd taken her to the woods to see his special place and dinner had burned. It was merely an accident.

"Sandy should be home soon," Brett said abruptly.

She could tell he attempted to lighten the somber mood. She nodded and handed him the used bowls and plates.

Frowning, Brett took the dirty dishes and went outside.

Tess tidied the table and put the remainder of the salvaged soup aside for Sandy. The blackened cornbread she threw out the window. A faint smile touched her lips as she recalled Brett chewing the black, crunchy substance.

Well, at least the coffee was still good, she mused. Tess filled two mugs and pulled a bench nearer the fire. She tossed a log on the low flames and they sputtered before

113

brightening the dim room. The single candle on the table would not give off sufficient light for a haircut now.

When Brett returned, Tess stood near the fire, his scissors in her hand.

"Sit down and let's get this over with," she commanded shortly.

His eyes widened and he hesitated.

Tess scowled at him. "Don't worry. I'm not mad anymore."

Brett nodded slowly and shuffled to the bench.

"I poured you some coffee," Tess said blandly as she began running a comb through his thick hair. She raked his head roughly time and again. The comb had to hurt, but he said nothing as she yanked the teeth through his tangled hair.

He reached for the coffee and tried to drink, but she tugged on the comb and he spilled the hot liquid on his trousers.

Tess sighed loudly. "All right. Take a sip of coffee first," she ordered.

Brett took a big swallow, then set the tin cup on the table. "Okay. Let the torture continue."

Tess bristled. "Do you want a haircut or not?"

Brett remained silent, staring into the fire.

Again, Tess pulled on the comb and snipped at the wild hair with the scissors.

Loud steps sounded on the porch and the door opened. Sandy held the Spencer rifle and glanced once at the pair before closing the door and replacing the long gun over the door. "Got me a big buck and delivered it to Warren. He said he'd mark it in his book." He kicked the other bench and sat down.

Tess leaned to the warming rock and retrieved the bowl of soup. She placed it on the table before Sandy and turned back to Brett.

The room remained silent except for the clipping of the scissors and the slight scraping of Sandy's spoon in his bowl. Firelight danced across Brett's taut features, but he hadn't said a word as Tess fought his snarled hair. Her annoyance grew as she worked. She'd tried to hurt him, make him yell or something. But he didn't complain.

Sandy watched the proceedings before him, ignoring the obvious tension in the air.

"That's a good haircut," he observed as he pushed the empty bowl from him. "I'd have you cut my hair, too, Tess, if I had any to cut." He ran a hand through his thinning hair, a narrow grin creasing his weathered face.

Was he making a joke? Tess smiled at the older man. "And I would be pleased to do it, Sandy."

"I saw my clothes on the line," he continued as he took the steaming cup Tess offered him. He blew on the mug before he went on. "Thanks for washing them. Did you find any that needed mending?"

Tess only nodded when she wanted to snort. Each piece of clothing needed attention. "All taken care of. Let me know if you need any more, Sandy. I don't mind." She stepped back to survey her work. "I think that's a big improvement." Tess walked slowly around Brett, reviewing him with a critical eye. "Now for the shaving."

Brett stood and shook himself, knocking loose hair from his shoulders and back. He bent to sweep the trimmings into a pile before tossing them into the fire. Flames leaped hungrily at the dark curls, and firelight gleamed on the peeled, smooth log walls as Tess mixed lather for the impending shave.

Brett took his seat again, and she forced his head back, studying his exposed throat. Expertly, she brushed lather on his neck and took a firm hold of his straight razor.

"You seem to have done this before." Brett muttered through clenched teeth.

"Be quiet," Tess commanded, dragging the sharp tool against his skin and up to his jawline.

"You don't have much of a beard." Sandy pointed at Brett with his empty cup. "You might as well take it off."

"Say the word, Brett," Tess threatened. She held the razor above his chin for emphasis.

"No." Brett held up a hand. "I like my beard. It makes me feel older."

Sandy snorted his disgust. "You aren't much older than this young girl, Brett. With the two of you around, I feel like an old man in the schoolyard."

Later, as the older man retired for the night, Brett followed and washed his face in the stream. Then he filled the coffeepot for the morning. Tess took advantage of the empty cabin to slip into bed fully dressed.

Brett soon returned with the blackened pot. He placed it near the fireplace and then blew the candle out, glancing at Tess in the semidarkness. She could feel his eyes upon her. Turning, he tossed more wood on the blaze. He pulled his blankets from their pile and prepared his bed, sighing loudly as he stretched out on the deerskin hide.

The firelight played on the yellow walls as Tess looked for Brett in the dark. She watched him, wanting to speak, to explain. She'd been so angry this evening. How could she tell him she didn't know what bothered her?

"Tess?" he whispered suddenly.

Her eyes widened and she tensed.

"Are you still awake?" He shifted on the floor, and she wondered if he were looking at her, searching for her in the shadows.

She hesitated. "Yes, I'm awake."

"I've tried hard not to ask too many questions about

you. I accepted you needed a safe place to stay and that was enough for me. But now I want to know more."

The fire crackled and the shadows danced. She worried he would ask things she didn't wish for him to know.

Tess said nothing, hoping he might go to sleep. She didn't want him to know everything about her. But, after a pause, he spoke again. "I know you wish to go to Chicago, but I don't think that's where you've been living. I know your pa died in the war. Where is your mother?"

Tess hesitated again. How much should she say about herself? Soon, she would be leaving. Being a runaway, she might endanger all that Brett had worked so hard to build, should she be discovered here. Still, he had saved her, given her a place to live. Didn't she owe him an honest answer? It was the least she could give in return for his generosity and kindness.

She sighed and looked up at the rafters. "I ran away from my stepfather. He lives in Omaha with my mother."

Silence hung heavy in the cabin and only the crackling fire disturbed the quiet. Then Tess heard Brett shift beside the table.

"Do they know you're in Laramie?"

"No. I don't think so. I rode a freight train here in a storm. I guess that's why I was so sick when I arrived. I intended on going east immediately, but I got on the wrong train."

Tess wondered at how easy it felt talking to Brett. Relief filled her, allowing the heavy burden she'd been carrying to slip away.

A long silence followed, and Tess was certain Brett had fallen asleep. She prepared to slip from her bed and go to the little chapel in the woods, but then he spoke again.

"Tess, thanks for telling me. You can trust me with your story. I know you're a minor and must do what your folks say, but I think I can guess what made you run away."

She tensed again as he paused, and Tess wondered if Brett truly understood what drove her from Omaha and Frank Mercer's shack. Could he guess the wicked truth?

"Tess," Brett continued, his soft voice clear in the still cabin. "What do you wish for now? I mean, now that you're free from your stepfather. What are your goals, your dreams?"

His question startled her. Her dreams? Why, she had no dreams. It had always been within her to simply get away from Frank. The last four years had been miserable.

Possibly, when she'd been a little girl, maybe then she had enjoyed dreams. But Papa had never told her she could do anything special. Tess had always believed she would simply grow up and find work, perhaps marry a man and have children, like Mama. The lack of encouragement or dialogue about her future had never allowed her to believe good things awaited her.

But Papa's death in the war and Mama's fear and timidity had afforded a chance for a man like Frank Mercer to step in and ruin any hope she'd had of dreams. Now, Tess desired safety. And love.

"Tess, are you still awake?"

This time, she didn't answer. Her thoughts confused and disturbed her. This handsome tie cutter made her think things she had given up long ago. Were dreams still possible for her?

Tess watched the shadows deepen as the fire died down. Brett's even breathing revealed that he had fallen asleep at last.

Tess waited a long while to make certain. Then, lifting the covers, she slipped from the warm bed and carried her shoes to the door.

CHAPTER ELEVEN

The heavy door did not creak as she carefully opened it a crack and slipped out, closing it behind her. She tugged on her shoes and moved swiftly to the path that led to the glade. The tall cross beckoned, calling her by name.

Moonbeams filtered through the trees, lighting her way, a patchwork of deep shadows and brightly lit avenues. Anticipation and expectancy filled her as she rounded large rocks, her heart thudding in her chest as she neared the special place.

Her prayers were lifted daily, but here, in this sacred place, she would feel his presence, Jesus, her hope and savior.

What would God tell her? Why was she here? What was happening to her?

Tess tried not to think about these things, concentrating on navigating the narrow trail to the extraordinary retreat, a refuge from the overwhelming fears of life that plagued Tess. There, God would speak. There, in front of the tall cross, Jesus would meet her.

Finally, the fallen monarch barred her path. Brett had cut away some of the bigger branches. This time, she had no help in surmounting the big tree. A glance told her she could not go around, tall ferns and stretching branches blocked her way.

Grasping a broken branch, Tess pulled herself up and onto the rough bark of the dead pine. She grunted as she threw her legs over and slid down the other side.

As if a light from Heaven, moonlight filled the clearing and shimmered on the stream's ripples in the pool. The waterfall played a reverent melody as Tess took her seat on the granite bench and leaned back, nestling into the solid rock.

Awed by her surroundings, Tess held her breath as she looked across the stream to the tall cross, illuminated in glowing moonshine. Tess stared at it, knowing he could read her thoughts. He knew her innermost worries and struggles. She sat there, waiting, longing for God to speak.

The gentle breeze that blew each afternoon across the mountains was gone now. The silent forest lay completely still save for the music of the gently tumbling water. Tess allowed her pent-up thoughts to spill forth. Now was the time to open her heart and hear God's wisdom. Now he would speak and tell her what was happening and why.

She wiped her sweaty hands on her dress and searched the bright glade, waiting. But nothing happened. Her nose twitched and she chewed the inside of her cheek. She wrapped her arms around her chest and pulled her legs up, huddling against the cold stone at her back. What was he waiting for? Where was Jesus?

She glanced again at the cross, its roughhewn surface almost glowing in the moonbeams. It reminded her of God's goodness and promises, never revealed as Tess expected but always faithful. God sent his own son to die for mankind's sins, her sins. He caused Jesus to rise from the dead, destroying the power of death over those who believe in Jesus as their savior. God will never leave me nor forsake me, Tess breathed, recalling Scripture verses that encouraged her in times of distress. Like now.

Nothing can separate us from the love of God. Not even Frank Mercer and his disgusting attentions. Not even the fear that comes when Tess considered Laramie and the

Moyer brothers. Not even the ache she held in her heart for her frightened mother. These things were not from God. He did not want wickedness and cruelty and fear to rule our lives. God is love. He desires good things for his people.

An image appeared in her mind, making her chest tighten. Brett Calloway. She tilted her head, seeing his bearded face with those gentle hazel eyes.

Brett was a good man. He was kind to Tess. He looked out for her.

Another thought crowded into her mind. Tess longed for real love. Someone to help her, someone to think of her in a good way. She longed to love and be loved. To be protected and to serve the one who loved her.

Again, her thoughts drifted to Brett, and she looked quickly at the cross, wondering if this thought had come from above.

Everything suddenly made sense. Her confusion, her anger, her shyness, her desire. Tess stared hard at the cross, praying for guidance and discernment. Was this what God had brought her here to reveal? Was this the reason she had boarded the westbound train in Omaha? Was this the reason she was now at this cabin in the woods?

In an instant, she knew the answer. Yes, this was the reason. There were no coincidences or accidents in God's plan. He was intentional. He had orchestrated these events to bring a lonely and scared young woman to Laramie.

With a shudder, realization swept over her, filling her with an unexpected and unfamiliar sense of joy. Tess was falling in love.

CHAPTER TWELVE

Her eyes filled with tears, and she began to weep. Slow rivulets rolled down her cheeks as Tess felt God's strong embrace around her. He wanted her to know love. Not only the love of God, an eternal and perfect love, but the love of a man who would hold her dear, protect her, and serve her.

Tess needed to love. Her father had never shown her real love and certainly her frightened mother had rarely been capable of looking past her own needs. Frank had entered the picture and had showed Tess only a perverted and selfish attention. Healthy and proper love from a Godly person had certainly never come Tess's way, except possibly from her old schoolteacher, Mrs. Sellers, who had introduced Tess to Jesus.

Tess loved her mother, but the woman seemed unable to overcome her fear at being alone enough to protect her daughter from an evil man. Tess's mother would allow wickedness to happen to her daughter if it meant she would not be alone. That was not real love.

Tess longed for the love of someone who would love her in return. To guard her and want good things for her. She yearned for such a love as this.

Brett Calloway seemed to be that very man. But Tess would be patient. She must not allow these new feelings to fool her. What if her feelings were simply infatuation with the first handsome man who'd paid her any attention? She didn't wish to emulate her own mother's record of falling for a deceptive man, to allow her desperation to hoodwink her. She must not permit her heart to govern her actions. No, she would wait and see if this proved real and true.

St. Paul said that when he was a child, he thought like a child. He wanted things that might not be good for him, being ignorant and immature. Now, as an adult, God challenged him to be intelligent, mature, and wise. Tess would resolve to do the same.

Again, she looked at the cross standing tall in the small glade. The wooden structure shone brightly in the brilliant rays of the moon, reminding her how Jesus had risen from the dead to overcome death and the power of sin. She would stay away from sin. Tess would not allow her heart to lead her astray.

"I promise to be patient, Jesus. I'll wait on you, Lord. You will show me what is true and good. Let me have an open and soft heart for you to shape into who you would have me be. Teach me what is right, and don't let my feelings get in the way and fool me. I want to love Brett, I think he's a good man, but only if it's what you want for me. You know what is best for me. Your will be done."

Tess finished her prayer and stood. She shivered, suddenly aware of the cold. Had the chill been here all along? She walked to the fallen pine and scrambled atop the trunk, glancing back down at the small clearing with its tall cross and stone bench and cheerful little waterfall. The place *was* special, she agreed, recalling what Brett had said earlier that day. She smiled and then clambered down the big pine and wended her way back to the cabin.

Tess shivered more now, rubbing her arms briskly. Smoke curled above the stone chimney, dancing like a ghost in the brilliant moonlight.

Pulling her laces, she slipped out of her shoes as she leaned against the log wall. The latch lifted quietly under her hand and Tess moved within, her shoes gripped tightly in one hand.

"Tess?" Brett's voice called softly. She froze, not daring to make a sound. Yet, he must have heard her enter.

"Yes, Brett, it's me."

He did not reply. He must've fallen back to sleep. Moving on, Tess placed her shoes on the floor and pulled her dress over her head. Swiftly, she slipped under the blankets and rolled into a tight ball. Tess shivered, shaking and trembling uncontrollably for a few minutes despite the cabin's warmth. Soon she became comfortable and relaxed.

Tess glanced once more at the rafters above her, invisible now in the darkness. She remembered her pledge to the Lord and closed her tired eyes. It had been a long day.

It seemed only a minute later when she heard Brett moving about the cabin. The fire blazed, crackling cheerily, and she could hear the coffeepot simmering on the hearth.

Tess shifted and stretched. Brett turned to look at her. "Good morning, sleepy head. There's fresh coffee and some sourdough biscuits." He paused a moment before he added, "They're not burned."

Tess frowned, tensing as she remembered the cornbread of the previous evening. But at his gentle chuckle, she realized he teased, and she let it go, relaxing once more, not having to prepare for battle.

"Sandy and I will work late today to make up for yesterday's break. See you for supper."

He took his coat from the peg beside the door and stepped out onto the porch, the latch falling into place as he closed the door behind him.

Tess smiled at the door, enjoying the sight of Brett and recalling her night visit to the woodland cathedral. She reached for her dress and then hesitated. She would bathe this morning and do some laundry before walking to Laramie.

She ran to the door and pulled in the latch string before rushing to the fire with outstretched hands. She glanced over her shoulder, uncomfortable in her thin nightgown, but no one peered at her through the window. The men had gone.

Tess lifted the coffeepot, feeling the weight—enough remained for her. She filled a tin cup, still feeling foolish in her nightgown, and reached for a biscuit.

A grin played at the corner of her lips. Well, it wasn't burned, she thought as she took a bite of the lumpy biscuit. She wrinkled her nose at the taste but kept eating.

The sun peeked between the trees when she brought the first of the laundry out to wash, shadows dappling the clearing before the cabin. Today, bedding must be cleaned along with the lone towel Brett owned and the gray dress Tess had worn.

Cold water lapped at her toes as she tested the pool, making a shiver race along her spine. But she waded in, eager to finish the wash. She would bathe later, after chores were complete.

Tess swept the flagstone floor with Brett's homemade broom and wondered what Sandy did for his dirt floor. Would he sweep it like Tess did for Brett's cabin? Certainly, her mother had always said that sweeping a dirt floor seemed a waste of time, yet she'd swept the shack's filthy floor in Omaha, nonetheless. Tess wondered if it'd been for cleanliness or because her mother feared Frank's criticism.

Tess chopped and stacked wood and tidied the cabin, making sure all was ready for when she returned to prepare supper. The thought of working at the café filled her with excitement, and she didn't want to be late.

Taking clean undergarments and another dress, Tess

strode down to the wash hole and bathed. The water was chilly, but the sun shone on her bare head and shoulders as she swam about the little pool.

Soon, she was clean and dressed as she stepped off the porch, her long hair still damp. Tess passed the small bridge and the narrow path that led to the wash hole. Her gaze traveled across the creek to Sand's cabin nestled among the dark pines before the log structure was lost from view. The track through the woods followed the stream as it flowed down the mountainside toward the Laramie River somewhere down on the flats.

In the distance, a train whistle pierced the morning air. She'd heard the train numerous times now as it arrived and left Laramie. Birds and squirrels chattered among the branches as Tess strode through the forest and thought she glimpsed a fox as it darted into the thickets. The woods thinned and ahead, she could see where the well-trodden road lay, following the shining twin tracks of the railroad.

Tess turned left to town and then stopped, tilting her head as she slowly spun on her heel and peered east. Sunlight shone on her face and Tess closed her eyes, soaking in the rays, feeling the warmth steal over her damp hair. This road led to Tie Siding where Brett and Sandy sold their ties. She wondered if she would ever see that little wayside hamlet. Brett said there was nothing there but tie cutter shacks and loading platforms.

Tess opened her eyes as she turned again and headed for town. A train pulled away from the depot as she crossed the wooden bridge over the river, and the engineer waved at Tess. She waved in return and even smiled, surprised at the unexpected feelings that assailed her. She felt happy.

She leaned on the railing and watched the train, black smoke billowing as the engine puffed along the rails. Tess looked down at the water, pretending to be attentive when she really wanted to study the unfamiliar emotion she now experienced. Happiness was a sensation she was not accustomed to—hard work and diligence were.

But something had changed in Tess. She could feel the difference. A great adventure had begun. Her time at the cross late last night revealed it was no accident that she found herself here in Laramie. Like Esther in the Bible, perhaps it was for such a time as this that she had come west instead of east. Brett acted kindly to her. When Tess had arrived in town, alone and sick, he'd taken her in. Now, her feelings for him bloomed.

A heavy wagon rumbled past, the wood planks trembling beneath her shoes. She walked on. Fear had been her constant companion for as long as she could remember. Only the Lord's strength and encouragement had allowed her to endure this far.

She glanced up as she walked. "You're with me, aren't you? I know you are."

She pursed her lips and moved on. Surely God's commanding words to not fear and be courageous had carried her into town and helped her find a job. Yet the old feelings hovered around her, telling Tess she couldn't do it, she wasn't strong enough.

Tess halted again. Tension settled in her stomach, tying knots that squeezed within. She wiped her hands on her dress as anguish threatened. She took a deep breath and then bit her lip, her gaze darting up and down the muddy street. Couldn't she just be happy for a little while without her unwanted companions showing up again?

Trust God. Trust God. Trust God, she repeated silently to herself, trying to regain her composure. Tess needed to hurry to the café, but she wanted to begin this day in prayer.

She dashed into an alley and stood behind a rain barrel.

She began to pray. She prayed silently, allowing her eyes to roam over the sprawling town on the Laramie River. She prayed for her protection and well-being, but she also prayed for the inhabitants and the businesses. Tess prayed the Word of God would penetrate this place and bring souls to a life changing relationship with the savior, Jesus Christ. Fervently she prayed and, slowly, the tension eased. The vise that gripped her heart let go and she breathed deeply, filling her lungs with fresh air.

Peace assailed her. God was with her. She was not alone. He had provided. She would not be alone.

Tess returned to the main street, eager to get to the café. She passed the horse trough and only glanced at the foul-smelling water. She saw Ivan Belmont seated on his bench, a stick and his knife in his hands. He nodded when he saw her.

"Good morning, Mr. Belmont." Tess needed to hurry on, but one look at the old man's somber face stopped her. "What is it? What's happened?"

He indicated the empty seat beside him. Tess scowled and looked down the street. No line appeared outside the café this morning. Perhaps she had a minute. She sat down, folded her hands in her lap, and waited.

Ivan peeled another strip with the sharp blade. "Charlie Denton is dead. Big Steve shot him in the Bucket of Blood. He says it was a fair fight. So do the Moyer brothers, they were witnesses. But I know they wanted his land."

Tess squeezed her hands. Omaha was rough and a girl had to be careful, but killings were not common there like they seemed to be here in Laramie. She remembered Brett confronting the Moyers and Steve Long about a killing the night she arrived in town. That seemed so long ago now.

"Cranston was killed only a week ago and now Charlie Denton. I heard Long shot a man in the Chinaman's

Palace too. There needs to be some real law and order in Laramie," Mr. Belmont said between clenched teeth as he pushed another curling strip from the stick.

Tess stood. "I'll stop by after my shift." She left the hostler behind and started on again for the café.

Big Steve Long was the law in Laramie, Tess knew, yet he also seemed to be a known killer. He'd shot a number of men and somehow taken their land.

Tess walked on, passing the Overland Stage Station before hurrying past the Bucket of Blood. Ace and Con Moyer lounged on the front steps, a cigar dangling from Con's mouth. He didn't seem to notice Tess, but she watched Ace tip his derby at her, a wide grin on his narrow face.

Fear bubbled within her, but she fought the panic down. She would not allow fear to rule her life anymore. She'd been so frightened in Omaha. Frank Mercer had been both a bully and a dishonest man. He often worked discreetly on the side, using company materials, to build and sell items. She knew she couldn't trust Frank and inherently knew the same about the Moyers.

Her bluff of strength had warded off Ace when he'd accosted her on the way home yesterday, but she knew only Sandy's timely arrival was what saved her from real harm.

The gaudy red and yellow Palace loomed as she hurried toward the café. The dragon carving over the door leered at her as she passed, and Tess dropped her gaze, suddenly intent on her shoes.

Only a few men were seated at the long tables when Tess entered the café. Mrs. Warren brightened when she spotted Tess. "I'm so glad you came." The plump woman untied her apron. "There's no rush like we have on doughnut days. I think you can handle today's lunch crowd."

Tess tied a clean apron around her slim waist. "Mr. Warren, I'm here."

The café owner waved at her from the kitchen and then turned back to Henry, giving instructions to the cook.

Tess moved easily among the men, filling coffee cups and fetching platters of meat and beans and bread. Venison was the meat of the day, and she wondered if it was the same big buck Sandy had delivered.

The rough men of Laramie were mostly courteous, in a rough sort of way, but she enjoyed the work. A few were overly familiar and bold as they looked her over, but none said anything inappropriate. Disrespect to a woman could get a man hanged. One man even proposed to Tess before the end of her shift.

Ace and Con Moyer came in and sat together at a table against the far wall. Tess served them like she would any other customer, but they were cold and quiet when she drew near.

Tess observed them covertly as she worked. The Moyers stared insolently at the other customers in confident, challenging looks. Occasionally, they leaned their heads together and whispered.

Were they discussing the shooting of Charlie Denton? Ace Moyer had bragged only yesterday that they'd soon be big men in the territory, landowners and ranchers. Was this part of their scheme? To kill men who had land they wanted? Suddenly, Tess recalled Ace mentioning something about Brett's homestead.

When Tess placed plates on their table, Ace looked up and sneered. "Enjoy your meal, gentlemen," she replied, almost choking on the polite words. But she needed the job. Besides, no sense letting Ace Moyer think he scared her.

The crowd swelled and Tess was kept busy. Her four-hour shift passed quickly. Mr. Warren made a mark in his book and then Tess ate her meal by herself. The table near the window afforded the best view of Laramie.

She scanned the wide street as she ate. The Chinaman's Palace lay closest to the café, but even the Bucket of Blood was visible from here. Con Moyer stood on the boardwalk now, leaning against the roof support, a cigar clenched in his teeth. There was no sign of Ace.

Tess frowned, hoping the little toad didn't plan on waylaying her again on the way home. The frown melted as she remembered God's words. It would not be easy, but she would try to avoid fear.

Tess left the café and made her way across the busy street to Ivan Belmont's livery, but the older man was nowhere to be found. A quick search of the stalls and the corrals behind the big barn proved unsuccessful, and Tess decided to head for home.

Thunder rumbled and Tess looked up. Black clouds bunched ominously in the west. Afternoon thunderclouds were not uncommon, and the occasional shower often accompanied these dark clouds. However, these looked more serious to Tess. With a cautious glance at the impending storm, she stepped into the road home.

A great clap of thunder made her jump. The sound echoed from the surrounding mountain peaks and finally drifted down the valley, the rumbles lessening in volume as they drifted farther away.

Tess turned again to look at the coming storm. Lightning zigzagged from above, striking the forest with brilliant jabs. Great streaks of light flashed faster than the eye could follow. Another rumble of thunder sounded, and Tess hurried on.

The sun had disappeared, and now a hazy, gray light pervaded. Darkness descended quickly and Tess picked up her pace, her bonnet swinging down her back as wind whipped her hair into her eyes. The thunder rolled and she peered ahead with worry. Where was the bleached tree? Her heart pounded as another clap made her duck her head.

Finally, the turn off to the cabins loomed, and Tess left the road and walked into the wagon track, branches swatting at her as she weaved among the trees.

The dark forest enveloped her, making her feel more alone than she felt on the open road. Where her journey to town that morning had been filled with hope and bright sunlight, she now felt chased by something intangible, something dark.

Tess leaned into the trail, the gentle incline making her anxious as she struggled to go even faster up the mountainside. She slowed at the sight of the little bridge to Sandy's cabin, her destination near now. Tess placed a hand to her chest, breathing hard as she walked to the clothesline. Laundry fluttered in the wind.

Huge raindrops struck her as she pulled the damp bedding from the line. She looked up when she heard the mules. Brett and Sandy came into the clearing, the wagon loaded with timbers.

With her arms full of laundry, Tess raced through the sudden downpour to the protective overhang of the porch. Her chest heaved as she faced the storm and its fury. Rain came in sheets and pounded the dry ground. The two men led the obedient mules around the cabin toward the temporary barn.

The men would want coffee. Tess went inside, pausing to listen to the rain pounding the cedar shakes above her.

Draping the damp clothes around the room, Tess hoped they would dry in the cool cabin air. Perhaps a bigger fire would help, she thought, as she nudged the smoldering embers, thankful she had the forethought to bank the glowing coals this morning before leaving for work.

The fire hesitated, licking tentatively at the fresh wood, then blossomed as the small, hungry flames were fed. Tess stared into the bright blaze and felt grateful to be indoors from the storm. She gathered her wet hair and twisted it, rubbing the long locks fiercely with the dish towel.

Tess frowned when she lifted the empty coffeepot. With a glance at the roof, Tess moved toward the door. The rain fell hard. She was sure to get soaked running to the stream.

She stepped from the warming cabin onto the porch. The pile of wood at one end would ensure dry firewood through this storm, she knew, and she silently thanked Brett for his thoughtfulness.

She hesitated another minute, watching the downpour, and then raced for the stream.

Her shoe slipped once in the mud, but she gained the bank and hurriedly lowered the pot into the rising stream. Rain from higher up on the mountain had already swelled the creek with new water.

Puddles formed around her as rainwater dripped from her to the rough planks of the porch. She watched the storm, reluctant to enter the cabin and walk on the recently cleaned floor with her wet clothes.

Another loud clap of thunder rolled across the face of the mountain and Tess shivered. Brett's yellow cabin felt snug from the storm, but she pitied anyone out on such a day as this.

Tess wondered if the railroad crews worked in this weather as she pushed the filled pot into the coals. Certainly, they'd be allowed to return to the safety of their lodgings. She'd seen the huge tents that sheltered the numerous workers for the Union Pacific.

A sudden pounding of boots on the porch alerted

her that Brett and Sandy had arrived. She thrilled at her eagerness to see the handsome young tie cutter. Tess hadn't forgotten her realization of the night before, though she tried to keep her confusing emotions in check. She wouldn't allow her heart free reign. Prudence and caution seemed best now.

She stepped from the warm fire to open the door. The two men stood on the porch, water streaming from them in little rivers. Brett arched his eyebrows as she handed them cleaned flour sacks to dry off.

Tess had noticed the café went through a lot of flour and a stack of the sacks piled in the corner of the kitchen. She resolved to ask Mrs. Warren for some of them the next time she went to work. They could be sewn together to make towels or curtains.

By the men's silence and somber mood, Tess sensed something wrong. Brett's forehead wrinkled with worry lines, and Sandy's lips pressed in a thin line.

"What's happened?" Tess asked, glancing from one man to the other. Usually, Brett seemed so positive and upbeat. His dour expression now did not rest well on his lean face.

He squinted at her. "Is coffee on?"

She nodded. "It'll be ready in a minute," she replied, irritated he hadn't answered her question.

Suddenly, she thought of the two wet men and their sodden clothes. "Brett, Sandy, leave your wet clothes out here and I'll fetch blankets. I can hang them indoors to dry. You should sit by the fire with something warm."

Without waiting for a reply, Tess closed the door and went to Brett's pile of bedding beside the chimney. She lifted two blankets and hugged them close for a moment, inhaling Brett's scent. She turned her head as she opened the door a crack. A hand snaked in and grasped the blankets and Tess closed the door. She dragged a bench near the fire.

The two men came in then, barefoot and wrapped in dry blankets. They shuffled awkwardly to the bench before the stone fireplace. Tess handed them steaming mugs before she hurried to the porch and gathered the wet clothes.

Tess draped them around the room, moving the chair closer to the fire for the heat. She stole furtive glances at the two glum men as they stared moodily into the fire, neither man speaking. Something weighed heavily upon them.

Finally, Tess could take the suspense no longer. She pulled the second bench closer to Brett and rested a hand on his shoulder. The tender touch drew his gaze and Tess could see the worry and dread in his hazel eyes.

"Brett? What is it? What's wrong?"

He stared at her a moment before responding. "The railroad cannot pay us for last month's work. We'd been waiting for this pay day to square our debt at the store in Laramie. All the cutters are angry. None of us have been paid in two months."

Sandy inhaled deeply and looked at Tess. "Big Steve Long was there and offered to buy the homesteads from cutters who have prime land. He offered to buy our place, too, but we said no."

Brett frowned and dropped his head. "We're through, Tess. We owe money in town and Long is marshal. He said that if men couldn't pay their debt, their land would be put up for sale. It's not right or legal, but he's the law around here."

Tess tilted her head as her gaze roamed the smooth log walls. This was Brett's cabin. He'd filed on the land properly. Could Big Steve take another man's land from him? Was there nothing the cutters could do?

"Are the other railroad men affected? Are they receiving

pay?" Tess wanted to know.

"No," Brett said, shaking his head. "But they're fed and housed by the Union Pacific. They can go a while without pay and still work. We need to buy supplies, or we can't keep working. Big Steve has ordered the store to stop extending credit to the tie cutters."

Tess chewed the inside of her cheek. "Well, when did the company say they'd pay you?" This seemed serious. If Brett was forced to give up his homestead, he wouldn't be able to move his family west. Nor would he be able to build his sawmill.

Again, the young man shook his head. "They don't know. Some bureaucratic mix up back east has temporarily halted pay to the Union Pacific. General Dodge says to keep working, pay will come. But we need supplies to do that. Sandy and I have been tapped out long ago and have been living on credit."

"I told you not to give all your money for that glass window," Sandy growled, pointing at the clear window in the front of the cabin. "You should've used butcher paper like me, and you might still have some cash money."

Brett nodded. "I know, Sandy. It's just that I wanted my cabin to be nice for Ma and Becky when they arrive."

His words struck her hard. She felt ashamed she could only think how their news might affect her. Brett and Sandy might lose their homesteads and be forced to return east for other employment, but she had nowhere to go. The small amount of money Mr. Warren owed her was for her return to Chicago and the friends she hoped to live with there.

But something had happened to Tess that made her think now about Brett Calloway. She believed she was falling in love with him. If her feelings were true, she could not be selfish and think only of herself. To experience healthy love, the kind God desired from his people, one must love in return. Tess must think of others, not solely what benefitted her.

Jesus came to serve, not to be served. His love was unselfish. Tess must think of serving the man she loved.

These feelings were new and strange to Tess. Her own mother had married Frank because the frightened woman couldn't think about what was best for her family, only what was easiest for herself. This single selfish decision had caused more problems than it solved. If Mama had been patient and waited on the Lord, perhaps finding work, maybe things would be different now.

Tess made up her mind. She knew God asked her now to think beyond her own needs and desires. The trip to Chicago would have to wait.

"Brett," she began quietly. "My job in Laramie will help with supplies. Also, I've been thinking of cutting hair after my shift at the café. I used to cut hair in Omaha. Perhaps I could help out while I'm here."

Abruptly, Tess felt better. Although she offered to give all she'd saved, the gift made her feel happy. She wanted to help these kind men, even if it cost her more time here in Laramie. She would get to Chicago eventually, she figured. If Brett wasn't the man for her, Chicago awaited. Only time would tell. Tess would give God that time.

Slowly, Brett's head lifted, and he stared wide-eyed at Tess. Sandy, too, turned to look at her, a glimmer of hope appearing in his tired, defeated eyes.

"You'd do that for us?" Brett whispered. "You don't even know us, Tess."

She grinned, liking the feeling that swept through her. The feeling of helping someone.

"Of course, Brett. You didn't know me when you took me in. I was a stranger, and you fed me and took care of me. It's the least I can do to repay you for your kindness."

His hazel eyes softened, and he glanced at Sandy before he spoke. "Thank you, Tess. I'll never forget this." He lifted a hand and placed it over hers where it still lay on his shoulder.

At the touch of his rough hand and the gentle look in his eyes, her heart swelled. An unfamiliar emotion, a sensation she couldn't name, filled her and she could only smile at him in return.

CHAPTER THIRTEEN

Tess marveled how her few words could so easily turn a somber moment into one of good news and hope for the future. With her offer of aid, Brett had gone from despair to excitement as he shared his desire to continue cutting ties and hope for a larger payout later.

"The pay master assured us that eventually the back pay would be doled out," Brett reported as he set the table with one hand, his other hand holding two corners of his blanket at his neck.

Sandy scowled at this. "I still don't know if I believe him. After all, they'll be getting free work out of us if they never come through," he grumbled. Tess heard the skepticism in his tone.

"They'll pay," Brett replied with confidence. His mission to create a home for his family and his dream of building a sawmill one day were suddenly restored.

Tess smiled, happy she was the reason for this encouragement.

She stepped outside while Sandy dressed in his damp clothes. The evening had turned pleasant, even though some doubt remained about the payout for the ties that had already been delivered to Tie Siding.

"I'll take you there one day," Brett had promised when Tess inquired about the small hamlet where the tie cutters delivered and stacked their ties.

Tess leaned against the roof support now and hugged herself against the cold. The sun had long disappeared, and the night was very dark, very wet, and very cold. The rain had decreased in ferocity but still lingered, falling with a steady rhythm. The swollen stream ran bank full now, and its usual gentle melody had been replaced with a low roar. Tess knew a lot of water had fallen, and she wondered if it might affect the little bridge that spanned the creek to Sandy's cabin.

She looked out at the gloom and praised God for these new and thrilling feelings she'd never experienced before. She'd always served her mother, but a lot of that had been from duty. Her mother had not really thought of Tess when she'd married Frank. Mama had been afraid of being alone and solely responsible for their upkeep—nothing more.

Tess felt amazed and overwhelmed at this strange feeling of satisfaction that welled within her. Doing God's will had brought about intense joy.

The door opened behind her and Sandy stepped outside. He closed the door and stood beside Tess a moment before leaning down and stamping his feet into his muddy boots. Then the tall man straightened and peered at Tess in the gloom. "I didn't get a chance to thank you in there," he said, jerking a thumb towards the cabin. "That was mighty kind of you, and I appreciate it."

He shifted and cleared his throat before going on. "I hope to return east this fall and fetch a wife."

"Is there someone in particular, Sandy?" Tess asked, smiling into the darkness. It seemed difficult to think of this serious man with a wife.

He drew in a deep breath of the fresh air before he replied. "I like it up here. You know, I only came along because Brett convinced me I could own my own place, and two men could handle heavy ties easier and quicker than a man working alone." He gestured to the homestead across the swollen creek. "This is my land."

He paused and Tess waited, smelling the damp pines around her.

"And to answer your question, yes. I have my mind set on a certain school mistress back in Ohio, if she's not already married. We kind of were courting before the war, and we renewed acquaintance before I came west."

Tess nodded, curious. If this quiet man could find love, was love available for everyone? If patient and persistent, could anyone find someone?

"I hope she's still available," Tess said softly.

Sandy nodded. "Me too."

The tall tie cutter chuckled suddenly and then strode off into the darkness. His long form disappeared, and then Tess heard his boots thud across the wooden bridge.

Tess felt eager to return to the cabin and be with Brett. He drew her like a sunflower to the sun. But first she needed to think.

She glanced irritably once more at the rain, which kept her from going to the chapel in the woods. Brett's special place had become hers too. She wished now she could go there and pray. With a sigh, she looked out into the inky night.

"I know you are with me. Thank you for showing me what love is. It's sacrificial. Only by thinking of Brett did I come up with the idea to give them my wages. You are wise, Father. Only by giving my life will I find life."

The door opened suddenly behind Tess, a shaft of yellow light streaming into the clearing and glistening on the wet earth. Brett stood there, fully dressed now in dry clothes. He grinned at her as he pushed the door wider. "What are you doing out here, Tess? Come in where it's dry."

With a final glance at the starless sky, she followed him inside.

The lone candle still burned on the table beside an open Bible. Tess glanced at the book and then at Brett, a question in her eyes.

Brett read her curiosity and closed the door before replying. "I like to read Scripture," he explained, moving around the table and taking his seat again. "Tonight, I'm reading about the mighty men of King David."

Tess smiled as she dragged a bench to the table. "I've read that story. My school only had two primers and a stack of Bibles, so I learned to read from Scripture."

"No better reading," Brett agreed, nodding, his face breaking into a comfortable grin. "I hope to teach my children to read from the Bible. It's truth and holds many wise lessons about life. What do you think?"

Tess wrinkled her nose. "What do I think about you having children or the Bible being wise?"

Brett's hazel eyes twinkled in the dim light. "Both," he replied, still grinning.

Suddenly, Tess felt nervous, unwilling to allow this conversation to proceed further. It seemed as if they were treading on dangerous ground. She feigned an extreme yawn. "Oh, I'm tired," she insisted, rising to her feet. "I need to get some sleep. If the railroad crews don't have to work tomorrow, the café will be very busy."

Brett frowned, obviously disappointed in the discussion's abrupt end. But Tess had already moved to her bed and was removing her shoes. She kicked them aside and paused, glancing at Brett expectantly.

"Oh, yes, of course," he mumbled, the bench scraping as he rose quickly and went outside.

Tess pulled her dress over her head and tossed it on the foot of the bed. Then she frowned as she studied the disheveled garment and hurriedly laid it out. She might wear it again tomorrow, she thought as she considered how unclean it might've gotten that day. The apron at the café certainly helped protect her dress from getting too dirty.

Brett returned, sticking his head in first. Seeing Tess safely in bed, he entered and blew out the candle. He pulled the blankets from his pile beside the stone chimney and dropped them to the hard flagstone floor. It took only a minute to arrange the makeshift bed on the deerskin rug. He sighed as he stretched out.

"I'd always planned on buying a lamp for the cabin. Candles are cheaper, but I wanted a nice lamp for when Mother arrived," he explained. Tess peered below the table, barely discerning Brett in the dim firelight, his arms crossed behind his head. "I guess the candles will have to do. And the wooden shutter over the other window. I won't be buying any more glass." He paused and then added, "Or a lamp."

Tess sat up in bed, pulling the covers close to her chin. "But your mother will appreciate the one glass window," Tess reminded him. "And the flagstone floor. Our little shanty only had a dirt floor."

"I suppose so," he agreed with a yawn.

Tess laid back down, staring up at the rafters, as silence filled the room. The warm cabin made Tess sleepy. She listened to the rain drumming the roof and snuggled deeper into the blankets.

The fire had already been banked for the coming morning, and the firelight flickered upon the underside of the roof. Tess stared at the light, enjoying the dances of the now familiar dark shadows.

She felt tired—it had been a long day—but she was pleased to know she'd made Brett happy. She vowed to work very hard to help his dreams come true.

"Tess?" Brett's voice called softly, disturbing her thoughts. Somehow, she didn't mind.

"Yes?" Tess replied, her eyes now open wide.

"Do you want children one day?"

She froze. He seemed to be moving too swiftly for her. Tess thought again of God. Patience and prayer were his recipe for success, she knew. She would follow his lead.

"Goodnight," she said, evading Brett's question.

After a long pause, he went on. "Well, tell me about your shanty with the dirt floor. I know your ma and stepfather live in Omaha. Any brothers or sisters?"

Tess bit her lip. The less he knew, the better. She didn't want any harm to come to Brett for harboring a fugitive from the law. She was, after all, a runaway and it might be best if he could plead ignorance if she were found here. She lay quietly, hoping he thought she'd gone to sleep. After a short while, he sighed loudly and shifted in his blankets. In a few moments, she heard his even breathing.

Again, she wished she could go out to the woodland chapel but knew it would be too wet. She said her final prayers of the day and turned over. Despite her fatigue, sleep did not come easily.

CHAPTER FOURTEEN

For two more days, rain fell steadily, forming puddles across the clearing. With the roads too muddy for the heavily loaded wagons, Brett and Sandy decided to work around their homestead.

Part of the Homestead Act required the owner to build on and improve the land he claimed. Their hundred and sixty acres spread in opposite directions from the stream with various opportunities for development, but both men chose to work around the cabins.

They cleared a better path to the makeshift barn on the small meadow where the mules were corralled. Brett even worked a little on the path to his woodland chapel, removing some of the bigger rocks from the trail while the ground was wet and easy to work with. He also moved sections of logs to be used as steps on either side of the giant fallen pine near the small glade where the cross stood.

Tess was forced to walk in the rain to Laramie, but Brett loaned her a thick, woolen blanket to use as a cloak to help protect her from the worst of the rain.

The trail through the woods lay muddy before her, and Tess left the cabin a little earlier than usual to make sure she gave herself ample time to arrive at the café before ten o'clock. Large puddles dotted the trail, and she used the deep mats of pine needles to step on and avoid the tiny lakes.

A train whistle startled her when she arrived at the main road that followed the tracks into town. She didn't know why she thought the rain might keep the train from moving on such a wet day. Then she remembered the stormy day she had arrived in Laramie. Could anything slow the Union Pacific?

She glanced at the tall, dead pine that marked the trail to the homestead before halting to watch the big engine chugging slowly to the east, pushing several empty freight cars back toward Crow Creek. Maybe they needed more supplies from Omaha, Tess wondered as she waved to the engineer and continued toward the café.

She turned at a rustling in the brush, and her heart leaped to her throat. Was Ace Moyer hiding there, waiting for her? The thought was immediately dismissed, though, as she realized the little thug wouldn't wait out here on such a wet day.

A large brown bear snorted in the brush but then rambled off at sight of Tess. She watched the animal lumber away, the bear glancing once over its shoulder before disappearing into the forest. She took a moment to let her heartbeat return to normal and then strode toward town.

As she approached Laramie, she could feel the old familiar fear well up within her. The Moyers and the many other crude men made her wary, but she fought these sensations down with the comforting words she'd formed a habit of reciting. God's Word gave her strength and courage.

The town seemed uncommonly busy for a weekday. Numerous men walked the muddy streets, and the music from the saloons blared noisily. Sodden tents sagged amid the occasional wooden shacks and buildings. Laramie sprawled along both sides of the rails and stretched out into the prairie, but clearly, most of its population roamed the bawdy businesses of the main street today.

She crossed the wooden bridge over the Laramie River and hurried to the livery barn where Ivan Belmont stood at his wide door. The livery man scowled deeply as he watched the railroad men move in and out of the various saloons and gambling houses.

"Mr. Belmont," Tess called as she navigated around a large puddle in front of the barn. "I see a lot of men are in town."

The older man muttered something under his breath and turned to Tess. "The bridge crews and the roadbed crews are unable to work in the rain. They were let off today, and they've filled the saloons." He spit into the mud and then growled, "The devil's playground, I call it."

Tess shrugged. "It must be good for business."

Ivan stared but said nothing.

Just then, a shot rang out from the Chinaman's Palace and then another. The music halted for a moment, and there was a sudden, still silence. Then, the music started up again and the chatter and hum of many voices continued. Someone laughed loudly.

Tess watched as a pair of men carried a lifeless body from the Palace and walked behind the row of saloons with their heavy, cumbersome load. A few minutes later, the two men returned to the Chinaman's saloon without the body. One of them carried a pair of boots and a gun belt slung over one shoulder.

Mr. Belmont squinted at Tess. He nodded his shaggy head, and Tess merely shrugged again. The Lord had brought her to Laramie, a rough and wild town. He had brought her here for a purpose. It was her job to blossom where he planted her. No one said it would be easy.

Tess shifted. "Mr. Belmont, I'm planning on being in Laramie a little bit longer than I expected," she began as she stood beside the livery man, watching the bustling street. She gripped the corners of the woolen blanket around her. "I need to make a sign. Any suggestions?"

"What kind of sign?" The old man turned his gaze from the saloons along the long street and studied her.

Holding her hand up, Tess gestured as if outlining a placard in front of her. "Haircuts and shaves, ten cents apiece."

He stared at her with unblinking eyes. "Are you serious?"

Tess nodded, ignoring his concerned look. "Yes. I need the money and I can cut hair. I used to give haircuts back in … uh, before I came to Laramie."

The old man rubbed his bearded chin. "It sounds like a good idea, but dangerous. I think the café is safe enough for you, Tess, but cutting hair might not be so safe. Where are you going to set up shop?"

"Right there," she pointed, indicating a shady spot under an old gnarled oak tree outside the livery barn.

Mr. Belmont looked at the spot and nodded. "Maybe it'll work. That is a wide, open place. Everyone in town can keep an eye on you there."

"I'd like to start tomorrow after my shift at the café," she suggested, looking at him for confirmation.

"All right, Tess. I'll have a sign for you by then," the old man promised.

Tess continued to the café. The café already held more men than usual, but it wasn't yet full. "Come get me if you get swamped," Mrs. Warren told her as the fat woman left the café to go home. Tess knew the Warrens only lived next door. She remembered the night she'd come to Laramie, and Brett stopped to talk to Mr. Warren.

Tess smelled liquor on many of the noisy and boisterous lunch crowd. A tall, wide-shouldered and dirty man leered at Tess, eyeing her up and down. She turned away, a familiar shudder moving along her spine as she recalled Frank. But the man grabbed her elbow and spun her around. "Don't walk away from me, missy," he growled between clenched teeth. Tess couldn't tell if he was grinning or snarling. Another man in the café stepped in and told the louse to shut up.

The dirty man turned on him. "I can do what I like. No one can stop me," he bragged, swaying on his feet.

The interloper grinned and motioned to a nearby table of Irishmen. He jerked a thumb toward his friends. "These Irishman are the toughest men in Laramie. They say you cannot speak disrespectfully to this young lady, Jones. Now, do you shut up, or do we throw you out?"

Jones stepped back and raised his fists. "I'd like to see you bunch of micks try and throw me out of this place."

The man nodded to his friends. With a rush, the railroad men moved and encircled the wildly swinging Jones. Benches toppled as men lunged to escape the fight. Laughing, the Irishmen carried the drunken worker from the café and threw him into the street.

Jones sprawled in the mud, the light rain falling on his back as he lay among the puddles in the middle of the street. The crowd cheered heartily as the Irishmen filed back into the noisy café.

Tess continued working, trying not to let the rough men around frighten her. She was supposed to be here, she kept telling herself. This was where God had brought her. Certainly, he would take care of her.

The Irish workers laughed and ate, but no one bothered Tess again. She later saw Jones rise and attempt to wipe the mud from his shirt and pants. Then, the staggering man wandered into the Bucket of Blood.

Tess heard three more shots while she was in town that day but didn't witness anymore men carried, boots first, out of the gambling halls or saloons. Men talked freely in front of Tess at the café, and discussions about the shooting at the Chinaman's Palace earlier were common. As was the idea that Big Steve Long had been right in shooting the cheating gambler.

A worker grumbled that Steve also claimed the man's large pile of winnings. His friend elbowed his ribs roughly and hissed, telling him to keep his opinions to himself.

"It's not safe to talk about Big Steve," the man warned his friend.

Tess pondered these things as she worked and listened attentively for any report of the homesteads of the tie cutters being bought up by Big Steve, but she heard nothing.

Mrs. Warren was only too happy to give Tess extra flour sacks when she asked later that day. The café went through a large quantity of flour, she told Tess, so spare sacks were always around. Tess felt excited at the prospect of turning the empty sacks into towels and curtains for the cabin. Maybe she'd make a curtain to conceal her bed if she stayed long enough.

The image of hanging curtains above the glass window of Brett's cabin occupied Tess's mind as she made her way precariously down the muddy street after her shift. The rain had ceased, although the sky remained gray and overcast and more rain threatened. Dark clouds still glowered over the mountains, signaling the storm had not departed.

Today's noon meal had consisted of beef steaks and gravy. Beef was still not common at the café. Most local ranchers kept their cattle to build their herds, but occasional steers could be had.

But it was not the tasty beef that filled Tess's mind as she passed the edge of town, the final buildings and tents behind her. Those curtains kept coming to her. Perhaps two panels, she mused, that opened in the middle and pulled to either side. Or maybe a single panel, wide and colorful, would be best. Cloth dye could be purchased or possibly made from Indian Paint Brush. Tess had seen some of the plants growing alongside the tracks on her way to town. Or perhaps the hulls of wild nuts could be boiled. She'd heard that during the war, Confederate soldiers had dyed clothing in beechnut hulls to color their uniforms when gray replacements were no longer available.

Tess had never felt the satisfaction of cleaning the shack in Omaha that she experienced when cleaning Brett's bright, yellow cabin. The cleverly fitted flagstones seemed such an improvement over the dirt floor of the shack.

And a real glass window. Tess marveled every time she saw the clear pane. Just last night at supper, Sandy had complained how his butcher paper window coverings had ripped from the rain. But the glass never tore and always allowed the sunlight indoors.

She wondered if Brett would ever be able to complete the other window in the south wall, boarded up now, waiting for glass. Or afford a lamp.

A great sense of belonging and being settled always filled her after sweeping the cabin floor and filling the wood box next to the stone fireplace. She even liked to dust the long mantle.

Her steps faltered and she paused, peering out over the prairie to the north, the distant sounds of town still coming to her on the breeze. The Laramie River flowed that way before turning east to join the Platte River. She stared, enjoying the freshness of the newly washed landscape. Bright green grass shimmered across the high plains, and lone trees stood as if roving scouts for the army gathered behind Tess. Her fists clenched at her sides and she frowned, knowing these pleasant thoughts could not last. Who was she fooling? Her stay in Laramie would not last forever. Soon, after Brett received his back pay for the ties he'd cut, she would be heading east to Chicago. She was only seventeen and Brett was twenty-one. They were young, much too young for her to be making plans of living permanently in the yellow pine cabin.

Besides, she didn't know how Brett felt about her, and she was wary of her own feelings for him. She feared her fickle heart, swooning at the first handsome man who was kind to her. Tess vowed not to be taken in like her mother had been.

A rider on a big black horse reined in beside her, and Tess was jolted out of her daydream as she looked up at the man, admiring his cowhide vest beneath his open coat.

He nodded politely. "Miss, I was wondering if you knew of a good eating place in Laramie. I haven't been to town since the railroad arrived."

Tess considered the man. He seemed courteous without being too familiar, like many of the railroad workers were to her. "Yes, sir," she replied, taking a step nearer. "The café at the north end of town is very good. I work there during the noon hour," she added, not knowing why she shared such personal information to this stranger.

"Oh?" He smiled, his weathered face softening. "Then I'll make a point of being there tomorrow." He lifted a hand to his hat and the movement pulled his coat open, revealing a tin star pinned to his vest pocket.

She watched him ride down the road, finally dismounting in front of the café. She wondered about the kindly man. He had a hard face, like he'd seen difficult times, but that wasn't uncommon. Many of the men on the railroad were veterans of the Civil War. At least he seemed respectful.

Beyond the stranger, Tess noticed Ace Moyer slouching in front of the Bucket of Blood. She pursed her lips as a cold shiver ran down her back at the sight of the little man. His narrow face was pinched in a cruel smile now, his dark eyes piercing into Tess, even at this distance. She turned and resumed her pace, eager to put Laramie behind her.

As if sensing his gaze, she glanced over her shoulder, her eyes widening as she saw he followed her.

Tess quickened her step, but the heavy, sodden woolen blanket she carried, and the bundle of flour sacks tucked under one arm slowed her. Her heart thudded as she pumped her legs, trying to evade Moyer. Too late, she realized her mistake at fleeing town. Too late, she realized he meant to intercept her. The lean, wiry outlaw halted her with a call.

"Hold on there, Tess," he said boldly as he stepped in front of her. His small eyes studied her face, and Tess didn't like what she read in them. "I saw you talking to Boswell. I hope you don't think he can do anything. He's only the sheriff in the territory and has no real authority here in Laramie. Big Steve is the law here," he boasted.

Something about the brazen arrogance of the little thief irritated Tess. The anxiety that had filled her at sight of Ace left her now and she straightened, squaring her shoulders as she faced him.

"It sounds like you and your brothers are running roughshod over Laramie, but you'll not get Sandy and Brett's homesteads. They have legal claim to the land, and they're proving out," she retorted, defiance lacing her words.

He blinked, her sudden bold front seeming to startle him. Clearly, he was not used to people speaking in this way to him. He frowned at Tess's confrontation and tilted his head.

"Well, maybe you haven't heard that any tie-cutting homesteaders who don't pay their debt at the general store can have their land confiscated. They must provide for themselves or their land is up for grabs again. And," he added, lowering his voice. "I happen to know they won't receive their pay for some time."

Tess narrowed her eyes. "And how could you know that?"

Ace grinned. "Don't you fret about that. Big Steve has a lot of power in Laramie. You better decide which side you want to end up on. With the losers," he paused and stabbed his chest with a thumb, "or with the winners."

Tess laughed. "And you believe you'll be the winners?" What did he know of the eventual pay day for the tie cutters? Tess thought he sought only to impress her.

Her sudden laughter annoyed the little man, and he scowled at Tess. He pulled the brim of his derby down low and stalked away.

A few sprinkles warned Tess that the rain was coming again, and she repositioned the flour sacks under her arm and draped her blanket around her shoulders. With a worried glance toward the bank of dark clouds, Tess started again on her way home.

Despite the gentle rain, Tess was not unhappy to be walking home on the muddy road. Her earlier pleasant thoughts of Brett's cabin returned, and she allowed her mind to wander over the fun and enjoyable improvements she would make if the cabin were her own. Of course, she smiled to herself, it would include Brett Calloway.

She felt intrigued by the way she enjoyed sharing the cabin with him. Never having had brothers, it surprised her how much she enjoyed taking care of a man. Two men, actually, if she counted Sandy.

Certainly, they contributed to the upkeep of the cabins, but Tess had shown her willingness to work hard and help the two men on their path to success. While she took care of things around the homesteads, they were free to continue cutting lumber from the hills above and make money.

Furthermore, Tess now contributed her wages from the café to ensure they would succeed in their venture. Mr. Warren assured her that he'd pay her every Friday. Tess also hoped to begin cutting hair for the local railroad men soon.

She wrinkled her nose as she remembered how Frank had insisted on Tess coming to the railroad yards in Omaha and cutting hair for the single men or those whose wives stayed back east.

"I don't want to," Tess recollected saying. She'd been only thirteen then.

"I don't much care what you want," had been Frank's insolent retort.

Tess recalled that she'd turned pleading, sad eyes on her mother, begging for her intervention. Her mother had hesitated a moment, looking intently at her young daughter. Tess could tell her mother struggled internally with what she should do or say. Finally, Cathy had turned to Frank.

"I'll go in her stead, Frank. I can cut hair very well."

Frank had merely chuckled, not even bothering to look up from his work. "Those men want to see a young girl, Cathy. Not an old, tired thing like you."

Her mother had stared hard at Frank for a full minute. Then, turning away slowly, she had simply walked back into the shack. Tess remembered that was the day when she'd begun to be fully aware of the disappointments she had in her mother.

So, she had begun cutting hair on pay days, making money that was promptly handed over to Frank. She'd even gotten quite good at giving shaves.

A sigh escaped, as Tess recalled the promise she'd made herself long ago. She had said that if she ever escaped from Omaha, she would never cut hair again. The men were often dirty and some of them had lice.

Never say never, she reminded herself with grim determination. Here she was again, about to cut hair for more dirty railroad men. But this time she wanted to. This time, it would help Brett.

The rain increased and she picked up her pace, though she had to be careful about where she placed her feet. Deep puddles stood everywhere on the muddy path, and she wished to protect her shoes as much as possible.

Her thoughts turned again to Brett. Did she love him? The thought nagged at her constantly. Tess certainly had no experience with love to truly know how it should feel. Sure, she'd loved her mother, but that was expected. Her mother had been very self-absorbed and worried about herself to love in a healthy way. She didn't put her daughter's well-being above her own selfish desires to avoid loneliness.

Tess sighed again as she sighted the tall dead pine and turned off the main road to the trail to Brett's cabin. Thoughts of her mother always made her feel sad. Real love had only been demonstrated to her in Scripture. God's love was real and sacrificial. By serving each other, Christians demonstrate God's love.

Tess prayed she would discern whether her feelings for Brett were right or not by comparing them to God's standard. She would not love by her standard only to gratify her own infatuations or desires. Tess vowed to only allow her feelings for Brett to grow if they were what the Lord wished for her. She wanted to do things God's way.

The slight incline caused her to slow, but Tess continued to plod through the afternoon shower. The dark forest around her did not frighten her. The big pines and the small stream she followed were familiar now. She liked living in the woods. It was certainly better than living on the flat, bleak prairie around Omaha.

Water dripped from the thick branches over her, and not even a squirrel chattered at Tess as she walked through the gloomy forest, but her heart warmed as she neared the cabin.

Later, she would slip away to the wash pool and clean the flour sacks she carried. They should dry easily in the warm cabin tonight. Then, she could decide what use they might provide around the place. Towels? Curtains? Tablecloth? The possibilities seemed endless.

CHAPTER FIFTEEN

The next day, Tess carried the scissors and shaving gear she'd borrowed from Brett with her to Laramie. She hoped Mr. Belmont had her sign ready.

The sun had peeped early under the layer of thick, dark clouds when Tess first arose. Now, though, the sun stood well above the cloud layer, and the day was gray and pregnant with the threat of more rain.

Sandy had said the rain would continue, but Brett had predicted the storm would be played out and only some dark clouds would linger to frighten people. He doubted the empty clouds could contain any more moisture.

Tess studied the swollen clouds as she walked now, thinking that perhaps Brett might be mistaken.

Sandy had only laughed. "You know nothing of these mountain storms. It rains here more often than down below. I wouldn't be surprised to see snow."

It was Brett's turn to laugh. "It's not cold enough for snow, you old codger. I'm from real snow country. I know."

The joking and bantering continued until the two men had walked from the cabins, anxious to return to the woods and continue cutting timber. The ground was still too soft for the heavy wagon, but they could cut ties and pick them up when the ground dried.

Tess grinned, remembering the morning conversation. The three of them worked well together and enjoyed each other's company. She felt warm and satisfied when she thought of them. Tess felt like she could live here forever.

Train to Laramie

The walk to town passed quickly, the downhill road allowing her to descend rapidly. She carried the damp woolen blanket under one arm today, grateful not to be walking in rain.

Besides, she hoped it wouldn't be raining when she found a spot under the old oak tree and set out her shingle.

As she approached town, Tess felt a few sprinkles on her head, causing her to quicken her pace. Eyeing the dark clouds, she tugged on the woolen blanket and draped the damp covering over her head as she ran toward the café. A wave from Mr. Belmont at the livery barn made her shout a greeting and then she was past him, hurrying down the street.

The drops grew bigger and suddenly a loud thunderclap boomed and reverberated among the high mountains. The sound was accompanied by the heavens opening and a downpour drenched Laramie.

Forced to seek shelter, Tess raced up the stairs to the boardwalk. She lifted her head, dropping the blanket to her shoulders, as she gained the protection of the long porch. Tess gasped and her eyes widened as she recognized the Bucket of Blood directly behind her.

Thankfully, Tess did not recognize Ace Moyer among the men who pushed through the door to watch the torrential cloudburst. Rain fell fast, pounding the wooden roof above her.

Tess shook the woolen blanket as she listened to the comments of the men around her about the fierce summer storm. She felt someone watching her and she glanced over her shoulder.

Con Moyer stared at her, his thin lips holding an unlit cigar. He removed the cigar and stepped closer, a wolfish grin creasing his sallow face. "You're wet," he said in a low voice, glancing up and down her slender figure. "But not as wet as that night I first saw you. You looked like a little kid that night."

The crooked saloon keeper nodded once and then continued. "You don't look like a little kid now. But Ace says he has his eye on you, so I won't interfere." With a devilish wink, Con Moyer turned and strode back inside the saloon.

The rain slackened and men moved from the overhang to go about their business.

Her gaze followed the retreating figure of Con Moyer and glanced past him to the long wooden bar that ran the length of the room, a huge mirror hanging on the back wall. She turned away, feeling dirty, and looked out at the rain that cleaned the countryside. Forgetting the heavy blanket she carried, Tess darted from the porch to the café, far down the saturated street.

Mr. Warren nodded at her when he saw Tess come from the storeroom where she'd taken a moment to comb her wet hair. "I'm glad to see you. Ma was tired today, and I let her go once the breakfast crowd thinned out. I was some worried you might not show up, with the storm and all."

Tess smiled as she tied an apron around her. "You can count on me, Mr. Warren." She reached for the platters of food in the kitchen window.

The café was almost empty, but Tess had to continue filling some coffee cups for men who were reluctant to leave or had nowhere to be. Otherwise, Tess was free to allow her mind to roam.

The words of Con Moyer haunted her. Tess was no stranger to the menacing glances of wicked men, and she'd seen the same look in Con's small eyes. What did the bartender mean by his remark about Ace? Did his brother have designs on Tess? Did the little thug think he had any claim on her?

She grinned to herself, thinking that her heart belonged to another. Even if she didn't have strong feelings for Brett, Tess could never love a man like Ace. The man was crude and ill-mannered, not caring or thoughtful like Brett.

Besides, Ace was shorter than she, but Brett had at least five inches over her medium height. The handsome woodcutter stood just the right height for Tess.

The Moyer brothers were both hardened outlaws, Tess was sure. Along with their half-brother Big Steve Long, they appeared to have Laramie up a tree and were planning on skimming everything of value from the western railroad town.

Could the homesteaders hold out against the ruthless trio of thieves? Somehow, Steve Long had been appointed town marshal when Laramie first boomed. Now, he was reported to have killed a few men and profited from their deaths. Was the marshal planning on using this same tactic on the landowners who refused to sell their land to him?

Tess worried for Brett and Sandy. They were both good men and God had been kind to lead her to them. They only wanted to work hard and make their homesteads permanent homes for their families. Soon, Tess knew, Brett would send for his mother and sister, and Sandy would go back east this fall looking for his sweetheart.

A little before noon, the rider from the previous day came into the café, interrupting Tess's thoughts. She recalled that Ace had called him Boswell.

The tall man moved to a side table where he could watch the door and the window from his seat. His lined face creased into a smile when he recognized Tess.

"Hello, miss," the man said as Tess placed a tin cup before him and poured coffee. "I ate here yesterday, and the food was good. My business is concluded in Laramie, and I'll be leaving today, but I wanted one more meal here before I hit the trail."

"I'm glad you did, Sheriff," Tess said, stressing the final word and hoping his known identity might draw him into conversation about the town's lawlessness. But Boswell only shot her a sharp glance and sipped his coffee.

As she continued to work, Tess noted that Sheriff Boswell keenly scrutinized all around him. The tall man with the tin star even studied the Bucket of Blood from his covert vantage point.

When the sheriff had finished his meal, Tess saw Mr. Warren come from the kitchen and seat himself across from Boswell. The two men spoke quietly together for a few minutes. Tess believed this would be a good time for refills.

As she neared the lawman's table, Mr. Warren pounded the table with his fist, his face reddening. Tess leaned close as she poured the coffee.

"Tom, I know you're mad," Boswell said as he reached for his mug. "But there's nothing I can do. I have no jurisdiction here. Besides, there's no evidence he's committing murder. He's produced witnesses after each shooting to prove his provocation."

"What about all the robberies of men who won big money in the Bucket of Blood? Surely that's proof they're killing men," Mr. Warren persisted.

"No, it's not," Boswell answered, a tone of bitterness in his voice. "My advice is to steer clear. Keep out of their way. They won't do anything to you if you stay out of their affairs."

Tess walked away from the table at that point, and the sheriff left the café soon after.

She untied her apron and handed the soiled garment to Mr. Warren when her time was through. The café owner seemed tense and distant. The older man took Tess's apron and threw it roughly onto the dirty wash pile of tablecloths and towels that Mrs. Warren cleaned every few days.

"Is something wrong, Mr. Warren?" Tess asked. Normally, this man acted mild and kind. His agitation surprised her.

Mr. Warren peered at Tess as if he just realized she stood before him. He nodded. "I'm sorry, Tess. I haven't seen Boswell since the war. We've both changed. Now, he's a sheriff and a rancher in Dakota Territory, and I run a café at the end of the tracks."

He paused, a faraway look in his eyes. "Who'd ever believe Colonel Boswell would herd cows?" He shook his head. "I was telling him of our troubles here in Laramie. He's already heard of them but can do nothing about them." Abruptly, Mr. Warren reached into his pocket. "I nearly forgot, Tess. It's Friday. Pay day." The older man dropped coins into her outstretched palm.

"Thank you, Mr. Warren. I'll see you tomorrow," Tess said as she slipped the money into her pocket. Gathering her belongings, she left the café.

Despite the earlier downpour, the streets were now filled with men conducting business. Horses lined the hitching rails and buckboards crowded before stores and the shops of the railroad blacksmiths. The dark clouds had vanished, replaced with a few scattered gray clouds, patches of blue sky peeking between them. The street lay dotted with small lakes of standing water surrounded with deep mud. Heavy freight wagons pulled by struggling animals labored through the thick muck, leaving deep ruts behind.

Tess hurried to the livery, purposely averting her eyes when she passed the Bucket of Blood. She did not want to see either of the Moyer brothers.

Mr. Belmont was waiting for her when she arrived. He held a wide board. His eyes twinkled with excitement.

"I have your sign, Tess," he announced as she drew near.

He turned the sign around. Tess read the painted red block words aloud. "Haircuts and Shaves Ten Cents." She looked up at him, smiling.

"It's perfect," Tess said quickly, and the old man beamed.

A section of cut log would serve as a seat. Ivan rolled the stump from the barn to the place Tess indicated beneath the big oak tree. He propped the new sign against a rock.

"There," Tess said, "I'm in business."

The shaving cream was quickly mixed and then Tess opened and closed the scissors several times, flexing her fingers.

Mr. Belmont stood near, his searching eyes scrutinizing likely customers as they passed on the street. A few curious men read the sign advertising haircuts and then walked on.

After ten minutes of this, Ivan turned to Tess. "I need to get back to the livery. I'll be close. Yell if you need anything."

The old man hobbled away, and Tess was left alone. She frowned, recalling how she'd bragged about giving her wages to Brett to save his homestead.

What if she was unable to produce much money? The small amount from Mr. Warren certainly wouldn't make them rich. Tess had sincerely believed the haircutting plan would be lucrative.

Suddenly, a shadow loomed over her and Tess turned to see Marshal Long standing before the sign. The big man read the words aloud and then grinned.

"Well, I'm sure I'm due for a haircut and a shave, miss," the marshal said loudly. He lifted a hand to caress his long moustache. "But leave this alone. I'm growing it out." He walked to the upended section of log and seated himself, pulling his gun belt around so the gun hung between his knees, the butt within easy reach.

Tess stared and then bit her lip. Did he recognize her? Brett and Sandy disliked Big Steve immensely. Sandy openly called the town marshal a crooked and dishonest man. With his half-brothers, the Moyers, Marshal Long had been killing off men for their land. But what could she do? He already suspected she was a runaway and Tess couldn't dare to give him more cause to take notice of her.

With a few more practice snips of the scissors, Tess haltingly stepped forward. Big Steve threw his hat aside and ran a large hand through his thinning hair. She heard him chuckle. "Well, maybe a haircut is a wishful thing. Trim it up some and definitely give me a shave," he ordered briskly.

Tess ran the comb rapidly through the dark hair peppered with streaks of gray. Despite the silver splashes, she suspected he was younger than he looked. Perhaps hard living had aged him prematurely, Tess pondered as she continued to comb and then cut the ends of his hair.

She walked around the still man, combing and trimming confidently, just like Frank Mercer had taught her.

"Make it look like you know what you're doing, and men will believe you are a real barber," Frank had instructed.

Frank had been right, she admitted grudgingly. A bluff of experience had carried her far. Soon, she had the experience and didn't have to fake know-how.

Marshal Long peered at her occasionally from under bushy eyebrows. He seemed puzzled, like he was unable to place her. "I've seen you somewhere before, haven't I?"

Tess bit her lip again and said nothing for a minute, wondering if she should tell the truth. In the end, she knew she would tell him. He would surely find out anyway. Besides, God would want her to be honest.

"Yes, Marshal Long. I met you a few weeks ago. I came to town on the night train."

Tess moved from his line of vision, afraid he would see the fear in her eyes. If he recalled that night, would he now follow up his threat to capture and hold a runaway? Tess hoped he wouldn't recall and would simply leave her alone. Perhaps her bland reply wouldn't draw attention. Run a bluff, like the haircutting. To be forced to return to Omaha would break her heart, especially now that she'd found a place where she felt safe.

The scissors flew around the marshal's large head. The man was not only tall, but his shoulders were wide, and his arms were long. Big hands rested on his knees as Tess moved around him, combing and snipping away. He held a protective hand over his long, drooping moustache when she neared his leathery face.

"I remember now," he finally murmured. Tess's heart sank with dread. *He's going to take me in and send me back*, she thought wildly as she kept working, her hands starting to tremble.

Tess paused and acted like she studied her handiwork as she attempted to control the shaking. It would not do to give this man a bad haircut. Tess painted on a fake smile, hoping to distract his focus. "There you go, Marshal. Time for the shave."

Hastily, Tess turned to Brett's shaving gear. She quickly stropped the razor on the length of leather harness Mr. Belmont had provided for this very purpose.

"I don't like to boast, but I think I give a close shave," Tess said as she approached the big man. "Lean your head back now," she commanded. Tess felt surprised at how calm her voice sounded as her mind whirled, anything but calm.

"Good," Big Steve remarked. "I like a close shave."

"Don't talk now, Marshal. I need you to be still," Tess instructed as she brushed the thick lather on his wrinkled neck. Gripping the razor, hoping her hand would remain steady, she stood beside him and dragged the sharp metal against his skin.

Her hand trembled slightly, but by keeping her hand moving and pressing against his neck, the shake was not so obvious.

"A good barber pulls the razor up on the neck and down on the cheeks," Tess said quietly as she moved in front of the crooked lawman.

She worked carefully, and soon the job was completed. Even his gray handlebar moustache appeared neat.

"I have no mirror," Tess confessed as an apology. "I was hoping to buy one if my business took off."

Steve Long stood, wiping his face with the flour sack Tess handed him. "Then I'm sure you'll soon have a mirror," he smiled. He dropped two bits on the short barrel near her.

Tess moved quickly to make change. "Your change, Marshal," she called as she frantically searched her pockets for a nickel. Would Big Steve use this minor infraction as an excuse to arrest her, knowing she was a runaway?

"Keep it." He waved a dismissive hand as he pulled the big gun back into place on his hip. He slapped the butt of the blue gun reassuringly and glanced down the street. "Now, back to work."

Tess stared as the big man walked away, her body quivering all over now. Clumsily, she picked up his quarter and stared at it before she dropped the coin in her pocket.

CHAPTER SIXTEEN

Near the end of July, Sandy discovered a meadow of good grass on his land, so he and Brett constructed a fence to surround the ample grazing area. They also blazed a new trail to this pasture and often allowed the big mules to graze there, but the men always returned the draft animals to the makeshift barn by nightfall. Grizzly bears and mountain lions roamed these mountains and would not hesitate to attack a mule.

Wolf packs were said to frequent the Rocky Mountains, especially farther north, Brett reported. He'd never seen them, though an occasional lone wolf could be heard baying at the bright summer moon.

Tess had heard the mournful wail once while she prayed at the chapel in the woods. The sound had curdled her blood, and she'd scampered back to the protection of the cabin. But nothing could keep her from seeking God's direction. After staying away for a night, she returned to the moonlit dell.

She'd made it a habit to visit the little glade next to the waterfall on most nights. After Brett fell asleep, she would creep carefully to the porch and then to the well-worn trail to the special place. Brett had worked to improve the trail, but Tess, knowing the path so well now, could navigate the route in the dark.

Stealing away to the rock bench in the boulder, she would sit for an hour, sometimes longer, and pray. Whether designed by Brett or purely accidental, the rays of the bright moon always filtered through the thick foliage overhead, shining directly on the tall cross. Tess lingered in the glade, studying the illuminated cross and listening to the rustling of the waterfall as her heart connected with her creator.

The serene melody of the small waterfall both soothed and vexed her as she sought God's peace, pleading with him for his guidance. Would the Lord answer her? She determined not to repeat the mistakes of her mother. Was Brett the man for her?

But the wooden cross proved to be a silent confidant, not disclosing what steps Tess should take next. Yet she could not deny the small things Brett did for her, always reminding her of his thoughtfulness. Was she reading the signs correctly?

Tess wondered if Sandy saw this too, but if he did, he'd said nothing to her about Brett's attentive manner.

This night, Tess felt especially eager to escape the confining cabin and race into the forest to her woodland retreat. Here, she talked with the living God. The cross reminded her of the sacrifice her heavenly Father made for her. Tess knew God loved her, but what of Brett? Did he return her love? Did she truly love him?

She shifted on the stone bench, nibbling on her lip as she pondered her predicament. She hated the way she drank Brett's encouraging words like nectar, unused to such kindness. The way she craved his attention scared her. Was she allowing herself to be hoodwinked?

She shook her head, not wanting to believe she could so easily be fooled. Why, even Sandy arched his eyebrows when Brett delivered wilted wildflowers for the table one night, shrugging when asked for the reason. The older woodcutter had glanced slyly at Tess, but she'd turned hurriedly to the fire, hiding her heated cheeks.

But was it enough? Her mother had settled for Frank

Mercer's diseased affections. She had allowed her fears and anxieties to cause her to lower her standards and accept less than what God wanted for her. Tess vowed not to follow in her mother's footsteps. Brett might be just the right man, but she would wait on the Lord for confirmation.

A soft wind wafted, making the forest sigh serenely. Overhead, branches nudged pine needles together and made a music that touched her, a salve to her fretful heart. But her own fears of the past still haunted her. She wanted to submit to God, not the selfish desires of her own heart. Only the man God chose for her would satisfy.

So, here she sat. Praying for a sign, a revelation, that Brett was or was not that man. Nothing kept her in Laramie now. The midday shift at the café allowed her to make some money, but the haircutting had proven very profitable. She'd even purchased a mirror. In addition, Tess had been paying weekly on Brett's tab at the general store, and slowly the debt had decreased despite the purchasing of additional necessary supplies.

Tess Randle was now known by most of the folks in Laramie and the railroad workers too. Some of the rough men were crude and forward, but most had been courteous and appreciative of her hard work, sensing a kindred spirit. They respected any person who worked as hard as they did, seven days a week. Only when harsh weather or unforeseen calamity halted their progress did they take a break. All these men understood they competed in a great race to lay as much track as they could. General Dodge pushed them, as did Dr. Durant, the director of the Union Pacific. The government paid for every mile of track the men laid, so speed was of the essence if they hoped to beat the oncoming Central Pacific from California. Eventually, with the historic tracks across the continent, the two labor forces would probably meet somewhere in Utah.

Tess pushed herself too, only taking Monday afternoons off from cutting hair, which seemed the slowest day. On those days, she'd hurry back to Brett's cabin to clean or chop firewood or prepare food for the two lumberjacks she cared for.

Sandy had told Tess her efforts allowed him and Brett to work longer in the woods, cutting more ties for the railroad. If it were not for her, they'd be forced to return home earlier each day to prepare their own meals and complete chores. She'd become an integral part of their team, their success due, in part, to her efforts.

Tess liked this arrangement and felt involved in the success of the two homesteads. Plus, she enjoyed Brett and Sandy's company. This new family was a much better one than she'd experienced. Chicago could wait.

When Brett discovered Tess home on Monday afternoons, he'd announced to the surprised Sandy that every Monday would be a half day in the woods. This would allow them time to work around their cabins and repair or sharpen tools.

With a curious glance at Tess, Sandy had agreed. When Brett turned his back, Sandy grinned knowingly and winked at Tess.

Tess sighed and squinted up at the cross on the other side of the stream. She, too, knew why Brett had stayed around the homestead on Monday afternoons. His company was pleasant, even if he sometimes got under foot. She tried to work hard on these days, but he often wished to take her on a walk or have her bake a special delicacy. Tess soon discovered his appetite for apple pie.

She couldn't complain about these interruptions—she loved them. Brett's attention made her smile, an unfamiliar warmth filling her chest. Despite the never-ending work around the cabin, Tess eagerly looked forward to any time spent with Brett.

But was that what God wanted for her?

Tess sighed again, folding her hands in her lap as she looked about the moonlit glade. She loved it here on Brett's homestead. She could see herself living here forever. However, she must be patient and see what God wished for her.

"Your will, Father, not mine. I wish only to do what you desire for me. You know my heart. I think I love Brett, but I don't want to go too quickly and make a mistake like Mama did. I don't think Brett is like Frank, but I want to be sure. Guide me by the power of your Holy Spirit," Tess whispered into the darkness.

She drew a deep breath and stood, uncoiling her stiff limbs. It would be dawn soon, and she needed to get some sleep. She strode from the glen, and with a backward glance at the tall cross, stepped atop the log Brett positioned as a stair to the crest of the fallen pine. Nimbly, she scurried over the big tree and made her way back to the cabin.

An owl hooted and she froze, locating the big bird perched on a high branch. The predator hunted at night, searching for mice and other rodents. The owl's lonesome call reminded Tess of her own lonely heart. Would she ever know God's plan for her life? Her heart ached with the need to be loved. She longed to be more than merely the girl Brett brought in from the rain.

Again, she felt the nudge of the Spirit cautioning her. She remembered the passage from Song of Solomon that warns young maidens not to awaken love before its time. Tess wondered what Mama would say about this Scripture verse now.

Her bare feet padded the cold flagstone floor as Tess carried her shoes and crept to her bed. Barely a glow showed in the stone fireplace—the coals had dimmed since she'd first left the cabin.

Tess pulled the covers up—the bed having grown cold with her absence—and she shivered as she snuggled deeper. Tess lay still, waiting for the blankets to warm as she searched the dark room for Brett. She heard his even breathing, but his dark form blended with the shadows. Propping an arm under her head, Tess stared to where he should be, stretched beyond the table.

Brett did the work of two men on most days and pushed himself to accomplish much. But he knew winter would descend in these mountains by November. Then, he'd told her, he'd allow himself to slow down—the snow would force him. Until then, Brett pushed himself to cut timber dawn to dusk. He needed to pay for his supplies and make money to send to his mother. Tess knew Brett hoped to have his small family reunited by this fall.

If only the tie cutters were ever paid for their work.

Tess lay back and stared up at the rafters, unseen now in the darkness. But she knew each knot in those logs, having memorized every detail of this beautiful wooden house.

Her thoughts turned to Brett's family and their hoped-for arrival. He needed money to pay their travel expenses. Would Marshal Long ever pay the tie cutters? The crooked law man forever 'encouraged' workers to sell their homesteads to him and move out. He'd already taken three sections of land from men who'd been unable to pay their debt at the general store. He and his half-brothers were becoming rich landowners.

The night before, Sandy had shared another story of a man killed in Laramie—now a familiar tale. Shootings, knifings, and robberies were becoming all too frequent. As town marshal, Steve Long had been asked to account for this increase in violence. He blamed the railroad. When the tracks moved on, the problems would, too, he claimed.

Tess yawned again, feeling too tired to think anymore tonight.

Courage. She must have courage. She resolved to wait on the Lord, trusting God had a plan for her. She pulled the blankets a little higher and peered again into the gloom toward where Brett lay. Tess smiled, the handsome woodcutter her final thought as she fell asleep.

CHAPTER SEVENTEEN

August came with dry, hot days. The fragrance of pine permeated the mountain air and there had been no rain since the big storm in early July. Local ranchers grumbled. Some of the smaller creeks had stopped flowing altogether.

But the stream between Brett's homestead and Sandy's land still ran strong, and the water remained clear and cold. Snow melting from the high peaks must water it some, Tess thought, along with water from natural springs.

Tess walked swiftly to Laramie this morning. Yesterday had been doughnut day at the café, the long tables crowded with railroad men and locals craving the infrequent delicacies. Tess received an extra two bits from one old codger who claimed he'd never tasted better doughnuts. Mr. Warren told her to keep the tip.

A train whistle accompanied Tess into town this morning. The bright sun warmed her back and shoulders, her dark hair tucked neatly into her bonnet. She crossed the bridge over the Laramie River without glancing at the rushing waters, yet she still eyed the horse trough outside the livery with a skeptical eye.

She stepped around a mound of horse apples in the street, flies buzzing angrily, but she didn't mind. Tess was coming to like this familiar frontier town.

Although the lawless element and the crime still concerned her, Tess hadn't known peace in her troubled life like she'd enjoyed in Laramie. She seemed to have found her place. Folks recognized her by name and called to her on the street. She kept her head down as she passed the Bucket of Blood and the Chinaman's Palace.

Ivan Belmont stood near the Overland Stage Station, reading Scripture aloud. Often, curious men would stop and listen. The old hostler shared his faith eagerly with those searching for salvation.

Sometimes, scoffers sneered as they passed Ivan, but he was not deterred on his mission to bring the Gospel to Laramie.

Tess smiled and gave a little wave to her friend as she passed him. He nodded to her and continued reading from the book of John.

Tess touched the letter in her pocket. Brett's family in Minnesota awaited word from him. Did Mama ever miss her?

The bustling market hummed like a beehive of activity when Tess entered, the bell above her head announcing her arrival. She inhaled deeply, enjoying the intoxicating smells of licorice, leather goods, and tobacco wafting through the crowded store.

"Hello, Tess," the man behind the counter greeted as she handed him Brett's letter.

"Good morning," she replied and hurried outside into the dusty street, the brilliant sunlight making her squint as she turned toward the café.

As she picked up her clean apron from the shelf in the kitchen, Tess noticed the café had slowed to its normal pace today after the explosion of business they always endured on doughnut days. Tying the apron securely behind her, Tess moved to the front room.

She waved as Mrs. Warren left the café, noticing a weary look in the older woman's eyes. She wondered how much longer the plump lady would be able to keep up the challenging pace of the café.

Mr. Warren had promised to hire a replacement for his wife when business slowed down—perhaps in the fall. But, for now, he'd told his wife he needed an experienced waitress to attend to customers. Mrs. Warren frowned as she wagged a finger at her husband, "Keep in mind, I'm not as young as I once was."

"Ah, but you're still just as lovely," Mr. Warren told her as he smiled and leaned to kiss his wife on her rosy cheek.

As Tess hurried to each table, refilling empty coffee cups, she considered the obvious love the Warrens shared. She was too young to remember much of her own parents' affection for one another, and the relationship her mother now had with Frank was nowhere near the kind and tender way Mr. Warren treated his wife.

A wistfulness came over Tess as she swayed among the tables and fetched food for hungry customers.

Would she ever know the security and love that Mrs. Warren knew?

Tess strode to the open window in the kitchen wall and grabbed another plate of apple pie. The dessert reminded her of Brett, and she wondered again if God meant for them to be together.

Much like Mr. Warren, Brett was an honest, thoughtful, hardworking gentleman. Despite their close quarters, Brett had never attempted to use his ownership of the cabin to his advantage. In fact, Tess and he shared the responsibilities and worked together, ensuring the success of the homestead. Like a team.

He was a good man, but was he the *right* man?

Tess frowned. God would show her the way. Be patient.

Oh, she wanted to be certain. Her fear of making a mistake clouded her mind. Tess couldn't stand to follow in her mother's steps.

For the thousandth time, she glanced heavenward,

asking for help.

The front door slammed, and Tess turned to greet the new customer. She smiled when she recognized the rancher, Mr. Boswell, his tin star pinned to his open cowhide vest.

He nodded at Tess and walked to a nearby table. Placing an empty cup in front of the man, she poured the hot black drink. "Sheriff Boswell, I don't know if you remember me. I met you about a month ago."

The rancher glanced around Tess to the kitchen beyond, nodding when he caught the café owner's eye. He smiled up at Tess. "Yes, miss. I remember you," Mr. Boswell replied as he reached for his cup.

"Well, I wanted to tell you that the tie cutters are waiting for back pay. Rumor has it Big Steve Long has fixed it with someone not to allow their pay to get to them. Then, he made a town law that all men who don't pay toward their tab at the general store could have their lands taken from them," Tess explained.

Mr. Warren approached the pair while Tess was still speaking and heard the end of her story. "It's like I told you last time, Boswell. Long is running this town into the ground. He's crooked and there've already been many killings and robberies. It's reported that any man who wins big in the Bucket of Blood is robbed before he gets a block from that dirty saloon."

The sheriff stared into his coffee mug and scowled, deep lines creasing his brow. After a sip, he put down his cup.

"Tom, you know there's nothing I can do about Long. This is a town matter. I have no power in Laramie."

Mr. Warren threw up his hands and stalked back to the kitchen, leaving the frustrated rancher to give his order to Tess.

She moved around the room, taking orders and filling empty cups. Disappointment settled within her as she pondered the rancher's words. She'd heard Mr. Boswell say something similar to Mr. Warren on his last visit to Laramie.

Tess gritted her teeth. What were the honest citizens of Laramie to do if the lawman of the town was crooked?

Everyone knew Big Steve Long was dishonest. In fact, the big man made light of the numerous complaints about the robberies and the killings. Over fifteen men had died here since May, making it seem unhealthy to gamble or drink in the Bucket of Blood saloon.

Con and Ace Moyer were his henchmen. Any man who won a big hand at the poker tables in his saloon was quickly stripped of his winnings in the nearest dark alley, often with a knife in his ribs for good measure. A variety of shootings had occurred in Laramie as well, all benefiting Steve Long. Most times, he claimed he'd had to draw his weapon on a bad man. Other times, the big marshal simply bullied drunken railroad workers into a gun fight. Regardless of the provocation, the outcome was always the same. Big Steve Long and the Moyer brothers came out ahead and were now some of the biggest landowners in the region.

After Tess ate her meal alone at two o'clock, she hurried to the livery barn to retrieve her sign. Everyone in town knew to wait until the painted sign was visible from the street before stopping for a haircut.

The old man met her as she entered the dimly lit barn. "Hello, Mr. Belmont. I heard you reading the book of John this morning. Did anyone come forward?"

The old hostler shook his shaggy head as he hobbled near to Tess. "No, girl, but that's not my responsibility."

Tess reached for her sign and then turned to stare at him, tilting her head. "But I thought it was our duty as Christians to share the gospel with unbelievers."

Mr. Belmont nodded, his eyes softening. "It is our

duty, that's right. But we share our faith out of love, not only duty. However, it's for the Holy Spirit to make new believers. I can only share the word of God. It's up to the Spirit to prepare the soil before I throw the seed."

Tess considered his words. "We're to be obedient, right? It's up to God to do the rest."

The old man grinned, a twinkle in his eyes. "I can lead a horse to water, but I can't make him drink. I believe I planted seeds today. Maybe someone else will water those seeds, but it's the Holy Spirit who brings them to life."

She agreed and then turned to go. "I'll see you later."

A few men lounged near the old gnarled oak tree, eyes turning expectantly at Tess's approach.

"Tess, shave Barney first. He's so ugly, I can barely stand to look at him," one sunburned railroad worker called loudly.

Another one stepped close to the stump as Tess set up her instruments and shaving lather. "Tess, when are you going to marry me?"

"She can't marry you, Bill. She's marrying me," a short, stocky Irishman retorted with a grin. Tess noticed the gaps in his smile.

The banter continued as Tess began cutting hair on the first man. She smiled as they chatted with one another.

"I heard the heat killed six fat mules yesterday." A man in a blue shirt spit into the dust. Men shook their heads.

"They push those critters hard. The mules are expected to work like the rest of us," another man grumbled.

"Sure is hot," another worker complained, wiping a sleeve across his brow.

"There's talk of moving base camp farther west before winter. Will that be the death of Laramie?"

"Good land hereabouts. Maybe ranching and lumbering will keep folks here," another suggested.

Tess listened, rarely saying much, enjoying their candor. She liked how comfortable the men were in her presence.

For the first time in her life, Tess made money and was able to choose how to spend it. She felt pride in the fact that she'd helped Brett and Sandy keep their homes, as well as maintain the snug, comfortable cabins. They were her family now.

Sandy had said they'd repay her when the tie cutters received their pay, but Tess knew she wouldn't accept the money. It was the least she could do for all the two men had done for her. Besides, it might take another month before the tie cutters received expected pay. But Tess no longer cared if the time was extended. Truth be told, she no longer felt rushed to relocate to Chicago.

Tess finished cutting one man's hair. He dropped a dime on the barrelhead before he vacated the stump. Another man, long hair curling above his shirt, took his place.

Tess suddenly realized she couldn't recall ever being happier. Her new life in Laramie included a lot of hard work, but she loved the feeling of accomplishment and the sense of belonging. She felt more content than any other time she could recall.

Tess combed the man's tangled hair into straight lengths and then her scissors flew about his head, expertly trimming his long, unruly hair, taming the mess.

The sun shone warm and bright overhead, but the shade of the massive oak tree remained a pleasant spot to gather. At least five more men stood in line and Tess considered her day's profits. Perhaps she'd walk over to the general store before she started for home and pay some more on Brett's debt.

She finished with the current customer and he tossed a dime into Tess's outstretched palm, giving her a roguish smile and wink.

"Maybe you'll want to walk out with me sometime, Tess."

She sensed the sincerity in the young man, but knew she'd have to let him down gently. Her heart belonged to another.

Before she could respond, a tall man shouldered through the crowd and grabbed Tess by her arm, his fingers digging into her flesh. Tess cried out and turned, her blood chilling as she recognized the grizzled face of her attacker.

Frank Mercer.

CHAPTER EIGHTEEN

It took a long moment for Tess's mind to comprehend what was happening. All her hopes, all her expectations had been suddenly dashed by the appearance of this evil man.

"I've got you now, you little sneak," Frank crowed loudly, his thin lips curved in an ugly sneer, revealing his stained, yellow teeth. Tess cringed at the victorious gleam in his dark, small eyes.

"Hey, mister." One of the railroad workers stepped forward. "There ain't no cause to grab Tess that way. Let her go." The other men of the group began to press closer.

Frank whipped a long knife from under his coat, the blade glittering in the sunlight. The crowd melted back.

Tess recognized the blade as one of those the whiskey peddler traded with the Indians for skins. Frank had made numerous such knives on his own time for the trader.

"Stay back," Frank warned, waving the knife. The railroad workers fell away from the threatening blade.

"Marshal Long!" the young man who had asked her out called. "Marshal Long!" he shouted again, gesturing wildly to get the marshal's attention.

Tess glanced down the street and saw both Con Moyer and Steve Long standing on the steps of the Bucket of Blood. The marshal leaped off the boardwalk and hurried toward the crowd of men under the oak tree.

Frank's fingers dug painfully into Tess's arm. She wanted to cry out, but she feared he'd strike her like he'd done in the old days when she'd angered him.

Big Steve Long held out an open palm toward Frank as he approached, appraising the situation. Tess noticed the crooked lawman's other hand gripped his holstered gun.

"Hold on, now, mister. What's this all about?"

Tess saw Con move to Steve's left, trying to circle behind her and Frank. Frank saw him, too, and pressed his back against the oak tree. "Stay back," he repeated, brandishing the knife. "This is my stepdaughter. She's a runaway, and I've come to take her home."

Big Steve stepped in front of the crowd of railroad workers, but Tess lost sight of Con. He must be somewhere behind her.

"Mister, if what you say is true," Steve said in a calm voice. "You're going about this all the wrong way. Now, put down the knife and let's talk about it."

Frank's eyes widened as he wielded the long blade. The crowd spread into a half circle, watching Frank and Tess with keen interest. His feet shuffled, but his grip tightened on the knife. Numbness replaced the pain that ran through her arm.

"There's nothing to talk about. She's my stepdaughter. She's a runaway. As a minor, she must come home with me."

Tess watched the marshal scowl, and something gleamed in Big Steve's narrowed eyes.

Impatience? Disgust?

Whatever the big marshal felt, he halted before the shifting Mercer and then straightened, tall and wide-shouldered, making an imposing figure.

Tess could see Steve's demeanor change from one of caution to one of intolerance for the situation before him. With almost a casual reach, the marshal pulled his heavy pistol and aimed the gun at Frank Mercer's head. "Mister,

I'm going to count to three, and then I'm going to blow your head off. Put the knife down or die," Steve said.

Tess marveled at Steve's calm voice. She didn't doubt he meant what he said.

Obviously, Frank thought so, too, for he hesitated only a moment and then lowered the long knife. Con stepped from behind the tree and yanked the knife from Frank's hand as Big Steve took another step forward, his gun still trained on Frank.

"All right, mister, who are you?"

Con tore Tess from her stepfather's hold, but Frank never took his eyes from Tess.

"I told you. I'm her stepfather. I'm Frank Mercer. From Omaha."

Con chuckled as he shoved Frank's knife into his belt. "I've heard of you. You make knives for that whiskey peddler. I've heard you've even done some night work. Some men get knocked in the head when they step off the train in Omaha. Rumor has it you did it."

Frank did not reply but turned on Steve Long. "You the marshal hereabouts? I want to let you know I'm taking this girl home. Her mama is worried about her. She ran off a couple of months ago, and I only just heard of a girl of seventeen cutting hair in Laramie. I knew it had to be her. I came right away."

Con stood near Tess, preventing her escape, as the tall marshal stared intently at Frank, rubbing his whiskered chin.

"Of course, we guessed Tess was a runaway. You have to take her home right off? Ace'll be disappointed." He paused and then lowered his voice. "Besides, I could use a man like you in my business." He glanced at the men milling about.

Tess looked around, too, and noticed the crowd of men

had now wandered off.

Frank's small eyes sized up Con and then returned to Steve. A knowing grin spread across his bearded face. "So, you have a little night business of your own, do you? Well, marshal, I confess I'd enjoy hearing more about it, but I have to get this girl home to her mama. The poor woman's been worried sick about our Tess," Frank said, his dark eyes now looking Tess over from head to toe. "You've grown up some, Tess girl," he muttered, his eyebrows arching appreciatively as he studied her slender form.

Marshal Long snorted in disgust. "Frank Mercer, you're a pig. But a pig we might be able to use. Consider my proposal and let me know. You might be what we've been looking for."

Con handed the knife to Long. "I need to get back," he said before stalking toward his saloon.

Frank shook his head. "No, thank you kindly, Marshal. I want to be on the late train to Omaha. I'll be getting the girl's things and heading home."

Big Steve nodded. "All right, Mercer." He started to turn away but then hesitated. "Let me take you to where she's been staying. I want to look the place over my own self. It might be that I'll be owning that land soon and I want to see it." Frank's eyes glinted as Long handed his knife back to him and together they walked with Tess between them to the nearby livery.

With both Big Steve and Frank beside her, herding her like a sheep to the slaughter, there was nowhere to run. Her mind whirled with multiple thoughts. Frank Mercer was in Laramie, and she would see Mama soon. But that meant leaving Brett. Would there be a chance to say goodbye to Brett and Sandy?

"Belmont!" the marshal bellowed when they entered the shadowy barn. Tess saw the old hostler hobble through the rear entrance. Tess cringed as the old man neared, the dimly lighted barn hiding her presence. Then Mr. Belmont halted, his eyes widening with sudden recognition and fear.

"Belmont, hitch me up a buggy. I'll have it back within the hour. Hurry it up. I don't have all day," Steve Long ordered.

Mr. Belmont hesitated only a moment and then complied with the marshal's demand. He returned a few minutes later, leading the buggy, hitched and ready.

He led the vehicle outside and Steve stepped in stiffly, the light buggy lurching from his weight as Frank made sure Tess got in ahead of him. She squeezed between the two men on the front seat.

"Well, Mercer, you about make this young girl sit on your lap. I can see how it is with you over her, but I won't say anything. It's none of my affair," the marshal said as he lifted the buggy whip and struck the bay horse with a light touch.

Tess noticed Mr. Belmont standing motionless in the big door of the barn, watching the buggy take off. She could see anxiety etched across his face and knew there was nothing he could do for her.

"That's right, Marshal, there's not a thing you can say. She's a runaway and a minor, and I'm her legal guardian. I'm taking her home to Omaha. But," he added leaning toward the other man, a cruel grin creasing his face. "It's a long trip to Omaha, and anything can happen."

He chuckled and Tess shrank at the sound of the mad glee and triumph in Frank's voice. Tess tried to pray, but the words got mixed in her worried mind. No amount of effort would put the words in proper order in her panic-stricken brain. "Jesus, Jesus," was all she could whisper.

They passed the Bucket of Blood and the Chinaman's Palace. Tess wanted to call for help as they passed the café, but the two men squeezed her between them, cutting off any chance she had. The buggy bumped over the log bridge at the edge of town. Tess wished she was able to throw herself into the swift river below.

Soon, the many shanties and tent buildings fell behind as the horse trotted easily on the hard packed dirt road paralleling the tracks east of Laramie.

The thick forest on their right drew Tess's attention. How she wished she could leap from the moving buggy and flee into the protection of these dark woods. She knew the way to the chapel by the small waterfall, and she suddenly longed for the peace she felt when she visited the little glade at night.

Desperate and resigned, Tess peered at Frank from the corner of her eye, the late afternoon shadows coloring his features. Soot smudged his cheeks from the train ride and his small eyes glowed with wickedness.

"How is Mama?" she asked quietly, hoping to catch him off guard.

Frank didn't even turn his head to reply, acting as if he hadn't heard her question.

Tess frowned as she faced forward, her eyes naturally seeking the dead pine that marked the turnoff.

Steve Long shifted on the seat, his big frame bumping Tess. "So, Frank, you came to bring your girl home."

Frank said nothing as Long paused.

"But Con says you like to make a little side money."

Again, Frank said nothing.

The marshal sighed and let the matter drop.

Soon they reached the turnoff to Brett's homestead and Big Steve pulled on the reins, forcing the horse to turn into the dimly lit trail that led to the yellow cabins. The horse slowed from a trot to a walk as he plodded up the gradual ascent, climbing the side of the mountain. Tess was shoved roughly aside as the marshal reached for his gun and held the weapon firmly in one hand, the reins bunched in the other.

Through the thick woods, Tess caught sight of the familiar cabins. She tensed as they approached, her thoughts turning to Brett. The smoothed logs stacked cleverly beneath the tall pines warmed her anxious heart. Tess's chest tightened as she spotted Brett striding through the woods from the lean-to barn behind the cabin. The handsome tie cutter stepped onto the porch and then turned at the sound of the approaching buggy. Tess watched fear flit through his eyes as the light vehicle pulled into the clearing.

Steve Long halted the horse with a pull on the reins, a cloud of dust circling them.

"Tess, what's this about?" Brett took a step nearer.

Marshal Long lifted his gun and pointed the barrel at Brett. "Just stay where you are, Calloway. I know you have a rifle somewhere around, and I don't want you to get any bright ideas of helping this girl. She's a runaway, and this is her pa."

"He is not my pa," Tess said through gritted teeth. She wanted to fly into Brett's strong arms and let him protect her from this evil man who sat next to her, but the gun in Big Steve's hand would allow nothing of the kind.

Suddenly, she looked at Brett and knew in that moment she loved him, and it was good with the Lord. The gentle and kind woodcutter was the right man for her. She knew it, she could feel it. The joy she felt in her heart confirmed the truth.

This sensation—in her heart and mind—was real and not just a selfish emotion.

"Girl," the marshal said in an even voice. "You go inside and fetch your things. If you try anything stupid, I'll shoot

Mr. Calloway."

Slowly, Tess rose on unsteady legs and lowered herself from the buggy. Tess walked to the door but hesitated when she stood next to Brett. They were out of earshot of the buggy here.

"Tess," Brett whispered. "I'll get you out of this. Don't worry. Trust me."

"Hey, stop talking to her," Frank demanded from the buggy. A look of jealousy lashed through his dark eyes, and Tess frowned. She loathed this man.

"You are a fool," Brett said, looking directly at Mercer. "You know Tess despises you, and you still want to take her home." Brett turned his attention to the marshal. "Long, you know I don't have any respect for your office, but even you can see what this man intends. Won't you step in and protect this innocent girl?"

Big Steve chuckled without a touch of humor. "Calloway, I have a pistol aimed at your belly and you still have the nerve to say that to my face. Well, no one can say you're yellow. No, I will not step in and save this girl. What is she to me? And I have my own plans working. Soon, Calloway, I'll have your land. Yours and your balding partner's."

Tess opened the cabin door and entered the welcoming room that had been her home for the past few months. She moved swiftly around the room, gathering her few garments and her Bible. She could hear the men speaking outside.

Out of sheer habit, Tess almost stopped in the collecting of her things to toss an armload of wood on the fire. Soon it would be supper time and she'd be preparing something for the men. The coffeepot, already filled with fresh water, stood on the corner of the hearth and she wanted to push it into the coals to warm.

Standing in the middle of the room, Tess stared around

the bright, cheery cabin, the fresh scent of pine mingling with that of wood smoke. This had become her home. She loved it here. She glanced at the deerskin rug before the hearth where Brett slept each night. She loved him too. She knew it for sure now.

"Tess, get out here," Mercer growled, a ring of impatience in his voice.

With a final glance at the big stone fireplace, Tess moved toward the door. She closed the heavy plank door softly behind her for the last time as she heard Brett's rapid whisper.

"Make them keep you in town tonight. I have a plan. I'll find you tonight. Look for me," he whispered from the corner of his mouth.

"What are you saying to her?" Frank snarled.

Tess walked forward to the buggy and climbed back in, scrambling over Frank to her seat between the two men.

"Nothing," Brett shrugged. "Only I hope you have a decent place to keep her tonight. A saloon is no place for a lady."

Frank laughed loudly at this. "You need not worry about that. I'll be on the evening train with my Tess girl. I'll be gone from Laramie before you know it and won't miss the dust of this town, I can promise you."

Big Steve cracked the whip over the horse and the animal started to walk from the clearing. Tess saw the little bridge spanning the stream and she looked once more at Sandy's cabin across the creek. She'd miss this place.

Tears welled in her eyes as Tess looked a final time at Brett. He stood tall, defiant, but she read the concern in his hazel eyes as she stared at him. The buggy turned in a tight circle and left the clearing. Tess watched the young tie cutter over her shoulder.

"Goodbye, Brett. Thank you for everything. Tell Sandy

I said goodbye," she called to him, but her voice cracked with emotion.

With a wave, Brett raced from the clearing. Tess wondered if he ran to tell Sandy the sad news of her departure or if he was running toward Laramie.

With a sigh, she turned, faced forward, and stared at the bay horse pulling the buggy. She gripped her Bible on her lap and hung her head, mouthing a silent prayer as the tears streamed down her cheeks.

CHAPTER NINETEEN

Tess lifted her head as the buggy slowed to make the turn at the bottom of the hill. She drew a ragged breath, her heart breaking, knowing she would no longer see Brett or the cabins or the little bridge. The bitter truth of her situation burrowed into her heart as she cried silently, her vision blurred as she peered at the twin rails pointing toward Laramie.

Frank leered openly at her and Tess turned away, wiping her wet eyes on her sleeve. There was no doubt in her mind what Frank would do when he got her alone on the train. He had always been a mean, cruel man, but had become lecherous and disgusting in the past couple of years as Tess aged.

Suddenly, she turned to Big Steve, his features still clear in the dim light of late evening. "Marshal, you know me. I've been working in Laramie for most of the summer. Can't you do anything to save me from this man? I don't want to return to Omaha with him."

Frank sneered. "Pay her no mind, Marshal. She needs to be taught who's boss, that's all. I'll see to that."

Big Steve shook his head. "Nope, I won't interfere. I know Ace'll be disappointed, but we must keep our eye on the prize. There are bigger fish to fry." He remained silent for a moment before going on, mumbling almost to himself. "The two homesteads are back to back, joined along the stream. The pair of them would be valuable for the ties they provide. The railroad would pay handsomely for that kind of timber."

Tess studied the marshal in the vague, gloomy glow of dusk, wondering what he rambled on about. She cringed as understanding dawned, comprehension sweeping over her. He planned to seize their homesteads. The marshal's gang would take Brett's land.

She slumped in her seat. The two wide men squeezed her tightly between them, but she tried to ignore the touch of their shoulders against her own. Her stomach churned and she felt nauseous. What would become of her? Dread overwhelmed her. God was not going to protect her. She would be returned to the same situation she'd tried to flee.

She thought about how the dim and gloomy shack she'd shared with her mother and Frank differed from the bright, warm yellow cabin Brett had built. The wonderful cabin she would never see again.

Despite the misfortune of Frank finding her in Laramie, she prayed the Lord was with her still. He promised to always be with her. She knew God's intent was not that Tess would fall into the hands of this wicked man, but sin made men do evil things.

Darkness had fallen and shadows stretched over Laramie ahead. Only faint yellow lights revealed where the main street and the many saloons stood. Even the livery was shrouded in complete blackness as the buggy rolled in front of the big barn. Mr. Belmont stepped quickly from the shadows, his face marked with apprehension as Tess neared.

"Belmont, tell Con I said you could have a few drinks at the Bucket of Blood—on the house," Big Steve called as he walked with Mercer toward the saloon.

"I don't drink," the old man answered quietly, but his reply was lost on the two men as they guided Tess along the boardwalk.

Tess peered over her shoulder at the old hostler. She wanted to say something to him, but Frank shoved her roughly toward the main street before she had a chance to speak. Now they were far from the livery and Tess knew she'd not be able to thank the old man for all his kindness and help.

The Bucket of Blood was in full swing when they entered. Eight lanterns hung from the ceiling in the crowded saloon, glowing brightly. Tess saw three women dressed in gaudy dresses, sleeveless and with low-cut necklines. One of the women, a large, pasty girl, squinted at Tess as she was ushered through the crowd to a hallway beyond the long bar. Tess stared at the woman, hoping the saloon girl perceived her plight. But the big woman looked hard and colorless, her eyes cold and hollow as she watched Tess being dragged down the dark hallway.

Tess passed a row of doors, wondering what went on behind them. Big Steve led the way to the last door on the right. Opening it, the big man indicated that Frank and Tess should enter.

"You can wait in here, if you wish," the marshal said. The dim lantern light cast from behind Tess revealed the small storeroom held a table and four chairs. A narrow cot sat propped against one wall. Boxes and casks lined the far wall. "I do business in here sometimes," he explained as Tess and Frank moved to the chairs and seated themselves. "Or a person can get some sleep here, if the need arises." The marshal leaned outside the doorway and called toward the bar. "Con. Bring us a light and a bottle."

The little man in white shirt and black vest soon appeared with a glowing candle, a brown bottle and two glasses. He grinned when he saw Tess. "Sorry, girl. We don't got no soda pop."

Steve and Frank chuckled as the small bartender poured

two stiff drinks. Setting the bottle on the table, he turned and left the room.

Long pulled a chair out from the table and seated himself, the chair creaking in protest. He lifted the glass and swirled the drink, studying the brown liquid before he took a big gulp.

"Ahhhh. That's what I needed." He smacked his lips.

Frank had grabbed his drink quickly when Moyer set the glass on the table, downing it thirstily. Now he reached for the bottle and poured himself another.

Tess stared with disgust at the two men. She was trapped and now forced to watch her captors get drunk.

Big Steve glanced at Frank. "Well, Mercer, I wish you'd reconsider my idea. You can stay here and work with me. There's no hurry to go back to Omaha so fast, is there?"

Frank poured his third drink. "I need time to tame this wild girl. Then maybe we can talk. I gave up my job when I began looking for Tess, so I'm in need of work," Frank confessed. Tess noted how his words already slurred. She remembered only too well how the drunk blacksmith sounded the drunker he became. "Besides," he continued, glancing around the little room. "I didn't realize you had connections with a saloon."

"I own this place," Steve boasted, gesturing to the barroom at the front of the building. "Con and Ace Moyer are my partners, not to mention my half-brothers. We run gaming tables and sell whiskey. We have a few girls working the cribs behind the saloon. And we're cleaning up the good range land and homesteads in the area. Soon, we'll be the biggest landowners in this piece of Dakota Territory."

"Wyoming Territory," Frank corrected the crooked lawman, his eyes narrowing. "How are you acquiring all of this land, if I might be so bold to ask?"

Big Steve grinned. "Perhaps we'd better move young Tess to another room before we discuss business."

Frank waved a hand, shaking his head. "No. That's all right. She can sit right here where I can keep an eye on her. I don't need to know about your business, anyway. I'm leaving town tonight."

The marshal frowned at Frank's reply but said nothing. The big man pulled a gold watch from his vest pocket. "Well, we'd better get you to the train. It arrived two hours ago. I heard the whistle. And now I'm sure the construction supplies have been unloaded and the train has to turn around and head back for more. Come on, I'll walk with you."

Frank leaned forward and hastily poured himself another drink, spilling a little of the dark liquid. He lifted the full glass and downed the contents in a few swift gulps.

The chairs scraped on the rough plank floor as they were pushed away from the table. "I make a lot of the spikes and fittings and brackets the railroad uses up here," Frank said self-importantly as the trio walked from the small room.

"You mean you used to, Mercer, remember? You have no job now," Big Steve reminded Frank as they strode through the crowded bar to the front door.

Frank scowled and squinted at the marshal's harsh words, making Tess wonder about Frank's confession of being out of work. How was Mama getting along without Frank's wages? She worried, anxiety filling her as they walked into the dark night to the train station.

Frank led Tess, keeping a firm hand on her arm. She could feel a bruise already forming above her elbow where he gripped. She knew escape was impossible, and resignation crept into her soul. Life had become so good for her here in Laramie. Now, she would return to the life she dreaded.

The August day had been hot, but the cool wind off the high peaks now felt refreshing as Tess trudged along, her heavy feet moving where her stepfather directed.

The walk to the train platform was a short one. A big black engine stood silently beside the raised loading docks, but Tess sensed something amiss as they approached. She tilted her head, studying the soundless engine in the dim light of the depot lantern. No smoke issued from the stack, no steam hissed from the boiler.

Frank seemed to notice it too. The blacksmith rushed forward, dragging Tess behind him, confused by the quiet engine. "What's going on here?" he bellowed as they ran onto the platform.

A pair of men appeared farther down the tracks, near the still engine. Tess could see by the men's garb they were the engineer and probably the brakeman, judging by the ember burns in his coat.

Steve Long accosted the two guilty-looking men. "You two," he snarled as they approached. "What's happened? Why isn't the train ready to move?"

The engineer scratched his head and pointed to the lever in the cab. He wore a blue bandana tied around his neck and held a bottle in the other hand. "A man came by and wanted to drink with us. We had a sip or two with the gent and then he left. But someone had pulled the pressure release when we weren't looking. There's no head of steam. It'll take hours to boil the water to move again."

"Who was this man who drank with you?" Steve demanded.

The two railroad men stared at each other, puzzled. The one with the blue bandana shifted, but the one with the cinder burns spoke up. "Well, I don't recall he gave us his name. An old man with a limp. Said he fought for

General Sherman."

"To General Sherman!" his companion roared as he raised the bottle high and tilted the neck over his mouth.

Suddenly, a glimmer of courage seeped back into Tess. Mr. Belmont. She remembered what Brett had said to her on the porch of his cabin. Be ready.

Her weary eyes flew open as anticipation coursed through her, filling her again with excitement and hope. Perhaps she was not through here yet. Ivan and Brett were up to something.

Cautiously, she peered around in the darkness, searching for any sign of her friends.

The marshal turned away in disgust. "Mercer, it'll take hours to gather another head of steam. You might as well come back to the saloon with me and spend the night. You can go home in the morning."

Frank gave a curt nod, eyeing the two railroad men with frustration. "I guess so. What about the old man who gave them the bottle?"

Marshal Long snorted and shrugged. "That description fits a hundred men in Laramie. Besides, they're drunk. It might've been a young dwarf for all these men can remember. Come on, let's go back. I'll find a room for the girl. You and I can talk business."

The two men turned to walk the short distance back to the Bucket of Blood. But then Frank halted abruptly. "I won't let Tess out of my sight. She's going with me when I leave Laramie."

Big Steve took Frank by the elbow and guided him toward the bar once more. "I have just the room. It has a window too small to crawl through. She can sleep in there while we talk. I want you to meet Con and Ace."

Frank hesitated again, shaking the big man's hand from his arm, obviously annoyed at the delay.

The marshal cocked an eyebrow at Frank. "There'll be a bottle when we talk."

Frank hesitated only a moment longer. He gave a single nod and licked his lips before he followed Long, dragging Tess behind him.

Tess struggled to keep pace with her stepfather but didn't mind the delay. Hope surged through her now, but she wondered how Brett and Mr. Belmont planned to help her.

Their boots thumped on the boardwalk, and they shoved through the front doors, a tight grip on Tess's arm as the trio entered the Bucket of Blood once more. This time, she saw Ace Moyer standing by the end of the bar, talking with his brother. The little thief wore his derby cocked to one side. Tess thought he looked ridiculous.

He smiled at them as they drew near. "Hello, Tess Randle," he greeted her, his eyes taunting and cold. Then he glanced at Frank. "I like your hat, mister."

Frank nodded and touched the brim of his own derby. Ace grinned at him and then Big Steve stepped forward.

"Ace Moyer, this is Frank Mercer. I'd like you to join us in the back for a little talk with Frank. Put this girl in the smaller storeroom. And lock the door," Steve ordered as they continued down the hall.

Ace fell in behind them as they returned to the small office they'd recently vacated. Frank stood in the doorway and watched Ace push Tess into the dark storeroom across from the office. "Let me see," Frank growled and peered around the little room before Ace reached for the door.

He grinned wolfishly at her and pulled the door closed tightly. Tess listened as the key turned in the lock. Darkness enveloped her. Stretching her arms out, she moved cautiously around until she bumped into wooden boxes. Liquid sloshed as she dragged a keg from the wall. With a sigh, Tess perched on the edge of the little barrel and leaned her elbows on her knees.

Muted music blared from the large bar room down the hall. Occasionally, she heard loud yells and twice she heard gun shots while doors slammed on the rooms between her and the main room. Despite the late hour, the saloon bustled with activity.

It was then she recalled the window Big Steve had mentioned.

Rising tentatively, Tess again put her hands out and explored the walls. With difficulty, she maneuvered the entire border of the storeroom, locating a small window on the back wall, level with her head. A piece of canvas dangled above the tiny opening, protecting the room from rain.

Her heart sank as Tess touched the narrow borders of the opening, too small to fit through. She wasn't even sure if she could pull herself up to the window. Sighing with disappointment, Tess was just about to turn from the little opening when she heard a whisper.

"Tess, it's me."

Her heart leaped and tingles raced down her back as she recognized Brett's voice. "Brett," she breathed, his mere name giving her strength. She peered into the gloom and lifted an arm through the small window. She waved, hoping to reveal her position. "I'm here, Brett," she whispered, frantically trying to keep her voice low.

A hand grasped hers and she wanted to scream with excitement. She couldn't see a thing in the deep shadows of the alley behind the saloon, but she recognized Brett's strong hands.

"Ivan is here, too, Tess. We have a plan to help you," he reported, his voice choked with eagerness.

"To get me out of here? How?" Tess released Brett's

hands and pulled on the sides of the small window. It felt solidly built and there was no give in the wall. Again, she gripped the bottom edge and stood on her toes. "The wall is strong, Brett. What do you intend to do? Use an axe?"

A worried glance over her shoulder revealed nothing but the dim crack of light below the door. An axe would make a tremendous racket. Frank would be here before Brett could free her.

A sudden whisper came from outside. "Tess, I cannot break you out. There's a guard on your door. I saw him. And any noise on this wall would draw too much attention."

Tess frowned in the darkness. "Then what are you going to do, Brett?" How could she escape if they couldn't break her out of the storeroom?

Her inquiry met with silence. "Brett?" Tess hissed, panic rising. "Brett?" she repeated in a frantic whisper.

"I'm going to marry you," he replied softly.

Tess stared at the dark window in disbelief and could feel her jaw drop. Did he say *marry*?

"Tess? Did you hear me? I can marry you, and your stepfather can't take you away. You're a minor and must obey him. That's the law. But you're old enough to get married, and then you're free from his guardianship," Brett explained rapidly.

Tess wiped her sweaty hands on her dress, her heart swelling with excitement. That was it. Brett had figured out the way to outwit Frank Mercer. And Tess would marry the man she loved. Everything would be all right.

She smiled into the darkness, happiness crowding out her fear and anxiety. Brett would save her. God had saved her.

Then she realized how this decision would affect Brett's life. Marriage was forever. He'd be trapped with her for all his life. She couldn't do that to him—it felt selfish. While he saved her, she would be ruining him. She shook her head as tears threatened. No. She couldn't do this to the man she loved. Tess shook her head again.

"Brett, I can't marry you. You'd be sacrificing yourself for me. I cannot ask that of you."

"Tess, there's no time for this. Trust me," he called quickly through the small window.

"No," she replied. "No. You must not do this for me, Brett."

She heard a scuffle outside the window and Tess worried the two men had been discovered. Instead, Mr. Belmont spoke.

"Tess, we must hurry. Is this what you wish to do? Is it your decision to marry Brett?"

"No, Mr. Belmont. I can't do that to Brett. There must be another way," she pleaded.

Another scuffle outside, and Tess heard Brett's voice again. "There's no other way, Tess," Brett said with a hint of impatience. "Now tell Ivan you'll do this and let's begin."

"I don't want to ruin you like this," Tess implored. She desperately wished to marry Brett Calloway, to escape Frank Mercer. But she also didn't want to cheat Brett out of marrying the girl he might fall in love with one day. What if there was to be another woman in his future? What if Brett was only marrying her to be kind, to save her?

"Tess," Brett hissed. "Stop stalling and tell Ivan you'll marry me."

Tess frowned and then thought of Frank and the life she'd live if she didn't marry Brett. She simply could not return with Frank to Omaha. Reluctantly, desperately, she nodded in the darkness. "All right. I will," she whispered, her heart in her throat, choking her quiet reply.

The ceremony was surprisingly swift and brief. Before

Tess knew it, she was married to Brett.

"I now pronounce you man and wife. You may kiss the bride," Mr. Belmont whispered.

Tess tilted her face to the window, eagerly craning to reach through the small opening. With disappointment, she felt Brett's lips on the top of her head. And then they were gone.

CHAPTER TWENTY

Tess peered out the little window into the gloomy alley but saw nothing. Brett and Ivan were gone. In the matter of a few moments, she'd become a married woman. Tess Randle, married.

Only, she was now no longer Tess Randle. Now she was Tess Calloway. Mrs. Brett Calloway. The thought stunned her. The suddenness of the transformation daunted her. A thrill ran up her back. But her knees felt weak. Tess stumbled through the dark room to the keg near the wall where she collapsed, leaning on her elbows as she prayed.

"God, what just happened? Was this your will? I'm sorry, Father, if my personal desires got in the way and guided me in my decision. I want only to do what you want me to do. But on the mountain today, when I thought I would never see Brett again, I knew I loved him. I pray I have not ruined his life by allowing him to marry me. Guide us and bless us, Lord," she concluded softly in the darkness of the storeroom.

Wild thoughts raced through her mind. She was married and Brett was her husband. Frank Mercer couldn't take her away now. She could finish the curtains she'd started for the yellow cabin. She had finally put aside enough flour sacks for the project.

The silliness of these last thoughts made Tess smile. Even locked in a dark room, she still planned how she would decorate her home.

Tess stood suddenly and nervously paced the floor.

Would she and Brett now share the one bed? But no, she must not think of that now. She had to still get free from this room.

She wondered if she was truly safe. The events of the last few months came flooding back over her as she walked back and forth.

Fear had lived with her and her mother in that little shack on the prairie in Omaha. Fear of Frank Mercer and fear for her future.

She'd come to Laramie on the wrong train, but Brett Calloway had proven a friend with his safe refuge and help. Tess had made other friends here also. Ivan Belmont, Sandy, the Warrens. Even the chapel in the small glade had become dear to her heart.

God had worked in Tess's life, she was certain. He had brought joy and safety and love to her. The rough and lawless town of Laramie with its tough element of railroad workers and the many saloons and the numerous killings and robberies had not detracted from the happiness Tess found in this raw frontier town.

Tess brushed against the keg, and tired from her frantic pacing, she sank upon the little barrel. She stared unseeing into the darkness that surrounded her.

A gasp escaped her, and she squeezed her hands together, twisting them into her lap. Married. Her whirling thoughts kept coming back to this one fact. She had married Brett, and Frank couldn't do anything about it.

She thought then of her mother and how she wished she could meet Brett. Maybe they would meet one day. But her mother had chosen to seek her own security rather than that of her daughter. Perhaps she wouldn't care if Tess was married.

For the remainder of the night, Tess pondered these things that haunted her thoughts. Through it all, she continuously came back to the fact that she was Mrs. Calloway. The thought astounded her. Regardless of the future, whether she still had a job at the café or would still cut hair or if she even still lived in Brett's cabin, she would be Mrs. Calloway. This single truth carried her through the maze of her active mind.

The noise in the other room had long since died down. Occasionally, Tess heard a door opening and closing down the hall. Tess stood and stretched, watching the crack beside the canvas flap slowly gray. Today would prove an important day.

Her hand reached for the curtain and pulled the cloth aside, revealing the dim gray morning sky, replacing the deep blue of early dawn.

A train whistle called from the station, and Tess felt her stomach knot. She clenched her fists and paced again, knowing they would soon come for her. How surprised Frank would be to learn she was now married. A smile crept over her face as it had done a thousand times this night. Tess would not be returning with Frank to Omaha.

The door down the hall opened once again and Tess heard footsteps coming closer. A key rattled in the lock and the door swung open. Ace Moyer stood there, bleary-eyed and rumpled. A three-day stubble covered his jawline, and he scratched his chin when he saw Tess. He looked as if he'd not slept in days.

"Good morning, Tess," he drawled, his gaze openly traveling up and down her frame.

Tess cringed, sickened by the little thief. She looked away.

He chuckled. "I guess we weren't meant to be. Frank tells me you're his. I'd disagree with him, but Steve says he figures into our plans now and to leave him alone."

Tess peered at him, an eyebrow arching. She narrowed

her eyes then, trying to contain the thrill that raced through her. She had a secret that Ace didn't know. Tess wasn't frightened by his threats.

Striding past him, she marched down the hallway toward the big room where the long bar stood. Ace hurried after her.

"Hold on, Tess. You can't go out there without me. Big Steve would have my hide." He laughed as he caught up with Tess and grasped her arm.

Tess didn't struggle or pull away. She felt eager, almost impatient, to see Frank. She wanted to see his face when the dirty man heard the news.

Two small groups of men stood on the platform as Tess and Ace approached, the black engine puffing in the early morning air. All of the men looked like Ace, rumpled and tired.

Big Steve Long saw her first. His hawk eyes watched Tess approach, the tin star pinned prominently on his vest shining brightly in the early morning sun. Con Moyer was there, too, along with Frank Mercer. Blood-shot eyes and haggard faces greeted her arrival, and Tess climbed the stairs to the platform, anxious and expectant.

Her heart leaped when she gazed farther along the platform. Brett Calloway and Ivan Belmont stood with Sandy beside the depot. Sandy held Brett's Spencer rifle.

As Ace and Tess joined the outlaw gang, a door slammed by the livery barn.

Tess turned at the sound, pleased to see Sheriff Boswell emerge from the big barn. Casually, the lawman sauntered toward the depot.

"Well, Frank, here's my lady love," Ace teased as he came up to the sour-faced man. Steve and Con snickered, but Frank bristled at the remark.

"I don't think that's funny," Frank growled, a dark scowl

on his face. He grabbed Tess's arm and dragged her away from Ace. She stared defiantly at him, smelling the night's effect of too much liquor on his foul breath.

"Oh, relax, Mercer. Keep focused. Ace was just joking," Big Steve snapped. "Don't let this girl get in the way of business."

Boswell halted below the platform and looked up. "I'm leaving town, Belmont. I wanted to square my bill with you."

Brett stepped forward and Tess thrilled as she watched him come closer, knowing what he was about to disclose. Yet her stomach coiled in knots, worried for him. What would Frank do when he learned his plans had been thwarted?

"Marshal Long?" Brett called, his gaze never leaving the crooked lawman. He spoke loud enough for all to hear.

Frank's grip hurt, digging painfully into her, but Tess ignored the agony, her attention on Brett.

The four men turned to face him.

"Yes, Calloway? You're up early this morning," Long added, his eyes scrutinizing Brett before he glanced at Ivan and Sandy.

Brett shifted. "Yes, I am. I wanted to introduce you to my wife." He pointed to Tess. Frank's grip tightened.

Tess froze and held her breath. All eyes turned to her and Frank.

"Your wife?" Big Steve arched his bushy eyebrows and threw a skeptical glance at Frank.

Tess saw Mr. Belmont lead Sheriff Boswell closer to the small group. Sandy stayed back, his hands holding the rifle in an easy grip.

"Yes, Tess and I were married last night. She has no intentions of going back to Omaha with this man." Brett gestured to Frank.

"It's a lie. A lie, I tell you," Frank snarled. His face twisted in fury as he pulled Tess protectively behind him, his hand still gripping her arm.

"It's no lie, I assure you," Ivan interrupted. The gray bearded hostler stepped forward, unfolding a piece of paper. He showed the marshal the marriage certificate.

"It is all legal, gentlemen. I've already filled out the necessary paperwork and will file it with the land office this very morning. Tess Calloway is not under this man's guardianship any longer." Ivan folded the paper and slipped the document in his shirt pocket.

A long moment of suspended silence hung in the clear air. Tess heard the rhythmic puffing of the nearby engine and the cry of a hunting hawk circling overhead in the blue sky. Clouds drifted lazily to the east, the morning sun peeking through, coloring them with splashes of pink.

She glanced at Brett. He held himself tall and she felt pride burst in her chest, knowing he was her husband.

"It's not legal, I say," Frank blustered, turning pleading eyes to Marshal Long.

Long shrugged. "Sounds legal to me. Looks like the girl really didn't want to go with you." He spread his hands wide. "Nothing I can do about it."

Frank tugged suddenly on Tess and dragged her forward. He thrust her hand up, revealing her fingers. "Where's her ring, then?" he demanded, his voice shrill and desperate.

Brett reddened as he cleared his throat. "I haven't had a chance to get Tess a proper ring, but she is my wife, nonetheless. Please let her go."

Tension filled the air, thickening as Frank's face clouded. Tess clenched her teeth, and her stomach tightened, afraid of what Frank might do.

He turned his gaze on Tess. His dark, piercing eyes burrowed into her soul, searching for the truth. "Are you and this man married?"

Tess could see the fear in his menacing eyes, smell the stale whiskey on his breath. She almost laughed in his face, wanting to inflict as much pain on him as she could. But she wasn't free of him yet. She bit her tongue, holding her fiery retort.

Suddenly, Tess felt a confidence she'd always lacked, a defiance that filled her with bravery. Her chin lifted and she nodded, returning Frank's intense gaze.

"Yes. I am his wife."

He stared at her, shock spreading over his features as the color drained from his cheeks. Then he sneered and bared his teeth like a cornered wolf. He pulled her behind him once more, dragging the girl so fast she stumbled and almost fell. His hand flashed and he drew the same knife he'd pulled the day before.

"Stay back. The girl is mine," he said between clenched teeth, his thin lips pulled back in a snarl.

Sheriff Boswell suddenly stepped beside Frank, his pistol held to the blacksmith's head. "You'll let go of the girl or I'll kill you, mister. I don't know who you are, but I know Brett Calloway. If he says this girl is his wife, then it's true."

"Boswell," Steve Long said calmly, waving a dismissive hand. "I have this situation under control. There's no need for you to interfere."

"Then handle it, Long," the rancher ordered. Without moving an inch, Boswell's gun didn't waver. He couldn't miss at this range and everyone knew it.

Big Steve moved forward a step. "Mercer, put the knife down. Calloway has outwitted you. There's nothing you can do about it now."

Frank hesitated a moment longer, and Boswell pressed the barrel to his temple. Frank frowned and licked his lips, the wild gleam disappearing from his small eyes.

Slowly, he lowered the long blade and released Tess.

She moved quickly to Brett's side, but the tie cutter swept her behind him, not taking his eyes from the men before him.

Boswell lifted the barrel of the short gun and stepped back, keeping his eyes on Frank as he continued to walk backwards to where Ivan stood near Brett.

Slowly, the tension dissipated, and Ace suddenly laughed out loud. "Well, Calloway, I wouldn't give a plugged nickel for your life."

No one said anything to this, and Brett turned with his companions and walked away. Brett placed an arm around Tess's slender waist and drew her along with them. His firm but unfamiliar touch thrilled her despite the gravity of the situation.

"Well, Mercer, it appears you don't have to hurry off now," Steve Long announced as they left the platform.

"This isn't over yet," was Frank Mercer's bitter reply, then they were out of earshot.

Brett and Ivan led the group toward the livery. Sheriff Boswell followed them, casting furtive glances over his shoulder as he walked to the big barn. Sandy brought up the rear, still holding the big Spencer rifle.

"Mr. Boswell, I hope you took note of those men," Ivan said as he hobbled to his barn. "That bunch is terrorizing Laramie. I fear they've recruited Frank Mercer to join them."

"None of my affair, Belmont. I have no authority in Laramie. I'd suggest you stay out of their way," the rancher said as he slipped his pistol back into his holster.

"You know it's not that simple, Sheriff," Brett added. "There are good people in Laramie, and they're afraid of those men. Steve Long and the Moyers have systematically acquired the land of murdered men. Those were not accidents or fair shootings that killed those men."

Boswell shook his head as Ivan led the sheriff's horse out. He dropped a few coins in the old hostler's hand. Grasping the pommel of his saddle, Boswell hesitated. He glanced at Brett. "You have no proof that those men were murdered, Calloway. I'd need proof. I have no jurisdiction in Laramie." He stepped into the saddle and nodded to Tess. "Congratulations, Mrs. Calloway." Turning his horse, he rode down the dusty street.

"I'm hungry," Sandy said abruptly. "Some excited young man pounded on my door in the middle of the night, and I haven't had anything to eat yet. And I dearly need some coffee."

"We all do," Brett agreed with a grin at Tess. "Let's go eat at the café. Tess's treat."

"I can't. Too busy. Congratulations, Tess. I'll see you later." Mr. Belmont smiled and patted her arm before he hobbled back inside his livery.

"Well, I can go with you, especially if Tess is buying," Sandy said. He leaned the long rifle over his shoulder and led off for the café.

As the trio of friends passed the Bucket of Blood, Tess shivered and glanced at the quiet saloon, remembering the long night there, locked in a dark storeroom. Then she smiled when she recalled she'd also been married there.

They passed the Chinaman's Palace and Land Office before the Overland Stage Station. Sandy stepped onto the stairs in front of the café and opened the door wide for Brett and Tess to enter.

"I would like to announce Mr. and Mrs. Brett Calloway," Sandy called loudly, interrupting the early morning crowd of customers.

There was a startled pause in the conversations around the room. Few people were present at this early hour. Then,

Mrs. Warren's plump face broke into a wide smile and she began to clap.

"Oh, Tess, I'm so happy for you," the big woman said as she hugged her. "I had no idea you were so serious about Mr. Calloway."

"It came as a surprise to me too," Tess confessed with a blush.

Breakfast was a merry meal, as Sandy made much of the newlyweds and teased Tess mercilessly. "Will you still do my laundry, Tess? Or will this woodcutter have you busy soon with little ones running around the cabin?"

Tess blushed again at the mention of children and carefully avoided Brett's eyes.

"Mrs. Warren, is there any chance Tess could skip work today?" Brett asked when the large woman came by to refill coffee cups. "I'd like to spend the day with her, if you don't mind."

Mrs. Warren rested the hot pot on the edge of the table. "I don't see why not. Doughnut day is the day after tomorrow, though, and I cannot do it without Tess. But she can certainly have today off." Mrs. Warren shot Tess another smile before she moved away from them.

"I guess that means I'll be working alone today," Sandy complained good-naturedly.

Brett stood. "Yes. You're on your own, Sandy. We'll see you later tonight."

Tess stood also, unsure where they were going. Was she to be alone with Brett now? How long had she hoped for this day and now that it was here, she was not certain how to react.

Sandy stayed seated, his hands gripping his tin cup. "Have a good day, Brett and Tess. See you for supper."

Brett retrieved the long Spencer rifle from the corner where Sandy had leaned the weapon, and then, together, he and Tess stepped from the café. More traffic filled the street now as they strolled slowly up the main street of Laramie. They didn't touch, although Tess eagerly wanted to hold Brett's hand.

Ace stood on the porch of the Bucket of Blood when they passed. Tess turned her face away, but not before she saw his taunting grin and the threatening gleam in his small eyes.

Ivan was nowhere to be seen when they passed the livery.

"You can take a day off from haircutting, can't you? Can we afford it?" Brett asked. Tess had been responsible for paying the tab at the general store and collecting coins in the coffee can atop the mantle. Brett had seemed relieved to hand that responsibility over to her.

Tess nodded. "We can afford to miss one day of work, Brett, but no more. We must stay on top of our debt."

"Our debt?" he repeated quietly. "I like the sound of that. We are truly a team now, Tess."

Together they crossed the log bridge spanning the Laramie River. Tess remembered that only yesterday, she'd considered jumping into the swift current to escape Frank Mercer. How different her plans had turned out in such a short time.

The small city lay behind them, and Tess could feel the warm morning sun on her bare head. Where had she left her bonnet? She must look a sight, she worried, in the same dress she'd worn since the day before. She lifted a hand to her hair and stifled a giggle.

"What's so funny?" Brett wanted to know.

Tess stared at the ground. "Well, I never imagined I would get married in this old dress. I always hoped for a special dress, something I put a lot of thought into," she said quietly. She touched her dark hair again and continued. "My hair must look frightful. I feel like I need a bath, and the quickness of the whole thing still takes my breath away."

Brett grinned before glancing around quickly and then handed the Spencer rifle to Tess. "Here, hold this," he ordered.

Tess received the heavy rifle awkwardly and watched as he scurried along the roadside, picking wildflowers.

"A bouquet for the bride," Brett said with fanfare as he handed the colorful bunch of flowers to Tess. He retrieved the gun from her.

Tess inhaled deeply, smelling the beautiful arrangement as she walked beside Brett, casting covert glances at him from the corner of her eyes.

They rounded the turnoff to the cabins and entered the deep woods. Blue jays squawked as they passed. A woodpecker drilled noisily into a dead pine, and fat, gray squirrels chirped warnings at sight of the couple.

Tess felt nervous. The intense tension of the previous night and the strain and fear she felt on the train platform had dissipated while they ate and chatted over breakfast. Now, with the crowd gone and Tess left alone with Brett, the same feelings of worry and anxiety creeped back into her. What would happen next?

Every step drew them nearer to the cabin, and Tess began thinking about what usually happens after a wedding. Was Brett thinking the same? Was that why Sandy had stayed in town, giving the newlyweds some privacy?

Suddenly, Tess felt frightened. She did not wish to be alone with Brett. Things were moving too swiftly for her.

The little bridge loomed into sight and then the yellow cabin where they would be alone. Tess frowned, realizing she'd been alone in this same cabin countless times before. But, now, something felt different. Nervous anticipation swept over her, causing her to blush and tremble.

"Brett," Tess spoke abruptly, breaking the long silence that had accompanied them up the slope. "What are we going to do now?"

They had reached the porch, and the young woodcutter halted, turning to face Tess.

He was handsome, she had to admit. His soft, hazel eyes sparkled as they studied her. He leaned against the roof support and smiled warmly.

"Well, I thought you said you wanted to clean up some. I figured to leave you alone to take a bath and put on a clean dress. I must tend to the mules and sharpen my tools for tomorrow. Then, if you're willing, I'd like to do what I always wished to do with my bride on the first day of my marriage."

Startled by his blunt and bold reply, Tess stared at Brett, her heart pounding in her chest. "And what is that?" she stammered, her eyes wide.

"Well, I'd like to spend some time in prayer, asking for God's blessing, giving our marriage to the Lord," he replied easily. "I hope to have a Christian union, where we mutually serve each other."

His reply startled her even more. Of course, she had wanted something similar for her marriage, but she'd wondered if such things were possible. Certainly, the marriage between Frank and her mother was nothing like what Tess hoped for herself. Still, she'd never actually believed she would find such a mate.

Silently, she thanked God for this man who stood before her. She smiled in return. "I would like that, too, Brett," she said softly.

Nodding, he leaned the rifle against the wall and turned away, starting for the trail to the makeshift barn. "I need to let the mules graze," he said over his shoulder. "Then do a few chores. I'll be back in a couple hours."

Tess watched him go, his easy stride taking him rapidly down the narrow trail until he was lost from sight among the tall pines. She stood on the porch a minute longer, simply looking around the clearing. This was truly her home now. She belonged here completely.

The bouquet of flowers she held reminded her that she was a new bride. Slowly, she turned and entered the cabin. The yellow of the pine logs still calmed her with their bright and clean beauty. Tess loved this spacious cabin, which smelled of fresh cut wood. And now it was hers too.

Locating a small pitcher, Tess placed the bouquet of colorful flowers in the center of the table. She looked at them, remembering Brett picking each one for her. He was being patient with her. This was his wedding day too, but he'd allowed her to prepare at her pace. She appreciated his thoughtfulness.

Tess wanted to go at her own speed. She was young and a little frightened of what was now expected of her, of any bride. That she loved Brett Calloway, this she knew. But everything had happened so quickly, and Tess wanted to process the previous night's events.

Gathering clean clothes and her flour sack towel, she strode down to the wash hole. A refreshing bath would do her good, Tess surmised.

The water felt cool and welcoming over her heated skin. Tess swam around the little pool a long time, allowing the water to comfort and soothe her. She kept a constant eye out for either of the returning men but saw no one.

Eventually, Tess crawled from the pool and dressed. She sought a warm, sunny place in the clearing to allow her wet hair to dry. Brushing the long tresses relaxed her and soon she felt unbelievably tired. The night before had been wearisome and long. Stress and anxiety had overwhelmed her for many hours, and now that she was able to relax, she found herself suddenly exhausted. Promising to only lay down for a few minutes, Tess walked back to the cabin and stretched out on the bed.

The sunlight streamed cheerfully through the glass window, and Tess snuggled into her cozy blankets. Her eyelids felt so heavy. Despite her excitement and anticipation for Brett's return, she could not keep her eyes open. Just a little nap, she said to herself. Tess closed her eyes and slept.

CHAPTER TWENTY-ONE

Tess awoke hours later. Shadows stretched across the clearing, dull light indicating dusk's nearness. She yawned, surprised she'd slept so long. The cabin seemed so peaceful and quiet. Then she remembered. She was a married woman. More than that, she was safe from Frank Mercer. All her fears had slipped away. This bed she laid in, in the cabin on the slope above Laramie, was her and her husband's cabin.

Tess smiled when she thought of Brett as her husband. The strong, handsome lumberjack was good to her. It was he who had come up with the plan to marry Tess and so thwart the designs of her wicked stepfather. Tess recalled the frustration that filled Frank's small eyes when he realized he'd been bested. "This was not over yet," he had said to Big Steve.

Suddenly, Tess felt afraid for Brett. Out of habit, she drew in a deep breath and exhaled slowly, allowing her thoughts to calm. *Be strong and courageous. Do not be afraid. God is with me. He will never leave me or forsake me.*

Tess crawled from the bed and stood, running a hand through her long hair. The bath had felt good. But she decided abruptly, she was hungry.

The door opened slowly, and Brett stuck his head in. "Oh, you're awake. I've been checking on you all afternoon. You must've been exhausted." He came in and moved close to Tess. "Are you starving? We haven't eaten since breakfast. And Sandy hasn't come home yet. He's being thoughtful, I guess," he added, turning away so she could not see the meaning in his hazel eyes.

"I was just about to fix toast. Will you join me?" Tess moved to the fireplace.

"Sounds great. I'll fetch some wood," Brett replied and went outside.

The fire had turned to gray ash. Any coals there might have been had died long ago. Tess put the kindling together and reached for the matches on the mantle. Rising, she walked outside to fill the coffeepot at the stream.

She saw Brett at the woodpile, stacking logs in his arms. She could only carry half of what he was able to hoist in one load.

Going down the bank of the creek, Tess stepped onto the plank bridge to the flat rock in the middle of the current. This plank had washed away once when the big storm had come and swelled the stream, but it'd only floated as far as the wash hole.

The water flowed fresh and clear. Tess remembered her bath from earlier and felt grateful that Brett had allowed her the time to freshen up and rest. He was very kind, thinking of Tess and her feelings.

She placed the now full coffeepot on the warming stone in the hearth while she prepared the toast. The last time she'd gone to the general store for supplies, she'd discovered a shipment of honey had arrived from back east. The sweet nectar would taste good on their bread now.

Brett prayed before they ate and then glanced at Tess as she reached for the toasted bread. "I would still like to go to the chapel and pray, if you don't mind."

Tess nodded, eager to comply. Could marriage really be this wonderful? If they were to make a proper go of matrimony, she wanted all the help they could muster. Walking with God would enable them to lean on the Lord's wisdom and help. His plan for marriage would ensure their success. Service to one another, love, forgiveness, support, encouragement, and patience was God's recipe for a solid union.

When they'd finished their meager meal, they started out to the chapel. Tess had walked the trail plenty of times in total darkness, but this time, Brett held out a hand to guide her over and around the rocks.

Tess placed her smaller hand in his broad palm, and the touch went through her like electricity, reminding her again they were together as man and wife.

Brett led her slowly toward the special place in the woods. Soon, they were crossing the giant fallen pine, and the gentle melody of the small waterfall came to her ears. The last gleams of sunlight fell on the tall cross at one side of the little glade. Brett walked to the rock bench in the boulder and sat down, still holding Tess's hand. Together they sat quietly for a few minutes, enjoying the musical sound of the stream at their feet and watching the final rays of sunlight disappear through the trees.

Peace filled Tess, and she felt amazed at how perfect this spot seemed. Only a few short months ago, she'd been wrought with fear and anxiety and troubles she could not carry alone. God had brought her here. Through accidents and coincidences that were neither, events had unfolded that brought Tess to this woodcutter's cabin. Laramie, not Chicago, had been her proper destination. The Lord knew that, even though Tess had not.

The easy friendship she shared with Brett had naturally evolved into love.

He turned to her, his eyes soft in the fading light. "I always thought I would begin my marriage by inviting the Lord Jesus to be at the center. Although our marriage didn't begin exactly like I thought it would." He smiled wryly. "I'm still overwhelmed that you're my wife."

He stared deeply into her eyes, and Tess thought she might drown in his gentleness.

"Tess," he continued softly. "I love you. You are a special gift to me from God. I promise to always treat you that way."

She said nothing, but watched him intently, afraid to spoil the moment with a foolish reply. He turned and bowed his head. For the next several minutes, Brett thanked God for his provision and the wonderful girl who now sat beside him. He prayed humbly, acknowledging the Lord's hand in all things.

He named God's many attributes and then asked the Lord for special things. Things like wisdom and guidance, humility and a gentle spirit toward his bride. He prayed for patience and the ability to serve when he was weak. He prayed for strength to be a good and godly husband. Finally, he ended his prayer and looked at Tess from the corner of his eyes. He gently squeezed her hand, letting her know it was her turn, if she wished to pray.

Tess often prayed aloud but not for anything so beautiful as that which Brett had just prayed. Her prayers had often been about her and her needs, her fears and her desire to escape Omaha. Tess had not spent much prayer asking for a loving spirit or the ability to forgive.

Now as she turned her thoughts to her new role as a wife, Tess prayed for these things. The ability to be patient and supportive to her husband. To be a source of encouragement and not one of frustration. She prayed she would always be open to the guidance and conviction of the Holy Spirit.

As the newlyweds prayed together, something pure and magical happened between them. Their spirits melted together. Christ fused their union in prayer and petition.

Finally, Tess concluded, and she gripped Brett's hand tightly. She had never felt so close to another living person.

He smiled down at her. "Thank you, Tess. I'm glad we began our marriage this way."

She returned his smile, shyly at first and then relaxed, pleased. "Me, too, Brett," she replied tenderly.

Slowly, he withdrew his hand from hers and lifted it to her face. Gently, he caressed her cheek before twirling a dark tendril of hair from her cheek, tucking the loose strand behind her ear. His glance shifted from her eyes to her lips and then back to her eyes and Tess tensed, guessing his intent. She'd never been kissed. Frank had never allowed any of the railroad workers to show her undue attention. Brett lifted her chin and Tess trembled, her eyes closing as their lips met.

As they kissed, Tess felt her heart leap as fire raced through her, igniting something unfamiliar within her. She leaned into Brett, wanting more, eager for his touch as he pressed his lips more firmly.

For a moment, time stood still, and Tess was drawn into a tornado, her mind whirling and stars bursting in her mind. Her arms encircled Brett's neck, holding him with a fierce grip.

They parted and Tess opened her eyes, her lids fluttering. She could see Brett was startled by the sensation, and he grinned at her. "Tess," he said, his voice now husky, "Can we … can we go back to the cabin?"

She dropped her gaze, saying nothing, nodding slightly.

Brett rose, and taking her hand once more, led Tess from the rock bench and over the fallen pine tree. She glanced one last time down at the beautiful clearing, etching the memory forever in her mind, and then stepped down from the giant tree to the trail below.

They walked slowly, as if in a dream. Brett held her

hand, guiding her lovingly around the rocks that still littered the path. Nervous anticipation filled Tess, but she didn't worry. She knew Brett would be kind and patient with her.

Pounding hooves disturbed her thoughts as they entered the clearing before the cabin. Tess stared as a buggy wheeled into the darkening yard.

"Hello, the cabin!" the driver called. Tess recognized Ivan Belmont's voice.

"Here, Ivan." Brett released her hand and stepped forward. The old hostler pulled hard on the reins and the horse snorted as it pranced, the buggy coming to a stop. He faced the young couple.

"Brett, Tess, I surely hate to intrude on your honeymoon, but I'm afraid I have bad news."

CHAPTER TWENTY-TWO

"What is it, old-timer? It can't be that bad, not on a day like today," Brett said with cheer as he shot Tess a warm smile, his hazel eyes sparkling in the dim light of dusk.

Mr. Belmont hesitated, glancing at Tess. The afterglow of twilight dimly lit his worried face. He rubbed the back of his neck and then gripped the reins tighter, leaning forward. "Perhaps you'd better go inside, Tess."

Tess stepped closer, placing a hand on the old man's arm. "What is it, Mr. Belmont? You can tell me."

He narrowed his eyes, staring bleakly at her before lifting a shaking hand to his bearded chin.

Tess felt her stomach tighten. "Mr. Belmont? You're scaring me. What's happened?" She sensed Brett move beside her.

The old man sighed. "Sandy is dead. I don't know how else to say it. He was found lying in the alley behind the Bucket of Blood, stabbed. No one saw anything or, at least, they're not talking. Big Steve says it was a robbery. Lord knows that's common enough in Laramie, but Sandy had no money. There's no reason he'd be dead."

Like a load of bricks, a heavy weight settled on Tess, overwhelming her. To go from the heights of happiness to the depths of despair so rapidly jarred her to the core. She bit her lip and reached for Brett's hand, gripping it tightly as she tried to comprehend the old man's message.

No one said anything for a long moment. Then, Brett shifted beside her. "I'll be back soon. Bar the door behind you and open it for no one." He looked into her eyes, and she could see the sparkle had vanished, replaced with something else, something dark and somber. He released her hand and strode rapidly to the porch to retrieve the Spencer rifle.

"Where are you going?" Anxiety swept through her as she watched Brett stalk to the buggy. She needed him. She wanted him to comfort her.

Brett scrambled into the buggy beside Ivan. "I'm going to town. I want to see Sandy for myself. Stay here, Tess."

Ivan slapped the reins, and the horse leaped into action. The buggy turned around, but Brett's eyes never left Tess as she watched them disappear down the trail to Laramie.

"I love you," he called and then they were gone.

Tess stood in the dark for a long time, retreating only as far as the porch as she listened to the sounds of the forest around her. A dry branch cracked and a pinecone tumbled among lower branches, but these were her only company as she searched the immense solitude that followed Brett's departure.

Finally, a distant train whistle wafted on the still air, drifting to Tess's straining ears, and only then did she turn to go inside the cabin. Closing the door securely behind her, she dropped the heavy bar in place and leaned against the plank door.

What would happen now? Who had killed Sandy? Only that morning, she'd shared breakfast with him. Now he was gone.

Tess remembered the rifle. Brett had taken the long gun. Was there to be a fight? Would he get injured, perhaps killed like Sandy?

With leaden feet, Tess walked to the fireplace and coaxed the glowing coals into life. She would not light a candle tonight.

God was sovereign. God was good. God had a perfect plan. God worked all things out for his glory.

Tess reminded herself of these truths as she knelt before the small blaze, feeding sticks into the hungry flames. It was God who'd brought her to this place. He was intentional. There were no accidents. A purpose had to be in this somewhere.

Through the long night, she prayed without ceasing. She prayed for Brett, for Ivan, for herself. She even prayed for the school mistress back in Ohio that Sandy had intended to ask to marry him.

Hours passed before she heard a horse coming to the cabin. The moon had passed its zenith, and only shadows remained where its bright rays had recently lighted the clearings and glades. Dawn waited, lurking in the final shadows of night.

A rough pounding sounded at the door. "Tess? It's me. Let me in," Brett ordered. She could hear the weariness in his voice.

Hastily, she removed the bar and opened the door. He stood there, hollow-eyed and haggard, as if he carried an unendurable weight on his shoulders. He placed the long rifle on the elk antlers over the door and then slumped on a bench. Staring into the flames, he ran a hand through his hair. "Is there any coffee?"

She reached for the blackened pot and hefted it, surprised by the heavy weight. When was the last time she'd made coffee? The events of the last few days swirled around her head like angry flies and she pushed them away, not remembering the last time she'd filled the coffeepot and not wanting to recall all of the recent troubling events.

Tess fidgeted around the cabin, stealing covert glances at her husband as she made the bed and swept the floor. Brett stared morosely into the fire. When the coffee simmered, she filled a mug for Brett.

Brett accepted the steaming cup with a nod. Tess could see how tired he truly was. He held the cup a long minute, continuing to stare into the fire, before he spoke again. "He was stabbed with a knife. Both Ace Moyer and Frank Mercer carry a blade. Many other men do too. But I think it was one of them who did it."

"Why do you say that? What did you see to make you think it's one of them?" Tess whispered.

Brett lifted the steaming cup and drank. "They were so casual about his death, like it didn't matter. I heard Big Steve tell Con Moyer to check the file at the Land Office tomorrow and see what claim Sandy had on the land. They're after the homestead."

Tess frowned, not understanding. "But Brett, that land is now yours. You told me so yourself that you and Sandy set it up that way from the beginning."

Brett nodded, lifting the cup for another gulp before continuing. "Yes, that's true. But they don't know that. They've been killing men for months, making the deaths look like robberies. Or Big Steve has been forcing men into gun fights and shooting them. Sandy had no gun. They killed him in the alley and left his body there. They'll discover tomorrow the land is now mine, and they'll be coming for me."

Tess gasped, her blood chilling at this news. If these brutes would kill men for their land, they would not hesitate to kill again, and Brett was an obstacle to their plans. Tess had heard Ace say so. Big Steve and his half-brothers were here to get rich, no matter the cost.

"What will we do, Brett?" Tess finally asked, wringing her hands. They had to prepare. Something must be done to get ready for an attack by these cold, hard men.

Brett bowed his head and then looked up and stared at

Tess. Tenderly, he reached a hand to her cheek and rested his palm there. "We will pray, Tess. I can shoot and maybe we can get one or possibly two of them, but in the long run, they'll get me. And that means you'll fall into their hands again. No, we must do something more than prepare to fight."

He lowered his head again, shaking it slightly.

She placed a firm hand on his arm. He looked up, weariness and defeat reflected in his eyes. She smiled. "If God is for us, who can stand against us?"

Brett nodded and his troubled eyes softened. "Thanks, Tess. I needed to hear that. You are just what I needed."

She patted his arm and then rose to get more coffee. The fire had gone low and a pale gray peeked in the eastern sky. Individual trees appeared, stepping from the dark mass of a dark forest.

Tossing a piece of wood on the fire, Tess stared into the flames for a moment. Sandy was gone. That fact still hadn't sunk in yet. And now, Brett held extensive land holdings. Three hundred and twenty acres, to be precise. Big Steve and the Moyers will probably find him a likely target. They'd soon discover they gained nothing from Sandy's death. Brett now owned the immense homestead.

Tess tilted her head. Or did he? Weren't the laws clear on that? A homesteader must live on the premises and show he's making improvements on the land. Brett and Sandy built cabins and were going to be partners in a sawmill. What now? Could Brett lose the additional homestead if he didn't occupy the land?

Troubled with the questions, Tess turned to Brett. The young man had fallen asleep at the table, his head resting on his folded arms.

She realized that he'd been awake the past two nights. She retrieved a blanket from the pile beside the stone fireplace. Tess draped the cover around his shoulders and then gently brushed her fingertips across his brow, tracing a path down his cheek. He was due for another shave, she mused.

Tess stood there a minute longer, praying for her new husband and hoping God had a plan for his protection. Things were about to heat up around Laramie, and Brett would be at the center of the commotion.

CHAPTER TWENTY-THREE

Brett still sat asleep on the bench when she silently left the cabin. She strode across the bridge, pausing for a moment in the middle to peer into the swiftly running stream below. Despite her resolve to give all her anxiety to God, Tess shuddered and hugged herself tightly, the apprehension welling within her.

A sense of foreboding crept into her bones, convincing Tess events were about to unfold they had not anticipated.

Brett and Sandy's goals of opening a sawmill and cutting timber for the building that was sure to follow the completion of the railroad had now stalled.

Could God handle this mess? Would he intervene on Brett's behalf? Tess knew that sometimes evil triumphed, even if only for a short time. Nevertheless, she hoped things would work out for her mate.

Sighing, Tess turned away from the clear stream and walked to Sandy's cabin. No one had been here since the occupant left yesterday morning. Someone should check in and make sure there was no food left out or anything else that needed attention.

Tess stepped hesitantly onto the hard-packed dirt porch. She was about to knock but stayed her raised hand. She didn't have to knock anymore. Sandy was dead.

Hinges creaked as she slowly pushed the door open. The stillness frightened her, and she tensed, not wanting to step farther inside. The air felt heavy, as if the empty cabin knew its owner was gone and would not return.

A gentle breeze fluttered the ripped edges of the brown paper window cover, the borders water stained and thin. Tess stared at it, watching the ray of sunlight stream across the dirt floor of the dark cabin. A dim, muted light shone through the greased paper, a marked contrast from Brett's own bright and cheerful cabin. Perhaps Brett would put glass in this window. It was, after all, his cabin now.

A frown tugged at her mouth. Brett would not place glass here, he still needed another pane for his own house. And a lamp.

Her glance dropped to the floor. Boot marks scuffed the dirt surface, pine needles scattered everywhere. Rubbish heaped in a corner, the same discarded pieces of leather and broken tools she recalled from before.

Tess's frown deepened. The cabin seemed as messy as on her former visit. Apparently, Sandy had not been much of a housekeeper.

Tess sighed as she rolled up her sleeves. Taking the broom from behind the door, she began to sweep, neatly arranging anything of value. She carried an armload of debris to the ash pile, a dim path revealing the way to the heap behind the cabin. Tess tidied things as she moved about the room.

As she worked, she noticed the mound of gray ashes covering the hearth. Another glance at the unmade bed made Tess wrinkle her nose. She began stripping the filthy blankets.

Although she hadn't intended on cleaning the entire cabin, now the idea struck Tess that it was good to keep busy. Tess liked to clean and feel the sense of accomplishment the task provided.

Dust swirled thickly as she swept, floating in the single shaft of sunlight that stole through the torn window paper. She tossed the bedding outside, promising to get to that later. She shoveled the deep pile of ashes into the metal bucket near the fireplace and made another trip to the heap behind the cabin.

She removed Sandy's spare articles of clothing from the pegs on the wall and added them to her pile of dirty bedding. Tomorrow might be a wash day, she surmised as she brushed her hands together and reviewed the mound of dirty clothes.

The sound of an approaching buggy drew her gaze. Tess stared across the creek as the horse pulled to a halt in the clearing. Ace Moyer and Frank Mercer studied Brett's cabin, still unaware of Tess's presence. The two men conversed quietly before stepping down and turning toward the small foot bridge. They had only stepped onto the wooden planks when they saw Tess.

She stood frozen in place, unable to move. She couldn't run, she couldn't scream to alert Brett. Tess looked at these two men who both had threatened her and her blood chilled. She was alone.

Her hand gripped the broom handle.

The breeze stirred, waving a strand of loose hair across her cheek, and she sensed the calm steal over her. She was not alone. God was with her.

The trio stared at each other for a long moment until Tess broke the awkward silence. "What do you want?" she demanded, brushing the rebellious strand with the back of her hand.

Frank grinned. Tess remembered that sinister smile and a shiver raced through her.

"We're here to see our new land," he said. "I didn't know it included you."

Ace laughed at Frank's crude joke. "Frank, this other cabin belongs to Calloway and Tess will be safe there. For now," he added with a wink.

Tess drew in a sharp breath and took a step forward, not retreating like she wanted to. Something pushed her forward with a strength she didn't feel. "This land is not yours. It belongs to Brett Calloway. Now, please turn around and leave."

She glanced over the two men's shoulders at Brett's cabin, but there was no sign he'd heard the visitors outside. If they wanted to, she knew they could simply throw her off Sandy's homestead. There was nothing she could do.

"Sandy is dead. His homestead is open again for claiming. We've claimed it and are taking possession," Ace explained. He took another step forward, Frank on his heels, but Tess raised a hand.

"Hold right there. You are mistaken," she said loudly, hoping Brett might hear them. "This homestead was filed with the particular understanding that should something happen to the owner, Brett Calloway would get first opportunity to file. He will be claiming this land today." She attempted a confident smile, but none would come.

Both men frowned and then exchanged skeptical glances. Ace shifted on the narrow bridge. "She's lying. She's trying to make us believe we can't get this land. Steve sent us and he would know what he's doing."

Frank nodded and scratched his whiskered chin. "Besides," he added sourly. "A homesteader must occupy the land they've filed on. Calloway cannot live here and in his own cabin. We'll get the land anyway."

Ace chuckled and started on again. Tess lifted the broom, unsure what she expected to do with it, but knowing she had to try something.

A rifle cocked in the clear air and both men halted, their malicious grins melting.

"The homestead is mine," Brett spoke from his porch. "And my wife will be occupying the cabin in my name.

We're married, so it's legal."

No one moved for a long moment. Tess could see the anger and frustration in Frank's cold eyes, and she smiled triumphantly at him. These men had not outsmarted her husband.

"Come on, Frank," Ace said, aware the big gun was still pointed at them. "They've won this battle, but the war is not over yet."

The little thief tugged on Frank's arm and together the two men retreated to their buggy, Brett continuing to cover them with the Spencer rifle.

As Frank lifted the reins, Ace turned to Tess. "This is not going to turn out the way you hope it is, Mrs. Calloway." He spat the title. "My advice to you is to leave now while your husband can still walk."

Frank chortled at Ace's veiled threat and then struck the horse with the whip. They drove from the clearing, dust hovering in the early morning sunlight after they departed.

The silence of the forest returned, and Brett lowered the long rifle. He carried the gun with him as he crossed the bridge to join Tess. The young woodcutter halted before her, and Tess read the weariness and strain that haunted Brett's hazel eyes. Suddenly, he smiled down at her, a sad smile of regret or fear as his hand went to her cheek.

Tess leaned into the warm, tender touch, closing her eyes and drinking in Brett's strength and gentleness. With abrupt comprehension, she realized she needed this man. He was her friend, her husband, her leader. Her eyes opened, and she smiled up at him in return, grateful he was with her.

"What are we going to do, Brett?" she whispered. She knew she would consent to anything he asked of her. He had given her sanctuary when she needed it, guidance and encouragement, too. Now she would submit to his leadership. She was his wife, come what may, she would follow him.

"They're after Sandy's homestead," Brett replied, dropping his hand to his side. "They'll stop at nothing to get what they want. They thought killing Sandy would give them this land. Learning that I now own it only made them turn on me. But they'll look for who has possession. I must go to town and check on the file. You have got to hold the cabin, Tess. No matter what happens, this land is ours."

She nodded, not saying a word, content to be near him. Brett nodded once before he turned and sprinted for the horse that Ivan had loaned him the night before. Clattering hooves pounded on the hard-packed dirt of the clearing and he was gone.

Tess remained where she stood for a moment longer. Then, finally, she turned away, praying for Brett's safe return.

For the remainder of the afternoon, Tess worked around Sandy's cabin. It felt odd saying it still belonged to Sandy when she knew the older man was dead. Nonetheless, she cleaned the house as if he would soon return and she wanted him to be pleased with her efforts.

The café would miss her this day, but there was little Tess could do about that. She hoped Mrs. Warren wouldn't be angry with her. Tess hadn't missed a single day of work since she'd begun at the café. She vowed she'd be there for the doughnut day tomorrow, though, no matter what.

She stopped abruptly, tossed her dirty cleaning rag into the wooden bucket, and sighed. Her gaze roamed the interior of her dead friend's cabin. Life had not turned out as she'd hoped. She tilted her head, grinning shyly, as she realized she didn't even know what she'd hoped for. Safety with friends in Chicago? Then what? That was as far as her shortsighted plans had gone. Now she was married to a wonderful man she hadn't known long. Love and happiness filled her, despite the troubles they now faced. God had known her innermost and true desires, and she'd been blessed with a Christian husband. Brett loved her and wanted good things for Tess. It was more than she'd ever hoped or dreamed. God knew Tess better than she knew herself.

She glanced heavenward and nodded. "Thanks," she whispered.

The day had far advanced by the time she finished cleaning Sandy's cabin. For the hundredth time, she looked down the road toward Laramie, but there was still no sign of Brett. Not wanting to sit and allow herself to worry, she chose to keep busy and carried the dirty laundry heap to the bathing pool. Tess spent another hour scrubbing blankets. Despite her resolve to not ponder on worrisome things, she couldn't keep her thoughts from Brett. Her mind whirled as she worked, acutely aware of the threat Ace Moyer had made before departing.

Tess scowled, her hands gripping the blanket beneath the water. Both she and Brett were now in danger. Frank Mercer would not leave Laramie when there was even a remote chance he might possess Tess again. With Brett out of the way, there would be no one to shield Tess from Frank's evil designs. The scoundrel would simply recapture Tess and be on his way.

No, she decided as she dunked the wet blanket one more time. She clenched her teeth as she wrung the water from the sodden bedding and shook her head. Frank Mercer would go nowhere with her.

CHAPTER TWENTY-FOUR

"Hello, Tess."

Brett's voice startled her, and she whirled. Despite her vigilance, he'd walked right up to her. His dark hair lay windswept over his furrowed brow and a heavy cloud hung in his hazel eyes.

She stared, concern sweeping over her as she dragged the wet blankets after her. Without another word, Brett reached for the heavy bedding and carried the load to the clothesline.

Tess helped Brett spread the blankets on the line, waiting impatiently for him to share his thoughts.

Finally, he turned, and Tess's heart ached at the sight of the deep scowl and torment on her new husband's features.

"Tess, let's go inside where we can speak freely. I don't trust these woods anymore. I feel the Moyers might shoot at me from cover if I stay outdoors." Brett glanced into the forest as he led the way to his cabin. Tess searched the dark woods, too, imagining sharpshooters behind every tree.

They were safe inside, and the door closed firmly behind them before Tess spoke. "Brett, I've been worried about you all afternoon. I've been praying for you too," she admitted, enjoying the relief she saw her words had on him. "Tell me everything while I put supper together." She moved to the sideboard and reached for the dough.

"I'll fetch some water and then I'll tell you all the news," he promised. Brett reached for the wooden bucket and, with a cautious glance outside, he hastened to the stream.

He returned quickly and filled the coffeepot as he spoke.

"I saw Big Steve when I returned the horse to Ivan. The marshal had the nerve to tell me to be careful. He's the one who hopes something will happen to me. I went to the Land Office and sure enough, the papers on Sandy's homestead were already laying on the counter. Ace and Frank had gone right away to the Land Office to check my story. It was all there, just like I'd said. Me and Sandy wanted it that way. Should anything happen to the other, there would be twenty-four hours for the other to claim the homestead before the land came up as unclaimed."

Tess made biscuits, listening attentively as Brett talked. He spoke rapidly, his words tumbling over one another, as if in a hurry to tell Tess all the details. He placed the coffeepot on the warming stone at the side of the fireplace before he lowered himself to a bench with a sigh.

"I paid the filing fee again," he went on with a bitter, humorless chuckle, one hand raking his unruly hair. "I used your wages to make the payment. I had no choice, Tess." A note of apology sounded in his weary voice.

Tess looked up, flour covering her hands. "Brett, my money is your money. You don't have to explain or apologize to me for what you did with it. I trust you."

Her simple statement seemed to mollify him and Tess watched as the tension melted from his strained features. "Thanks, Tess," he mumbled.

He took a deep breath. "Well, they were all on the boardwalk of the Bucket of Blood when I came out of the Land Office. They knew why I was there. The Moyers and Frank Mercer watched me closely as I went around town on my business, watched me like a hawk."

He scowled and glanced at the fire, watching the flames dance. "I wondered why they allowed me to come to town and file the new paperwork. Why not simply waylay me and put me out of the way? Then I understood. They wanted me to put the two homesteads into my name. Then, with me gone, they got double the land for half the work."

Tess could see the merit of the plan but realized again she'd be alone if anything happened to Brett. What would Big Steve and the Moyers plan for her with Brett out of the way? Would they kill her like they'd done to Sandy or was there a deeper game they played? Her stomach tightened as she thought of how both Ace and Frank looked at her. A shiver rippled down her spine.

Brett leaped to his feet, as if suddenly aware he wasn't helping the situation. He fetched bowls from the cupboard and held the pair up for her inspection.

"Only two bowls tonight," he said softly. Tess nodded. She missed Sandy too.

Dinner was a quiet affair. Both Tess and Brett's minds filled with their own troubling thoughts. Brett did say that he'd seen Mrs. Warren while in town and the kindly woman had understood the situation when Brett explained the reason for Tess's absence from the café.

"She told me she'd see you tomorrow," Brett reported. "She said it would be a doughnut day, and she couldn't do it without you."

Tess smiled to herself, wondering how the plump woman had managed before Tess's arrival at the café. "I'll look forward to being there tomorrow," Tess replied. Her gaze dropped to her coffee cup and then rose to meet Brett's across the table. "We'll need the money," she added quietly.

Brett nodded, the worrisome look coming back into his eyes. "I know, Tess. But we must have faith. The Lord is well aware of what's going on in Laramie. He'll take care of us," he said with a confidence Tess did not share. Where was her courage she'd worked so hard to develop?

She reached across the table and placed a hand on his arm. "What are we going to do, Brett? Sandy is gone and we have two homesteads, but you haven't been paid in weeks. How long can we hold on here?"

The events surrounding her coming to Laramie had taught her to trust God, but things were only getting worse. Was it truly God's will that she be here? She wondered if she and Brett would need to clear out of this wonderful mountain refuge.

She gritted her teeth and gripped her mug as she glanced at him from the corner of her eye. He would not go easily, Tess knew. Brett had worked hard to create this home and knew his mother and sister would be arriving soon.

The bench scraped as Brett stood. The lines of worry had come back to his forehead, making him look older than his years. Tess hated to see him this way, but she was frightened for their safety and future too. Would God intervene?

"God has a plan," Brett said definitively, as if reading her thoughts, but then paced like a caged cat. "We'll pray and trust."

He returned to the bench, and for the next half hour, the newlyweds prayed before the fire. Tess wished they could've gone to the chapel in the woods, but she knew it wasn't safe. Frank or the Moyers could be prowling around, waiting for an opportunity to kill Brett.

"I'll walk you to Sandy's cabin, Tess." Brett strode toward the door when they had finished praying.

Brett laid a hand on the latch and glanced at her. "We must be in possession of the homestead if we hope to keep it," he explained quietly after reading the question in her look. He turned his gaze away when he saw the anger spark in her eyes.

"You mean I will sleep over there alone?" she demanded, although that was precisely what she expected. Their sudden wedding had amazed her, but the days since that event had been filled with danger and death. Was she never to know a peaceful time with her new husband? Tess was angry, but she felt hurt even more. She turned away when she felt the tears well in her eyes. She wiped her face and glared at Brett, knowing this was not his fault.

Again, Brett refused to meet her heated glance. "I'll walk you over," he repeated, not replying to her question.

The two young people walked without speaking to the cabin across the stream. Brett carried blankets from Tess's bed and a candle. Not even the gentle murmur of the swift stream or the brilliant stars above could diffuse Tess's frustration. She didn't want to sleep alone in Sandy's cabin. Despite the cleaning she'd performed that very day, a somberness pervaded the dark cabin and filled Tess with memories of the recently killed older man she had shared the summer with.

Brett halted on the dirt porch of Sandy's cabin and handed the blankets and the dimly glowing candle to Tess. Glancing around, he spoke without looking at her.

"They will be looking for any excuse or opportunity to claim this land. The Homestead Act clearly says that the person who claims the land must occupy it. You are my wife, so that is why you must stay here. We don't want to lose this land."

Without another word, Brett strode rapidly back to his own cabin, his boots thudding on the wooden bridge.

Tess watched him go, frustrated by his leaving her alone at Sandy's cabin, but something more too.

The night was dark under the tall pines, but the clearing was brightly lit by the countless stars above. She watched Brett cross the bridge. A yellow rectangle of light flashed across his porch from the opened door and then he was gone. A moment later, the light in the window dimmed, and Tess knew he'd gone to bed.

For the entire time Tess had lived here, Brett had slept on the floor before the stone fireplace. The bed had become her bed, although it belonged to Brett before she'd arrived. With their new marriage, Tess had believed they would share it.

Slowly, sadly, Tess turned and entered the gloomy cabin. The hinges groaned as she pushed the door open. The glow of the candle reached dimly into the corners of the log cabin but was enough for Tess to maneuver the now familiar room.

Torn butcher paper rustled at the window, a gentle breeze invading her privacy. A chill ran down her back and she trembled. Should she start a fire? It wasn't too cold, but it would be by morning, Tess knew. At this elevation, it always grew cold at night.

She decided to worry about it in the morning. Miserably, she stared at the unmade bed. Sandy had slept here and now he was dead. The morbid thought disturbed her.

Tess placed the candle on a bench and threw the blankets onto the low bed. The room felt eerie and lonely.

Still dressed, Tess lay on the unfamiliar bed and pulled the covers up to her chin. She'd forgotten her night shirt in Brett's cabin.

The slight wind from the open window harassed the candle, making the yellow flame flicker and dance as Tess watched it, her despair mounting. That God had brought her to Laramie, she accepted. God had brought her to this place to meet Brett Calloway. That she was already married to the young tie cutter seemed unbelievable.

But the arrival of Frank and the killing of Sandy had left her wondering what God was doing with her. And now

Tess was alone in the dead man's cabin while her husband was in his own cabin across the creek. This was not how she thought she'd spend her wedding night.

Tess huddled under the blankets, wishing she could go to the peaceful chapel in the woods. Perhaps time there would bolster her courage or convince her of the wisdom of Brett's decision to put her in Sandy's cabin. But she knew this was not possible. Intruders might come in her absence.

Suddenly, a gust ruffled the ripped edges of the butcher paper, and Tess glanced at the small window just as the candle sputtered and went out. Total darkness enveloped the cabin. And her heart.

Tess gripped the blankets tighter and contemplated lighting the candle again. The matches lay on the mantle. Tess had seen them there today when she'd been cleaning. She wished now she'd started a fire. Even a glow from the coals would give off some friendly light.

Clutching the blankets to her throat, Tess stared into the darkness of the cabin, feeling reluctant to leave the scant security of the bed now and light the candle or start the fire.

Brett had not even looked at her when he'd left. Was he regretful of marrying her? With his partner now gone, was Brett unsure of his plans to build a sawmill? She worried that he'd know he'd made a mistake in marrying her. Perhaps he hadn't thought the whole marriage idea through very well.

Huddling in the dark, lonely and frightened, Tess cried herself to sleep.

CHAPTER TWENTY-FIVE

Tess awoke at dawn, exhausted and cold. Haunting dreams had plagued her all night, not allowing her to rest. Disturbing thoughts of Sandy, Frank, and Brett ran through her mind the entire endless night.

Something had awakened her. Tess lay in the still early morning chill, wondering what had brought her from her upsetting slumbers. Then, she heard the knock.

Quickly, she threw the blankets from her and padded swiftly to the door in her stocking feet, grateful now that she'd gone to bed fully dressed. Hesitant, she opened the door.

Brett stood upon the porch. "Tess," he said without any greeting. "I need to get to work early. With Sandy gone, my load has doubled. I'll be late coming home too. Please have supper ready," he commanded.

Without another word, Brett turned and stalked across the bridge to the waiting wagon. "Come on, Tip. Go, Mike," she heard him call to the big mules, a slap of reins and the wagon lurched in the dark blue of predawn.

She heard the lumbering wagon make its way down the lane and she listened until even his departure faded into the forest.

Slowly, Tess closed the door. She hadn't said anything to Brett, and he hadn't seemed to notice. Shivering from the morning chill, Tess hurried to the fireplace. She reached for the box of matches on the mantle and struck one quickly, bending to toss the flaming stick on the prepared pile of kindling. The fire caught slowly, then hungrily reached for the small pieces of wood. Soon, a blaze filled the fireplace.

Tess straightened and narrowed her eyes, studying the stark cabin in the light of the fire. She did not wish to stay in Sandy's cabin for breakfast. Indeed, there was no food in this cabin anyway. The three of them had always taken their meals in Brett's house. She reprimanded herself for not considering this before starting the fire. Tess sighed, knowing she'd just wasted a perfectly set fire for no good reason.

A tentative hand went to her dark hair. The long tresses needed to be brushed, but she didn't even have her personal toiletries here. The move to Sandy's cabin the night before had been so sudden and unexpected, Tess had no time to prepare.

It took only a minute to make the bed and push the bench under the table. She placed the short stub of candle in the center of the table with the box of matches. If she had to return here tonight, she would know where the lighting materials were located.

Tess pulled the bigger sticks from the blaze, allowing the fire to die down a little before she walked from the warmed room. She would return to Brett's cabin for some coffee and her clothes. Tess could not be absent from the café today. The Warrens counted on her to help on doughnut day.

As if trapped, cold air hovered above the stream as Tess hurried across the little bridge. She hadn't even brought her coat the night before.

Eagerly, she pushed into the cabin Brett now lived in alone. The air within felt warm, much warmer than Sandy's with the torn window cover. A bright glow from the hearth told Tess that the fire would be easy to encourage.

She tossed a few sticks on the coals and the fire blazed

cheerily. Tess brushed her long hair with patience, wanting to take time to put her anxious thoughts in order.

She cared too much for Brett to see him harmed. Despite his possible regret of their marriage, Tess had none. But she admitted this feeling might be one-sided. His actions the last day seem to indicate this.

Of course, he'd been overwhelmed with the death of his partner and the demands of keeping the land, Tess mused. Brett's fate and that of his hard-earned home surely must be weighing heavily on the young man.

Tess laid the brush aside and walked to the coffeepot. Liquid sloshed heavily inside the blackened pot and she grinned. He didn't have to leave some coffee for Tess, but he had.

Recalling the tears of the previous night, Tess looked up. "Lord, don't let me think ill of Brett. Let me be patient with him. Perhaps there's good reason for the things he's doing. Let me give him grace and hope for good things."

There was still one clean dress hanging on the pegs in the wall. Tess dressed, promising to wash her clothes before walking to Laramie. The sudden thought of the woodland chapel made her hurry and clean the cabin after preparing a hasty breakfast. Soon, she made her way through the forest toward the tall cross in the small glade beside the waterfall.

Sunlight dappled her path and warmed her shoulders as a fat squirrel with bushy gray tail barked irritably at Tess. The familiar trail seemed to beckon, and she found herself quickening her pace, eagerness mingling with anticipation as she neared her destination.

The fallen monarch of the forest posed no obstacle now as she mounted the steps Brett had fashioned alongside the dead pine tree. Clambering down the other side, Tess found her way quickly to the stone bench. A crow flew by, and Tess saw the gleaming black of his wings. Only this visitor disturbed the deep solitude of her woodland refuge.

Tess looked at the roughly hewn cross Brett had fashioned and placed in a low hummock across the warbling stream. The Lord Jesus had died on such a cross as this. Died for her, Tess knew. Mrs. Sellers, Tess's schoolteacher, had told Tess about the cruel way Jesus had died. He suffered so we did not have to, his ransom paying our debt to a holy God, our sins washed away.

The truth of this redemption given to Tess still amazed her and caused her to wonder. Why would God do that for evil people? Why send his son to die for *all* our sins?

The answer came to her, surrounding her with the truth, embracing her with its simplicity. Love. God's love was why he'd sent Jesus to pay our debts. For God so loved the world that he gave his only son.

Tess felt the peace she'd been seeking slowly creep into her restless soul. Whatever Brett's feelings about regret or frustration or anxiety, Tess would wait on the Lord. Like Esther in the Bible, Tess had been uniquely placed in this moment and place by God. She would trust that, believe that a purpose was still to be revealed to show why she'd been brought here. God did not make mistakes.

Abruptly, Tess smiled. The Lord was eager to help his people. He was the perfect father, perfect in his actions. His guidance, his trials, even his discipline were all intended to grow his people in love, mercy, and understanding. God loved her, Tess knew, and she gloried in his presence.

She glanced at the sun, marking its location above the trees. It was time to start for town. Tess didn't want to be late today after missing work the past two days. The Warrens had been very kind to her, and she wished to show them respect and diligence in return.

A glance at the cabin across the stream revealed nothing

seemed amiss when she returned to Brett's house. After gathering the scissors and the shaving brush and razor, Tess closed the door behind her and headed down the trail toward Laramie.

Ace and Big Steve came to her mind as she stepped silently on the trail, the thick mat of pine needles spongy under her shoes. Big Steve Long was the most disreputable lawman that had ever existed, Tess surmised. The large man used his office as a cover to perpetrate crimes and stay above justice, and no one could do anything about the marshal's shootings.

Not even Sheriff Boswell could stop this crime spree in Laramie. And now Frank Mercer had joined this dangerous group. These thoughts filled Tess's mind as she strode to town. She must believe that despite the terrible situation she now faced, God was present. He might be silent, but he was not absent.

Again, Tess wondered about God's plan but forced the questioning thought from her mind. He was the potter, she was the clay. His will would be done. She need not understand, only obey and submit to his perfect will.

Do not fear, Tess coached herself again. Be strong and courageous. Wait on the Lord.

Mr. Belmont's livery loomed before her. She hadn't even remembered the turn onto the main road that followed the tracks. She'd been so engrossed in thought that she hadn't paid attention to her location.

She frowned. That was not good. Any of the Moyers or Frank Mercer could've easily surprised her on her way to town. She promised herself to be more alert from now on.

The stump where she cut hair was still in position, and Tess would be there that very afternoon, Lord willing. She had missed the conversations with the railroad men and the talks with Ivan.

Con leaned easily against the porch support as Tess walked past the Bucket of Blood. The bartender held a cigar in his teeth but removed it when he sighted Tess. Nodding to the girl with a threatening sneer on his narrow face, Con stabbed the thick cigar between his teeth. Tess stiffened and the small hairs along the back of her neck bristled, knowing his small, beady eyes followed her as she passed the Chinaman's Palace and then onto the café at the end of the long street.

Tess tried to ignore the little thief, but her curiosity got the better of her and she glanced behind her as she climbed the steps to the café. Sure enough, Con still watched her. She felt the heat rise to her neck as she gripped the doorknob. She would try hard to practice what she preached. Despite her fears, she would hold her head high and truly trust in God's protection.

Mrs. Warren greeted her warmly when Tess entered the crowded café. "Doughnut day is always crazy," the large woman reminded Tess as she watched the young girl hasten to tie her apron. She began moving about the room, delivering doughnuts to seated groups of customers.

Mr. Warren and the cook could not make the doughnuts fast enough. Tess knew they'd both arrived early on this day to begin the intensive work of producing hundreds of doughnuts.

Many of the men greeted Tess by name. She had worked in Laramie all summer, working at the café or cutting hair. Tess realized she liked the feeling of being a part of the railroad town. She'd become familiar with many of the regular customers and was often able to remember their names.

Tess grabbed a large platter of doughnuts from the window between the dining room and the kitchen, and then rushed them to a noisy table of Irishman who hooted gleefully when the plate clattered before the hungry workers. "Thanks, Tess," they called boisterously. She moved away quickly to fetch more of the tasty delicacies.

She recalled then how these same men had tried to protect her the day Frank had come to town and she smiled.

Cutting hair later that day reinforced this feeling. Some of the men were not due for another haircut yet but insisted on getting a trim anyway. Tess readily complied, grateful for the dimes they paid her.

That night, she'd placed supper on the table just as a very tired and haggard Brett came home. The young man could barely keep his eyes open while he ate the soup Tess served him.

"I'm working twice as hard as before," he explained, but Tess already knew why he was so weary. "With Sandy gone, I must do his work too. I need the money and soon snow will make it difficult to cut ties. I'll be making less when the snowstorms come," Brett said.

She hoped he'd be able to rest a little when winter finally did arrive, possibly allowing him to take time off from the back-breaking pace he'd set for himself.

For the next few weeks, the young woodcutter pushed himself to heroic lengths. He would begin early each day and come home only when it was too dark to swing an axe. His steady work pattern impressed Tess.

Brett was often too exhausted to undress for sleep but never failed to converse with his young wife. He seemed hungry for her words, her presence. He demanded every detail of her day, hanging on every word, yet sometimes he even slept in his dirty clothes.

Tess was more than concerned at the incredible workload Brett set for himself each day. He seemed to be killing himself for his dream. "I must make as much as I can while the weather holds," he informed an anxious Tess one night when she expressed worry over his exhausting workload. "Besides," he added quietly. "We need to occupy both cabins. There is no real need for me to come home early anyway."

Despite his incredible fatigue and amount of work, Tess continued to pray for her new husband and hope that one day things would improve between them.

It was the old hostler that gave Tess her first inkling of how hard Brett was truly working and why. One day, as she trimmed the old man's gray beard, she had begun to tell the interested man about her life at the cabins.

"Brett comes home very late every day," Tess complained, leaning the old man's head back and dragging the razor up his neck. "He's working so hard, I wonder if he even wants to come home. He's only there long enough to eat and sleep. He's obsessed with cutting ties as long as the weather permits. He says snow will slow him down."

The razor moved expertly around Ivan's neck, taking the small hairs off without a nick or trace of blood. Tess wiped the blade on her shaving towel and took another swipe.

"Have you wondered why he's keeping such an intense pace?" Ivan spoke between clenched teeth.

"Hush," Tess commanded as she snipped at his scruffy beard with the scissors. "Well, of course I have," she snapped, bending down and trimming carefully.

"The boy is in love with you, Tess, and he wants to provide for you. With Sandy gone, Brett hopes to make enough money soon to hire a new partner."

Tess stepped back from the livery man's surprising words. She gazed at him skeptically, her eyes narrowing as she studied the old hostler. "How do you know this?" she demanded.

Mr. Belmont leveled his head once more and looked

sternly at Tess. "He comes to town sometimes to get new supplies or have his tools sharpened at the blacksmith's shop. I talk with him when I can. Not only is he hoping to find a new partner, but this mess with the Moyers and Big Steve has made him very concerned for you."

"Me?" she asked. Had he truly been so preoccupied with other things that it would not allow him to enjoy his new marriage?

"He's greatly worried that something will happen to him and you will be left all alone with no one to protect you. Besides the worry he has about you, he's trying to bring his family here from Minnesota. They've been waiting for Brett to get established before he sends for them. The sawmill was to provide a living for his mother and sister," Ivan explained.

His words startled her. She'd only been thinking of herself. Of course, these other situations must be weighing heavily upon Brett too. Suddenly, Tess felt sorry for her husband. She'd been wrong to judge and only see things through her perspective.

Her comb lifted absently and she worked on, her mind elsewhere as she trimmed his beard. The old hostler tipped his head back again, allowing Tess room to work.

They remained silent for a few minutes, each preoccupied with their own thoughts. The sun felt warm on Tess's back. Memories of the bitter cold winters she had endured in the little shack in Omaha made her appreciate the sunny days of summer here in Laramie. The cabins Brett owned were a big improvement over the drafty shack she used to live in with Frank and Mama. Winters in the plains city had been brutal from the fierce northern winds as much as from the drifting snow.

Would she still be here when the first snow fell? Thoughts had begun to creep into Tess's mind about leaving Laramie and returning now to Chicago. Her marriage to Brett had saved her from Frank but nothing more.

Regardless, if Brett didn't care for her anymore, Tess was now in a position to leave for Chicago with a little money in her pocket. Despite the financial demands of the homesteads, Tess had managed to make enough at the café and haircutting to put a small sum aside. She was prepared to depart for Chicago if she deemed the move a wise one.

But she was no quitter, and Mr. Belmont was confident she was overthinking things. Brett was simply worried about many concerns, he said. Before, he had Sandy to help carry the load. Now, Brett was alone to make the decisions and plan for his future.

Tess smiled as she finished with Ivan. Shaking the towel vigorously, she stepped back from the old man. Ivan was right. She would be patient. It was too soon to make hasty decisions that might have long lasting repercussions. To leave for Chicago now would mean walking away from her new marriage, her job, and her future. She still loved Brett. He was a good man, although lately he'd seemed preoccupied, despite his nightly conversations.

The hostler's sincere words had struck home for Tess. She would remain the patient and supportive wife, as the Lord would have her do.

"All done, Mr. Belmont," she said as she stepped away from him.

The livery man rose, running a hand up his smooth neck in appreciation. "Thanks, Tess," he said as he tossed a dime on the stump. He turned to go but not before Tess reached quickly for him, grasping his arm.

The old man turned, and his clear eyes twinkled with fondness as he stared down at her. They'd grown close, their friendship deepening as the summer passed.

"Mr. Belmont, thank you. I needed to talk. Thank you

for your wisdom."

He smiled. "It is always a pleasure to talk with you, Tess. You've come to be like a granddaughter to me. God is good. Trust in him." He patted her hand before turning and limping toward his livery barn.

Tess watched him go, her thoughts turning to Brett. If he was troubled as Ivan suggested, how could she help?

Tess carried the painted sign to its place in the big livery. Turning toward home, she pondered ways to show Brett she was still committed to supporting him.

September had come to the mountains and frost dotted the open places among the pines each morning. By afternoon, the still warm sun scoured the forest, releasing the fresh pine scent that lingered among the trees.

Her mind wandered back to their first day together as man and wife, when they had walked hand in hand to the woodland chapel. There, among the pines of the hidden nook, they had prayed to be servants to one another. She and Brett had enjoyed their first kiss. But since then their marriage had been stalled by the demands on Brett and the threat of the Moyer brothers.

Tess walked steadily now, tired from the day of work in Laramie but excited by these new resolutions to think of ways to serve Brett. She could not go into the woods with him and cut timber. Tess had seen how the men swung the long axes, swift and accurate. She had often watched Brett cut a pile of firewood in minutes—the task would have taken her over an hour to accomplish.

No, she couldn't work with him, she admitted. But she could work *for* him. Already, Tess was responsible to make all the meals for Brett and do the normal cleaning. She felt adept at these chores and completed them quickly and confidently, as he did his own work. But she hadn't tried to do extra. Perhaps she should show Brett how much she appreciated his efforts.

Abruptly, Tess halted. Glancing over her shoulder, she decided she hadn't gone too far from town. Spinning on her heel, Tess hurried back into Laramie. It took only a few minutes to retrace her steps to the café. Mrs. Warren expressed surprise to see Tess when she reentered the busy café.

"I was hoping I could take a pie. I'll pay for it out of my wages," Tess said hastily, hoping this delay wouldn't hamper her plans to do something nice for Brett.

The plump woman readily agreed. "There is a fresh apple pie right here."

"Thank you, Mrs. Warren," Tess replied as she accepted the pie and departed.

In addition to the pie, Tess carried a dozen flour sacks bunched under one arm as she trudged along the tracks. Mrs. Warren had given Tess several such bundles over the last few weeks. Hopefully this winter, while storms raged across the mountains, she'd have time to make the curtains and towels she wanted. Her eyes sought the rare wildflower that lined the trail. Only a few months ago, the road had been lined with flowers of all colors. Now, at this late season, none of the colorful plants remained.

Balancing the pie precariously in one hand, the flour sacks still tucked under her arm, Tess stooped to pluck a few long-stemmed grasses. She would now have to hurry to return to the cabin and prepare something special for Brett.

Ahead, the dead pine tree indicated the turnoff to the cabins, and Tess went swiftly into the trail. The dark forest wrapped around her, but this time Tess didn't notice, intent on her evening event.

By the time Brett arrived later that night, dusk had fallen, the sun having just disappeared over the mountains. Tess heard him drive the team past the cabin and tossed another log on the fire, the blaze leaping cheerily. She brushed the bark from her hands as she glanced at the candle, noting with satisfaction the merry glow reflected on the glass window.

Tess met Brett that night at the door. She'd brushed her long dark hair and had replaced her dress from earlier with his favorite pale yellow one.

He stared at her, and she saw his weariness slip away.

"I'm glad to see you, Brett." She smiled warmly, hoping he sensed her desire to please him. He straightened and his eyes widened as he surveyed the room behind her. "I have a surprise for you."

Brett followed as she led the way inside the yellow cabin.

The pine walls gleamed brightly, a sense of cheer permeating the spacious log cabin, warm and welcoming. The usual candle sat on the table, but an additional one sat on the cupboard, lighting even the darkest recesses of the room. She had placed her bouquet of long stems and cattails on the table too, adding a splash of color to the room. She hoped he noticed that a load of additional logs had been stacked beside the chimney, his after dinner chore already completed. The smell of fresh bread filled the air, and Brett's eyes sparkled as he turned to look at her. She stood near the fire, her hands folded demurely in front of her. "I don't know what to say," he stammered. "The cabin has never looked so good."

He walked slowly to the bench. Tess turned so quickly that her dress twirled with the sudden movement, her heart pounding with anticipation. Soon, she placed a steaming cup of coffee before Brett along with a thick slice of bread and a bowl of soup.

Seating herself across the table, Tess bowed her head. "Dear Lord, thank you for this meal and help make me a good wife. Let me be patient and understanding with my new husband. Let me remember always that you brought us together to serve one another. Amen."

Tess took up her spoon and began to eat. "How was your day?" she asked after a moment. "Did you get to that stand of pine over east of here like you wanted to?"

Brett stared. "I didn't know you heard me say that."

"Of course, I did. I hear everything you tell me."

Brett frowned but then reached for his piece of bread and tore a huge chunk from the crust. "How was the café today? It wasn't doughnut day, was it?"

⁣⁣⁣⁣⁣⁣⁣⁣⁣

Tess looked at him as he stuffed the bread into his mouth, pleased at his interest in her day. "No, that was yesterday. I should've brought you some. I will next time," she promised. "I had a good day, thanks for asking. I even gave Ivan Belmont a shave today," she added. She wondered if the old hostler's advice was working.

Brett smiled. "I spoke with Ivan a few days ago. He's a good friend."

"Yes, he is," Tess agreed. This was going better than she'd expected. Rather than merely hanging his head tiredly until he was through with supper, Brett was participating in a real conversation, not merely listening to her recital of the day's events. Tess liked it.

The meal passed easily, and Tess realized how much she'd missed Brett. A little effort on her part had drawn him into the evening and she smiled, pleased at his attention. She enjoyed getting reacquainted.

Tess rose, taking the dirty dishes with her. "I have apple

pie for dessert. I know it's your favorite." She refilled his empty cup and then placed a large slice of pie before Brett. She watched him as he ate, enjoying each morsel, until his plate was cleaned. "Well, tomorrow will be here soon enough. I know you need your rest," Tess remarked as she rose to leave. "I'll clean the dishes tomorrow."

Brett stood quickly, almost upsetting the bench under him. "Thanks for the wonderful supper, Tess. I really appreciate it. May I walk you home?"

Tess didn't reply as she dropped her gaze and then smiled softly at Brett. He hurried to help drape her shawl around her. Resting his hands lightly on her shoulders, Brett leaned down and whispered in her ear. "Please, Mrs. Calloway. Can I walk you home?"

His warm breath made Tess tingle. She loved the feel of his strong hands on her shoulders. "Of course, Mr. Calloway," she replied.

Brett reached for the door and held it open. Together, they strode to the bridge, Tess's stomach churning with butterflies. When they'd walked half its length, Brett put a hand on Tess's arm and halted her there.

Silently, they stood over the swift running stream, a sliver of moon peeking through the dark trees. The musical melody of the gurgling water below them seemed to calm Tess's quickening heart. She suddenly felt both awkward and excited.

The dim moon shone bleakly, and a foreboding chill filled the clear air, as if nature warned of impending colder times. An owl hooted from down the lane toward the tracks, but the darkness of the forest did not bother Tess tonight with Brett standing so near, his arm looped tightly around her slim waist.

Tess shivered and leaned into him, liking the firmness of Brett's hold. He felt her shudder and, mistaking its meaning, spoke hurriedly. "I'm sorry, Tess. It's cold out here and I'm selfishly keeping you outside." Brett guided her toward Sandy's cabin. He did not, however, remove his arm from around Tess's waist.

The young couple stepped together onto the dirt porch. Tess turned to face Brett, and the woodcutter drew her suddenly into his arms. Without hesitating, Tess leaned forward, her eyes closing as she tilted her face to his. She felt his warm lips press against her own, her mind suddenly whirling around and around.

Thoughts of their first kiss at the small clearing by the cross came to her, causing Tess to blush with the memory of her eagerness for his touch. This was her husband, and she wanted to stay in his arms.

She felt him draw from her, breaking the magic spell, his breathing deep and raspy. Her eyes remained closed, not wishing to see Brett retreat from her. Perhaps if she kept her eyes shut, he might kiss her again.

"Goodnight, Tess," Brett whispered softly, then he was gone.

CHAPTER TWENTY-SIX

Tess's eyelids fluttered open in surprise of Brett's sudden departure. The closing of his cabin door across the stream confirmed that Brett had indeed fled.

She touched her lips, the warmth of their second real kiss still lingering. That hasty one she'd received on their wedding night certainly couldn't count as a kiss. Not compared to this one. Tess smiled.

But why had Brett raced away? Perhaps he felt the same apprehension and unfamiliarity she now experienced. Or maybe he feared the inevitable conclusion of such an inflammatory kiss if he stayed. Regardless, Tess promised herself to be patient. Brett was her husband now and she would wait for him.

Besides, the perfect moment would arrive in God's timing, not hers. Tess was convinced the kiss would not be their last. She turned to enter the cold cabin.

Despite the chill, Tess chose not to start the fire. Instead, she hurried to light the candle she'd left on the table. Her searching fingers found the matchbox and soon the match flared brightly in the dark room. Placing the candle again on the bench within easy reach, Tess undressed rapidly and hung her pale yellow dress on a peg.

The bed creaked as she leaped into the cool blankets. Tess huddled beneath the covers, recalling Brett's tender kiss. A thrill ran through her, but she wasn't sure which had caused the shiver, the cold or her joy.

As the chill slowly receded beneath the warming

blankets, she thought again of the evening.

Mr. Belmont had been right. The hard work of these past weeks along with Sandy's sudden death and the heavy responsibility burdening Brett had made him distant and neglectful. Tess needed to be patient and forgiving. To show support to her new husband rather than blame and demand his attention. Tess had anticipated his preoccupation with other demands and concerns at the start of their marriage, but now Tess longed to fulfill her duty as a good wife.

Supper had been no amazing meal, but Brett had certainly thought of it as such. The apple pie, however, had been a nice touch, Tess thought, pleased she'd remembered his favorites. The result of the thoughtful meal had turned out better than she'd hoped for. The pie, the wild foliage, and Brett's favorite dress had all worked together to make him feel special and loved.

Slowly, the bed warmed under Tess and she relaxed, her giddiness slipping away as her tense muscles loosened. Puckering her lips, she thought of the kiss again and blew out the small candle.

She lay back, staring up into the dark rafters above and sighed, feeling utterly content. Despite having Frank on her trail, possibly hunting Brett, despite sleeping in a dead man's cabin, despite the prospect of endless toil and hardship, Tess felt grateful for the brief moment of peace and security she'd enjoyed in Brett's strong embrace.

She sighed again into the darkness as a gentle breeze rustled the torn paper at the window. Yes, even the cold couldn't dispel her joy. She loved Brett Calloway, and Tess looked forward to serving her mate all the days of her life.

"Dear God," she breathed softly into the darkness around her. "I love you, and I know you love me. Thank you for taking me from Omaha and bringing me here. I found what I was looking for. I thought it was supposed to be in Chicago, but you know the desires of my heart. Thank you, Father, that you know me so well. I have love, safety, happiness. I pray that these wicked days that surround us will end soon. I will continue to pray for this to happen, but in the meantime, let me be patient, trusting, and a servant. Goodnight, Father."

||||||||||||||||||||||||||||||||||

The next day began like so many others with Tess making Brett breakfast and promising to have supper waiting for him when he returned that night. The ease and comfort that they'd always enjoyed with one another returned, and yet, a new joy had entered the yellow cabin as well.

Brett pulled the mules to a halt before the cabin. He seemed to sit taller upon the high wooden seat. A few rebellious tufts of hair showed from under his hat. Tess reminded herself that he needed a haircut as she stood on the porch, watching him closely. The bright hazel eyes she had come to love were hidden now in the shadow of his wide brim.

"I look forward to seeing you later, Tess," he called with a casualness that couldn't conceal the intensity in his voice. Then, lowering his head, he shifted and fumbled with the leather reins but then looked up again. "I love you, sweetheart," he said swiftly and slapped the reins.

The mules pulled against their harness and the heavy wagon lurched forward as she stared at Brett's retreating form.

Tess spent a pleasant hour cleaning Brett's cabin, noticing again how much light the glass in the window allowed inside, reflecting cheerily on the yellow peeled logs of the walls and glistening on the freshly mopped flagstones. She would have to remind Brett of the torn butcher paper that still hung over the window in Sandy's cabin. He'd have to replace it before winter truly arrived. In the meantime, she'd fill the space with flour sacks to keep out the chill.

Tess stopped abruptly, her broom in her hands. Perhaps she should stop calling it Sandy's cabin. The log house across the creek belonged to her and Brett now.

She frowned at the thought of her and Brett in separate cabins. Weren't a man and wife supposed to share a house?

Tess blushed at the thought of sharing a bed with Brett but lifted her chin defensively. Well, why not? They were married now and that's what married people did and … where babies came from. She giggled, a little embarrassed at this idea. And then her chin lifted again. Why not babies? Certainly, Tess had always assumed she'd have children when she married.

These muddled thoughts followed Tess as she walked to the wash hole. She scrubbed their dirty clothes and hung the garments to dry on the long clothesline attached to the corner of Brett's cabin.

After a quick swim in the wash hole, Tess put on her simple calico dress. She would not wear her pale yellow one today. That outfit was Brett's favorite, and she'd attempt to save it for special occasions. Mr. Belmont had talked of starting a Sunday church service under the big oak tree where Tess cut hair. Perhaps she would wear it to such an event as that, if she were ever off on Sundays. Tess had also considered asking Brett to come home early one day so she could treat him to a meal at the café. It would be a date, she thought excitedly, and she could wear the special dress then.

Fall had come to Laramie, and with it were the concerns of impending winter. Extra stores of wood and the window coverings, of course, would have to receive attention soon enough. But for today, Tess allowed her mind to wander along less difficult challenges. She thought of Brett and their life together. The thought of one day living in a house together and of children.

She ignored the fat, gray squirrel that chattered angrily at Tess as she passed on the wooded trail. The fear of Frank and Ace and the numerous robberies and killings in Laramie faded as she considered how many baby things she could sew with the flour sacks from the café. Perhaps, if they made enough money after Brett was paid for the railroad ties he'd already cut, they could buy real store-bought fabric.

Was there any rush to make baby clothes when she and Brett didn't even live together? A heated surge of frustration coursed through her veins, but Tess fought the sensation. She would be patient. Things would be better one day. Brett needed her to be supportive.

Would the threat of having their homesteads taken from them ever be gone and allow them to live together? Would the Moyers and Big Steve Long always be watching for any opportunity to strip them of their land?

Again, she pushed these unanswerable questions aside and focused on what she could do now. Tess would work hard, hoping for better times. She could love Brett and serve him as he continued to struggle with the incredible responsibility that weighed on him.

The buildings of the frontier town loomed ahead as a new thought came to Tess. What if things never got better? What if she and Brett were destined to always struggle?

The words from that fateful night she spent in the Bucket of Blood came flooding over her. For better or worse. In good times and bad. Tess had made a vow before God to try hard to be a good wife, despite the circumstances that surrounded them.

The livery barn appeared, but Mr. Belmont was nowhere in sight. Tess peered into the wide doors of the tall barn as she passed, hoping to see her friend. Undoubtedly, she would see him this afternoon when she returned for her sign.

She passed the Bucket of Blood next and increased her pace, anxious not to be noticed by its inhabitants. The Chinaman's Palace always intrigued her curiosity with its bright red and yellow paintings, but she did not slow down.

The café was busy and noisy when Tess entered. Mrs. Warren patted her sweaty brow with her apron before she greeted Tess. "The shift change has come in, and the café is crowded. I'll have to stay with you today, Tess," Mrs. Warren called, her plump face shining from exertion.

Tess felt relieved to have help. She enjoyed working at the café, but it was hectic when they were too busy. She'd appreciate the older woman's assistance.

The four-hour shift passed rapidly. By time the shift had ended, Tess was even more grateful Mrs. Warren had remained. Many more customers than usual had dined at the café today. Now, however, only a few old timers sat at their tables and enjoyed coffee refills.

Tess thought of the hot meal she'd soon enjoy. The smell of good food had teased her this past hour, and Tess was ready to relax and eat something.

"Miss? Could I get another piece of pie?" An older man called to Tess, waving his fork in the air. She frowned to herself, eager to be off duty.

The Overland Stage rumbled noisily past the café, a cloud of dust following. Tess felt only vaguely aware of the coach's arrival as she moved to the kitchen to retrieve another slice of pie.

"Miss? More coffee, please," another customer called.

The man shook an empty pot at Tess. She recognized Sheriff Boswell.

Tess huffed, impatient and hungry, as she took the pot with a forced smile and hurried to the kitchen. Mr. Warren glowered when he saw her leave the pot on the counter. "Don't leave an empty there," he growled. "Fill it at the pump and put it on the stove."

Tess hastened outside and then sighed, filling the empty pot before picking up a fresh one to fill empty cups.

She'd only begun to untie her apron, her thoughts on her upcoming meal, when the front door slammed. Looking up, Tess saw a woman enter with a girl about Tess's own age. They carried valises, and their dresses were travel-stained and covered in dust. She could plainly read the fatigue on their faces.

"I hate that dirty old stagecoach," the woman complained as Tess eyed her. "But it's still better than that big ugly metal train that puffs smoke and shoots steam."

The girl patted the woman's arm. "Now, Mother, it's all over now. Let's get something to eat and then we'll rent a buggy. I'm sure there is one to let at the livery."

Something about the young woman drew Tess's attention. There was a familiar look to her, Tess thought as she hung her apron on the hook and turned to step away.

"Miss?" the woman's call halted Tess.

Tess pursed her lips, turning slowly to glance at the pair of ladies. "Yes?"

"We need some coffee." The woman pointed to an empty table near the front window. There was a note of command in her voice Tess didn't like.

Looking around quickly for Mrs. Warren, Tess squinted, failing to locate the plump woman. Scowling, she retied her apron and strode to the table where the two women sat.

Tess placed a pair of tin cups on the table and quickly poured the hot drinks. The young girl smiled appreciatively up at Tess. Her eyes seemed familiar, Tess thought again as she turned to go when the older of the two stopped her.

"I will have whatever this place can serve at this time of day," she said as she brushed crumbs from the edge of the table with a disdainful glare. "I am sure it cannot be much worse than the other food we've endured on this trip."

The comment irritated Tess. "All of the food served here is of the best quality. Everyone says it's delicious." Tess lifted her chin.

The woman rolled her eyes, not bothering to conceal her annoyance. "Well, there is no accounting for some people's taste."

Tess stared, startled by the remark. The young woman interjected. "We've had a long and difficult journey, miss. We are tired. Whatever you have will be wonderful, I'm sure." She seemed apologetic, and she cast concerned glances at her mother from the corner of her hazel eyes.

Her mother said nothing, the woman's keen gaze surveying her surroundings, a dissatisfied air about her.

Tess moved to the window in the wall and placed the order. She was eager to have her own meal but knew she must now wait while the women needed to be served. She eyed the pair while she put away clean dishes.

"Order, Tess," Henry called through the window. Tess placed the hot meal before the ladies. "Thank you," the young girl said as Tess turned to go.

Before Tess took two steps, the older woman halted her. "Miss, I am sure this meat is not even cooked. It is undercooked, to be sure." The woman poked experimentally at the venison steak with her fork. "What is it?" she asked.

Tess sighed louder than she intended, then snatched the

woman's plate and whisked it away. "I'll get you another, ma'am," Tess called curtly over her shoulder as she sped back to the kitchen.

Mr. Warren was much more forgiving than Tess. "Maybe the lady isn't used to venison. Whatever the case, I'll give her a fresh piece, well cooked."

Before Tess could lower the plate with the new piece of meat to the table, the woman spoke. "Never mind, miss. I've changed my mind about the meat. Do you have any soup?"

Tess slowly withdrew the plate, glancing at the steak hungrily. "Well, I think we still have some from lunch."

"What kind is it?" the woman demanded. The girl fidgeted in her seat, obviously embarrassed by her companion's behavior.

"Bean soup," Tess replied, trying her best to remain kind and attentive when she wished she could throw the disagreeable woman out on her ear.

"Oh, I only like my own bean soup. Everyone makes it differently, you know. I think I will just have some bread. You *do* have bread, don't you?" she questioned, her eyebrows arching.

Tess nodded as her fists clenched. She felt tired from her shift and hungry too. Her joyful mood of earlier that morning had fled, partly due to this woman's ill-mannered treatment.

Tess spun quickly on her heel and marched to the kitchen where she grabbed two thick slices of bread, placing one on a plate. Tossing her apron at the wall, Tess carried the two pieces of bread out front.

"Here you go, ma'am," she said, sliding the plate of bread in front of the startled woman as Tess headed for the exit. As the door slammed behind her, Tess heard the woman's plaintive plea for butter.

Train to Laramie

Laramie lay quiet now at this hour after the shift crews left town. Only the hammering at a new construction site marred the afternoon solitude. Tess munched bread as she made her way toward Ivan's livery, glancing at the large building going up across the street. They needed the money, but Tess found herself hoping that not many men were waiting for haircuts. She was ready to head home.

The workmen scurrying around the half-finished structure drew her attention as she came near. Must be another saloon or mercantile, she reasoned, judging by the large dimensions. A shudder rippled down her back as she surveyed the incomplete building, wondering at the unexpected foreboding that filled her. Stark wall studs and bare rafters outlined the immense building, but there was nothing that warranted such a frightening sensation. The skeletal frame of the structure looked innocent enough.

Shaking her head, Tess walked on.

Small dust clouds lifted from her shoes as she made her way down the main street, sidestepping horse apples and the occasional wagon. It hadn't rained for quite a while, Tess recalled. But the stream by their cabin still ran with clear, fresh water. Brett had chosen well when he'd selected the site for his homestead.

Ace Moyer lounged on the boardwalk before the Bucket of Blood as Tess passed, wearing his derby at a jaunty angle as always. Tess could feel his beady eyes following her as she walked toward the livery and she slowed her pace, not wanting him to think he frightened her. Despite her tough façade, she shivered. The little outlaw gave her the creeps.

Tess herself had heard the threats of these men, and she believed they were criminals. So did Brett and Ivan, although nothing could be proven. Even the Warrens disapproved openly of the lack of law and order in Laramie with Big Steve Long as town marshal. Tess recalled Mr.

Warren's discussions with Sheriff Boswell.

Only three men waited under the wide spreading branches of the big oak tree as Tess retrieved her sign from the tall barn. She hurried to lean the shingle against the stump and pointed to the seat with her scissors. The first man sat down, and Tess began cutting his hair.

As she worked, Tess noticed the two women from the café walking toward the livery. No doubt they were on their way to rent a rig. She wondered who these women were. The railroad brought many spectators and settlers and businessmen to Laramie. But not many women ended up at the end of the tracks, especially women of this caliber.

Tess watched them enter Ivan's barn, searching for the hostler. For some reason Tess couldn't explain, her gaze followed the newcomers with curiosity. She watched them from the corner of her eye as she moved around her customer.

The second man wanted a shave, and as Tess mixed the cream, she saw Ivan speaking with the two ladies. The older one seemed to do all the talking, Tess noted, pursing her lips. The woman seemed to hold a high opinion of herself, and no doubt was giving Ivan an earful right now.

Tess lathered the man's neck and began with the razor, finding it difficult to watch the proceedings at the livery and shave the man at the same time.

Suddenly, Ivan gestured toward Tess and the women looked her way. Tess cringed as a frown creased the older woman's face. Then, all three turned away.

Ivan disappeared for a few minutes and then reappeared with a horse hitched to a buggy. Slowly, his limp pronounced, the old hostler led the women to the shade of the big oak, near Tess, while he fussed over the buggy.

The women stared and whispered, the older one crossing her arms tightly over her chest. Tess gritted her teeth and ignored the knots in her stomach, curious but also annoyed that they watched her work.

Finally, Ivan approached, the two ladies in tow. He scuffed his boot against the stump and glanced at the dirt. "Uh, Tess? This lady says she needs to go to Brett Calloway's homestead. This is his mother, Mrs. Calloway."

Tess jerked at his words, the razor nicking the customer. "Ouch!" he howled. Tess quickly wiped the blood from his neck and continued to work, her hands trembling.

"Sorry, Roger," Tess whispered, patting the man's shoulder before glancing at Brett's mother. Tess nodded stiffly. "Hello, ma'am." She squinted and tried to steady her hands. What was she to do? This woman would scream at the unexpected news of Brett's wedding. She might gouge out Tess's eyes or strangle her.

The young woman nodded courteously, but her mother only stared, ignoring the greeting. Mrs. Calloway tilted her head, her brow puckering. "How is it that you know my son?" Her eyes narrowed as she studied Tess.

Tess glanced at Mr. Belmont. The old man stood wide-eyed, clasping his hands together anxiously. She glanced down at Roger's neck, pleased to see he'd stopped bleeding.

"Well, I'm a good friend of Brett. Perhaps he mentioned me in one of his letters home. I know he writes you regularly."

Mrs. Calloway scowled at this comment. "You seem quite familiar with my son's personal affairs," she remarked in an icy tone.

Tess nodded. "I know he's been waiting on your arrival this fall." Tess turned to the young woman. "That must mean you're Becky. Pleased to meet you."

"Pleased to meet you, Tess." The warm glow in the girl's eyes bolstered Tess.

Mrs. Calloway gestured to Ivan, now standing

sheepishly near the buggy. "This man says you can show us Brett's place. Are you willing?"

Tess nodded as the shaved man dropped a coin in her hand. The final customer seated himself on the stump.

"I would be happy to take you there after this last haircut." Tess took up the scissors. Despite her confident front, she shared Ivan's anxiety about the arrival of Brett's family. How would it affect her and Brett's marriage? Would Mrs. Calloway approve of her?

"I am eager to see my son now. I want to complete the final leg of our journey," Mrs. Calloway insisted.

Tess hesitated. "Well, I'll be done in a few minutes." She peered down at her customer and frowned at his thick and tangled long hair. This would not be a fast haircut.

The man stood abruptly and grinned at Tess. "I can wait until tomorrow, Tess. I've waited this long anyway." With a nod to the other women, he walked away.

"There," Mrs. Calloway waved. "We can go now. Are you ready?" Without waiting for a reply, Mrs. Calloway strode to the buggy.

With a worried glance at Ivan, Tess followed.

CHAPTER TWENTY-SEVEN

Mrs. Calloway allowed Ivan to assist her into the buggy. "We will have to go by the station first and retrieve our luggage," she ordered Tess as the two younger women took their seats. "The stage driver said there was nowhere to leave baggage at the Overland building," Mrs. Calloway explained while brushing dust from her rumpled dress.

"I'll put your sign away, Tess." Ivan shot an uneasy look at Brett's family and leaned close to her. "See you tomorrow," he mumbled. He winked as she turned the buggy and headed for the train station.

Dust billowed around them as Tess maneuvered down the street toward the train tracks. Mrs. Calloway coughed and held a handkerchief over her nose. Tess tried to move slower, hoping to keep the dust to a minimum. Although it was autumn by all accounts, the days were still very warm, and the lingering summer heat had turned spring's mud into summer's dust.

Marshal Long eyed the buggy of females with interest as they passed the Bucket of Blood. Frank lounged beside the tall lawman, and Tess could see his reddened eyes from her vantage on the buggy. He stared sullenly at her, and his sallow face puckered into a scowl. Tess pretended not to notice the two men, but she watched from the corner of her eye as Big Steve abruptly straightened from his casual stance and hastened into the saloon behind him, intent on a sudden errand.

Her eyes narrowed at his retreat as she finessed the

horse around a wagon stopped in the middle of the wide street and then pulled to a halt in front of the train station. A porter stepped forward to assist Mrs. Calloway from the buggy, but Tess climbed down on her own.

Mrs. Calloway instructed the porter which pieces of luggage belonged to her, directing the lifting and placement of each item into the small buggy. Precise packing became paramount, and repeatedly, the exasperated porter was forced to remove and shift various bags and trunks to make room for others. Mrs. Calloway's stern guidance only seemed to frustrate him more.

Becky stood next to Tess, watching with an amused eye. No doubt, the young woman had witnessed similar proceedings before.

"Your mother is quite capable of taking care of herself," Tess observed mildly, as she watched the porter drop a heavy trunk and incur Mrs. Calloway's stinging remarks.

Becky grinned. "I cannot recall a time when Mother could not take care of herself and us. Brett and I were always taught to plan ahead and be intentional." She paused, giving Tess a sidelong glance. Then she added, "How long have you and Brett known each other?"

Tess groaned inwardly. The secret had to come out, but she was unwilling to be the one to share it. "Not as long as I would've enjoyed," Tess replied evasively. "Excuse me," she added as she hurried away from the inquisitive girl.

Becky seemed shrewd, and Brett's mother would not long be fooled. Tess hoped Brett would soon right things.

Tess strode to the end of the platform, pretending to study the heaving locomotive while workers swarmed aboard, unloading incoming building supplies. Tess heard at the café that the tracks west of town were moving at a rate of almost a mile a day.

Acting as if to read the train schedule posted on the

depot wall, Tess glanced over her shoulder toward the two women. She needed to keep her distance from Becky's interrogations until Brett could explain.

A man in a cowhide vest leaned against the telegraph agent's booth, speaking in low tones. Tess recognized Sheriff Boswell. Curious, she sidled closer.

"There might be need of soldiers in Laramie soon if the robberies continue," the rancher was saying. "Maybe a garrison from Fort Russell could be moved here temporarily."

"The Union Pacific will do little to prevent its workers from blowing off some steam now and again," the agent warned from within the small shack. "They believe the saloons and the gambling halls are good for morale." Tess took another step forward, listening attentively.

"But I'll need help stopping these crimes," Boswell snapped. "Steve Long saw me coming to the telegraph office and ducked into his saloon. He knows I'm up to something, but I cannot do anything without support. I have no jurisdiction in Laramie and Long knows it."

"Then you suspect the marshal and his brothers?" The agent persisted.

Tess could hear the two men arguing from her vantage point behind the telegraph booth. Though frightened at her nearness, eagerness to listen in on this important conversation forced her to take the risk.

"Yes," Boswell replied, his voice conveying resignation. He sighed loudly. "I've heard more than one man in Laramie suspect the same thing. Big Steve and the Moyers have been killing workers to gain their homesteads and robbing customers who won large pots at the gaming tables in the Bucket of Blood. It's been going on all summer. Almost fifty men have died here in the last two months, a dozen of them at Long's own hand. And now they've added this Frank Mercer to their gang. He's a back stabber if I ever saw one."

Tess shivered at mention of her stepfather. She moved back a step, a board creaking beneath her.

Boswell hissed sharply and leaped around the corner of the shack, his gun in hand. Tess's eyes widened at sight of the leveled pistol aimed directly at her. Boswell blinked in recognition. He straightened, sheathing the big gun. "It's okay," he called over his shoulder. "It's just the waitress from Warren's café."

The rancher stepped closer to Tess, his head tilting as he approached. "Well, hello, Tess. How much of that did you hear?"

Tess gulped. "Some of it, to be honest. But I won't say anything, Sheriff Boswell."

The lawman scowled, then drew a deep breath. "You know, after the war, I was headed west for Oregon when my wagon broke down." He gestured to the distant plains. "Only about twenty miles from here. I decided to stay, to build a ranch, run some cows and forget the carnage I saw back east. I only accepted the sheriff job to bring in some steady cash. And now I find myself in the middle of this mess."

He paused and let his breath out slowly, shaking his head. Tess stared but said nothing. She turned and walked quickly to rejoin her group. Mrs. Calloway had only just finished supervising the packing of their numerous bags, and a slight frown pulled at the corners of her mouth as she watched Tess approach.

"Are you ready, Mrs. Calloway?" Tess asked, eager to be going home. The confrontation with Sheriff Boswell had unnerved her somehow.

Not waiting for a reply, Tess scrambled into the heavily loaded buggy and grabbed the long leather rains, her thoughts whirling. Boswell had particularly mentioned Frank. Tess knew the corrupt railroad blacksmith had thrown in with the Moyers and Big Steve, but apparently everyone else knew it too. What would happen to her mother if Frank were implicated in the murders and robberies of Laramie? Would the lonely woman have any means to support herself?

The annoyed porter helped Mrs. Calloway to her seat in the buggy, his heated, sweaty face shining brightly in the afternoon sun. He quickly helped Becky up, too, as if eager to have the ladies depart. There was no room for Becky in the rear of the flatbed vehicle and was forced to squeeze between Tess and her mother.

Thank God, Tess thought as she slapped the reins, that Mrs. Calloway wasn't wide like Mrs. Warren. There simply would've been no space for Becky.

No one stood on the boardwalk outside of the Bucket of Blood this time, Tess noted as they passed. She flicked her wrist, the reins slapping anew, and the horse quickened its gait from town.

Ivan Belmont stood in the wide doors of his livery, watching the women drive from Laramie. He grinned at Tess and waved when he caught her eye.

"Now what was that old fool smiling at?" Mrs. Calloway muttered when she saw Ivan. "I declare, western folk have few manners." She clicked her tongue.

Tess stewed, apprehension creeping into her as she drew nearer to the homesteads. Brett quite possibly would be there at this time of day. Perhaps, after last night's kiss, he had even arrived earlier, looking forward to supper with Tess. She pursed her lips as she felt the heat steal up her neck and warm her cheeks. She glanced away, hoping no one noticed.

She'd thought of that tender kiss many times today.

Embarrassed to admit it, even to herself, she eagerly looked forward to more of the same. Brett's embrace had made her feel safe and secure, something she hadn't felt before. Last night's kiss had awakened the desire to be together more than ever, to concentrate on their special friendship.

The thought made Tess smile to herself, remembering how Brett's lips had touched her own.

"Well, that simple porter was unable to load all our trunks," Mrs. Calloway complained, spoiling Tess's daydream. "Brett will have to go to town and fetch it tomorrow." She leaned forward, craned her neck around Becky, and peered at Tess. "How far is Brett's homestead?"

Just then, the dead pine came into view. Tess pointed with her chin. She slowed to turn into the dark aisle between the tall trees. "We're almost there," Tess offered quietly. The horse slowed even more for the gradual pull up the slope and Tess allowed him to walk at his own pace, remembering the buggy was heavily loaded.

The stream gurgled alongside the trail, and Tess could see the water as it leaped from pool to pool, racing around rocks and downed trees as the stream rushed to meet the bigger Laramie River near town. A deer leaped from its hiding place and bounded swiftly away. Its white tail made it easy for Tess to follow through the dense forest. The fat, gray squirrel that always greeted Tess stood on its legs to watch the buggy pass. The creature chattered incessantly and danced before darting away into the underbrush. Tess wished she could follow the forest creature, not sure she wanted to see how things played out with the Calloways.

They rounded the final turn of the road as first the foot bridge came into sight, then the two cabins standing on either side of the stream. Brett stood on the porch of his house, intently watching the trail. Tess saw his eyes widen with recognition, and her stomach tightened anew as the inevitable confrontation neared.

CHAPTER TWENTY-EIGHT

"Mother!" Brett shouted and leaped off the porch, striding toward the buggy, his face breaking into a wide grin. "Becky!" he called with a wave.

Tess pulled on the reins as Brett reached for his mother and helped her to the ground. They embraced and then, laughing, he lifted Becky down, grabbing his sister and pulling her to him. Tess wound the reins to the brake and climbed down, feeling somehow detached and excluded.

"Why didn't you write me when you'd be arriving? I could've met you at the station," Brett said but didn't wait for an answer before he glanced at Tess.

A tremble started in her fingertips and moved up her arm. Tess thought she might be sick. Her legs felt suddenly weak, and she wished she could crawl under a rock and hide. This was it. This was the time she'd have to come clean with her true identity. She, like Brett's mother, was also Mrs. Calloway.

The older woman turned to face Tess. "Miss, you can put our bags on the porch, if you would, please," she instructed in a crisp tone.

Tess saw a shadow of confusion cross Brett's tanned face as he looked at his mother. "What are you talking about, Mother? I'd never allow Tess to unload these heavy trunks. I can manage." He moved to the rear of the buggy. "And why call her miss? This is my Tess, as you must know." He hefted a large trunk and carried the luggage to the porch.

Becky, sensing something amiss, stepped forward.

"Brett, we only met Tess in town and really don't know her at all. She was very kind to bring us out here."

Brett dropped the trunk to the plank porch and glanced at Tess. "Didn't you tell them?"

"Tell them what?" Mrs. Calloway demanded. She stared at Tess, watching her as a hen watches a fox stalk her chicks.

Brett turned back to his mother. "Well, Mother, Tess is my … my … wife," he stammered. Complete silence followed, and the horse stamped an impatient hoof.

"Your wife?" Mrs. Calloway echoed, her eyebrows arching as the color drained from her face. She pursed her lips, and her gaze narrowed as she studied Tess. Tess squirmed under the piercing scrutiny.

Becky squealed and hugged Brett again. "Oh, you've gone and done it. Like you always said you would. You've married one of these western girls. Brett, I'm so happy for you." Becky looked at Tess, still standing motionless beside the buggy. "Congratulations, Tess. I'm sure we'll be like sisters, when we get better acquainted," she said, smiling a sincere smile.

"Thank you, Becky," Tess murmured.

"Well," Mrs. Calloway finally said. Color had returned to her cheeks and she turned her gaze back to her son. "I am exhausted and need to get cleaned up. We can discuss this more later. Which of these cabins is yours, Brett?"

"Both of them," Brett said, indicating the cabin across the stream with a gesture. "They're both mine."

"I mean, which one do you live in?" his mother clarified with a huff.

Hooking a thumb over his shoulder, Brett pointed at the nearest cabin. "I live here."

"Then I assume that cabin over there is for me and Becky?" Without waiting for a response, she strode toward the bridge. "Bring my luggage over immediately," she commanded to those behind her.

Becky grinned at Tess and then grabbed a small valise and started after her mother. "I'll see you later, Tess," the young woman called.

Tess looked at Brett. The woodcutter stared in consternation after his mother and sister. With a sigh, he glanced at Tess.

"I'm sorry, Brett. I didn't know how to tell them. I thought you'd better break the news."

He nodded. After a pause, he spoke. "Take the buggy back to Ivan. I'll get them settled and we'll have supper together. That'll allow us time to talk."

Tess watched as Brett removed all the bags from the buggy, placing each item on his porch. Tess climbed to the wooden seat again, and with an apologetic glance at Brett, slapped the reins and the horse began to walk. As she passed the bridge, Tess glimpsed the open door to Sandy's cabin, but no one was in sight.

The shadowed trees surrounding her pressed in as the buggy plodded back down the hill. Her thoughts, too, felt constricted and suffocating. Had she been wrong to conceal her identity from Brett's mother and sister? Should she have told the truth from the beginning? Tess didn't want to upset Brett or make him embarrassed or ashamed of his choice to marry her.

The train whistle brought Tess out of her gloomy disposition, and she realized she was already back in Laramie. It took only a minute to draw up in front of the livery and climb down.

Ivan watched her approach and then hobbled forward to hold the horse as Tess reined before him, his bushy eyebrows dancing as he watched her dismount. "Well, Tess. How'd it go? Brett's ma sure pulls no punches. She lets you have both barrels, huh?"

Tess pinched her eyebrows together. "Mr. Belmont, she hasn't even spoken directly to me yet, except to give me instructions on how to handle her luggage. She seems angry that Brett and I are married." She wrung her hands and glanced nervously toward the café.

Ivan placed a comforting hand on her shoulder. "Don't fret none, Tess. The good Lord has a plan. It was right that you and Brett married, I'm sure of that. Now, wait on the Lord and see what he says. Don't let Mrs. Calloway upset you too much. It'll all work out."

Tess sighed and looked at the old hostler. "You're right. Thanks. I'd better head for home." She tried to give him a smile despite her somber mood. He'd been a real friend to her since her arrival in Laramie.

The walk home was slow, her stride short, as if she were reluctant to arrive at the cabins too soon. She'd made this journey a hundred times, but this evening, her feet dragged. Her unexpected trip to Laramie had brought her here to this frontier town, a place she'd never wanted to visit. Indeed, the railroad town seemed little more than a sleepy stage station before the train had arrived. Now, it was the end of the tracks, thriving, and the work camp for thousands of men needed to build the railroad.

Somehow, Tess had found a place among these rough men. She knew that was wholly due to the Lord's intervention. Surely, she couldn't have achieved anything without the Lord's guidance and support.

Brett had been a surprise too. Finding love in this mountain land was exactly what she'd needed, although she didn't know it. Finding someone who loved her and thought of her protection and best interests shocked Tess. Certainly, neither her own mother nor Frank ever thought like that.

Now, her new husband's family had arrived to move in with them. What would happen now? Would she be absorbed into the family unit as one of them or simply be ignored as before as an outsider living among them like she'd experienced in Omaha?

Shadows lengthened around her, the sun on her back as it dipped far to the west by time Tess made the turn into the forest. The summer day was far advanced and already a gentle breeze brought cooler air down off the mountains above as she trudged through the darkening woods.

The loud caw of a crow startled her, and Tess came out of her deep thoughts to look around. Up ahead, she could barely make out the little bridge that spanned the stream. She was almost to the cabin. She should've walked faster, she chided herself abruptly. She'd be expected to prepare supper for their guests.

Guests? No, she realized with a start, these were not guests. They were family. Her new family.

Tess stared wide-eyed when she found Becky and Mrs. Calloway working over the fire when she entered the cabin. Mrs. Calloway turned sharply to glance at Tess but then quickly looked away. Becky smiled warmly at Tess.

"Oh, I'm glad you're back. We have a dozen questions, and Brett had to go feed the mules." Her eyes, so like Brett's, sparkled with excitement. Tess smiled at the young woman's attempt at including Tess. But her smile faded as she glanced at the distant, taciturn mother. It would take a great deal to win over Mrs. Calloway.

Tess took a hesitant step forward. Out of the corner of her eye, she glimpsed a pile of her goods and clothing atop her old bed. Brett must've retrieved them when he moved his family into the cabin across the creek.

"How can I help you?" Tess glanced to where Mrs. Calloway bustled over the steaming pots, not sure where she belonged. Or, *if* she belonged. Although this technically was her cabin, Tess gripped her hands and resolved to stay out of the way.

Becky indicated a seat on the nearby bench and Tess lowered herself to the wooden seat. She'd sat little today and was suddenly aware of her tired and sore feet.

Becky retrieved a tin cup from the cupboard and filled it with coffee before handing the mug to Tess.

"For starters, how long have you and Brett been married?"

Tess tilted her head, remembering that horrible night in the Bucket of Blood. Could that only have been a few weeks ago?

"Less than a month," Tess replied. "So much has happened in that short period of time."

A dark shadow crossed Becky's face and she nodded. "Yes, Brett explained about the poor man who used to be his partner. How terrible. Brett said that you were a great comfort and help through that difficult time."

Tess's eyes fluttered wide. "He did?"

"Oh, yes. Brett said he couldn't have gotten through without you." Becky placed a firm hand on Tess's arm. "Thank you for what you've been to Brett. It's obvious he loves you dearly, and I will love you too."

The simple words made Tess's heart swell, and she felt her gloom and fear fade away in the light of this gentle girl. Tess wanted to hug Becky but held her impulsive desire in check.

Just then, the door swung open, and Brett entered as Mrs. Calloway called everyone to the table. The mealtime conversation felt strained, but Brett tried valiantly to include everyone in the discussion. He explained about the Union Pacific and how far the tracks were being laid each day. Slowly, the rails were stretching to the west and soon they would cross the Rockies and connect the entire continent. Brett explained how he cut ties all day from the forest and delivered them to Tie Siding just east of Laramie, providing the ties the heavy iron rails would rest upon.

"Of course, I haven't gotten paid in well over a month, and the railroad owes me quite a bit of money," Brett informed his mother and sister. "Tess has been working at the café in town and cutting hair to pay our debt at the general store and make sure we're not kicked off our homestead. Marshal Long has already removed many of the settlers from their land and taken over their claims."

"Can he do that?" Mrs. Calloway asked. "I mean, he is the law, right? Shouldn't he be helping people?"

"Well, yes, he should," Brett agreed as Tess poured him a second cup of coffee. "But he's dishonest. There have been numerous killings and robberies at his saloon, which he owns with his half-brothers. Together, they're a gang of thieves."

"Have they made attempts to acquire your land, Brett?" Becky wanted to know, a worried look in her eyes.

Brett nodded. "Yes. I believe that's why Sandy was killed. But they didn't know we'd prepared for such an event. In case one of us was unable to maintain their claim, Sandy and I wished the other to have the homestead."

"In preparation for the intended sawmill?" Mrs. Calloway persisted. "The whole intention was to build a permanent structure for business and ship lumber, right?"

Brett nodded again. "Yes. That was why I wanted you two to join me here. This is going to be our new home. We will settle here as a family permanently."

"Oh, I can see it now," Becky added, eyes glowing as she looked at Tess. "You and Brett will have children soon, and the Calloway family will be lumber people. Lots of sons to help run the family business and help Brett in the mill."

Tess blushed at the implication while Mrs. Calloway glared at her daughter. If only they knew how far that was from the truth, Tess thought bitterly. She and Brett did not even live as man and wife.

The chair scraped as Mrs. Calloway stood, a disapproving look on her ruddy face. "Well, if we're going to live here, we will not give up knowing current affairs back east. In fact, this land has been officially designated as Wyoming Territory, no longer part of Dakota."

She lifted the pot of coffee to the others, but there were no takers. Mrs. Calloway pushed the blackened pot into the coals and straightened. "Also, President Johnson was not impeached. And a number of those southern rebel states regained their seats in Congress. I guess Mr. Lincoln kept the Union together after all."

She didn't sit down as she spoke, her eyes roaming the yellow cabin. The political concerns of the east seemed so far away, and Tess stifled a yawn as something soft crept into Mrs. Calloway's stern features. Tess frowned, studying her mother-in-law. Was she remembering the humble beginnings of her early life?

"It's late and we've only just arrived. I am tired. Tomorrow will be soon enough to discuss our plans. Goodnight," she declared stiffly and moved toward the door.

Brett rose, also. "Goodnight, Mother." He gave his sister a warm hug. "I am so happy to see the two of you," he went on as he and Tess followed the two ladies onto the porch.

"Perhaps soon you will see fit to put glass and a wood floor in our cabin, son," Mrs. Calloway called over her shoulder as Becky followed her across the bridge.

Slowly, Brett closed the door and turned to face Tess. Her chest tightened as she looked at him for a moment and then began to gather the dirty dishes. She must not look at him any longer. She was worried what he might say.

Despite the incredibly tender and sweet kiss of last night, had Brett now realized he'd made a big mistake? It was obvious his mother didn't approve of Tess. Becky seemed kind, but perhaps the two ladies had hoped for better for Brett.

Tess kept her gaze from Brett's as she cleared the table, but she felt his eyes upon her. He began to assist and together they washed the dishes in the stream and filled the coffeepot for the morning.

As they returned to the cabin, Tess glanced at Sandy's house. A dim glow showed through the brown paper window covering. No doubt the two ladies were making the single bed for the two of them.

Her eyes widened. Bed? Where was she going to sleep? They hadn't spent a night together since they were married.

Tess followed Brett back to the cabin, her arms loaded with the cleaned dishes, her mind whirling with wild ideas. She drew a deep breath and calmed herself, making her mind up before her feet stepped onto the porch. She would prepare for bed as before. Without saying a thing, Tess would get into the bed she used to occupy.

Dishes were stacked on the cupboard and Tess moved to her corner. Her few things from Sandy's cabin had been quickly stowed in their former places before supper, and now Tess pulled her sleeping gown from under the bed. She felt uneasy as she held the linen garment up, wondering if Brett watched her from beside the fireplace. Apprehension filled her, a knot forming in her stomach.

She loved Brett and they were married. God intended husbands and wives to sleep together. Would Brett move toward the bed? She trembled with expectation.

Her heart sank when she heard him pull his blankets from the stack beside the fireplace. He deposited the heap on the floor, and Tess whirled in time to see him spread the bedding over the deerskin rug. Sadness filled her. He was not going to sleep in her bed.

The candle was blown out, and only the dull glow of the dying fire lit the spacious room. Brett couldn't leave the cabin while she changed, and Tess crawled into bed and removed her dress under the covers. Pulling her night shirt on under the blankets was awkward, but she managed.

Neither of them spoke. It was as if they were both thinking the same thing but were afraid to say the words out loud. Tess stared at the old, familiar rafters above her. She could hear Brett's breathing, and he seemed to be fidgeting in his blankets, searching for a comfortable place on the hard floor.

"You haven't slept on the floor in weeks," Tess finally whispered into the darkness.

There was a long pause before he replied. "That's all right, Tess. I want you to be comfortable."

How could she tell him she wished he would come to her bed? A husband belonged in his wife's bed.

Firelight danced dully on the walls of the yellow cabin. The same comforting shadows Tess remembered from before, when she used to live here with Brett. Those had been good days for her. She'd come to love Brett in those early days. Now, they were married. Shouldn't they be in the same bed?

Perhaps Brett thought this was the best way. Tess stifled a gasp as she wondered if he considered not ever truly being man and wife.

A sudden, sharp banging at the door startled Tess, pulling her from her troubled thoughts. Brett leaped to his feet and padded to the door in his stocking feet. Then, thinking better of it, he turned and grabbed his pile of blankets off the floor and tossed them beside the fireplace.

He opened the door. Becky held a candle and looked first at her brother before nodding at Tess. "Thank God I caught you before you were in bed." She giggled. "I'm sorry to bother you. Mother says we're too cold. The window must be repaired tomorrow, Brett. We left our trunk with the bedding at the station. She noticed spare blankets by your fireplace."

Without waiting for a response, she hurried to the pile of blankets and gathered them together. "Sorry," Becky mumbled as she strode from the room, the latch dropping into place as she closed the door behind her.

For a moment, they both stared at the door. Then, slowly, Brett turned his gaze on Tess. "Now where am I going to sleep?" he grumbled.

With a shy smile, Tess flung the covers wide and made room.

CHAPTER TWENTY-NINE

In the morning, Brett whistled as he hitched the mules to the wagon. He would not work this day. His mother's trunk was needed, and Brett would pick it up at the station. With a smile and a wave, he drove from the clearing and headed down the trail.

Tess stood on the porch, watching him drive away. A deep and satisfying feeling of contentment filled her. She drew in a deep breath of the tangy, pine-scented air, wrapping her shawl tightly against the chill.

The door to the cabin across the stream opened, and Mrs. Calloway stepped out. "Where is Brett off to?" she called, her voice carrying easily in the clear air. Tess noticed the woman still wore her night clothes, her hair hanging loose.

"He has to order a window and fetch your trunk," Tess called back. She considered retreating indoors but hesitated. "Come over for coffee, if you're of a mind," Tess invited.

Mrs. Calloway shifted and tilted her head but then nodded. The older woman turned and hurried indoors.

Tess warmed the breakfast she'd already shared with Brett, feeling nervous. Mrs. Calloway seemed angry about Brett marrying without her knowing of the arrangement. Perhaps the woman was simply hurt she'd not been at the ceremony, Tess mused. She grinned, remembering the alley behind the Bucket of Blood. Would Mrs. Calloway have wished to be at her wedding if she knew where it'd taken place?

The door opened and Brett's mother entered. Mrs. Calloway was dressed now, her hair tucked tightly in place, and she closed the door firmly behind her. Tess blushed when she saw Brett's mother look at the bed with its rumpled blankets and the pillows bunched closely together.

"I've never slept in so late in my life," Mrs. Calloway admitted as she seated herself at the table and waited for coffee.

"It's this mountain air. And I'm sure you were very tired after your long journey," Tess excused as she placed a steaming mug before Mrs. Calloway. She hastened to reach for a plate.

"Just coffee for now, Tess. Come join me. I want to talk to you."

Tess's stomach tightened as she moved to comply. She watched Mrs. Calloway carefully, wondering if now was the time she would attack Tess, while Brett was gone. Cautiously, Tess poured herself a cup of coffee and seated herself across the table from Mrs. Calloway.

"I feel like the news of your marriage to Brett was so sudden yesterday. I certainly had no idea he was even courting someone. He never mentioned you in any of his letters. Of course, Brett had fought in the War Between the States and hasn't been home in a couple of years, but I'm still his mother. I always wished to be at his wedding and know the woman he married," she explained. She paused, blowing on her coffee as her eyes measured Tess over the rim of her cup before she took a sip.

Tess lifted her own mug, hiding behind the tin cup. Was Mrs. Calloway apologizing for her rudeness of the previous day?

"I am happy for you and Brett. He's always had good judgment, and I was pleased to hear how much you've done for my son. He says you've been a great help."

Tess shifted on the bench. "I've tried. I think Brett and I work well together, Mrs. Calloway."

The older woman smiled. "Please call me Delia. And yes, I'm sure you and Brett make a good team."

Pausing again, Mrs. Calloway sipped her coffee before going on. "I'm also very grateful he married a Christian girl, every parents' hope for their believing children. What I'm trying to say is, welcome to the family."

By midmorning, Brett returned from Laramie and joined the women for a short break from morning chores. Tess thrilled as he took her in his arms and kissed her softly before sitting at the table. "There's a lot of talk in town. The railroad pay has finally arrived in Tie Siding for the tie cutters. I wonder what made the marshal allow the funds to come in."

Tess nodded, pondering the effects of Sheriff Boswell's telegraph. Did the threat of an investigation make Big Steve release the funds?

"And Marshal Long has shot another man. The fellow apparently tried to shoot another worker and the marshal intervened. Ace Moyer is the only witness," Brett added dryly. "I don't believe any of the details surrounding the killing."

"I, for one, do not wish to hear about another shooting." Mrs. Calloway waved a dismissive hand as she fetched her son a cup of coffee. "I had no idea what kind of wild town we were moving to. What about the glass windows for our cabins?"

Brett held his mug in both hands, a tendril of steam rising slowly. He glanced at the boarded window in the south wall before he replied. "I ordered the windows, and they should be here within a few weeks. Things come so swiftly from Omaha now with the train."

Tess remembered the speed in which the machine shops of Omaha received materials from Chicago. The train allowed goods to be shipped so quickly.

"I'll not be able to do anything about the floor until spring."

His mother sighed. "Well, I've lived with a dirt floor before. I hate it, but I guess we can manage until spring."

"Tomorrow, I'll pick up my back pay at Tie Siding. I won't go this late in the day and risk driving back in the dark. Too many robberies to suit me," Brett remarked. A frown creased his tanned face and he shifted. "When I was in Laramie, I talked to some men about that shooting of Big Steve's and saw Sheriff Boswell. He was asking a lot of questions about the killing and what kind of land holdings the fellow owned. Apparently, he had a nice little ranch on the river just north of town. I heard one man say that Ace Moyer had tried to scare the man off his land a month ago, but the man wouldn't leave or sell. I guess his land is up for grabs now."

"Well, I don't pretend to understand all that is going on around this wild frontier," Mrs. Calloway grumbled with a scowl. "But I do want my cabin ready before snow flies. Why, it's already September, and October is just around the corner. There was frost on the north side of the cabin shakes this morning. Snow will be falling soon up in these mountains, if I don't miss my guess."

Brett nodded. "Yes, Mother, snow falls early up here. But don't worry," he said, placing a comforting hand on his anxious mother's arm. "That window will be here soon, and I'll put it in immediately. Hang in there and bear it as best you can in that cold cabin. I nailed a canvas cover over the window until I can install the glass."

"But now the cabin is completely dark," Becky complained.

"Patience," Brett advised as he rose from the table. "You can cook in here and only need to sleep in your cabin." He winked at Tess as he reached for the door. "I need to tend to the mules."

The days passed quickly with much work for all the homesteaders to perform. Added to Brett's many other duties was the chore of dragging more wood closer to the cabins for the winter supply of firewood. The women were not able to wield the heavy axe as quickly and easily as Brett, so the burden of cutting wood for two cabins fell on his shoulders.

Tess ran what errands she could while in town for her jobs. She asked the Warrens about hiring Becky part-time and they agreed. With winter coming on, they'd been praying for someone to replace the weary Mrs. Warren. Becky, they said, was an answer to their prayers. She could start in November.

Mrs. Calloway was kept busy mending and making new clothes and items from the flour sacks that Tess continued to deliver each week.

Tess noticed Sheriff Boswell around town more often these days. On more than one occasion, the rancher was observed in earnest conversation with Mr. Warren. The encounters always left the café owner agitated and nervous.

A tension seemed to settle over the town of Laramie. Everyone felt the strain. Even Tess could not deny the somber, expectant mood that enveloped the railroad encampment. It was as if everyone knew something was about to happen.

The Bucket of Blood, the Chinaman's Palace, and the other saloons of Laramie were open around the clock. There was talk of relocating the Hell on Wheels farther west to establish an end-of-tracks site since the rails had extended so far from town. But with winter so close, most believed this was only idle speculation. Laramie boomed with numerous shift crews, causing robberies to increase and shootings were almost a nightly occurrence.

Big Steve Long seemed oblivious to this crime spree and was often involved in the various shootings that ensued. By the time October rolled around with the season's first snow fall, Marshal Long had already killed no less than thirteen men since May.

Frank had joined the Moyers and was involved in many of the criminal activities of Laramie. Tess had sent her mother a letter back in Omaha, detailing the whereabouts and activities of her husband.

The thousands of railroad workers that called Laramie their home were constantly in danger of losing their hard-earned wages in the countless gaming halls that lined the main street. Despite the danger and risk, the drinking houses were filled to capacity each night.

Laramie was a powder keg ready to explode.

Tess had introduced Mrs. Calloway and Becky to the woodland chapel that Brett had carved from the forest. As often as possible, the women took turns stealing away to the solitude of the quiet glade. There, beside the gentle waterfall and in the shadow of the tall cross, they prayed.

The homesteads had become homes to the Calloway family.

Brett worked harder than ever. The deep snow of winter would slow his efforts to keep the Union Pacific supplied with ties. But he hoped the winter months would allow him time to plan and prepare for the sawmill he wanted to construct next summer. He'd already located a site for the mill with an easier access road to Tie Siding on the far end of Sandy's homestead. A steam donkey to power the saw blade had been ordered from Omaha and would be delivered by spring. Brett planned to make the sawmill his permanent occupation.

Mid October found Tess afraid to disclose she thought she might be pregnant. But in spite of her concerns, the excitement overtook Tess as she shared her news after dinner. Everyone was overjoyed at the prospect of the next generation of Calloways. Brett's mother started sewing baby clothes from the flour sacks.

The longed-for windows for the cabins still had not materialized. Because there had already been two light dustings of snow, Becky complained the cold was intense in the cabin. Brett promised the windows would arrive soon.

"Tess," Becky asked one cold and windy morning before Tess left for work. "Will you please make it a point to stop each day at the general store to check on the windows?"

Tess readily agreed. "I promise, Becky. But I'm sure Brett is right. They'll arrive soon."

One morning in the middle of October, Brett had left early for work. "A storm is coming," he'd warned, pointing to the darkening clouds forming on the horizon. "I need to get a lot done before it blows in. I might be a little late tonight. This might be the first of the severe winter storms," he predicted with a solemn tone. He pulled on his gloves and drove the heavy wagon from the clearing.

Tess turned to Mrs. Calloway. The older woman had made it a habit to rise early and see her son off to work each morning. "Delia, I'll be going to work early too. It's a doughnut day, and the Warrens said I can show up as early as I wish on these busy days. We could use the extra money," Tess explained as she pulled on her heavy coat. A hint of snow hung in the air, and Tess didn't want to get caught in a storm unprepared.

"You go right ahead, Tess," she smiled at her daughter-in-law. "I'll work on laundry today. Perhaps this storm won't allow us to get out tomorrow." As Tess stepped off the porch into the early morning gloom, Mrs. Calloway called after her. "Don't forget to stop by the store, Tess."

Tess strode swiftly down the dark trail, the sun hidden behind a curtain of black clouds. Even the blue jays and crows that greeted her daily were quiet, signaling the imminent weather. Not even the fat, gray squirrel that chattered incessantly at Tess made an appearance this morning.

The day felt gloomy, but Tess was not. The new life she carried within her and the new family she'd been accepted into made her feel alive and loved. The Calloway's were everything she'd ever hoped for in a family that supported and encouraged one another. She was pleased they shared her and Brett's excitement about the coming baby.

The wild frontier town had frightened her at first, with its violence and lawlessness, but now she took it in stride. God was with her, and he would protect her. He'd shown that when she was saved from Frank back in August.

Tess pursed her lips. No, more than that, she realized. God had saved her from Omaha, bringing her to Laramie. Tess grinned, knowing now it was the train she was meant to be on. God had provided protection in Brett's cabin. God had given her a job at the café. God had brought her the love of her life. How many unseen things that Tess was not even aware of had the Lord done for her?

The constant ups and downs of the summer with its fears and frightening events had taught Tess to trust in God. He was continually with her, even when he seemed absent. Despite her shortcomings and concerns, the Lord had always protected her. Through it all, he'd developed her faith. Through trials, courage had blossomed.

Tess turned into the wide path that followed the tracks to town and continued to ponder this.

In the open once more, released from the low canopy of

the dark forest, Tess could plainly see the ominous clouds bunched along the face of the mountains. Indeed, a storm was coming. Before nightfall, for sure, it would be upon them. She hoped she'd be safe at home before the storm arrived in all its ferocity. The bright yellow cabin felt so warm and fun now with others to share the workload.

Tess jumped at the unexpected rustle in the bushes, her heart leaping to her throat. A man with a red bandana tied over his face stepped from the undergrowth. Tess stared at him, seeing a derby pulled low over his small eyes.

Despite the disguise, Tess recognized the highwayman. His derby hat was cocked to one side in the fashion the thug preferred, and the familiar gaze peered roguishly at Tess. He held a big pistol in one hand and the long knife he always carried was tucked into his wide belt.

"Ace Moyer," Tess breathed, a hand rising to her throat. "What are you doing here?"

The gun lowered, but he didn't at once reply. He stared at Tess as if unsure what he should do with her. Finally, he shifted and tilted his head. "I was waiting for wagons to pass. I didn't expect you. But now that you saw me, I'll have to do something."

Tess froze at his meaning. She knew he was quite capable of following his threat with action. But she also knew he was not a shrewd man.

Tess chuckled abruptly, hoping her casual manner would distract the outlaw. "There is nothing you will do with me, Ace. I know Big Steve and I cut his hair. He'd be angry if you laid a hand on me. Also, it's doughnut day in Laramie. If I'm absent, a thousand men will turn this town upside down looking for me. You wouldn't last the day," she warned, speaking with a confidence she did not feel. "Besides, I'm a married woman with child. You would be hanged on the spot if you molested me and you know it.

So, go hide again in the bushes and I'll be on my way."

Without waiting for a reply, Tess turned on her heel and strode away. Whether it was her bold affront to Ace's attack or the protection of the Lord or simply her pragmatic argument, she left the little man standing in the road, his gaze boring a hole in her back as she walked toward town.

Tess wanted to run, but she kept her pace while she shook all over. Despite her brazen disregard for the thief's menacing words, she'd been terribly frightened. She glanced once more over her shoulder and was just in time to glimpse the outlaw as he slipped back into the bushes.

Tess scowled. Robberies had increased along the roads, but the boldness of the man during daylight hours shocked her.

The customary train whistle from the station greeted Tess as she walked rapidly into the limits of Laramie. Bustling men were moving like busy ants, moving freight and materials that would be needed on the railroad. Perhaps the impending storm caused the men to hurry about their work. Laramie seemed busier than Tess had ever seen the frontier town. More men than usual roamed the streets today.

She grimaced. Doughnut day at the café would be unmanageable. She wished she'd asked Mr. Warren if Becky could start work today.

In spite of the early hour, Tess stopped by the general store. She stepped into the warm room, brushing a windswept tendril of dark hair from her eyes as she closed the door behind her, drinking in the delicious scents she'd come to love when visiting the frontier market. Fresh coffee beans and licorice and leather and tobacco mingled to waft through the air, perfuming the crowded store.

The clerk spotted Tess and waved as she shouldered her way through the mob. No doubt others shared the idea of shopping before the storm arrived. "The windows are in, Tess," he called. "I can't get to them now but stop by later and I'll dig them out of the pile from Omaha."

Tess smiled at the clerk and nodded, signaling she'd heard his instructions above the din of the noisy room. She hurried from the store, anxious to get free of the crowded, stuffy building.

The pungent odor of mud and horse manure assaulted her as she stepped once more into the street. The gray clouds hovered, threatening, and Tess shivered as if it were the cold that struck her rather than a sense of foreboding that hung like a shroud over Laramie. She paused to allow a wagon to pass, then Tess hurried on toward the café.

Tess glanced over at the Bucket of Blood. Marshal Long lounged on the boardwalk with Frank Mercer. The two men watched her, collars pulled up high on their thick coats. Even at this distance, Tess could see Big Steve's long, gray moustache needed trimming.

Emboldened by her escape from the little outlaw on the road, Tess slowed and returned their stare. She knew she shouldn't do it, but she couldn't resist. She felt like she could take on the whole world today. The Moyers and Frank Mercer could do nothing to her. God was with her. She was married to the man she loved, and now she carried his baby.

Big Steve snorted and pointed at Tess. "You see there, Mercer. That little girl isn't afraid of you." The marshal chuckled as he looked from Tess to the sour-faced man beside him. "You'll never break that girl's spirit."

Frank scowled, lines forming across his wide forehead. "She'll be broken, mark my words. I'll break her," he growled loud enough for Tess to hear as she hurried on. He straightened as Tess turned away and shouted after her. "Did you hear that, Tess girl? I'll break you. Soon you will be mine."

Tess rushed away, reprimanding herself for her challenging behavior. Why provoke the wicked brute? Even though she was married now to Brett, Frank still worried her.

Tess well knew that should something happen to Brett, all three of the Calloway women would be fair game for these vulgar, dangerous outlaws. She prayed silently for her husband's protection and safety.

A sudden gust of wind buffeted her, drawing her attention back to the muddy street of Laramie. The chilled wind heralded the impending storm, billowing the soiled canvas walls of the tents, cracking loudly with each blast. The zephyr whined through the near-finished large building Tess had noticed before. Nobody worked on the half-finished building today. Either the coming storm or the rising tension within Laramie had stalled construction. Almost completed, the structure no doubt would be another saloon, Tess thought, observing the long bar along one wall.

She shivered, hunching her shoulders against the tremor that wasn't wholly caused by the bitter wind. Tess glanced once more at the lowering clouds before pushing through the crowd of hungry men at the café.

A frantic Mrs. Warren waved to Tess when the plump woman sighted her. "Tess, hurry with your apron," she called breathlessly, her face flushed. "We already have a large crowd and more outside."

"Why are so many men in town?" Tess tied her apron loosely over her tummy.

Mrs. Warren leaned closer. "The men are upset about the killing last night at the Bucket of Blood. They say Frank Mercer killed a worker who was drunk."

Tess was not shocked. This was what she'd expected

from her stepfather. It seemed fitting that he would join the Moyers and Big Steve at taking homesteads from settlers and robbing men with money. Hadn't she just seen Ace out on the road holding up unsuspecting wagons?

Shaking her head, Tess turned to begin work when she saw Mr. Warren speaking with someone at the back door. She tilted her head and glanced over her shoulder before sidling closer. She could barely make out the words of her employer and the unseen man.

"I can't hold the men back much longer. They want justice, jurisdiction or not," the man out of sight from Tess said. She recognized the voice of Sheriff Boswell.

"I know, and they should have justice, but I'm afraid for the innocent folks in town. There's liable to be shooting," Mr. Warren countered.

"There's shooting now," the sheriff hissed. "Things have gotten out of control. No one is safe any longer."

Frantic whispers followed that Tess couldn't make out. Men from the dining area clamored for more doughnuts. The din grew louder. Finally, she hurried back to the cut-out window in the kitchen wall and began distributing platters of the sweet cakes.

A blast of cold wind accompanied each customer that entered the café, reminding Tess of the pending storm. Again, she hoped she'd make it home before the snow arrived. She delivered a platter to a raucous table of workmen near the front window, glancing outside into the blustery street. Tess prayed fervently the storm would hold off as she hurried around the tables crowded with hungry, talking men.

More than once she heard discussions about the crooked and dangerous Bucket of Blood. All the men agreed it was not safe any longer to visit the biggest saloon in Laramie. Too many men had died or been robbed there.

"My best friend was killed there two weeks ago," one man with yellow teeth lamented loudly.

Another man in a heavy sheepskin coat suggested it was Ace Moyer who'd knocked him on the head and stole his winnings. "I swear I saw that derby hat he always wears on the man who robbed me," he declared.

Tess heard this remark and recalled that Frank wore the same style hat. No matter, she thought dismally, it could've been either Frank or Ace who'd robbed these men. What difference did it make?

Tess grabbed another platter from the cook in the kitchen and hurried to pass them out to the railroad men. Tempers were running short, and she could see it would take very little to light the fuse.

"I think Sheriff Boswell should do something about it," one big burly railroad man suggested.

The topic of justice and jurisdiction was debated throughout the café for an hour before most men agreed something must be done about the lawless element in Laramie.

At two o'clock when Tess was released from the café, the town had become full of angry, shouting men. Tess saw more than one brown bottle passed through the crowd from hand to eager hand. Why these men were not at work troubled Tess as she walked through the blowing gale toward Mr. Belmont's livery.

No one was in sight outside the Bucket of Blood when she passed the saloon. Usually crowded and noisy, today the gambling den seemed quiet and sedate, as if closed for business.

Tess felt grateful there were no men waiting for a haircut under the huge oak tree, its wide branches swaying wildly in the wind. The temperature had grown colder by the hour, but she wouldn't have been surprised to see a lone man or two waiting. Thankfully, not a single customer lingered this day.

She stopped in the lee of a building, watching the street fill with noisy men, clustering in raucous groups. Tess could feel the tension, thick enough to cut with her scissors.

Perhaps the advent of the winter storm would prevent any violence taking place today, Tess mused wistfully as she watched the hovering, dark clouds above the mountains. This storm would soon drive all the loitering men indoors.

Ivan appeared at her elbow. His wrinkled face wore an expression of anxiety Tess was not used to seeing there. "The crews have knocked off early today because of the coming storm. It's only given them time to drink before it arrives. Something's going to happen," the hostler noted grimly, shaking his gray head.

Tess knew he was right. Perhaps she should head home before something happened. She turned quickly to the old man. "Mr. Belmont, the windows Brett ordered are in. Could I borrow a rig to take them out to the homestead?"

He shook his head. "No, I'm afraid not. This weather is about to bust wide open. In fact, I was wondering how you were going to get home. If you hurry, you might make it before she opens up."

Tess clenched her teeth and glanced once more at the massing clouds. Darker now, they crowded low over Laramie. A fierce gust of wind struck them, and a few scattered flakes of snow swirled around Tess. As more flakes began to swirl, Tess wondered if she'd make it home safely.

She pulled her coat collar higher and turned to say goodbye to her friend when Ace stumbled into town, his red bandana hanging loosely around his neck. The derby hat he loved was gone. He lurched past Tess without seeing her, glancing worriedly over his shoulder as he ran. He faltered again in front of the livery, favoring one arm, and as he regained his balance, his gaze locked with Tess. She read the deep fear in the little man's beady eyes, his thin hair blowing wildly in the gale.

He tore his eyes from her and continued his staggering gait down the wide street, men in tight groups watching him as he made his way to the Bucket of Blood. The little thief struggled up the few stairs to the boardwalk, still holding one arm awkwardly. He shoved a shoulder against the doors and almost fell within, the doors slamming behind him.

CHAPTER THIRTY

The rumble of a galloping wagon made Tess look up the street again where Ace had come from. The driver stood shouting, the reins held in both hands as he lashed the racing team.

The plunging, snorting horses ran into town past Tess and Ivan, then reared as the driver hauled on the reins. The pair of horses pranced wide-eyed as men ran from both sides of the road, gathering around the heaving horses as the driver pointed to the wagon bed behind him. "A man in a mask tried to hold us up. My partner got shot. I winged the robber and he ran this way. I had to load my partner into the wagon before I could follow," he explained swiftly to the listening throng of onlookers. "Did anyone see a wounded man running this way?" the driver of the wagon demanded, scanning the faces of the men around him.

"It was Ace Moyer!" a man yelled from the crowd. Others took up the outlaw's name.

"He ran into the Bucket of Blood," another man yelled.

Suddenly, Sheriff Boswell stood beside Tess, his tall frame taut like a stretched cord, his gleaming eyes narrowed. "Boys, we've had enough of the Moyers in Laramie. Grab some ropes from the barn here and follow me."

Tess could only watch as men shouted and pushed into the barn behind her and returned with coiled ropes. Mr. Belmont said nothing but gripped Tess by the shoulders, as if holding her in place, afraid she might join the boisterous mob. Together, they stared as the horde pressed as a single mass toward the silent saloon.

Tess vaguely felt the cold wind blow around her, wrapping her dress about her legs, she kept her eyes trained on the large crowd of men as they surged up the stairs to the boardwalk and into the saloon. The locked doors seemed to have no effect on this unstoppable tide of men and the twin doors crashed open, forced by the sheer power of the pack. Other groups of men from farther down the street merged into the growing body of railroad workers as they poured into the Bucket of Blood.

Tess heard a shot and then another as the yelling crowd seemed to pour into the saloon like water through a bursting dam. Then, suddenly, the tide turned, pouring out again, this time with a few men held securely by the relentless crowd.

In horror, Tess watched as the group of crazed men moved their captives toward the nearly completed saloon farther down the street. The bare rafters gleamed like dull bones, exposed to the ominous sky.

Unable to look away, Tess watched as Sheriff Boswell stepped forward and tossed a rope over one of the rafters. She quivered as a shout went up from the surging crowd of angry men. Boswell fitted a noose around the short man and then the sheriff nodded to the men on the other end of the long rope.

As the man was lifted off his feet, Tess recognized the dark face of Con Moyer. The bartender kicked, boots flailing, hands tied behind his back.

As Tess watched Con kick his last, another nod from the sheriff and a second rope soared over a rafter. She saw the wounded Ace Moyer follow his brother into the sky, kicking with all his might.

A third pull on a rope brought the head of Big Steve Long above the swelling crowd. Tess recalled how she'd shaved this man only a few short months ago.

The crowd seemed to have come off its hinges now, screaming, whooping, and hollering with abandon. Nothing, not even the fierce cold wind, could be heard over the shouts of the crazed vigilantes. Tess could not turn away from the gruesome scene.

Suddenly, another man was shoved into position beneath the sagging rafter, a fourth noose tossed over the timber. Tess saw a derby hat knocked aside by Sheriff Boswell as he looped the noose around the man's neck. A jerk on the rope pulled the man from the ground. As he kicked and spun wildly in the air, Tess recognized her stepfather, Frank Mercer.

His face turned a ghastly hue, gray at first, then shaded to a deep purple. His eyes bulged, and for a moment, Tess felt their eyes lock over the crowd.

She gasped but still could not look away. Her heart froze in her chest, her blood ran cold, as she willed this man to feel her anguish, the way he had hounded her, the fear he'd instilled in her. Frank had made her run away from Omaha, away from her mother. This horrible man had caused so much hurt and pain.

She gawked at him, almost pitying him at this awful moment. And then, he spun, his legs jerking one last time before stilling, his limp body swaying in the fierce wind.

Tess stared, horrified. The four men swung lazily in the wind, and the milling mob below the bodies grew quiet but restless now that the grisly work was finished.

Her gaze shifted at a huff from the old hostler beside her. "Tess," Ivan called. "Don't tell me you saw all of that?" The gray-haired man squeezed her shoulders tightly. She could feel the tremble in his hands.

Tess nodded, unable to speak. Turning again, like steel drawn to a magnet, she looked at the men standing in and around the unfinished building where the lynching had taken place. Slowly, men drifted away, feeling the cold of the storm now and moving to find shelter.

"I'm sorry, Tess," Mr. Belmont mumbled as the old man released her and ran a shaky hand across his whiskered face. Tess ignored him, filled with her own disturbing thoughts. The windows at the general store now forgotten, she needed to flee. The only thing that mattered was returning to Brett's cabin. Her husband would take care of her. She needed to go to Brett.

CHAPTER THIRTY-ONE

Vicious wind tore at her long hair as Tess bent and raced into the storm. She heard the hoarse shout of the crippled hostler behind her, but she refused to halt, laboring on. The storm mattered not, it was something inanimate, something she could ignore. She had to get home.

She passed the water trough in front of the livery, and she dully remembered drinking the filthy water from the old wooden trough on her first night in Laramie. So much had happened since that night in June. The mud under her feet felt stiff and solid now. The storm was upon her, just as it had been the night she'd left Omaha. The violence and fierceness of the wind seemed to fit the whirlwind in her mind. As in Omaha, her thoughts then had been troubled too.

Tess ran on, past the last of the shacks and cabins and tents of Laramie and over the log bridge until she was alone on the empty road, following the twin iron rails.

The small, whirling flakes of snow now came in a blinding torrent. Like a veil, the snow shrouded the landmarks Tess knew so well. The elevated tracks on her left and the dense dark forest on her right were still vaguely visible through the swirling snowflakes. The road remained wide and open, an easy trail to follow, but she needed to hurry before the snow concealed everything. Her breath came in gasps now, and Tess slowed to a walk.

The Moyers were dead. Big Steve was dead too. And Frank Mercer. Grimly, Tess recalled her stepfather's dark face as it seemed to peer at Tess over the crowd. He would bother her no more. Her mother was now free to do as she pleased. Perhaps Tess would write to her and invite her to Laramie.

A strong gust of wind pushed Tess and she slipped on the frozen mud, sprawling on the cold ground. She lay there a moment, debating whether to get up or not. In this intense cold, it wouldn't take long to die, she thought.

A long moment passed before Tess struggled to her feet. There had been a time when she would've been willing to stay on the ground and let things happen. Frank had almost broken her spirit in Omaha and made her wish she were dead. But not now.

Be strong and courageous.

The comforting words came to Tess as she plodded on, the wind fighting her every step. Despite the wickedness of Frank Mercer and the despair that surrounded Tess in Omaha, God had not abandoned her. He'd been watching Tess with his loving eyes upon her. It was his hand that had guided her here to Laramie. To Brett.

And now a baby grew inside her. She must not forget that. A legacy of love she would create with her new family that hadn't existed in her own. The love of God would be passed on from her to her children and one day to their children.

A large bush on the side of the road drew her attention, and Tess studied the leaning foliage. The fierce wind buffeted the bush, making it sway madly, almost tearing the plant from its moorings. Was this the spot where Ace Moyer had hidden to rob wagons? It did look a little familiar to Tess as she peered around. Perhaps this was the very spot where he'd shot the man as the driver shot Ace.

Don't think about that now, Tess advised herself sternly as she trudged on. *They're dead and they will not bother me anymore.*

Suddenly, she scowled, glancing around. Where were her familiar landmarks? Tess squinted, peering through the snow as she searched for the dead pine tree on the side of the road, wondering if she'd be able to locate the narrow turn-off into the forest. The path to the cabins was not well marked. She'd placed a pile of stones once long ago when she'd first come to Laramie, before she located the now familiar lightning-struck pine tree. But she didn't even remember where she'd built the cairn. Tess had gotten used to the routine path home, and now all was obscured in the blizzard.

Moving forward more hesitantly, Tess peered into the forest for a clue to the whereabouts of the little trail. The wind blew mercilessly now, and the snow rushed horizontally at her unprotected face, stinging her cheeks like piercing needles. The force of the wind pushed at her and made it difficult for Tess to stay on her feet. Desperately, she hoped she was still pointed in the right direction.

While she'd been running, the intense cold had been endurable. Now, as Tess searched carefully for the small opening into the forest, the growing cold penetrated her coat. She knew she would not be able to withstand this intense cold much longer.

Panic welled within her and Tess wondered if she should attempt to return to Laramie. Perhaps she could make it back to the protection of the café or even Ivan's livery. But the desire to be at home, with Brett, drove her on, forcing her to search harder for the trail to the homesteads.

Tess prayed. Surely God would not allow her to die here on the plains of Wyoming. Not after finally escaping her pursuers and marrying Brett.

The blizzard blasted Tess as the fierce northern winds bent the trees with powerful force. Tess shivered, recognizing her body's final attempt at keeping her from freezing. A fallen tree loomed on her right that she didn't remember seeing before. Had she gone too far? Had she missed the turnoff? Perhaps she should take cover behind the fallen tree and wait out the storm.

The folly of this plan struck her at once, and Tess resolved to continue her frantic search. To not gain the protection of the cabins was to die.

"Oh, God, help me," she called into the wind. Her words were torn away and lost on the gale, but Tess felt her spirit lift once again. God would want her to succeed. He wished Tess to keep looking, no matter how cold she became. *Have courage*, she whispered to herself.

Suddenly, she kicked a pile of snow-covered rocks along the side of the road at the same moment she glimpsed the narrow aisle between the trees. The trail. A sob tore from her as she stumbled into the dim path. Relief swept over her and she ran, forcing her legs to pump, as she followed the narrow gap between the trees to the cabins beyond.

Only the roar of the blizzard filled her ears this time, masking the familiar melody of the now invisible nearby stream. Snow had already hidden the creek from view.

Her shoes slipped again, and Tess fell hard. This time, her elbow struck on the frozen ground and a sharp pain ran up her arm all the way to her shoulder. Struggling to her feet, the wind still pushing her cruelly, Tess regained her footing and continued. She moved much slower now, her frozen body barely able to hobble, although the wind was at her back. But she knew the cabins were not far.

Great sheets of white snow pelted her, threatening to disorient her, but she bowed her head and plowed on, knowing safety was near at hand. She could only dimly see the dark trees around her, but she kept doggedly on. One foot in front of another.

Suddenly the foot bridge loomed out of the silvery swirl

and Tess felt her heart leap. Home.

The cabin took shape as she neared the porch. She managed to lift her leg and step onto the wooden boards and then her hands numbly fumbled with the latch.

The door pulled open and Brett stood there, a panicked look in his hazel eyes. Another sob wrenched from Tess as she fell into his arms. Without a word, he grabbed her by her coat and dragged her into the warm room. Mrs. Calloway led her to a seat by the fire, and Tess heard the door slam behind her. Becky stood by the table, her hands holding her apron to her mouth, her eyes wide with fear.

For a few minutes, no one spoke as Tess shivered uncontrollably. The hot cup of coffee she held shook with every tremor of her cold body as Brett removed her shoes and rubbed her frozen feet. She could barely hear the prayers from Mrs. Calloway as the older woman muttered under her breath and draped a blanket around Tess's shoulders.

Brett gazed at her face and then searched her feet, aching now as they thawed. Tess could feel the relief in him as he worked, rubbing vigorously. Somehow, it touched her deeply to know he was so thoroughly upset for her safety. She felt loved. This was her home, and she was among her new family. Slowly, the tight grip of cold left her and she relaxed. Sipping the hot drink, Tess stretched her legs to the blaze, her toes tingling with stinging stabs.

Snow drifted down the chimney, making the fire spit and hiss as the wind howled outside. Tess shivered again, knowing she was blessed to have reached the cabin in such a storm.

"Are you all right?" Mrs. Calloway finally asked. Tess hesitated and then nodded. No sense in telling these good people that her fingers prickled painfully, and her feet felt like blocks of wood. However, their love and concern did much to warm Tess after the bitter cold of the blizzard.

"What made you try to walk to the cabin?" Brett demanded, a hint of reprimand in his tone. "You might've gotten lost in the blizzard or frozen to death out in the forest."

Tess only nodded and lifted her mug to her lips, hiding her face. Brett was right, she well knew. But she'd had to get out of Laramie. How to tell these people about the vigilantes? About Frank Mercer?

"There were some hangings," she blurted. No one said anything to this, although Brett's eyebrows bunched. "Some men were hanged," Tess continued. "Men were being robbed on the road to Laramie and one of them shot Ace Moyer. He fled into the Bucket of Blood and then a mob rushed the saloon and dragged four men out."

She paused, allowing her words to sink in. She drew a deep breath and let it out slowly.

Brett's eyes narrowed as he wrapped Tess's feet with a warm towel. He glanced up at her. "The Moyers?"

Tess frowned and nodded, recalling how the little thief had scared her.

Brett blinked and his jaw twitched as his tan faded. "Big Steve Long?"

Tess bobbed her head once.

Brett pursed his lips and reached for one of her cold hands, gripping it tightly. "Frank Mercer?"

Tears welled in Tess's eyes, and she squeezed Brett's hand. That was all the answer she could give.

Mrs. Calloway and Becky said nothing as they fussed over the fire and began making soup.

Tess bit her lip as the tears rolled down her cheeks. With an encouraging smile, Brett moved to help the women, leaving Tess alone to stare into the fire. How could she explain she wasn't crying for Frank but for herself? Tess would not miss Frank. They had never shared a relationship. From the very beginning, Frank had frightened Tess when he'd moved into the house she shared with her mother. But now she suddenly felt safe and free from the constant fear Frank had introduced to her.

Tess stared into the fire, her shoulders shaking gently as she cried. Now, finally, Tess was free. Free to live and love. The marriage to Brett had started a new life with the Calloways that Tess already cherished. A new adventure of family and beginning a new career filled her days with good thoughts. Suddenly, her life was full and happy.

Tess hung her head, bowing gratefully to God. Humbly, she thanked him for his overwhelming love and intervention. God had orchestrated these events enabling Tess to be here.

"Thank you, Father. My perfect Father," she whispered, tasting the salty tears on her lips. "I can never thank you enough, Lord. Although my adventure was difficult, you never left me alone. You were right to tell me to be strong and courageous, for you had a plan all along. A good plan. You never left my side. You are always with me. Thank you for your promises," Tess breathed, her heart swelling with love and hope.

CHAPTER THIRTY-TWO

The blizzard continued for three days. The wind howled ruthlessly outside, but inside the cabin was filled with warmth and love. Mrs. Calloway and Becky were given the bed, while Brett and Tess slept before the open fireplace, snuggled atop the deerskin rug.

Repeatedly throughout the long nights, Brett was forced to feed the hungry flames. They temporarily abandoned the cabin across the creek during the snowstorm, its inhabitants excited at Tess's news about the arrival of the window glass. Brett promised to install both panes once the storm broke.

Finally, the day dawned clear and blue. Outside, the snow piled high, drifts ridging the clearing like creamy white butter. Deeper drifts blocked passage anywhere except the small trail Brett had cleared to the makeshift barn to check on the mules during the storm.

The stream had frozen over, and Brett gathered buckets of snow to melt for drinking water and coffee. Plans were discussed for the digging of a well come spring.

On this first day after the blizzard had blown itself out, Tess stood on the porch, looking up at Brett on the high wooden seat of the wagon. "Are you sure about this?" he asked, waving a letter in one hand.

"I think so," she answered quietly, a slight frown puckering the corners of her mouth.

Brett's eyebrows arched as he drew in a deep breath. "Okay." He slapped the reins and the heavy wagon lurched, the mules leaning downhill. Tess watched as the team broke the drifts of snow that had formed across the trail to the tracks.

Becky appeared beside her, watching Brett depart. She shivered in the cold and drew her shawl closer around her.

"Are you still bothered by that letter?" Becky asked softly, glancing at Tess from the corner of her eye.

Tess said nothing for a moment, then turned to Becky. She smiled at the concern she read in her new sister-in-law's hazel eyes. So very much like Brett's, Tess realized for the hundredth time.

"Yes, Becky," she admitted. "I know in my heart that God would want me to send it, but I'm still frightened. I don't want things to ever go back to how they were before."

Mrs. Calloway joined the girls on the porch. Together, the trio trudged through the deep snow toward the small woodland glade to where the tall cross towered. They had to help each other over the fallen tree near the little clearing, giving Tess special attention, despite her protests.

"I can manage myself," she grumbled.

Mrs. Calloway huffed, and Becky smiled. "We know you're tough, Tess. But you have a little Calloway in there, and we want to help."

Tess sighed and patted her tummy.

Mrs. Calloway brushed snow from the rock bench with her mitten. "Sit here, Tess, and rest. You're carrying my grandchild, don't forget."

Becky giggled. "How could she, Mother? You remind her often enough."

A frozen cascade of ice shimmered where the waterfall used to flow. Sunlight glistened like diamonds on the crest of drifts, and Mrs. Calloway brushed a seat for them on the stone bench cut into the boulder. They huddled in the cold as Tess peered with wonder at the tall cross across the stream, her heart swelling in the beauty and solitude of the silent forest chapel.

No one had again mentioned the hangings. Although Frank was now dead, Tess still felt bothered by the lasting effects of the man's evil influence on her family. Could things change for her mother now or would the timid, frightened woman simply fall into the same pattern of searching for another controlling, violent man?

Only prayer and hope would give Tess the peace she sought, and she knew things would be different for her now. Brett was a good, Christian husband.

Although some crime continued, the robberies and killings that had plagued Laramie all summer disappeared as winter descended upon the land. Sheriff Boswell kept the local peace until a new town marshal could be located. The Chinaman from next door quickly laid claim to the Bucket of Blood and no one opposed the takeover.

November brought more snow, but the Union Pacific pushed on across the plains to the summit of the Continental Divide. Nothing could halt the progress and the building construction of the railroad.

ııııııııııııııııııııııııııııııı

A week before Thanksgiving Day, Brett drove the wagon into Laramie. Mrs. Calloway sat on the high seat beside him while Tess and Becky rode in the bed, covered in thick buffalo robes.

The sharp, shrill whistle of an arriving train split the frigid air. Huge billows of smoke rose from the black engine as the locomotive made the curve east of town and rolled slowly into the station. Escaping steam hissed, announcing the train had arrived.

Tess glanced once at the still unfinished saloon, its bare walls and exposed rafters lying empty now, the ghastly bodies of the outlaws absent. She shivered, thinking of those awful men, then turned her gaze to the huffing train once more.

Brett helped each of the women from the tall wagon.

Tess brushed past him, her anxious gaze searching the platform as she pushed through the small crowd.

Be strong and courageous, she reminded herself grimly. Only with God's strength could she endure this new challenge.

God is with me, Tess coached herself as her eyes scanned the windows of the train cars. *God loves me, He has good things for me*, she continued. *He promises to never leave me or forsake me.* Tess recalled how she had told herself these promises over and over again on that wild ride from Omaha to Laramie. With thankfulness, Tess realized these words had been proven true.

Again, she recalled that train ride so many months ago. A train to Laramie had delivered her into an adventure of a lifetime. The wrong train? Tess smiled. No, not the wrong train. The train God had intended all along.

Now, she stood, peering up and down the length of another train to Laramie. Would this prove to be the one that God would use for her future, the future of her family? She would have to trust it was.

Suddenly, the figure of a slight woman stepped from a train car, her hand gripping the railing. She hesitated, while frightened eyes scanned the bustling platform.

"Mama!" Tess called, waving as she rushed forward. The woman sighted Tess, a hesitant smile coming to her lips.

Tess ran into her mother's arms, hugging her fiercely. Mrs. Calloway and her children moved forward tentatively. They grouped around Tess and her mother as the pair embraced.

Finally, with tears streaming, Tess stepped back. "Mama, this is my husband, Brett Calloway."

Brett shook Cathy's hand firmly. With a grin of welcome, the tie cutter turned to introduce his sister and Mrs. Calloway. His mother stepped forward quickly, her hand extended warmly.

"I'm so happy to meet you, Mrs. Mercer," Delia Calloway said.

Tess's mother frowned. A dark shadow crossed her features and a muscle twitched in her jaw. "Please, it's Mrs. Randle. Cathy Randle. Call me Cathy."

Mrs. Calloway smiled. "Then, welcome, Cathy Randle."

The small group moved toward the wagon.

Tess gripped her mother's arm. "Come on, Mama," she said, her eyes shining. "Let's go home."

ABOUT THE AUTHOR

ANDREW ROTH taught American History for twenty-two years at the middle school level before beginning his literary career. He lives in Bakersfield, California, with his wife and is a proud father and grandfather. A native of Kansas, Andrew was raised with a deep love and appreciation for history, particularly the Old West. A Christian for more than three decades, Andrew's hope is that his writing will encourage readers and rebuild lives. The passage he feels is his guiding verse is Jeremiah 31:4, "I will build you up again and you will be rebuilt." Andrew's website is: http:// andrewrothbooks.com.

OTHER BOOKS BY ANDREW ROTH

Wildfire for Rose
Renewed Redemption

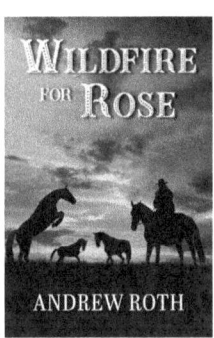 

www.ingramcontent.com/pod-product-compliance
Lightning Source LLC
Chambersburg PA
CBHW051135030726
47504CB00004B/886